BEACHED

BEACHED

A MER CAVALLO MYSTERY

MICKI BROWNING

*To Linda —
Thank you for
diving into Beached
Enjoy!
Micki
Browning*

— AAUW —

Published by Blue Shadow Mysteries ~ PO Box 1346, Port Salerno, FL 34992-1346

Paperback ISBN: 978-0-993806-1-1

Ebook ISBN: 978-0-9993806-0-4

Library of Congress Control Number: 2017960545

Printed in the United States of America

Beached is a work of fiction. Names, places, and incidents either are products of the author's imagination or, if real, are used fictitiously. Any resemblance to actual events, locales or persons, living or dead is entirely coincidental.

PRAISE FOR MICKI BROWNING

An action-packed read from beginning to end with a resourceful and engaging heroine. I defy you to read this book and not immediately want to dive into the next Mer Cavallo mystery! This book is a winner.

— LAURA DISILVERIO, NATIONAL BEST-SELLING AND AWARD-WINNING AUTHOR

As a sequel, *Beached* does not disappoint. The taut thriller builds on Browning's adept storytelling and character development. The historical elements of this undersea mystery are an immensely satisfying addition.

— MANDY MIKULENCAK, AUTHOR OF THE LAST SUPPERS AND BURN GIRL

This riveting thriller combines lost treasure, suspense, and an ocean-loving heroine with a snarky wit that will make you laugh aloud. As good as *Adrift* was, *Beached* is even better.

— AUTUMN BLUM, CEO STREAM2SEA AND FOUNDER OF SCUBA GIRLS

For Sissy

Meredith Cavallo had questioned her decision to stay in the Florida Keys plenty of times over the past few months, but never while standing on the deck of the *LunaSea*.

Two days remained until Thanksgiving and she had a lot of blessings to count. She had only to look around her. The waves above French Reef sparkled in the late morning sun, a welcome contrast to the squall that had passed through last night. She drew a big breath of salty air. No. This was home.

At least for now.

Next month, charter boats would be full of divers on their winter holiday, but today a family of four made up the entirety of the *LunaSea's* manifest. That left plenty of elbow room on a vessel large enough to accommodate twenty-six divers.

Mer scanned the water out of habit. They had the dive site to themselves and the divers had splashed ten minutes earlier. The reef was shallow. They had at least another half hour to explore.

Captain Leroy Penninichols poked his head out of the engine hold. An ever-present plastic straw peeked beyond his silver-streaked beard. "Maggie wants to know what she can make for Thanksgiving." A slight drawl tempered his baritone voice.

Mer gathered the tools at the edge of the hold. "Not a thing. I've got it covered."

"She said you'd say something like that." He pulled himself out of the hold and onto the deck. Sweat dampened his T-shirt and he wiped his hands with a rag. "I'm supposed to insist."

"Really. I got it." The toolbox was its usual jumble and Mer sorted the equipment into specific compartments. "Recipes are just like experiments."

"How many of these have you done?" he asked.

"Experiments? Lots."

"I meant Thanksgiving dinners."

"Before this one?" Mer asked. "None."

Leroy folded the rag and placed it on the camera table that rose from the rear of the deck. "Oh, goodie. I'll tell Maggie to make pies...and maybe the turkey."

He dropped the lid of the hatch. It slammed with a metallic bang and she flinched.

"Sorry." He indicated her leg. "That still bother you?"

She found herself rubbing her thigh and forced herself to stop. The wound had healed. "What bothers me is your skepticism regarding my ability to construct a pie."

"You don't even look like you know how to eat one."

"Well, if your waistline is any indication, you have enough experience for the both of us."

He patted his belly. "The proper terminology is baked, not constructed. Do you even have a cookbook?"

"That's what the Internet's for."

"Great. We'll bring the dressing, too."

"It's stuffing. It goes in, not on." The last wrench properly sorted, she shut the toolbox and snapped the latches. "Seems pretty self-explanatory." She slid the heavy box under one of the aluminum benches that ran the length of the deck on both sides of the vessel.

"How about we all just go out to dinner?"

Mer shielded her eyes against the November sun. Still no bubbles, but a dark shape in the water caught her attention. She stepped onto the bench to gain a better vantage and pointed off the starboard side. "Any idea what that is? I can't make out it out."

Leroy glanced over his shoulder and then turned, giving the object his full attention. "Looks like we got us a square grouper."

Her curiosity stirred. "I've never heard of a square grouper. Are they indigenous to the Keys?"

He shook his head. "How can someone as smart as you act like a calf at a new gate?"

"It's a logical question. The Arctic Ocean and the Florida Straits have completely different environments."

"This isn't your old research boat, so before you warm up for a lecture I'm not interested in, don't." Leroy picked up the gaff. "A square grouper is a bale of marijuana, not a fish."

"Oh." The news disappointed her. "I didn't encounter any of them in the Arctic."

The current pushed the black object toward the *LunaSea*. Smaller than a bale of hay, it appeared to be wrapped in black trash bags and bound with twine. When it was close enough, Leroy leaned over the side, hooked it, and pulled it to the swim platform. Together they dragged it onto the deck.

Mer dropped to her knees next to the sodden bale and ran her hands over the contours. It felt as if there were smaller squares inside. "What now?" she asked.

He stowed the gaff. "When we're on our way back to the dock, I'll alert the Coasties. They'll come pick it up."

"Why wait?"

"No sense announcing to the world what we've got on board. You never know who's looking for their lost property." He squinted toward the horizon. "Or what they'll do to get it back."

The gaff had torn the outer wrapping. Mer tugged at the plastic and enlarged the hole. "It looks like a bunch of duct-taped bricks."

"Let me see." He unfolded his pocketknife and stabbed one of the bundles. White residue clung to the blade when he extracted it.

"Not that I have much experience with it," Mer said, "but I'm pretty sure that's not marijuana." The breeze fluttered the outer plastic and Mer glimpsed the corner of a clear plastic freezer bag stuffed between two of the silver bricks. "There's more than drugs inside." She dug into her shorts pocket for her cellphone and opened the photo app.

"Not enough to be a marine scientist? Now you're an archeologist, too?" Leroy teased.

"Never hurts to document things *in situ*. Sometimes it's not the item so much as what's near it that's important. Besides, there's a whole field dedicated to nautical archeology." She tugged on the baggie but it remained wedged. She yanked harder. The plastic ripped, flinging a small circular object end-over-end until it clinked onto the deck. Leroy stomped on the disk before it disappeared off the edge of the dive platform.

Mer's attention remained glued on the stained piece of paper that peeked out from the plastic. She nudged two bundles aside to avoid tearing the brittle page and gently removed it. Names covered the sheet. "That's odd." She laid it across her lap and snapped a couple of photographs.

"Bet I got you beat." Leroy examined the coin in his palm and held it out to Mer.

She placed the list on the dry table, where it fluttered in the breeze. Mer weighted the page with her cellphone so it wouldn't blow away and took the coin. It felt warm and heavy in her hand.

Sun glinted off the portrait of an elaborately coiffed man. "Seventeen thirty-three? I didn't think they dated coins that early." She flipped the gold piece. Latin words circled a coat of arms topped by a crown and Mer read them aloud, "*Initium sapientiæ timor domini.*"

"Wisdom begins with the fear of God," Leroy said.

She gaped at the captain. "I don't know what surprises me more. That I'm holding a coin that's nearly three hundred years old or that you know Latin."

The thick thatch of beard hid his smile, but his eyes crinkled. "Guess you ain't the only huckleberry on the bush."

A glint drew her attention back to the bale and she placed the coin on the table next to the list. "There's something else." She pushed two of the bundles apart and dug out a small electronic device. "What do you suppose this is?"

Leroy snatched it out of her hand and dropped it on the deck. "GPS tracker." He brought the heel of his Croc down on the device and smashed it. "Call up the divers. Good chance we're about to have company." He disappeared up the ladder that accessed the bridge deck.

She sprang to her feet, grabbed a dive weight, and rapped it three times against the handrail of the swim ladder that hung in the water.

Thirty seconds elapsed and she repeated the emergency recall.

Now all she could do was wait.

Mer scanned the horizon, squinting behind her sunglasses. The glare made it difficult to see. The itch of someone watching her prompted her to spin, but she was unable to locate the cause of her unease. She refocused on the water's surface, searching for the trail of bubbles that would reveal the divers' locations. She hit the ladder again. Imagined the sound traveling through the water. Willed it to alert the parents and their eleven-year-old twins, Grace and Logan. Bring them back.

She rubbed her thigh and did the math. The divers had been down twenty minutes. Even if they returned immediately, it could still take them several minutes to swim back to the boat, plus a three-minute safety stop before they'd surface—if they heeded the signal at all.

Another minute ticked by. Still no bubbles.

A tiny dot separated itself from the horizon.

"We got company," she shouted.

2

A moment later the captain was at her side.

"There." Mer pointed. "Three o'clock. Moving fast."

Bubbles broke the surface along the port side of the *LunaSea* and inched toward the ladder. The family's daughter surfaced first and handed up her fins. Mer grabbed the blades and helped Grace up the swim ladder and steered her to the bench. "There you go." Mer kept her voice bright. "Let's get you out of this gear." Her fingers flew between the buckles and loosened the vest.

The mother, Lydia, surfaced next. Once she climbed aboard, Leroy walked her to the bench and guided her tank into the rack as she sat. Mer leaned close to the woman's ear and spoke low so the girl wouldn't hear. "I need you to stow your equipment and take your daughter into the V-berth. Stay there until I let you know it's safe."

The woman's eyes held questions, but she nodded.

Mer returned to the stern.

The boy bobbed on the line that floated behind the boat and struggled to remove his fins. Mer could feel the other boat racing toward them. She motioned to him. "Logan, I need you to hurry."

He replied, but the regulator in his mouth muffled his words and he took it out. "It's stuck." He put his face in the water so he could see the strap.

Blake surfaced a yard from his son and spit out his regulator. "There better be a good reason you're shortening our dive. I paid good money for this charter."

"Emergency. I need you and your son on the boat," Mer said. "Pull off your son's fins and push him to the ladder."

"They're expensive fins."

A boat engine rumbled like distant thunder. Growing louder. Closer. Mer's jaw tensed. No time to argue. She dove into the water and popped up next to the boy.

"Hey there, Logan. Let me see if I can help." She inhaled a few shallow breaths and dove beneath him. Her hands circled his ankles and ripped the fins off his feet. She hooked them over her wrist, then broke the surface and pushed him closer to the boat. "Up you go."

The sharp retort of a gunshot rang out. Mer froze. She knew that sound. Her leg throbbed.

The boy twisted in the water. "What was that?"

She grabbed his arm. They had to hurry.

A blow struck Mer from behind. Logan's father flailed for the ladder, not caring that his son was closer. She twisted and dodged his arm as it came around in another wild stroke. His knee slammed into her belly and drove the breath from her lungs. Then Blake was upon her, pushing her underwater in his panic.

Mer lost her grip on Logan. Salt water stung her eyes. The father thrashed the water above her head and her lungs burned.

The first rule of rescue was not to become another victim, and if Blake fell backward in his panic, two hundred pounds of man and an aluminum tank would smash into both Mer and Logan. Kicking away from the danger zone, Mer yanked the boy out of the way and surfaced, gasping for air. Fear widened Logan's eyes. His buoyancy compensator kept him afloat, but he wasn't moving.

Blake scrambled up the ladder. Leroy latched onto the father's tank valve to steady him as he lurched aboard the vessel.

Mer faced Logan. "We have to get on the boat. I'll help you."

Without his fins, the boy lacked the propulsion to move himself quickly through the water. Mer grabbed the ladder with one hand and stretched her other arm toward him. "Give me your hand."

Leroy leaned over the edge. "No time like the present, Cavallo."

"Get ready to get us out of here. I'll help Logan on board and stow the ladder."

Leroy nodded once and disappeared.

Mer clutched the shoulder of the boy's vest and drew him the last few feet to the boat. She wrapped his fingers around the rung of the ladder and swung behind him, her arms outside his, protecting his body with her own. "What say we get out of here?" She kept her voice calm as she prodded him up the ladder. Nothing wrong. No madmen hurtling across the water to intercept them. No one shooting at them. Just a typical day on the water. Her vision narrowed until all she saw was the path to the V-berth.

"See the opening to the lower deck?" She didn't wait for a response. "I need you to go down there." She peeled his fins off her wrist and gave him a gentle push. "Go on."

The growl of the high-powered boat grew louder. Low profile. Built for speed. Close enough, now, to distinguish two men in the cockpit.

Mer heaved the rope to raise the swim ladder and secured it. Leroy fired up the engines and she raced to the bow to unclip the boat from the mooring ball.

"Off line," she shouted.

The *LunaSea* surged forward. Wind tore through Mer's wet clothes as she sidled along the gunnels and swung back onto the main deck. The father cowered in the corner, still in his gear. The rest of his family huddled in the V-berth, staring at Mer through the hatch.

Mer dropped to her knees next to Blake. "You need to go below." She loosened the straps of his buoyancy compensator and undid the waist buckle as if helping a child. "Let's get this tank off you."

He didn't move.

She bit the inside of her lip to keep from venting her frustration.

"Don't worry, I've got it." Her fingers fumbled with the remaining clips. She peeled the vest from his body and dropped the tank into the rack, snapping the bungee cord around the valve. The last thing they needed was a forty-pound tank rolling around the deck. Although at the moment, hitting him on the head with it held more than a little appeal.

She knelt next to him again. "I know you're scared." The *LunaSea* swung sharply to port and her hand shot out for balance. "We all are. But I need you to help me. Help your family."

Another shot rang out. Adrenaline flooded her body. Mer grabbed Blake's chin and forced him to look at her. "Your children need their father. Like it or not, that's you."

He swatted her hand away. "I know how to take care of my family." He stared at her a long moment before he crawled toward the berth.

Mer ran her hands through her hair. They were hopelessly outclassed. Even at top speed, the *LunaSea* pulled twenty-four knots. Respectable, but not racing material. Not like the sleek cigarette boats favored by smugglers. The narrow beam and long hull of their pursuers' go-fast boat enabled them to hurtle through the water at more than eighty knots.

Leroy steered the dive boat in a wild zigzag across the water. The harbor loomed closer, but not nearly close enough.

The go-fast boat steadily gained on them.

Mer climbed up to the bridge. Leroy had his hands on the controls. His head swiveled back and forth between the smuggler's boat and safe harbor.

"You know how to give a distress call?" he asked.

Mer grabbed the radio and keyed the mic. "Mayday, mayday, mayday. This is Mer Cavallo of the dive boat *LunaSea*." She released the button and waited for a response. A male voice crackled across the air. She could barely make out his words over the whine of the engines, the wind, and her pounding heartbeat. "Request immediate law enforcement assistance."

The two men were too far away for Mer to get a description, but close enough to see the driver raise his arm. He fired another shot. The bullet struck the railing by Leroy's head. They both flinched.

"We are being pursued and fired upon. Repeat. They are shooting at us." Mer's voice climbed an octave as she reported their coordinates and approach path to Port Largo.

Without waiting for a response, she slammed the mic into its cradle. "Be right back," she shouted.

Sweat moistened her hands and she slid down the ladder rails, landing on the deck with a shin-banging thud.

Another shot. This one aimed at her. She ducked. Tried to make herself as small a target as possible.

The V-berth to her right offered safety. A place to hide. She turned her back to it and dashed toward the bale.

The plastic-wrapped bundle sat in the open on the stern. Mer slid behind it. She pressed her back against the camera table for support, wedged her feet against the water-soaked bale, and pushed. Her legs strained. The bale barely moved.

The driver raised his arm again and aimed. She scrunched lower. The open transom of the boat left her exposed. The only thing between Mer and a bullet was a sodden bale of drugs. The very thing she needed to get off the boat.

Her hand went to the pendant around her neck. With a growl, she redoubled her efforts. The table leg bit into her back as she shoved the bale across the skid-resistant deck, making agonizingly slow progress. Finally the bale teetered on the edge of the swim platform, and with a final jolt it fell into the churning whitewater behind the *LunaSea*. The dark plastic disappeared under the wake. For a horrible moment, Mer thought the bale had sunk, but then it popped up and bobbed on the swell.

The captain of the go-fast throttled back and broke away from the chase to retrieve the bale.

Mer's entire body shook as the adrenaline ebbed, leaving her weak-limbed and unable to get up. The angles of her seahorse pendant dug into her palm and she forced herself to relax her grip.

Fifty yards away, the smuggler pulled his boat alongside the black bundle and idled. The dark-haired passenger leaned over and tried to raise the bale into the boat. He couldn't do it on his own and the captain left the helm to help. Together they pulled the contraband into their vessel.

Leroy coaxed every bit of speed from the *LunaSea* he could, and it bumped and slammed across the waves. The distance between them and the smugglers grew. Mer drew a deep, steadying breath, but blew it out in a huff of renewed fear.

What if it wasn't the bale they wanted?

She clambered to her feet. Her cellphone was wedged in the corner of the camera table, still trapping the tattered remains of the list of names. But the coin was gone.

The flutter of fear returned. She had to warn Leroy. They weren't out of danger. Not yet.

3

Mer and Leroy looked over their shoulders the entire way back, only powering down the *LunaSea's* engines when they hit the no-wake zone at the entrance of Port Largo. A Coast Guard patrol boat fell in behind them and escorted them safely through the main canal. Even so, it wasn't until Mer saw the Monroe County Sheriff's deputy on the dock that some of her tension eased.

The dock had never looked so welcoming. Behind palm trees, the Aquarius Dive Shop loomed into view like a weary sentinel. In the six months she'd worked here, she'd looked upon it without really seeing it: an aging two-story building with a retail shop on the upper level and the nuts and bolts of the charter business below. This afternoon, though, everything was in sharper focus—the snap of the dive flag tickled by the breeze, the beauty of the bougainvillea crowning the retaining wall between the parking lot and the dock, the worn wooden handrails alongside faded turquoise steps.

But it was the south wall of the building that held Mer's attention. A riot of blues created an underwater vista across the entire side of the building. Sweeping lines rendered sea life in evocative strokes. Painted just the month before, the mural drew even non-divers to the shop. They stood for photos in groups or used selfie sticks for solo snaps. Mer preferred the artwork in the quicksilver light of dawn when everything shimmered with life. Then, like now, it helped center her.

And at the moment, she needed to be centered. The shaking had subsided, but the confrontation had left her jumpy. Even surrounded by law enforcement and friends, she wasn't convinced the danger had passed.

The timbre of the *LunaSea's* engines changed as Leroy spun the boat in the canal and eased it parallel to the dock.

Bijoux, the owner of the Aquarius Dive Shop, walked down the dock to meet the boat. The tall woman carried herself like a ballerina, graceful and strong. She handed Mer the bowline and the bracelets stacked on her thin wrist jangled like chimes. "Is everyone all right?" Concern softened her Haitian lilt and creased her forehead.

"No one got hurt." Mer wrapped the line around the cleat. The children had weathered the crisis better than the adults.

"That does not fully answer the question."

Mer stared down the canal to reassure herself that they hadn't been followed. She didn't want to lie to her boss—her friend—so she didn't answer. Instead she edged along the side of the boat and hooked the stern line around another cleat. Using her body weight, she leaned back and the rear of the boat swung toward the dock.

The boat was still in motion when Blake tossed his dive bag over the gunnel and onto the dock. "Who do I see about getting my money back?"

"That would be me." Bijoux extended her elegant hand to help him off the boat. He ignored her offer and jumped the small gap between the boat and the dock, almost striking Bijoux.

Lydia stood in the middle of the boat with an arm around each of her children. "Blake."

"They *shot* at us, Lydia."

Logan wiggled out of his mother's grasp. "Can we do this again tomorrow?"

Blake blinked at his son and worked his mouth, but nothing came out. He left his family to gather their gear and stomped toward the Coast Guard patrol boat that was docking behind the *LunaSea*.

Bijoux addressed Lydia. "Of course you will get your money back. And you are more than welcome to return whenever you like. As our guest."

Lydia lifted her gear bag off the boat bench. "I'm sorry about my husband. We're from Canada. We're not used to guns."

Mer picked up one of the children's rental wetsuits and turned it right side out. "I don't think anyone is."

Grace stepped around her mother and approached Mer. "Thank you for keeping my daddy safe."

"You're welcome." Mer kneeled in front of the little girl. "I couldn't have done it if you and your brother hadn't been so brave."

"Weren't you scared?"

"Yes."

Grace cocked her head to the side and wisps of blond hair fell into her eyes. "You didn't look scared."

Mer glanced at the black scuff on the deck where she'd pushed the bale overboard. "You can't always tell how scared someone is by looking at them."

Grace twined her hand into Mer's. "I was scared, too," she whispered.

"You know you're safe now, Grace, right? Your mother would never let anything happen to you."

"I know."

Lydia stood behind her daughter and put her hands on the girl's shoulders. "Thank you for taking that risk. I have to agree with my daughter. You are a brave woman."

The compliment left Mer without words. She'd been terrified. Her thigh ached from the exertion of pushing the bale overboard. That and something more. Phantom pain? It felt real enough. Too real. She dropped her hand to the top of her thigh but caught herself before she rubbed the round, puckered skin just below the hem of her shorts. The reminder that she'd been shot. Seventy-four days ago.

She dragged herself back to the present. "It's your children who deserve the praise."

Lydia's gaze shifted down the dock to her husband. "Yes."

Blake gesticulated wildly in front of a stoic Coast Guard ensign.

A deputy, clad in the dark green uniform of the Monroe County Sheriff's Office, approached the boat. His bald head gleamed with sweat. "Are you the one who placed the distress call?" His jaw worked a piece of gum while he waited for her to answer.

Mer nodded.

Bijoux took Lydia's dive bag and helped the mother navigate the small drop between the boat and dock. "Perhaps we should talk over here." She herded the family toward the picnic tables to give Mer and the deputy some privacy.

The deputy propped one leg on the gunnel and took a notebook from his shirt pocket. The tide was coming in and the *LunaSea's* position in the water placed them at eye-level.

"Name?"

"Mer. Dr. Meredith Cavallo. We found the bale—"

"How 'bout letting me finish getting what I need first. Okay?"

Mer pressed her lips together.

The deputy rapid-fired questions. How did she spell her name? Where did she live? How long had she worked at the dive shop? She answered each dutifully and he scratched down her answers.

His pen stopped and he studied her face as if seeing her for the first time. "Hey, aren't you the one who was involved in that *Spiegel Grove* mess a couple months ago? Detective Talbot's case?"

Her jaw tensed. "Yes."

"Huh." He closed his notebook, straightened to his considerable height, and stared down at her. "What happened today?"

"We found something we shouldn't have found floating in the ocean. Curiosity got the better of us. We dragged it aboard."

"We?"

"Captain Penninichols and I," she clarified.

"Why?" he asked.

"To turn it in."

"What time did you call to report it?"

A flush spread across her cheeks. "We didn't."

"Huh." He snapped his gum. "Why not?"

"We didn't want to give away the fact that we had a cache of what appeared to be cocaine on board the *LunaSea*."

He shifted his stance and faced her squarely. "Would've had a pretty high street value. Were you going to report it?"

"Of course!"

"How did you know it was coke?"

"When we pulled it out of the water, the gaff ripped a hole in the plastic covering. I looked inside. I'd never encountered anything like this before. I'd never even heard of a square grouper. That's what they're called, you know."

He hooked his thumbs in his gun belt. "I'm aware of that."

His demeanor irked her. "Well then, you also probably know that when people lose something valuable, they often go looking for it," she said.

"How'd they happen to find you? It's a big ocean. Did you alert them on a different channel?"

"What? No!"

His gum snapped. Again. "So they just happened upon your boat and somehow knew you had their drugs?"

"It was the GPS tracker."

"So now there's a tracking device. Ever seen one before?"

His scrutiny unnerved her. He had the same flat eyes as a bull shark. Even though he hadn't moved, it felt as if he was circling her.

"No, but after I found the coin and the—"

"Coin?"

"Yes," Mer said. "I found a gold coin. It looked to be in mint condition. Odd considering it was dated 1733."

His eyebrows nearly shot off his face. "Seventeen thirty-three. Where is it now?"

"I don't know."

Another gum snap. "You don't know."

Mer folded her arms. "Are you going to repeat everything I tell you?"

"Let me make sure I understand. You found a bale that had drugs, gold coins, and a GPS tracker?"

"I only saw one coin. Oh, and a list of names."

"What sort of names?"

"See for yourself." She'd be damned if she was going to get it for him. "What's left of it is on the camera table." She motioned toward the back of the boat.

"Wait a minute. You mean to tell me that you saved a piece of paper but not a gold coin? Most everyone I know would have done the opposite."

"I didn't intentionally save either."

"What happened to the coin?"

"I don't know."

"Re-a-lly." He drew the word into several syllables.

The last of her patience packed up and headed north to catch up to her blood pressure. "I've been shot at, Deputy..." She peered at the nameplate above his pocket. "Cole. Things were rather hectic. Pushing a commercial dive boat to top speed across three-foot seas makes for a bumpy ride. The *LunaSea* has an open transom. That's how I was able to push the bale off when the bad guys—the people you should be looking for instead of giving me the third degree—were chasing us. Maybe the coin rolled off. I don't know. And frankly? I no longer give a damn."

Deputy Cole boarded the boat, forcing Mer to take a step backward as he blocked the exit. "Do you mind turning out your pockets?"

The deputy's implication felt like a slap. She grabbed the inside of her pockets and yanked them until they hung like limp flags outside of her shorts. "Do you want the lint for evidence or are we through?"

"For now."

4

M er reached above her head and grabbed the safety rail that ringed the bottom of the upper deck. She swung herself over the gunnel and onto the dock, leaving Deputy Cole alone on the boat. Leaning over, she wrenched two of the thirty-five pound tanks from their holders and settled them by her feet. She readjusted her grip and stomped toward the equipment room.

A satellite media van pulled into the parking lot. Its tires crunched across the limestone gravel and raised a plume of dust. A dark-haired woman sat in the passenger seat. Wendy Wheeler. Mer's foul mood darkened.

The equipment cage stored the shop's rental gear, air compressor, and ice machine in a room on the ground level of the building. She set the tanks on the concrete floor and spun them so the valves faced the same direction as the other cylinders waiting to be filled.

When she looked up again Wendy had cornered Blake, her teeth bared in a predatory prime-time smile. Further down the dock, Deputy Cole interviewed Lydia.

Mer returned to the boat for two more tanks. The Coast Guard ensign and Leroy both leaned against the rails, chatting as if they were old friends.

The ensign looked up at her approach. Acne peppered his face like buckshot. "Nice move, pushing the bale off. No telling what would've happened if they'd boarded you guys."

"You get much of this around here?" Mer asked.

"Nah. Not like the old days."

Some of her anger dissipated. The ensign didn't look old enough to drive, let alone reminisce about olden days. "When was that?"

"Oh, this was the place to be in the eighties. Mother ships used to transport tons of drugs from South America and the Caribbean. They'd stop offshore and transfer the drugs to smaller courier boats. Back then there was no way to patrol all the marinas. Too many canals and too much shoreline." He puffed up his chest and continued. "Florida City, up Everglades way, built a whole industry around collecting square groupers and running dope. No way to catch them in all the mangroves up there. Least not 'til the Feds came in. Busted the whole town. Course, that was before I started."

"Of course. Did you need to speak to me about what happened today?"

The ensign shook his head. "I got what I needed from the Cap'n here. We'll document it, but sounds like all the fun stuff happened in state waters. The Sheriff's Office will handle it from here. Glad everyone's safe." He raised two fingers to his brow in a casual salute and headed back toward the patrol boat.

Mer watched him go. The ensign paused next to Deputy Cole and handed him a small piece of paper—probably a report number, something administrative. Cole didn't reciprocate.

She grabbed the last tanks off the boat and retreated to the equipment room.

A few minutes later, a whiff of expensive perfume warned Mer of the reporter's arrival and Wendy's shadow passed in front of the cage door like an eclipse that refused to move on.

"Fancy seeing you again, Meredith."

Silhouetted in the doorframe stood five feet, two inches of pure nosiness. Clad in a posh sheath dress, the reporter wielded her microphone like a weapon. The arrival of her cameraman darkened the room further.

Mer straightened. "Wendy."

"The key to Keys News," she chirped. "I want to ask you a few questions."

Mer fished one of the wetsuits out of the rinse bucket. Water splashed on the concrete floor and spattered the reporter's suede pumps. "I'd rather you didn't."

Wendy burst out laughing. "Silly me. I almost believed you."

Past experience convinced Mer of the futility of trying to avoid the reporter. If Wendy sniffed a story, she worked it until it paid off or fell apart. A small part of Mer admired her. Too bad it wasn't from a greater distance.

"Let's get a shot of you over by the boat," Wendy said. "It'll only take a moment."

Mer wove a hanger into the neck of the wetsuit and hung it on a drying rack. "You should talk to the deputy. I already told him everything."

"Oh, he's so stuffy. I'd rather hear it from you."

The thought of rehashing the event left a sour taste in Mer's mouth. She'd done her part.

She attached compressor whips to the tank valves. "It's about to get loud in here." She clapped on ear protection.

"But I'm—"

Mer pressed the button and the compressor kicked on, overwhelming the small room with noise.

Wendy took a step back but gave no indication of leaving.

Mer considered her options. If she lowered the compressor's flow rate, she'd have maybe fifteen minutes before the tanks filled. Fifteen blissful minutes that Wendy couldn't ask her any inane questions.

Not nearly long enough to dissuade the self-proclaimed "key to Keys News."

The smart course of action would be to put as much distance between her and the event as possible. Being the lead story on the local news wouldn't help maintain a low profile. That said, the coconut telegraph—the island's mouth-to-ear network—transmitted gossip more effectively than any news outlet. The smugglers had been close enough to see her. They'd definitely been close enough to note the *LunaSea's* distinctive hull paint and name. Nothing Wendy put on the air would be new information to the smugglers, but if there were more bales floating around, the news might deter other boaters from pulling them aboard and becoming targets.

The sound of Mer's sigh died in the cacophony of the compressor. Stripping the ear protection off her head, she left the tanks to fill and stepped toward the door.

Wendy signaled her cameraman to follow them. As the compressor noise faded, the reporter pressed her advantage. "I promise. We'll be done before you know it. Then you can tell all your friends and family you'll be on the news."

"You realize most people don't aspire to make the evening news."

The rapid click of Wendy's heels stopped and she spun, the hair of her precise bob falling back into perfect alignment. "Oh, but they do. People clamor to get their face on TV. Fifteen minutes of fame and all."

Mer never broke stride. "You've got two." She stopped in front of the boat. "And no names."

The cameraman lifted the rig to his shoulder in a practiced move and focused on Wendy.

She snapped the microphone beneath her mouth. "Something's fishy in the waters of Key Largo. A high-speed chase almost ended in disaster for the crew of the Aquarius Dive Shop. I'm here with one of the crew members who survived this harrowing ordeal. I understand there was an exchange of gunfire." She shoved the microphone into Mer's face.

"No. They fired at us. We didn't shoot back. We were unarmed."

An annoyed expression flitted across Wendy's face. "Terrifying. How did that make you feel?"

"Scared," Mer admitted.

Wendy waited for her to elaborate. When Mer didn't offer more, the reporter launched into another question. "Word on the dock is you located a bale of contraband drugs. So, tell me. Is this the square grouper that got away?"

That. That right there was why people hated reporters. They spoke in sound bytes and headlines, making puns and jokes out of everything instead of recognizing that someone who just had their wits scared out of her might need a bit more seriousness injected into the moment.

"It was an inanimate object. It was incapable of getting away. I pushed it overboard."

"Well thank goodness for your quick thinking." Treacly sarcasm dripped from the words. "Bold, brainy and brave. The community is lucky to have you. This is Wendy Wheeler, the key to Keys News."

The day's tasks completed, Mer sat on the top of one of the wooden picnic tables and stared at the canal. A slight sheen of oil floated near the stern of the *LunaSea*, creating a rainbow slick that faded as dusk fell. She wrapped her arms around her knees and pulled them to her chest. A splinter snagged the fabric of her shorts.

Nothing remained untouched in the Keys. Wood warped. Metal rusted. What was its effect on people?

"You look like someone licked the red off your candy and gave it back to you." Leroy sat on the bench and leaned his back against the table, his elbows splayed behind him for support.

"You ever wonder where you belong?" Mer asked.

"In the grand scheme of things?"

"Geographically."

"Don't think I've ever had that concern," Leroy said. "I figure it's all God's green earth. As long as I'm respectful, I can go where I want."

"But you stay here."

"Haven't worn out my welcome yet."

A green iguana skittered along the concrete retaining wall that ran parallel to the dock, and then disappeared into the parking lot. They didn't belong here, yet they flourished. Locals considered them pests, little more than island gophers that wreaked havoc on their gardens. If they could, they'd send every last one of them back to Central America.

"How long's it been?" Mer swatted at a mosquito on her leg and missed. "I mean since you came to the Keys?"

He scratched his head. "Gotta be coming up on twenty-five years."

"So just a short-timer." Mer resumed her inspection of the canal.

"Maggie's waiting on me to make sure I didn't collect any bullet holes today, so hurry up and get to the tail of the dog."

"Wendy Wheeler said the community is lucky to have me."

"I bet the Tremblay family is still thanking their stars you were on the boat today. Well, not Blake. I'm fair certain if he'd had his way, you'd have gone overboard with the drugs."

She couldn't tell if he was smiling behind the beard.

"You should skeedaddle, too," he said. "You got yourself a man waiting on you who's every bit as worried as Maggie."

Selkie. A warm feeling chased away some of her melancholy. He had factored into her decision to stay in the Keys. Not the only reason, but the one that had the most obvious short-term benefits.

"He's on one of his trips. He should be home tomorrow." She waved her hand. "You go on. I'll be right behind you."

"Bad things happen in the Arctic, too, Cavallo." He stood. "You're spooked. We both are. Now's not the time to be making any decisions about geography."

"Give Maggie a hug for me."

"Will do."

Without watching, she tracked his movements. A crunch of gravel, a metallic groan as he wrenched open the door, the three-crank false start before his old truck roared to life. All notes that belonged to the complex music of the Keys. A harmony she hadn't quite mastered.

If she were honest, it wasn't geography that kept her staring at the canal. It was a much larger issue.

Her family was like a dandelion gone to seed, and the breeze had dropped them across the nation. Her brothers occupied opposing coasts; one in New York, the other in California. For as long as her father still taught at the university, her parents would stay in Santa Barbara—but they planned to retire to Sedona, where her mother had been born and raised.

The five of them had tried to maintain holidays together, but colleges, a police academy, a seminary, education abroad programs, and research jaunts practically guaranteed that someone would be absent from the family feasts. This year it was her parents and their long-postponed second honeymoon cruising the Caribbean.

She missed her family. She missed home.

Only she didn't know exactly where home was anymore.

5
———

The November sun didn't rise until nearly seven, and a patina of silver and gray shrouded the dock when she arrived at work. She'd slept hardly a wink all night. Every time she'd nodded off, an imagined gunshot startled her awake.

Sound traveled easily in the pre-dawn quiet and the wheeze of Leroy's approaching truck placed him about four blocks away from the dive shop.

Together they'd prep the boat for the morning dive. While Leroy checked the engines, she'd handle everything else. Finish on time and they'd leave port just as the sun rose and painted the underside of the clouds with splashes of color.

She'd arrived before Kyle, the equipment tech, and she unlocked the equipment rental cage. Grabbing two tanks by their valves, she set a course for the dock. The bottom of the cylinders bumped against the top of each of the five wooden steps, the dull thud reminding her of a muted church bell. On the dock she readjusted her grip and turned. A man slept on one of the three picnic tables.

She took a step back.

The wide concrete dock ran parallel to the canal and invited strollers. Occasionally a reveler from one of the nearby bars stumbled down to the dock at closing and used the shop's tables as a waypoint. Twice she'd had to roust someone off the boat itself. But after yesterday, the appearance of a stranger put her on high alert.

He snored, the sound remarkably similar to Leroy's truck in both decibels and timbre.

Mer set the aluminum tanks on the walkway harder than necessary and startled two wild parakeets out of a nearby palm. The man stirred and then bolted into a seated position. A piece of paper fluttered to the ground but she kept her eyes on his hands. Empty.

"Good morning," she greeted him. "Diving with us today?"

Blinking sleep from his eyes, he patted the bench until he hit upon a pair of heavy black frames that he pushed onto his face. The lenses magnified Labrador brown eyes. "No. I am looking for a man named Bijoux?" He spoke with a heavy Cuban accent.

Job candidate. After all the excitement of the day before, she'd forgotten Bijoux had scheduled interviews this morning for a relief deckhand.

"If you're looking for a job—" Mer pointed to the paperwork he held. "You probably don't want to call her a man."

"No." He scrambled to his feet and gave a little bow while smoothing back his hair. "Are you Miss Bijoux?"

Standing, they were similar in height, which placed him at about five-foot-nine. Tall for a woman, not so tall for a man. His brown hair was a shade or two darker than hers, and even though he'd just smoothed it back, the bangs had already fallen into his face. It gave him a youthful appearance despite the faint lines that extended beyond his glasses. He reminded Mer of a friend she'd had in grad school who'd been her favorite lab partner.

She extended her hand. "I'm Mer."

He grasped it and then covered their two hands with his free one and gave a single pump. "Oscar Vigil. It is my pleasure to meet you." He indicated the tanks. "Please, you must let me help you. They are heavy."

"Thanks, but I've got them. They don't seem as heavy in the morning as they do at night."

He cocked his head and then smiled. "That is true of many things."

Wrinkles marred his shirt as if he had wrung it out but not smoothed the fabric before it dried. Or perhaps he had slept in it. She didn't remember seeing another car in the parking lot. "Do you have an appointment with Bijoux?"

"No. I just learned of this job. I hope I am not too late. I am a good worker."

Just another job seeker. Mer relaxed. "Are you PADI certified?"

Before he could answer, the crunch of gravel in the parking lot announced Leroy's arrival.

"Excuse me," she said.

Another bow, this time so deep that a gold crucifix slid out from under his T-shirt. "Of course."

Bijoux's red Jeep nipped at the rear wheels of Leroy's truck. She parked in the adjacent spot and slid from the seat, looking as bright as a parrotfish. She paused briefly and spoke to Leroy through his truck window.

Mer looked down at her own khaki shorts and tan T-shirt and wondered if she'd ever have the courage to wear even a fraction of the color palette that resided in Bijoux's closet. Probably not.

Mer hailed her friend. "If you have a moment, I'll introduce you to another applicant. He's on the dock."

Bijoux left Leroy rooting in his truck and fell in beside Mer. "Are you sure you are up to working today?"

"Someone's got to keep Leroy out of trouble."

Bijoux drew Mer to a halt. "Funny, he just said the same thing about you."

Mer worked the toe of her flip-flop against the gravel. "It's better to be busy."

"I understand."

They returned to the dock and found Oscar bent over picking up a discarded soda. His other hand held several more pieces of trash.

Mer cleared her throat. "Oscar."

The man startled upright, dropping the can. It clattered against the cement, overloud amid the morning hush. He colored and stooped to retrieve it. "I do not want such things in the water." He jogged to the trash can.

Years training as a scientist had impressed upon Mer the need to protect the environment. She nudged Bijoux. "He's got my vote."

He hurried back to the women and arrived slightly out of breath.

"Oscar, I'd like to introduce you to Bijoux Fouchard, the owner of the Aquarius Dive Shop."

Oscar swiped his hand across the front of his shirt, staining it with a trail of syrupy cola. A stray bit of paper still clung to his palm and he dropped it to his side. "Perhaps it is best that I only say hello." He inclined his head.

Bijoux gifted him with one of her dazzling smiles, showing the slight gap between her front teeth. "I understand you would like a job. I have interviews scheduled all morning," Bijoux said. "We can talk over lunch. Would you be able to come back at noon?"

"Twelve o'clock. Of course. If you do not mind, I will stay here. Watch. Learn how I can help."

Bijoux considered him. "Why don't you go out on the morning boat? That way you can see how we operate."

Oscar bent at the waist. "That would be very nice. Thank you."

"No working." Bijoux raised a manicured finger in playful admonishment. "Just watching."

Mer stepped forward. "Let me show you the *LunaSea*."

Sunlight punched through gathering clouds and speckled the ocean. The wind had picked up steadily throughout the morning, and while a dozen divers enjoyed Molasses Reef, the *LunaSea* bobbed in four-foot seas.

Leroy, Oscar and Mer had gathered at the stern of the boat. Leroy leaned against the handrail that stepped down from the deck to the swim platform, his arms crossed in front of him, casually chewing his coffee stirrer.

"And no bananas on the boat, either." Leroy instructed Oscar. "It's bad luck."

"A ridiculous prohibition based on supernatural causation that's known in the scientific realm as hooey," Mer said.

"This from the woman who touches a charm for luck before every rescue," Leroy countered.

Her hand rose to the seahorse that dangled from her neck, but she otherwise ignored his jab. What could she say? He was right. "Used to be considered bad luck to have a woman aboard, too."

Leroy swung the red stirrer to the side of his mouth. "Based on yesterday, I'd say it still is."

"Yesterday?" Oscar asked.

"A highly unusual situation," Mer said, wanting to close the discussion before it began. Still, she couldn't help but squint at the horizon. Just in case.

"I could hedge my bet. Throw you overboard," Leroy added.

Mer moved to the cooler. It squeaked as she lifted the lid. "Again?" Pushing aside cans of soda, she selected two oranges, and then removed a scratched cutting board and a serrated knife.

Oscar's attention seesawed between the two and finally settled on Leroy. "You have a history of this?"

"She's as smart as a tree full of owls, but occasionally one or two of them need to be knocked down to earth."

Oscar's brow furrowed. "I do not understand."

"She has a tendency of getting too big for her britches," Leroy said.

Mer placed the cutting board on the camera table, then worked her thumb into her waistband and held out the loose fabric. "I don't think that's the criteria you're using."

"Sure hope you brought a towel," Leroy replied.

Oscar grabbed the rail around the table to steady himself against the growing chop. "This is not a good day to swim."

Leroy glowered but it fell somewhat short of fierce. "That's because you were whistling earlier."

Oscar pushed his glasses higher up his nose.

Mer took pity on him. "For those silly enough to believe in superstitious nonsense, whistling into the wind is a challenge that conjures storms."

"Exhibit A." Leroy pointed to the steel band of clouds on the horizon racing toward them.

"As long as it doesn't delay us getting back in from the afternoon charter," Mer said. "I have to get out of here on time tonight."

"Hot date?"

"Only if you consider grocery shopping at Winn Dixie a good time."

Leroy tightened the line securing the ladder. "A bit behind the curve, aren't you?"

The knife sliced through the orange and released a sharp citrus scent. "Thanksgiving isn't until tomorrow."

"No sense rushing things." His beard twitched. "I'll add sweet potatoes to the list of what we're bringing."

"You'll do no such thing. I've got things well under control," she said. As long as one didn't count the weather.

A curtain of gray fell from black clouds. The divers would be coming up in the rain, and the dry table would no longer be dry. Mer lifted the cutting board and moved it back to the cooler. No one liked soggy oranges.

The massive Coleman was secured to the cabin floor, its flat surface perfect for an impromptu table. A large swell hit the *LunaSea* broadside as Mer leaned over, and she jammed her knee against the ice chest to absorb the shock. The knife teetered at the edge of the board and then fell to the deck and slid to a stop with its point wedged under the plastic corner. Setting down the board, she leaned over. Something gold glinted.

The hair on the back of her neck prickled. She used the knife blade to leverage the cooler up an inch and created enough space to hook the item with her fingernail. The missing gold coin slid into view.

"Wisdom begins with the fear of God," she whispered. The coin looked remarkably similar to an old silver dollar her father carried in his pocket for luck. Both had letters circling a portrait and lines scoring their edges.

"King Philip the Fifth of Spain."

Oscar's voice startled her with its nearness and she almost dropped the coin. "How do you know that?"

"It is marked on the coin." Pushing his glasses up, he leaned closer. "Seventeen thirty-three." He pursed his lips as if to whistle, but then glanced at Leroy and stopped. "That is a very old coin."

"Hey, Cap'n," Mer raised her voice to be heard over the burgeoning wind. "The prodigal coin returns."

"You have seen this coin before?" Oscar asked.

"Yesterday," she answered absently. She flipped it and studied the crown-topped coat of arms and the Latin words on the reverse side.

"King Philip. He is the first king to have his portrait on a New World coin," Oscar said.

Leroy joined the duo. "Well, I'll be a monkey's uncle."

"Guess you should rethink how lucky it is to have me aboard," Mer said.

"Luck comes in two flavors, Cavallo."

"I'm holding a gold coin in my hand. I think we can all agree what kind of luck that requires."

"It could be bad luck," Oscar said. "Like the Thirteenth Galleon."

"Thirteenth Galleon?" Mer asked.

His dark eyes never left the coin. "It is an old legend that tells of cursed gold," he clarified.

"And here I was starting to like you," Mer said.

Leroy clapped Oscar on the shoulder. "Don't worry. I'm liking you more and more." He grew serious. "What now?"

A drop of rain splatted the coin. "Try not to lose it again before giving it to the police."

"*Ay! Dios mío!*" A horrified expression twisted Oscar's face. "The police? This needs to go to a museum. Not into some officer's pocket."

The thought that an officer might keep the coin had never crossed her mind. The legal system in the United States wasn't perfect, but it wasn't rife with corruption like many other countries. She wasn't particularly fond of Deputy Cole, but she had no cause to believe that he would do anything other than book the coin into evidence. Detective Talbot? Despite finding herself the focus of one of his recent investigations, she still had no reason to doubt his integrity.

But Oscar had a point. Unless the coin was fake, it had value. Maybe even museum quality considering its pristine condition. How long would it languish in the bowels of an evidence locker? The coin had surfaced in a bale of drugs. She doubted anyone would walk into a police station to claim it.

"The police will know what to do with it." She closed her fingers around the coin. Her civic duty demanded she turn it in, but it certainly wouldn't hurt to research the coin's provenance a bit before she did.

"Ready for another lesson?" Without waiting for Oscar to answer, she wended her way to the V-berth and descended into the cramped musty quarters where her backpack nestled against a stack of bright orange life jackets. She unzipped the pocket holding her wallet and tucked the coin into an empty credit card slot so it wouldn't slide against the harder metals of modern coins.

The V-berth darkened and Oscar stood hunched in the hatch opening. "Will you really give it to the police?"

"It's the right thing to do." She zipped the pack. "Isn't it the same where you're from?"

"That is complicated."

She checked her watch. They still had a bit of time before the divers would surface. Sidestepping, she made room for him in the tight area. "What did you do back home?"

The glasses had slid down his face and he took his time pushing

them back into place. "I was a historian. I worked in *Habana*—
Havana," he corrected himself. "The *Archivo Nacional de Cuba.*"

A fellow academic. That explained the instant affinity she'd felt
for the soft-spoken man. "What brings you here?"

"America is the land of opportunity, is it not?" The wistful
expression on his face brightened. "I am here for the adventure."

"Then we need to make sure you impress Bijoux."

6

Mer considered herself a reasonably intelligent woman, but smart wasn't the word used to describe a person who went to the grocery store the night before Thanksgiving.

The lack of parking was her first clue. Almost getting run over before she even hit the door was the second. Yet neither prepared her for the mass of people milling in the aisles when she entered Winn-Dixie.

Armed with her shopping list, she had one goal. Get what she needed and get out.

A lone grocery cart remained in the foyer. She grabbed it, steeled herself for a full-contact game of bumper carts, and joined the fray.

Thanksgiving dinner took a surprising amount of things she'd never used before and she started at the far side of the store.

Four steps into the third aisle, she realized she didn't need anything down it, but retreat was impossible. A man wearing a New York Mets ball cap and red Converse tennis shoes drafted too close behind her to maneuver around without creating a multi-cart pileup.

Two more aisles of shopping left her yearning for the sanctuary of her apartment. Holiday tunes, price checks, and young children mid-meltdowns created a constant din. Pallets blocked the center of already crowded aisles as clerks frantically tried to restock shelves.

She rounded the corner of the spice aisle and collided with an empty cart.

The man in the Mets cap scowled and threw a package of sugar into the top basket. "Watch where you're going."

In the spirit of the holidays, Mer swallowed an uncharitable retort. "Sorry."

He turned his back on her and knelt to examine something on the bottom shelf. Boxer shorts stuck out of the top of his black jeans.

A woman stood on the other side of the aisle holding a can of evaporated milk in one hand and condensed milk in the other. Not enough space existed to allow Mer to pass.

The woman nudged her teenage daughter. "Which is it you use for Key lime pie?" She had a heavy New York accent.

The daughter shrugged and continued to study her phone.

If there was one thing people who lived in the Keys knew, it was how to make a Key lime pie. Even in her short time on the island, Mer had been bombarded with recipes—none of which she'd actually tried, but she still knew the answer. "Condensed."

The woman eyed Mer as if trying to decide her credibility and then put both cans in her cart and poked it forward a centimeter.

Not nearly enough.

Mer tried not to let her exasperation leech into her voice. "Mind if I squeeze by?"

The woman ignored her.

Mer glanced at her watch. Seven o'clock. The store closed at ten, and the way things were going, she wasn't sure she'd finish. She lifted the back of her cart to get a better angle and calculated the velocity required to smash through. Just before Mer attained ramming speed, the Met's fan stood. His shoulder caught the underside of her backpack and lifted it off her shoulder. The bag slid the length of her arm, but he caught it before it hit her wrist.

"Sorry," he said. "Let me help." He twisted the backpack, trapping her elbow.

"I've got it." Mer tugged, but it was still caught up between them. A second yank tore it from his grasp and she resettled the bag on her shoulder. She backed away, wary.

"Happy Thanksgiving." His lips moved, but the smile didn't register with his eyes. He knelt again and studied the items on the shelf. Packaged stuffing.

The crowd was getting to her. He was just another hapless soul trying to prepare for tomorrow. "Happy Thanksgiving," she echoed.

The produce section looked as empty as the water aisle before a hurricane. A stock-boy busied himself opening new boxes of carrots and celery. Mer waited for the three women ahead of her and then claimed her own bags.

Finally the only thing left was the turkey. She rolled through the frozen section and paused in front of the pot pies. They looked a whole lot more appealing than the mound of food in her cart. She'd only thrown a handful of dinner parties—and they'd been impromptu affairs involving fellow grad students—nothing steeped in tradition and expectation.

The pot pies beckoned, singing their siren song of convenience from behind a fogged freezer door. Unable to resist, Mer deposited six boxes in her cart—just in case.

Three steps later, she changed her mind. Backtracking, she replaced the pot pies on their cold shelf. She could do this. Breaking bread was a long-held tradition for establishing a community bond. She'd decided to stay in the Keys. That meant she needed to make it a home—and tomorrow, that required turkey. Not pot pies. Turkey.

A sign hanging above an open chest freezer at the end of the aisle advertised holiday birds. Mer leaned over the cavernous void. Two turkeys remained—one the size of a quail, the other a twenty-six pound monster. She did the math. Half a pound apiece, six people. Even with a margin for error, she'd be eating turkey until Easter.

Served her right for putting off shopping until the last minute.

She hoisted Birdzilla into her cart and embarked on a quest for a register.

An abandoned cart with a bag of sugar in it blocked her path. No sign of the Mets fan. Who could blame him? Even the express line moved at a glacial pace.

At last she unloaded her items onto the conveyor belt. She estimated the cost in her head and gulped. No one worked on a dive boat to get rich. But this meal meant so much to her. It had to be perfect—and perfect cost an appalling amount of money.

Each item pinged as the cashier mechanically swiped things over the sensor. Dark circles shadowed her eyes and she couldn't even pretend to smile. "Do you have your Winn-Dixie card?"

"Oh, yes. Just a second." Mer swung her backpack off to retrieve her wallet.

The front pocket was partially unzipped. And empty.

Her heart lurched.

She ripped open the main compartment and rummaged through the contents in case she'd dropped the wallet in there by mistake.

The cashier scanned more items and slid them toward the bagger.

Mer propped the backpack against the cart and yanked out her towel to get a better look. Dive slates, sunscreen, EpiPen, first aid kit, lip balm, glasses. Before leaving the boat, she'd rewrapped the coin in her sunglass micro-cloth to protect it, and she felt the reassuring weight of it in the bottom of her backpack. But no wallet.

The cashier announced the total.

Mer's mouth went dry. "I don't have my wallet."

The woman behind her exhaled loudly.

Mer flushed. "I'm sorry. It was right here." She addressed the cashier. "Can you hold my groceries aside? I'll come right back."

"There's perishables, we need to restock them before they spoil."

The thought of going through the entire store again was almost worse than not having her wallet. "Please, I just have to run home. I'll be right back."

The circles under the cashier's eyes seemed to darken as Mer waited for an answer.

"Hurry."

Mer ran to her car. A quick search confirmed that her wallet hadn't fallen from her backpack and wedged under the seat. She jammed the key into the ignition. Nothing in Key Largo was very far from anything else, but with only one thoroughfare, getting there could be a challenge.

Her fingers tapped the steering wheel. Four cars waited to get out of the parking lot ahead of her. The clock on her dash ticked off another minute. Where had she put her wallet?

A truck pulled in behind her. Higher than her Subaru, its lights struck her mirror and blinded her. Great.

The line crept forward.

She considered herself a cautious driver. Never had a ticket. No accidents. All that went out the window the moment it was her turn. Six miles separated her from her home and an envelope of emergency cash. Never had it seemed so far. She darted onto the highway, quick as a dragonfly. The truck sucked up to her bumper and entered, too.

The speed limit on the Overseas Highway capped out at forty-five miles an hour, but the holiday traffic hobbled it to a much slower pace. The truck continued to tailgate her Subaru and she merged into the left lane to escape the headlights. It followed. A dull throb started behind Mer's eyes.

"Fine, the lane's all yours." She shifted back into the right lane. It wasn't enough she'd lost her wallet. Now she had an idiot who wanted to ride in her backseat.

The driver ahead of her signaled and slowed for a driveway. Next to her, the driver of the truck mirrored her speed, backing up the already congested traffic. Someone honked.

Unease swept through Mer's body. As soon as her path cleared, she stomped on the gas and her car jumped forward. The other driver revved the diesel engine and caught up to her, the light from the headlights striking her side mirror.

She gritted her teeth. It had to be intentional.

The traffic light at Tarpon Springs neared. She checked the dashboard clock. Another two minutes gone. She didn't have time to spare, but she wanted to get away from the maniac in the truck. The left turn lane loomed and Mer swerved in front of the truck and caught the light into the shopping center. The truck turned, too. Her heart rate surged. With a whispered apology to her car's suspension, she floored it over the speed bumps, and then made a U-turn to take her back onto the highway.

The truck turned down one of the crowded lanes and the driver parked the black Ford under a light.

Relief washed over her. What a ninny she was. Her last name was neither Bourne nor Bond. She didn't warrant this type of attention and it was asinine to think she did. She clicked on her turn signal.

The traffic light turned green and Mer eased back onto the highway.

A long honk behind her drew her attention back to the mirror. The pickup fishtailed through the intersection.

Mer jerked her backpack across the passenger seat and dug into the pocket that held her cellphone. At least she still had that.

The phone rang twice and she held her breath, hoping that it wouldn't go to voicemail. It rang a third time.

"Please, oh please, oh please," Mer whispered. "Please be home from your trip."

"Hey there!" Selkie sounded slightly winded.

"I'm being followed. I need you to meet me at the gate."

"What's your ETA?"

That's what she loved about this man. No unnecessary questions. Just action. "Driving time from the post office."

"Got it."

The truck followed from a distance, as if the driver was afraid to spook her. *A little late for that.*

"If I shout directions, just do it, okay?" His voice exuded confidence.

Mer took a deep breath. "Okay. I'm ready." She could do this. Whatever this was.

"I won't let anyone hurt you."

"See you in a minute." Her voice shook.

The digits on the dash clock changed again, but now, time seemed to slow.

The Ford remained in the right lane. She neared her street on the left, but didn't signal. At the last possible moment, she veered into the turn lane. And stopped.

The swell of traffic carried the truck past her.

But only for a moment. Cutting off a car, the driver bounced a U-turn across the grass median, and headed back her direction.

Mer's heart clogged her throat.

"Come on." She pounded her fist against the steering wheel.

Finally a break.

She gunned the car and shot through a tiny opening in the oncoming traffic. Horns blared. She didn't care. She had to get away.

Less than a mile of empty roadway and she'd be at the security gate.

Her breath escaped in a whoosh. If she arrived before Selkie, she'd be screwed.

He'd be there. He had to be. She accelerated.

Behind her, headlights turned onto the street.

The chain-link fence of the marina and boatyard flew by on her right. Closed up and dark, it offered no protection.

The road narrowed as she neared the gate. Lush landscaping rose on her left. Shadowed and foreboding.

The window took forever to lower. Warm air blasted her face and carried the scent of hot asphalt and salt. No sign of Selkie.

Mer leaned out of the car and tapped the code onto the security keypad.

Headlights flashed behind her. Closer.

The gate lurched, traveling on its narrow track at a woefully slow pace.

Where was Selkie?

No time to dwell upon that now. She was on her own.

She leaned over and opened the glove compartment, searching for a weapon among the owner's manual, tissues, and spare tank O-rings.

Headlights flooded the Subaru. Exposed her.

Her hand slid into the pocket behind the passenger seat and closed around an old flashlight. Not great. Better than tissues.

The gate rumbled. Still not enough space for her to shoot the gap.

A door slammed behind her.

She gripped the flashlight. Glanced in the side mirror. A figure advanced. A man.

The canal was on her right. She might not be able to outrun someone, but the boats would hide her. If he had a gun...

She threw open the door and clicked on the flashlight. Five hundred lumens of light blasted her pursuer in the face. He raised his hand against the glare just as Selkie burst from his hiding place and tackled the driver.

By the time she recovered her wits, Selkie had his knee in the small of the man's back, winding zip cuffs around his wrists.

Mer knelt next to Selkie. "Oscar?"

Selkie tightened the restraint. "You know this guy?" The angled planes of his face looked sharper in the half-light.

"I met him at the shop."

For the first time she noticed his car. A white Corolla. She swallowed. "This isn't the guy."

"Why's he following you?" He yanked Oscar into a seated position. "You got business here?"

Oscar's glasses framed his face at an awkward angle. "I found her wallet. I just want to give it to her."

"He wasn't following me." Mer placed her hand on Selkie's broad shoulder. "It was someone in a black truck."

Selkie unclipped the knife in his shorts pocket and unfolded it in a practiced move.

Oscar jerked back, eyes wide.

"Relax," Selkie said. He cut the plastic.

Freed, Oscar swung his arms to the front.

Mer held out her hand to help him up. "I'm sorry. Someone followed me home from the grocery store. I thought it was you. Are you okay?"

He backed away from Selkie and rubbed his wrists. "I only want to return your wallet."

"Where did you find it?" Mer asked.

"In the Aquarius parking lot. Miss Bijoux, everyone, was gone. I think it best to keep. Give it to you tomorrow. But then I see your car." He indicated the highway. "So you are correct, I followed you. But I had a good reason."

"I feel terrible."

"I would worry, too, if I were followed." He stepped toward his car, then stopped and glanced at Selkie. "May I?"

Selkie stood slightly bladed to Oscar, his military posture relaxed, but alert. A black T-shirt stretched over his muscular frame and he towered over the shorter man.

Mer stepped forward. "I'm sorry, Oscar, this is..." She indicated Selkie. How was she supposed to introduce him? Her neighbor? Lover? Boyfriend?

Selkie thrust out his hand and saved her the trouble. "Selkie. Sorry about the misunderstanding."

Oscar reluctantly shook hands but broke contact quickly and scurried to his car.

Mer rubbed the area between her eyebrows. "I feel like such an idiot."

Selkie watched Oscar as he leaned through the opened window into the Corolla. "I want to know where the truck is."

Oscar returned and held out Mer's wallet. "I opened it, to learn of the owner. I found your license, but California is a long drive. No?"

Her parents' address. Maybe it was time to visit the local DMV. She had so many safety nets in place. How could she move forward if everything kept pulling at her like a riptide? She opened the wallet. Her sole credit card remained tucked in its slot, next to her license.

"I have bad news," Oscar said. "The coin. It is gone. Your money, too. I do not want you to think bad of me."

"Nothing's gone. The wallet must have fallen out of the backpack when I slung it over my shoulder." She would have sworn, though, she'd zipped the pocket.

Oscar visibly relaxed. "That is good. I do not want you to think bad of me."

She owed him a reward. The empty bill slot precluded cash. Gratitude didn't buy a meal. *A meal.* On impulse she blurted, "Tomorrow is Thanksgiving. I'm cooking dinner. Why don't you join us?"

Surprise registered across his face. "Thank you, but I do not want to intrude. This is a family holiday, is it not?"

"Please. It's the least I can do."

Oscar contemplated the invitation and then smiled. "I am honored."

She had to work the morning boat. The shop was running a special sunrise charter in honor of Thanksgiving, but unlike other shops in the area, Bijoux was closing right afterward to allow her employees time to enjoy the holiday. Mer would be home by eleven. "Dinner's at seven."

He bowed like an old world gentleman. "I am anticipating it greatly."

The security gate closed again. She hesitated. Give him the code? He'd just returned her wallet, after all. But she was still shaky from being followed. "When you arrive, scroll through the directory. Look for Orlando—like the city. That's my landlord's name. Press the button and I'll be able to open the gate for you. I'm the second house from the end." She looked at her watch. "I'm sorry, I've really got to go."

7

S elkie insisted on acting as her bodyguard while she retrieved her abandoned groceries. His presence gave her comfort even as his heightened vigilance threatened her composure. It wasn't until the security gate clattered shut behind them on their way home that she drew a normal breath.

The neighborhood was built on a converted twenty-three-hundred-foot airstrip that served double duty as a breakwater between Port Largo Marina and the Atlantic Ocean. Palatial homes backed up to the ocean on one side of the road and overlooked their personal docks on the other side of it.

Mer lived in a not-to-code granny flat on the ground level of a flamingo-pink mansion owned by an international banker she'd yet to meet. The arrangement suited her.

Selkie's home was built at the very end of the defunct runway. Originally, both houses had belonged to one owner. The properties still shared a driveway that forked about six feet from the road. From there, a thick hedge ran the remainder of the property line and ended at the ocean.

Mer pulled into the driveway and veered left. Bougainvillea and a collection of brightly colored bromeliads surrounded the carport that sheltered her front door. Together they shuttled the groceries inside.

Selkie placed the last bags on the crowded counter. "I still don't understand why you won't cook Thanksgiving dinner at my place."

She squeezed past him to open her refrigerator.

Preparing dinner at his house would certainly simplify things. His kitchen had space, modern appliances, and a large counter she could use as a serving buffet. Her apartment had a galley kitchen with enough space to comfortably accommodate a small child. Practicality screamed at her to accept Selkie's offer, but this was her home. Her first Thanksgiving dinner as a hostess should be at a place where she wasn't a guest herself.

She placed a bundle of celery into the refrigerator and held out her hand for more groceries. "Because."

He gave her a package of carrots. "Quite the eloquent argument."

She closed the crisper. "I don't know how to explain it. But it's important to me." She kissed him. "Besides, I thought the way to a man's heart was through his stomach. Isn't it about time I cook something for you?"

"Did you know that Thanksgiving is one of the busiest days at the emergency room?"

She smacked him with the cloth bag. "Remember that when you're giving your compliments to the chef tomorrow."

Mer jigsawed the contents of the fridge until she'd created enough space for the turkey. The shelf sagged, and she wedged a carton of milk sideways to bolster it. Not an inch of space remained. "Can I chill the white wine at your place?"

"Of course. What else do you need?"

A dozen things sprang to mind. "Not a thing. I've got it all under control." She'd organize everything tonight. Bake the pies. Double-check the recipes against her timetable.

"Then can I interest you in an adult beverage? You've earned it after the night you've had."

"You don't know the half of it."

Selkie stopped and gave her his full attention. "What's that mean?"

In all the night's excitement, Mer hadn't had the chance to tell him about her encounter with the pirates. "It means a glass of wine sounds wonderful."

The door closed behind them. They crossed the driveway to Selkie's property and climbed the sweeping staircase that led to his main entry.

He opened the front door. "Is this a conversation for wine or something stronger?" he asked.

She continued to the deck. "Wine for me. You may want to break out the Jameson."

The balcony ringed the upper level of his home. Teak furniture created an outdoor living space replete with conversation nooks, a dining area, and a hammock for lounging. She dragged her hand across the table. Heat from the day still lingered in the smooth wood.

Waves crashed against the rocks below and drew Mer to the rail. The crescent moon sat low in the sky and a ribbon of light shimmered across the water.

Selkie rejoined her. "So?" He handed her a glass of Pinot Gris and clinked his tumbler of whiskey against her glass.

Mer took a quick sip of wine and recounted her high seas adventure.

Selkie interrupted her. "What do you mean, they shot at you?"

"Technically, only one did."

He plucked the glass from her hand, placed it next to his, and gathered her into his arms. "You seem remarkably calm about this."

"I was scared witless. Which is probably why I freaked out about the truck."

"Fear is a defense mechanism." He drew back to be able to see her face. "Don't ever discount how something makes you feel."

She nodded.

"Talk to me about this Oscar person," Selkie said. "What do you know about him?"

"He's from Havana. Used to be an archivist. Quiet. He spent the morning on the boat with me and Leroy. He impressed us both."

"I see."

Mer broke free of his embrace. "Stop."

"What?"

She swept her hand toward the ocean and almost knocked over her wineglass. "It's a beautiful night. Can't we talk about something else?"

Selkie rescued the glass, but it was a long moment before he handed it to her. "You should report this."

"I'm going home now."

He wrapped his other arm around her waist. "I can't believe it's already Thanksgiving."

She leaned her back against his chest. "I have so much to be thankful for." Recent events notwithstanding.

He nuzzled her ear. "I'm thankful for you."

His voice, low pitched and smooth, gave her goosebumps. "Even after tonight?" she asked.

"You definitely make life interesting." He rested his chin against the top of her head.

"That's a nice way to put it." They stood together swaying slightly. She was acutely aware of the pressure of his hand against her belly. She nestled closer.

"I worry about you, though," he said.

Warmth flooded her body. She wasn't used to having someone worry about her—at least not someone within a three-thousand-mile radius. Her mother had worried about her the entire two years she spent conducting research in the Arctic. But this was different. "Can't have you getting bored."

"No need to worry on that account." He grabbed her hand and kissed her fingertips. "I love you."

Mer froze. Love. He *loved* her.

She drew her hand back. She'd spoken those words to him years ago. Before everything had changed.

Selkie squeezed her hand.

Her mind snapped back into operation. "I don't know what to say."

"You don't have to say anything. I just thought you should know."

"It's too soon," she mumbled.

He spun her around. "Technically, we've known each other twelve years." His voice remained gentle. Light. "That hardly qualifies as too soon."

She'd been a smitten undergrad and he'd been her older brother's friend. Theirs had been a summer fling. Nothing more. At least that's what she'd tried to convince herself at the time. After he left.

"I'm not sure bringing that up helps your case." The wineglass shook in her hand and she tightened her grip so he wouldn't notice.

"It's okay to be scared, Mer. I get it."

Her chin came up. "I'm not scared." But they both knew she was lying.

The only thing Mer was privy to regarding Selkie's career was the education that qualified him for it. He'd attended the U.S. Naval Academy in Annapolis as an undergrad. Then came the Naval Post Graduate School in Monterey. His master's degree was in Defense Analysis and he'd written his thesis on psychological operations and deception. His ability to discern her thoughts unnerved her more than a little. She gulped the last of her wine in three swallows. "I should go. Get some things prepped."

Selkie puffed out his cheeks and released his breath in a rush. "Need any help?"

She shook her head. "I can handle it."

"That was never in doubt."

She hesitated. "Are we good?"

He took her empty glass. "Better than."

"Be prepared to be wowed tomorrow."

"I wouldn't miss it for the world."

Mer kissed him goodnight and hurried down the steps.

There were times Mer wished she could read his expression with the ease he read hers. Selkie had said he loved her and she'd acted like a dolt. He wasn't the problem. She was the one who couldn't get over the fear that history would repeat itself.

Not the falling in love part; the ending of it.

Once inside, the familiarity of her apartment soothed her. A framed photograph of her family anchored the corner of her walnut desk. Her parents wore the beleaguered expression common to adults who wondered exactly when they'd lost control of their children. For their part, Mer and her older brothers had grown into a trio of overachievers. A priest, a cop, and a scientist. Add a bar and they'd have the setup for a bad joke.

The rest of the apartment was furnished in white wicker provided by the landlord. The only other thing that belonged to Mer was her aquarium and it served as a partition between the tiny living room and her bedroom. She walked over to the tank and pinched some flakes into the water. Small mollies and bright damsels darted around the large tank, hiding within the live rock. She never tired of watching them. Their presence conditioned the tank for its next occupant—an octopus. A symbol of her commitment to stay in the Keys.

Best not to trip down that particular lane at the moment.

And watching fish didn't get the Thanksgiving prep work done. She'd promised everyone a perfect dinner and that was exactly what she planned to deliver.

Food covered every inch of available counter space in the tiny galley. She drew a deep breath, determined to conquer the chaos. Once the mess had been tamed, she grabbed the pie recipes.

Despite the new order, it took several minutes to locate the can of pureed pumpkin. Personally, she'd never found pumpkin pie particularly appealing, but it was Selkie's favorite and she wanted to impress him. Maybe he was still awake. She peered out her kitchen window, but the hedge blocked her view of the house and she couldn't tell if any lights were still on.

She picked up her cellphone to call him, but the camera icon distracted her. *The photos.*

In all the recent excitement, she'd forgotten about them.

Opening the app, she navigated to her saved images. The last one showed the list of names she'd retrieved from the contraband bale—taken on the *LunaSea* before the wind from their getaway tore the brittle page to bits.

The small phone screen and the feathery handwritten scrawl thwarted her efforts to read the words. She attached the images to a message and emailed them to herself.

The photos were waiting in her inbox by the time her laptop booted up, and she deleted them from her phone. The photo filled the screen, large enough that she could decipher the tortured script. Nearly all the names were Hispanic.

Pushing aside a stack of holiday recipes, she pulled out a legal pad and then paused. She'd planned on completing some of the cooking prep tonight. The individual dishes seemed easy enough; it was the timing that worried her.

She leaned back in her chair and stared beyond the walls of her little home and her mind slid back to the list. Who was she kidding? The pies could wait.

By the time she finished transcribing the names, the wall clock above her desk read eleven o'clock. She should shut off the computer and call it a night. After all, her day started earlier than normal tomorrow with the holiday sunrise charter.

She prepared for bed, but her mind wouldn't abandon the task. Who were these people, and why were their names hidden in a bale of contraband drugs? Discovering their identity seemed a straightforward proposition. After all, she had their names. Waiting until tomorrow to investigate would only ensure she'd have a restless night. She started at the top and typed the first name into her search engine. Within seconds she had a list linking to Spanish language sites.

Growing up in California, Mer had learned Spanish by osmosis. Enough to get by, but nowhere near fluency. In school she'd studied Latin for taxonomy and French because she'd always wanted to know something about romance, even if it was just the language.

Fat lot of good that did her tonight.

Had she screwed up? Selkie was a puzzle with so many pieces she didn't know where to start. The one constant was that she loved him, even if she couldn't manage to spit it out and tell him. She rolled her shoulders back in a stretch and a vertebra popped into place. She should have called him earlier. Now it was too late.

She typed another name. Nothing.

The next one gave her too many results to contemplate.

Frustrated, she picked up her pencil and scanned the list looking for a distinctive name. Lots of Josés, Dons, Franciscos, and Josephs. Very few women's names, and the ones that were recorded shared the same surname with at least one other person. The logical assumption would be that they belonged to the same family. But she hated to make assumptions without something more substantial to support it.

She tapped the eraser of her mechanical pencil against the pad and contemplated the list.

Mateo Eques de Soto y Berdugo. That was a distinctive name. She dropped the pencil. Using quotes, she typed the entire name into the search engine.

Nothing.

The first two words she recognized. Mateo was Spanish for Mathew. Eques meant a horseman or rider in Latin. Based on the "de" that preceded it, she suspected Soto referred to a place, although it could be a family name.

This was getting her nowhere. She had plenty of data and yet nothing lent itself to a conclusion.

She dug out the coin.

Like any specialized field of study, she figured coinage would have its own vocabulary and hierarchy of categorization. Thankfully, Google spoke the vernacular.

She typed *gold King Philip V 1733 coin* and hit the return key.

Less than a second later, she had a staggering amount of results.

She yawned. Research would have to wait. Morning had technically arrived and in a few hours, she'd be on the *LunaSea* with a boatload of divers welcoming the sunrise.

Tomorrow, she'd call the police and give them the coin, mention the truck—although what good would that do? How many black trucks were there in the Keys?

She snapped several photos of Philip and his heraldry, and then tucked the gold disk into an envelope from her desk and stashed it in her backpack.

After tomorrow's dinner, she'd try again to identify the coin. Satisfy her curiosity. Be done with this whole curious affair.

8

The sunrise charter ran without a hitch. Fourteen divers from a scuba club in Pennsylvania had escaped snow to take advantage of the warm weather and clear water of Key Largo. They'd even tipped well— a welcome holiday bonus that helped defray the cost of today's feast. Now it was time to cook.

Lost in thought, Mer strode nearly to her front door before she realized it stood ajar. She stopped mid-step and slowly lowered her foot. Pry marks dented the doorjamb near the bolt, exposing fresh, splintered wood.

She scanned around her, half expecting someone to jump out of the bushes. Not even an iguana moved. She held her breath and listened at the door, but only heard her own pulse beating loud in her ears.

Poised to bolt, Mer pushed against the door. It banged against something inside. She pushed harder and poked her head around. An upended wicker chair scraped across the tile.

For a moment, she could only stare, her mind processing the chaos in small increments, as if that made it easier to comprehend.

Every drawer, every cabinet, every single thing had been upended. Strewn across the apartment. Even the refrigerator had been emptied, food tossed, bottles and jars broken—their guts seeping across the floor.

Mer entered. Glass crunched under her feet and she almost slipped in a puddle.

"No!" Her eyes sought the aquarium and found the damselfishes and mollies on the floor among the rubble of rock.

Her throat tightened and she slowly turned circles in the center of her home.

Mer dug inside her backpack for her cellphone and picked her way to the desk. Her legs wobbled and she leaned against it for support. A deep gouge scarred the spot where her laptop normally sat. Cracks spiderwebbed across the portrait of her family. She righted the photograph across the gash, hiding as much of the desk's injury as she could with the small silver frame.

Heat burned upward from her toes and flashed through her body. She clenched her fists and the phone dug into her palm. Who would do this?

"*Mon dieu!*"

Mer spun.

Bijoux stepped into the apartment, her head swiveling, trying to take in everything at once. "Are you hurt?"

Mer didn't trust her voice. She shook her head.

"Have you called the police?"

Bijoux's question focused Mer. "Just..." Her voice caught and she cleared her throat. "Just about to." The numbers seemed to swim on the touchpad. Finally she tapped out the three digits that would connect her to the Monroe County Sheriff's Office dispatch.

"Nine-One-One. What's your emergency?"

Mer answered all the male dispatcher's questions and hung up. Her anger simmered at a low boil.

"I came over to see if you needed any help." Bijoux moved closer to Mer, but didn't touch her. "I can see that you do."

A lump rose in Mer's throat. "Why would someone do this?"

"Because there are always those who believe that if they can take it, they deserve it." The taller woman placed her hands on her hips.

The stack of bracelets on her wrist settled loudly into their new position while she scrutinized the apartment. "At least you were not home," Bijoux said. "Property can be replaced. Wounds take time to mend."

They stood in silence for several long minutes.

Finally, Mer spoke. "Happy Thanksgiving." Oh shit. *Thanksgiving.* Her gaze took in the kitchen again. Flour dusted every surface as if the bag had detonated while she was away. On the floor, Birdzilla nested brazenly on a bag of cranberries. "I knew I should have bought those pot pies."

"Don't be absurd. This isn't Colorado."

"Not that type of pot pies."

"Exactly what type of pot pies are you talking about?" Deputy Cole stood in the doorway, his bald head shiny with perspiration. Despite the devastation of the apartment, his eyes remained solely on Mer.

"I didn't hear you drive up," Mer said.

He cracked his gum. "You weren't supposed to."

No greeting, no words of comfort. Mer's hackles rose. "Congratulations, then."

"You're avoiding my question."

"*Turkey* pot pie, Deputy. It's Thanksgiving."

"And yet I'm here," he said. "What happened?"

"Isn't it self-evident?"

He shrugged. "For all I know, you're a lousy housekeeper."

Bijoux gasped.

"I assure you, I am not," Mer responded icily. "If you care to look to your right, you'll observe pry marks. I certainly didn't invite anyone in to do this."

He dug in his pocket for his notebook. "Makes me wonder about the company you keep."

"How now, fair mistress?" Only one man she'd ever met managed to work Shakespeare into everyday conversation. She supposed it was inevitable that he showed up.

Detective Josh Talbot pushed past Deputy Cole and whistled.

"Wow. Last time I was here, this place looked a lot better." He wore slacks and a white linen *Guayabera* shirt that contrasted with his sepia-colored skin. Subtle notes of sandalwood cologne followed him, an unusual scent in an ocean town. He nodded to Bijoux. "Ms. Fouchard."

Bijoux smoothed her brightly colored head wrap. "Detective Talbot."

Deputy Cole glanced up from his notebook. "Dispatch called a detective out?"

"No, I heard the address on the radio. Figured I'd check in on my favorite troublemaker." His gaze flitted across the small space, cataloging the damage. "What was stolen?"

"My computer. Who knows what else."

Talbot scanned the apartment. "Strange. Burglaries don't normally entail this much damage. Risky, too. They had to notice the Thanksgiving-themed groceries. Know someone was coming back."

"They?"

"There are two different types of shoe impressions in the flour that's spilled on the floor."

The detective squatted at the edge of the kitchen and the two women leaned over him. Deputy Cole remained by the door.

"I suppose the smaller set could belong to a big woman," Talbot continued. "But I'd guess you had two guys stomping around looking for something."

"Drugs, maybe?" Deputy Cole stopped writing to gauge Mer's reaction.

The words earned him a glare. "Feel free to search." She faced Talbot. "The one thing I have of value is a gold coin that I found."

"You told me you didn't have it," Cole said.

"I didn't." She cut him from the conversation again. "Do you know what a square grouper is?" she asked Talbot.

"I grew up in the Keys. Of course I do."

"Huh." Apparently, her Keys knowledge needed fine-tuning. "Anyway. I found it in a bale of drugs."

"That was *you* the other day?" Talbot laughed. "I should have known."

She slapped her hand on the desk. "Nothing about this is funny."

Talbot's mirth dissolved. "You're right. I'm sorry. Please go on."

She made them wait a minute while she gathered her thoughts. "I'd discovered a coin in the bale. There may have been more, I don't know. Anyway, I thought I'd lost it during the chase."

Deputy Cole snorted, but never looked up from his point-and-shoot camera as he snapped photographs of the footprints.

A teenaged girl peeked her head around the door and glanced at the damage. "Dad, are you going to be much longer? Dinner's almost ready. Mom wants to know when we'll be there."

Mer raised her eyebrows. Dad? The girl was a child of autumn: sun-kissed skin, russet hair, and blue eyes. Nothing in her appearance lent a clue to her parentage. Neither man wore a ring. Not that all men wore a wedding band, but Detective Talbot had struck her as a traditionalist. Deputy Cole struck her as single.

"Go back to the car, baby girl," Talbot said. "This will just take a few more minutes."

She rolled her eyes. "You always say that."

"This time I mean it."

The girl disappeared like a wraith, but her voice trailed through the door. "You always say that, too."

Mer looked expectantly at Talbot.

He cleared his throat. "My daughter, Gabriella. Takes after her mother."

"So I gathered."

"You were talking about a coin?" Talbot prompted.

Deputy Cole lowered his camera. "A gold coin. Seventeenth century."

"Eighteenth," Mer corrected.

He widened his stance and the leather of his gun belt creaked. "You claimed you didn't have it."

She spoke through gritted teeth. "I didn't. I found it yesterday, wedged under the cooler we keep on the boat."

Deputy Cole tapped Talbot's shoulder. "Can I speak to you?" He jerked his head toward the door. "Outside?"

"Sure."

The two men stepped into the carport. Bijoux moved closer to Mer as if to give her support.

Despite the distance, the deputy's words carried. "What's the scoop on this lady?"

Talbot's voice was lower and she couldn't make out the words, but she could guess. After all, he'd once looked upon her as a suspect, too. But that was before. They'd moved beyond that misunderstanding. She thought.

"Looks like a drug deal gone bad to me," the deputy said. "None of the passengers saw them find the bale. What if they already had it on board? They rendezvous with the other boat while the divers are in the water. Only they didn't pony up everything they were supposed to. She signals an emergency to the divers to make it look good. By then, the other guys realize they'd been double-crossed. Come back for the gold. Now her apartment is ransacked? Something stinks."

More indistinguishable murmurs from Talbot. Was he defending her?

Her hands shook. She needed to do something. Anything. She coiled the laptop cord they'd left behind, then leaned over to pick up the notepad and papers strewn across the floor. The top page of the pad had been torn off, but a slight impression remained on the next sheet. Curious, she straightened her desk chair and sat. Scrutinized the page.

The names.

Blood rushed to her head. "They stole the list."

Talbot leaned through the doorway. "What?"

Her foot pushed off the floor and her chair spun. "The list of names that I found with the coin. It's gone."

Deputy Cole moved forward and towered over Mer. "So what list did you give me?"

"It's the same list. I had taken a photograph of it. Last night, I transcribed it."

"What a strange thing to do." Deputy Cole let the silence drag out.

"Speak up, Deputy. There's obviously more on your mind."

"There is. Everything is too coincidental for you not to be involved."

Mer flung her hand out to take in her apartment. "I am involved. All you have to do is look at my apartment to know that. But I'm not mixed up in this in the way you obviously think. I'm a victim here, Deputy Cole. I am not your suspect." She addressed Talbot. "I was followed by a black Ford pickup truck last night."

"Did you see the driver?"

"No."

"The license plate?"

She shook her head. "But it's all got to be connected, don't you think? Somehow?"

"Theories?"

She deflated. "I don't know. Up until two days ago, I didn't even know what a square grouper was." Her expression dared the deputy to snort or disagree. "The names could be distributors, maybe customers?"

Talbot frowned. "Or a roster of people being smuggled to the U.S. along with the drugs."

"People?"

"Cubans, mostly," Bijoux said. "But other islanders too. People trying to make a better life for themselves. The Keys are the closest place to land."

"But the bale was in the water. Were the people, too?" The thought horrified Mer.

"There was a squall Monday night," Talbot said. "You found the bale on Tuesday. The Coast Guard didn't pick anyone up."

"So that leaves three possibilities."

"Two," said Cole. "They either made shore or drowned."

Mer set her hands on her hips. "Three. We don't know for certain that it was a list of people trying to immigrate."

Cole snorted. "Need permission for it to be *immigrating*."

Mer sprang from the chair, causing Cole to take a step back. "But why was the list important enough to steal?" she asked Talbot.

"I'm more inclined to think they were looking for the gold coin. Did they get it?"

She shook her head. "No."

"Where is it?" Cole demanded.

Mer thrust her hand into her backpack and dug out the envelope. "I meant to call the station today, but time got away from me." She presented the coin to Talbot.

"That's believable," Cole said. "What else aren't you sharing?"

Her patience toggle flipped. "You know what? Get out." She spun on Talbot. "You, too."

He held up his hands. "I believe you."

"Which is why you let him insult me."

Talbot surveyed the room again. "At least let us dust for prints."

"No reason to." Cole freed his patrol car key from the leather keeper on his gun belt. "I found a latex glove on the driveway when I walked up. Whoever was inside wore gloves."

"Faulty reasoning, but there you have it." Mer stomped to the door and held it open. "The deputy has everything he needs."

Talbot hesitated.

"I have guests coming this evening. I have enough to clean up without your damn powder."

Bijoux placed her hand on Mer's forearm. "Perhaps—"

"No." She shook off Bijoux's hand. "They're done. So am I."

9

Mer slammed the door behind the two officers. At least she tried to. A piece of wicker bounced the door back into her shoulder.

Unacceptable. She kicked the chair out of the way and grabbed the knob, her hand tightening around it until her knuckles whitened.

Bijoux stepped in front of her. "Perhaps you should allow me."

Mer slowly released her grip. Took a small breath. Nodded, not trusting her voice.

The deadbolt no longer aligned with the strike plate and the metal scraped as Bijoux pushed the door closed. That tiny sound resonated through Mer's entire body. Only she didn't quite know what to make of it. Didn't know what to make of any of this.

But that would have to wait. She had guests arriving in precious few hours and she'd promised them a proper Thanksgiving meal.

Bijoux cleared her throat, but Mer spoke first. "Well, this may impact what time we eat."

"I am certain everyone will understand that circumstances have changed."

The seahorse pendant dug into Mer's closed fist and she

wondered how long she'd been holding it. "I just have a bit of...last-minute housecleaning before I start cooking."

Bijoux surveyed the mess and then Mer's face. "Where is your broom?"

A smile was still beyond her abilities, but a tiny spark of hope flared. She could do this. "Thank you. I have to attend to my fishes."

Careful to avoid the glass, Mer sat back on her heels, heedless of the water puddled on the tile. The vibrant colors of the fishes had already dulled. Tears pricked the back of her eyes and she blinked them away. The burglars had stolen her laptop, could have taken her camera. Why did they feel the need to destroy the tank?

She carried the fishes through the backyard, knelt at the end of the lawn, and placed them in the ocean. At least they'd remain part of the sea.

When she returned to her apartment, the two women righted the landlord's dinette, and then attacked the remaining furniture. The mattress had been shoved off the box spring and it jutted into the air. They slid it into place, but when Bijoux started to tuck in the sheets, Mer stopped her and stripped the linens from the bed. "I can't. Someone touched..."

"I understand." Bijoux gathered the linens in her arms. "Where is your washer?"

Mer gave her the key to the garage. "Thank you."

Standing there alone, the devastation seemed worse. Someone had been inside her home. Shoe prints marked the path of destruction and ended at Birdzilla. She stared at the prints. The larger impressions had tread that reminded her of the bottom of her sneakers. The other was just an outline that left an impression similar to her own flip-flops.

She forced herself to compartmentalize. Tackle one task at a time. She fitted the garbage can with a fresh bag. Birdzilla's twenty-six pounds overwhelmed the container and Mer shook open a separate bag. All the defiled produce, the opened packages, the rolls pulled out of their bag, all trashed. Even spice bottles had been opened and tilted as if the burglars expected to find the coin buried under a tablespoon of sage.

At least the kitchen smelled good.

"Such a waste," Bijoux said when she returned. She held another bag up against the counter and swept the dregs of an oregano jar into the trash.

Mer picked up a can of corn. "They didn't open the canned goods. We have corn. And pureed pumpkin."

"Are either of the markets open today?"

The clock on the wall wasn't there anymore and Mer looked at her wrist. "Half day. Both closed an hour ago." She swiped her hand across her face, realizing too late that it was dusted with flour. "The only places open now are gas stations, pizza joints, and maybe Walgreens."

Not that she could afford to replace everything, even with the tip she'd received earlier.

A car pulled into the driveway. Mer recognized the hum of Selkie's Range Rover. The engine cut and a perfunctory knock tapped on her door before he burst inside wielding a bouquet of gladioli.

"Mer." In three strides he crossed the room and gathered her into his arms in a forceful hug. The flowers smacked the back of her head. "Are you all right?"

Mer was used to the reaction by now, but she was too angry to want comfort and she wiggled from his grasp. "You should have seen this place forty-five minutes ago."

He stepped back. Before her eyes, the military operator in him came out. His chiseled features hardened while he thoroughly scrutinized the interior—assessing, noting damage, determining threats. "Have the police been here?"

"Yes."

"She kicked them out," Bijoux added, innocently sweeping sprigs of woodsy-scented rosemary into the trash.

Mer raised her eyebrow at her friend and then faced Selkie

again. "They think I'm a player and this was all just a drug deal gone bad," Mer explained.

"Who's *they*?" Selkie asked.

"Deputy Cole primarily. But Detective Talbot didn't spring to my defense."

"Josh was here?"

"He heard the call on the radio. I suspect curiosity got the better of him. He had his daughter with him."

"Gabriella."

"Do you know everyone in the Keys?"

"Pretty much." He still held the flowers. "Did they pull any prints? Take photos?"

"Cole snapped some. He found a glove, so he said there was no point in dusting."

"To be fair," Bijoux said. "They didn't have much time."

Mer snuck a sideways look at Bijoux. She'd wait until they were through cleaning, but then, sadly, Mer would have to kill her friend.

Selkie sighed and belatedly handed over the cellophane-wrapped flowers.

The wrapper crinkled as Mer admired the soft lavender blooms. The remains of her vase were scattered across the floor and she ran water into a saucepan. That would have to do.

"Cole was the one I was telling you about," Mer said. "He seems convinced I'm orchestrating some grand plan to use the *LunaSea* to smuggle drugs into the Keys, and that I was intentionally withholding contraband."

"He knows you pushed the bale into the sea."

"Not that. The coin."

"You still had it?"

Mer flushed. "I gave it to Talbot."

"Did you report finding it before turning it in?"

"I wanted to learn a bit about it first."

"So, no," Selkie answered for her.

Mer raised her chin. "No."

"And that brilliant mind of yours never considered how

suspicious that might look to Deputy Cole?"

The mere mention of the deputy stoked her anger. "Don't be absurd. Since when did it become criminal to be curious?"

A succession of emotions crossed Selkie's face before something indefinable settled upon his features. He wrapped his arms around her again, gently this time. "You sure you're okay?"

It was a serious question requiring serious thought. The furniture was back in place, but it would be awhile before any semblance of normalcy returned to the apartment. Her aquarium was destroyed. Her fishes killed. Someone had rummaged through her underwear. No. She wasn't okay. Not even close.

Selkie squeezed her shoulder. "What do you need?"

"Your trashcans."

"I meant you. What do *you* need?"

She shrugged off his arm. "Ten minutes with whoever did this."

Bijoux snorted. "That hardly seems adequate."

Mer rummaged through several desk drawers before locating a pencil on the floor. "It's all the time I can spare. I have a dinner to make."

"You can't be serious," Selkie said.

"Of course I am."

"At least have it at my place. It'll be a lot easier."

It would be easier. And maybe on a day when she hadn't invested so much in an outcome, she'd welcome the opportunity. Today wasn't that day. She wouldn't allow the burglars to take that from her, too.

She placed her hand on his chest and looked up into his face. Willed him to understand. "Please. May I borrow your trashcans?"

He clasped her hand and sighed as he brought it to his lips. "Be right back."

Mer found the pad of paper. She needed a plan. A list to wrangle her scattered thoughts and force them into some semblance of order. "If we focus on the kitchen counters first, that will give us a workspace."

She stepped over a broken plate and rescued a sponge from

the sink.

Bijoux grabbed the broom. "At least let me clear you a path so you don't step on something that slices through your flip-flops."

"The way my luck is going, I'd hit an artery."

Chunks of glass and china clinked discordantly as Bijoux gathered them into a pile. She stooped and rescued several canned items.

The kitchen was barely large enough for the two of them to work at the same time and they danced around each other as Mer poked through the cabinets. Most of the plates and glassware had been destroyed.

Selkie returned with two trashcans and a flat-edge shovel. Leaving one can outside, he dragged the other fifty-gallon monster into the apartment. The women stepped out while he made short work of the pile Bijoux had created.

Free of large debris, a sticky cocktail of syrup, ketchup, and orange juice covered the floor, and sucked noisily at her sandals when she returned. She eyed the salvaged items. Not much to play with. "How's spaghetti sound?"

"Like Thanksgiving at the Gambino house," Selkie said.

"It's either that or pickled beets and pumpkin puree over tuna fish."

"Spaghetti sounds lovely," Bijoux said.

Selkie pushed the can toward the door. "You know you can raid my cupboards."

"I hope I don't have to take you up on that, but thank you." She pulled out her cellphone and opened a browser. "Walgreens is open. Do you mind picking up paper plates and napkins?" The photograph of her family stared at her from the desk. She pried open the little tabs on the back and removed five one-hundred dollar bills sandwiched behind the photo. She handed one to Selkie. "And a couple of bottles of red wine, too. The bastards stole the pinot."

Bijoux leaned against the broom. "At least that's one less thing we have to clean up."

"Your relentless optimism is really annoying." Mer smiled as she said it.

"I will *happily* go to Walgreens for you." Bijoux snatched the bill from Selkie's hand. "Call me if you think of anything else you need."

"An industrial strength espresso machine with a frothing wand and a barista to operate it."

"Walgreens has Folgers."

"A sad day for us all," Mer lamented.

When Bijoux left, Selkie gathered Mer into his arms again. "At least you weren't home."

"What kind of a simpleton breaks into someone's house on Thanksgiving?" She leaned back to look in Selkie's face. "Everyone's home on Thanksgiving."

"Which when you think about it, leaves a lot of vacant houses if you're traveling to family elsewhere."

"This has something to do with the coin. I know it. I just need to figure out why."

"You don't have to figure out anything. That's what the police are for."

"Great. According to Deputy Cole, I'm their number one suspect in a new drug trafficking cartel."

"Josh is smarter than that. Besides, he likes you."

"Detective Talbot arrested me three months ago."

"Ancient history." He kissed her forehead. "You've redeemed yourself since then."

"Lucky me."

"What's next?"

"Figure out the coin's provenance. The names on the list were a dead-end, but since the list was the one thing stolen in addition to my laptop and wine, it must have some importance I haven't discovered yet."

"I meant what's next in the apartment?"

"Oh." The kitchen wouldn't be earning a Michelin star anytime soon, but it was a step closer to functional. She heaved a sigh. It was time for a harder task.

10

Together, Mer and Selkie lifted the broken fish tank. The rock liner formed a coarse sludge across the bottom of the aquarium that sloshed as they carried it outside. Everything else could be fixed or replaced, but not this.

A yellow VW bug pulled into Selkie's driveway and parked under the carport.

They set the tank down and Selkie tipped it on the edge of the grass to drain. "Be right back."

Selkie's younger sister, Fiona, barely had her feet on the pavement before Selkie swooped her up in a bear hug and swung her around.

"Put me down you big ox." She pounded on her brother's shoulder. "You'll hurt the baby."

Selkie nearly dropped her. "Baby? Wha—"

She skipped out of his reach. "You're so gullible. How'd you ever earn that degree of yours?"

"So, that's how we're going to play, eh?" He lunged for her.

Fiona darted behind Mer. "Save me from this madman."

Mer laughed. It felt good. "You've got more experience than I do."

Selkie threw up his hands. "One at a time, maybe. The two of you together? I've got more smarts than that."

"A new acquisition that I credit to your neighbor." Fiona gave Mer a hug. "Happy Thanksgiving."

Freckles played across Fiona's pale skin. Strawberry blond waves, so different from her brother's darker hair, brushed her shoulders and framed eyes that shone with a thousand laughs. "Oh, I almost forgot. I've got something for you."

She retraced her steps to the car and lifted an insulated wine tote out of the trunk.

"A sophisticated dry Riesling for Mer, a brash Beaujolais for my brother. And champagne for me. Cuz I like the bubbles." She crinkled her nose.

"I see you're still matching wines to the drinker and not the meal," Selkie said.

She handed the Beaujolais to her brother. "Be nice or next time I'll bring you vinegar."

"Duly noted."

She raised herself on tiptoe and kissed his cheek. "I've missed you."

"I'm looking forward to missing you again." He turned to Mer. "I'll be back in a flash. I forgot something next door."

"Don't let him fool you, he's probably checking the score on the game." Fiona said to Mer. "Now, what can I do to help?"

Mer led her into the apartment. "Funny you should ask."

At the threshold Fiona gasped, but quickly regained her composure. She indicated the trashcan. "Interesting design element. Very avant-garde."

"It's temporary."

"Glad to hear." She sidestepped the can and stashed the two bottles in the refrigerator. "Wine's chilling. What now?"

"Can you find a locksmith willing to respond on a holiday?"

"One locksmith coming up." Fiona slipped out onto the patio with her phone.

Bijoux returned laden with bags. Leroy and Maggie arrived a few minutes later.

Leroy's gaze swept the room and his frown deepened. "Good thing I told Maggie to bake pies." He placed a wicker hamper on the dinette and Mer could have sworn she heard the table legs groan.

Maggie bustled forward and enveloped Mer in a hug that smelled of cinnamon and sympathy. "Don't let him fool you. He doesn't *tell* me to do anything." She opened the lid. "Bijoux called and warned us. I whipped up a few things to go with spaghetti. I hope you don't mind."

Garlic perfumed the air as Maggie handed Mer two long loaves of bread wrapped in tinfoil. "The one with parsley is plain butter."

"Thank you."

Fiona pulled open the rear slider doors and called across the small bedroom. "Locksmith will be here after he eats and finishes watching the game." She approached the group with her hand out. "Hi, I'm Fiona."

Mer completed the introductions. "Let me set the table outside and you can enjoy some wine while I start dinner." She grouped the box of crackers and a can of tuna fish together, then set about finding her can opener. "I'll bring out some appetizers in a minute."

"Quite the traditional—"

Maggie jabbed the stack of paper plates into her husband's belly as she addressed Mer. "That would be delightful. I also grabbed some cheese I had in the back of the fridge." She excavated a wheel of Brie and a wedge of Parmesan from the carrier along with a grater. "Just on the off chance you needed this."

"How did Leroy ever land you?"

"Oh, child." She placed the items on the table. "He was bigger than life and twice as handsome. It was all I could do to reel him in."

Leroy nuzzled her neck. "She baited the hook with pie."

"Shush." Maggie swatted her husband playfully and returned her attention to the basket. She removed a divider, and then two pies. One had a lattice crust, the other a meringue topping. "Leroy said you wanted me to bring these."

Mer turned accusing eyes on her captain.

He shrugged. "One bite, you'll be thanking me."

They left the pies inside, but gathered the other items and carried them into the backyard.

The main house above Mer's apartment also covered her patio, and the cozy space bore none of the scars of the break-in. The chairs had all their cushions; the table remained undamaged. For a moment, Mer reveled in the normalcy of it.

Leroy set the plates on the edge of the table. "Nice view you've got yourself."

The vista never grew old. Four brightly painted Adirondack chairs dotted an expanse of lawn. Soaring coconut palms, dense thickets of sea grapes and clusters of colorful bromeliads created an impenetrable hedge between the neighboring homes. A series of cragged coral boulders dotted the edge of the grass where it met the sea, and a break in the stone created enough space to launch a kayak. Beyond that yawned the diamond-dotted Atlantic.

"I've got many reasons to be grateful." She placed the two bottles of wine on the table and came to a sobering realization. "Having glasses isn't one of them at the moment."

Maggie patted her on the shoulder. "You just worry yourself with dinner. I'll set out the cheese and crackers. It'll all work out."

Mer managed a tight smile. "I had everything planned."

Selkie arrived, carrying a large carton. "I brought over a few things I thought you might need." Crystal clinked when he placed the box on the table and he handed Mer a vase before turning to Maggie. "It's good to see you, Maggie." He bent over and planted a kiss on her cheek.

"Hi, Sugar."

Mer peeled back the box flaps and gaped. "Wine glasses? I'm not sure what I did to deserve you."

He leaned close to her ear. "You must have been very naughty in a former life."

Her face flamed and she busied herself unloading the glasses.

The last thing she drew out was an eighteen-year-old bottle of Jameson.

Selkie promptly relieved her of it. "All things considered, it seemed like a fine idea."

"I'll leave you to it while I get dinner started." Mer retreated to the kitchen.

A few minutes later, Bijoux entered. "Here." She thrust a glass of whiskey in front of Mer. "I know it's meant to be savored. But not today."

They clinked glasses and shot the amber liquid. The Jameson burned a trail down her throat and settled in a warm puddle in her gut. "That's vile."

Bijoux set down her glass. "Not to aficionados, it isn't."

They stood next to the stove. A film of olive oil slicked the surface of the water set aside for the pasta. Another pot held a mixture of diced tomatoes and tomato paste.

Mer put her palms on the counter and leaned forward as if she could press her troubles into the Formica. "They killed my fishes." She spun on Bijoux. "What kind of jackass *does* that?"

"You are going to need some time off. Get things settled."

Mer paced the confines of the small kitchen. "I won't leave you in a lurch. It's a holiday weekend."

"Taylor can work the boat. Oscar starts tomorrow. If I have to, I can pull Kyle into the store. We'll survive."

"Leroy needs me." The walls closed in around her. Caged her.

"How very pretentious of you," Bijoux said.

Mer stopped mid-stride and pivoted to face her friend. She inhaled a deep breath and exhaled noisily. "That was, wasn't it?"

Bijoux indicated the rest of the apartment with her hand. "You will have enough to do the next several days."

Mer slumped against the counter. She picked up a long-handled spoon and tapped it against her palm. She couldn't expunge the idea that a coin, a list of names, smugglers, and burglars were somehow all bound together and she was trapped in the middle. "I'm so angry," she whispered.

"Of course you are. I'm angry for you. When you are ready to cry, call me. In the meantime, there is pasta to make and I am hungry."

A light knock on the door caused both women to turn.

Mer glanced at the clock. "It's seven o'clock already? No wonder you're hungry." She left Bijoux in the kitchen and answered the door.

Oscar held out a handful of wildflowers. "I found these behind the church." His bewildered gaze flitted around her home.

"Thank you. I'm glad you could make it," Mer said. "I'm sorry, things are a bit messy. Someone broke into my home."

"That is terrible."

He'd slicked back his hair and his jeans had a slight crease as if he'd tried to press his pants with an iron that refused to get hot.

"I know you were looking forward to a traditional dinner, but I hope you don't mind spaghetti."

"This is a feast of gratitude, no?" He pushed up his glasses. "Does it matter what is on the table?"

Laughter from the patio carried into the apartment.

"No," she answered. And it didn't. But for just a moment, she wished she'd bought the pot pies.

Every creak, every palm frond scratch against the house startled her into wakefulness. Selkie had wanted Mer to spend the night at his house, but after all that had happened, it was important she slept in her own bed. She had to or she'd never overcome her fear.

They'd eventually reached a compromise and his deep breaths next to her lent some comfort. Beyond his sleeping form, a tiny bit of moonlight slipped through the curtains and glinted on the steel barrel of his Springfield Armory 1911 pistol on the nightstand.

But even with Selkie next to her, sleep had been elusive.

The morning shadows hid the lingering devastation of the day before—the furniture that needed repair, the drapes that needed mending, her tattered confidence.

Lavender scented the freshly laundered sheets, washed clean of the intruders' touch, along with her underwear, bathing suits, anything else that ever brushed her skin.

But she couldn't wash away the violation.

At thirty-three, Mer had an education, the prestige of being a doctor. She'd lived on both coasts, traveled to foreign continents, immersed herself in different cultures, and explored four of the seven seas.

But.

She didn't own a home, wasn't married, didn't have children. All the things that made her question her career choices and nudged her to consider life beyond academia—in Key Largo.

Maybe she'd made the wrong decisions. To date, life in the Keys hadn't worked out so well.

Selkie stirred.

Or had it? Maybe it was all within reach, but she was too scared to grab it.

The sheets trapped her in their folds. She eased out of bed, not wanting to disturb Selkie. His arms had found her throughout the night. Calmed her when she'd cried out. He deserved to sleep.

The edges of the room lightened to gray as the first hint of day crept past ruined drapes—ruined because of what?

In the half-light, her thoughts from the day before coalesced, and she made a new decision.

This was more than a break-in. Someone had shot at her. Ransacked her home. She had no idea what was so important about a coin that someone was willing to kill her in order to reclaim it.

But it was time to find out.

11

"I need your help," Mer said.

One side of Selkie's mouth curled. "Mark the calendar, this is a day of firsts."

They had relocated to Selkie's for breakfast. The morning sun flooded the breakfast nook with warmth and light and an extra helping of sarcasm to go along with the omelet cooking on the stove. Bacon drained on a folded paper towel.

"I ask for help all the time."

He tilted the pan to allow the egg to spread. "Name one time."

She considered the question seriously. "I let you open the champagne bottles."

"You let me," he teased. "Give me an example that's meaningful."

"That is meaningful. Popping the cork scares me."

"Corks. Not on the top of most people's what-scares-me list."

That particular list had grown in the past several days. "Are you going to help me, or not?"

"What exactly am I helping you with?" he asked.

"For starters, figuring out who broke into my home."

"For starters."

"After we learn that, I'm sure it will be a snap to figure out how the coin plays into it all."

"Let's think about this for a moment," he said.

"Way ahead of you." She didn't need a lecture on why it wouldn't work. Those reasons had already presented themselves to her in the dark of night. She didn't care.

He barreled ahead, anyway. "You think the burglars were after the coin."

"Yes."

"The only people who knew you had the coin were co-workers, cops, and the smugglers, correct?"

She nodded.

"I think we can safely assume neither the cops, nor your co-workers, broke into your home. Agreed?"

She crossed her arms. "I'm never going to eat, am I?"

Selkie ignored her. "Process of elimination suggests that the smugglers are also the burglars, ergo, you must want to confront a person who shot at you."

"Actually, using deductive reasoning, you can only conclude that the smugglers are the burglars. It's a common mistake. If every A is B and this C is A, then—"

"That's your takeaway?"

She blinked twice. "I don't want to confront anyone, I just want to learn who they are. Big difference."

"And it never occurred to you that chasing smugglers is a bad idea?"

"I thought you'd help me."

"I am helping you." He flipped the omelet. "You're a scientist. You research things. Study things. You have no tactical training, no protective gear, nothing."

"But you do."

Selkie possessed a skill set she lacked. He didn't have to tell her the details of his job for her to know its dangers. She'd first seen his scars twelve years ago, mementos of a helicopter crash. In the ensuing years, he'd added to his collection. It frightened her sometimes—not that he was dangerous, but that someday he wouldn't come back.

"Smugglers aren't nice people, Mer. As smart as you are, this isn't the kind of fight you'd win."

"I certainly won't win if I don't try." And she had to try.

"No."

"No, you agree, or no, you won't help?" But the set of his jaw had already answered her question.

"This is Monroe County's jurisdiction, not yours."

In hindsight, she should have known better than to approach him without something actionable. Once she dug up some information and devised a plan, then she'd ask again. Until then, there was no point in trying to change his mind. "I'm thinking of taking a kickboxing class."

"Best idea you've had all day."

She stood behind him and kissed the back of his shoulder. He probably wouldn't think it was such a great idea if he knew the class was more about personal safety and less about fitness. "If I locked myself in a tower you'd think it was a good idea."

He reached around with his free hand and pressed her closer. "Depends. Stone or ivory? From a security standpoint, one is far superior to the other."

"I don't need a tower." Although in light of recent events, maybe it wasn't such a bad idea.

"You should come out to the range with me this morning. Let me teach you how to shoot."

"I'm pretty good with a flare gun." Her stomach growled. She reached around him and swiped a piece of bacon.

"I saw that."

"I wasn't trying to be sneaky."

Still holding the spatula, he turned to face her. "What am I going to do with you?"

She batted her eyes, but she'd never mastered the flirt and she knew it came across as if she had something embedded in her cornea.

He laughed and it eased the tension. "Stay with me."

"I am with you."

"I mean permanently." He sobered. "Move in."

A piece of bacon caught in her throat and she coughed it clear. *Move in?* She placed her hand on his chest. His heart beat strong and steady. "You can't watch me all the time."

He had the good grace to look abashed. "True, but that's not the only reason why I'm asking. It's not even the most important reason."

"What happens when I become a kick-boxing ninja? You could be placing yourself in unnecessary danger."

"Consider it incentive to keep you happy."

Mer tipped her head toward the smoking stove. "What would make me happy is a scorch-free breakfast."

"Shit." He shoved a spatula under the omelet and slid it onto the plate. "Good thing there's bacon." He lifted the edge of the egg to determine the extent of the damage. "I can make you another one."

"Don't you dare. This one is fine."

"I'm trying to impress you."

"Help me then." She shoveled a bite into her mouth. Even slightly well done, the omelet was better than anything she'd be capable of producing at the moment. First off, he had feta cheese. And spinach. Fresh tomatoes. She had two pieces of leftover garlic bread and a slice of Key lime pie.

He wiped the pan with a paper towel in preparation for the next omelet. "So what do you think of the idea?"

He'd glossed right over her request. She lowered her fork. It wasn't a casual invitation—and it wasn't just about where she laid her head at night. Moving in meant more. A whole lot more. "I'm honored."

"But."

She hesitated, but he deserved the truth. "What if it doesn't work out?"

"We practically live together as it is," he reminded her.

"But we don't," she said. "I've got a good thing next door. If I move in here and it doesn't work, I'm the one out in the cold."

"So keep it. Keep it until you feel comfortable giving it up."

"It's not that easy."

"Yes, it really is." He kissed her gently on the forehead and turned back to the stove.

The scent of bacon hung on his clothes and mixed with the last remnants of aftershave. He smelled like happiness. It was intoxicating.

"You mean the world to me," she whispered to his back and was glad when he didn't turn around. "You know that, right? Even though I couldn't say it the other night?"

He broke an egg into a bowl, still not looking at her. "I know."

She set down her plate and her fork clattered onto the granite counter. "So you'll know this isn't about you when I say the time isn't right for me to make this particular decision?"

"Strikes me as the perfect time. You'll certainly be safer here, with me."

The omelet congealed into an uncomfortable lump in her belly. "No."

"You're going to have to elaborate. Because I'm pretty sure you'd be safer." He lobbed the eggshells into the sink.

Physically maybe, but emotionally? "It's a big decision," she said slowly. "I need some time."

"Analyze it, ponder it, list the pros and cons on a spreadsheet if you have to." He finally turned around. "It's a standing offer."

He meant it to be comforting, but in the end, all the analysis in the world wouldn't help make this decision. He'd broken her heart once before. It wasn't her head that needed convincing.

12

———

T en o'clock in the morning, and already her day wasn't turning out as planned.

Move in with Selkie?

The idea had merit—lots of it—but it was too weighty a decision to make when she was feeling vulnerable. Mer wrangled the thought into one of the many compartments inside her brain and firmly pushed it closed.

Instead, she contemplated the coin. She needed answers, and for that she turned to her old standby—books.

The Key Largo Library anchored the corner of the Trade Winds Plaza, equidistant between Kmart and Publix, and lost among the usual strip mall fare. It wasn't the voluminous Davidson Library of her student days, but considering her alma mater was located on the other coast, this would do.

Inside, the smell of books calmed her frayed nerves. She understood books. They encouraged thought, provoked questions, held answers.

And right now, that was a good thing.

Today she ignored the Friends of the Library nook to her right and the shell displays on her left, and headed to the main reference counter. Two librarians chatted while they placed books on different trolleys. The older librarian looked to be in her sixties. Rail thin, she sported spiked pink-tipped hair and a short strand of pearls. Her partner looked fresh out of middle school and had glossy black hair that fell to her waist. Her name tag read Rosa.

Rosa noticed Mer first. "Hey there. Can I help you?" Her voice held the slightest trace of an accent.

"I'm looking for information on Spanish coins."

"Let's see." The librarian consulted her computer. "Numismatics and sigillography are in seven-thirty-seven." She wrote the number on a piece of paper. "Sigillography. There's a great word for you. Sounds like a subject at Hogwarts." Her fingers typed in another search. "Hogwarts. Wouldn't you just love the chance to study there? You may also find some information in the history section. Not on Hogwarts, of course. That'd be literature. Spanish Colonialism." She added more Dewey decimals to the list. "But let's start over here. Follow me."

Rosa wove through the stacks. "First stop, reference." Her hand grasped a five-inch thick tome and dragged it off the shelf. "A little light reading." She giggled. "Look through that. Coin collecting is in our nonfiction stacks over there." A general sweeping motion of her hand took in nearly three-quarters of the library. "Holler if you need anything."

Mer found a quiet table in the back and opened The Catalog of World Coins, 1701-1800. The front pages explained how to identify coins: date, method of manufacture, denomination, mint markings, and assayer initials. Five clues that taken together made her realize she'd chosen the right profession. At least octopuses were easy to identify.

In an act of self-preservation, she skipped to the pictures. The book was truly a catalog. Divided by country, each coin was presented with an actual sized photograph of both sides followed by a description and the estimated number of existing coins.

The photo on her cellphone provided the information she needed. Within minutes, she'd found a match. A Spanish eight *escudos.* The book listed several mint locations and she ran her finger down the list. Madrid. That explained the mystery M stamped on the coin.

The same letters that surrounded the king's portrait graced several other coins. Curious, she flipped to the legend index. It proclaimed Philip the fifth king of Spain and the Indies by the grace of God. No wonder it was abbreviated.

She returned to the coin listing. Not a lot of them were still floating around. Most of the other coins had availability stated in millions. These *escudos* listed their mintage in the thousands. Sure, the one she'd held was in good condition, but it hardly seemed worthy of destroying her apartment.

A loud bang made Mer flinch and she spun out of her chair, poised to run. A woman picked up the book her toddler had dragged from a shelf. Embarrassed, Mer smoothed her shirt, sat back down, and closed her book.

Identifying the coin gave her a sense of satisfaction, but still left her unsettled. She was no closer to learning the connection between the coin and the list—and why both were in the clutches of a smuggler.

She needed more information, something to put things in context.

Maybe Oscar could shed some light on the coin. He was an archivist. More importantly, he'd known that Philip was the first monarch to have his face on a New World coin. No telling what else he knew.

Oscar wasn't at the dock, but then again, neither was the *LunaSea*.

Mer rounded the corner to the rental cage, expecting to see Kyle, the equipment tech. Instead, Taylor, the captain of the *Dock Holiday*, leaned against the lower half of the Dutch door, staring wistfully at the water. She'd twisted her blonde hair into a messy bun and the escaping strands made a starburst behind her head.

"Where's Kyle?" Mer asked.

"Upstairs. Bijoux wanted to cross-train him to help out in the shop."

"Bet he's loving that."

"About as much as you'd expect for an equipment tech who wants to earn his captain's license." Taylor noisily sipped the last of her iced coffee. "What are you doing here?"

"Looking for Oscar. Is he out on the boat?"

"I haven't met him yet." She rattled the ice as if to confirm there wasn't a sip hiding at the bottom. "You'll have to ask the boss."

The boss. The same woman who had ordered her to take a day off. Relax. But every time Mer slowed down, her thoughts slid back to topics she wasn't ready to revisit.

Reluctantly, Mer climbed the steps to the shop. She wanted to find Oscar and Bijoux would know where he was. She'd be in and out in a flash.

The blended scent of neoprene and coffee tickled her nose the moment she opened the door. Wetsuits and equipment lined two of the walls of the shop. A large armoire displayed T-shirts. Rounders of postcards and dive maps flanked the counter, which held the more expensive knives, watches and jewelry.

Kyle peeked at Mer from behind a mound of T-shirts piled on the counter. "Have you come to rescue me?" He sounded hopeful.

"The new shipment came in, I see," Mer said.

He raised the plastic shirt folder. "A mere sixty-five more to go."

Bijoux's voice drifted from the back. "You're not supposed to be here."

Mer walked to the office and stopped on the threshold. "I work here."

"I distinctly remember telling you to take some time off." Bijoux made a point of looking at her watch. "Congratulations, you lasted three hours."

"Nearly a whole shift."

Bijoux arched a delicate brow. "And why has Madame Scientist decided to ignore my wishes?"

Selkie's invitation to accompany him to the gun range flashed through her mind. "It was either this or shoot something."

"Go home."

A wooden yo-yo acted as a paperweight on Bijoux's desk. Mer grabbed it and threaded the string around her middle finger. "When does Oscar start? I was hoping to catch him today."

"I was not able to hire him after all." Bijoux leaned back in her chair. "He has no paperwork."

"You can verify his certification online." She flicked her wrist and sent the yo-yo toward the floor where it stalled in a spin.

"I'm not speaking of his scuba credentials."

"Oh." Mer bounced the string and the toy returned to her hand.

Scuba instructors were a transient lot. Often young, they chose the profession as a way to travel the world. The Keys were a popular jumping off point for the Caribbean, and many of the instructors in the area spoke with an accent. But despite their disparate nationalities, they all had one thing in common. A work permit.

Oscar was at least Mer's age, maybe even late thirties. He had an established career as an archivist. She didn't know much about Cuba, but employment in any government usually offered benefits and job security that the private sector lacked. Was he here on a travel visa? Restrictions between the U.S. and Cuba had eased. Surely he could obtain the necessary permits.

"Do you know where he's staying?" Mer asked.

"His car, I suspect. I gave him the address of St. Justin Martyr Church. They operate a food bank."

Mer unwound the string from her finger and set the yo-yo back in its place. "He's not here legally, is he?"

Bijoux lifted a shoulder. "I did not ask. He strikes me as a proud man. I am an employer. That entitles me to confirm he has a current work permit. Nothing more."

"So, that's that." Mer resumed pacing.

"I run Coast Guard-inspected vessels. He cannot work the boats. But that does not mean there is nothing I can do. The bougainvillea in the parking lot requires trimming and the picnic tables need to be sanded and refinished. I told him I could pay him cash as a day laborer."

Mer rubbed her necklace. "Will he?"

"That is his decision." Concern softened her words. "You really should go home."

To what? She'd already gleaned everything the library offered about the coin. She'd hoped Oscar's insight would help plot her next step. Now she didn't even know where to find him. If she went home, she'd be surrounded by an apartment full of reminders that she wasn't as safe as she'd thought herself to be.

Mer spun from the office. "Kyle needs me." She swept up an armful of shirts and set them on the adjacent counter.

Bijoux followed. "I'm quite sure Kyle is capable of folding T-shirts without assistance."

"I don't mind help," Kyle said.

Bijoux ignored him. "Have you seen the *Winchester* yet?" she asked Mer.

"The rifle?"

Bijoux ducked behind the counter, and deposited the shirts back in front of Kyle. "It's a wreck north of us."

The *Winchester*. Mer wracked her brain. Most dive shops in the Keys had set dive sites that they visited repeatedly. In the months that she'd been working in Key Largo, Mer had familiarized herself with the sites on Molasses and French Reefs. She'd dived all the local wrecks. Occasionally, they motored up to the *City of Washington* shipwreck above North Dry Rocks, but fuel costs cut into the bottom line when you were pushing a boat as big as the *LunaSea*.

And the *Winchester*? Mer shook her head. The name meant nothing to her.

"Good. Grab your gear. If you won't go home, at least go diving." Bijoux unfolded the waterproof map of the Florida Keys and spread it on the cleared counter. Her finger traced a path north of Elbow Reef and stopped. "A group of students from Miami chartered the *Dock Holiday* this afternoon to go to the *Winchester*." She tapped the map to show Mer the site. "I called in Taylor and Tom to take them out, but there is an empty seat. Take it. Listen to the briefing, explore the wreck."

Mer opened her mouth to protest.

"And then report back to me," Bijoux continued. "Let me know if we should consider the site for special charters."

Why argue? Bijoux needed her. Mer got to dive a new site.

And it beat going home.

13

A t one o'clock, five people in University of Miami T-shirts arrived at the dock, carrying their gear in brightly colored mesh bags. An androgynous figure wearing loose cargo shorts broke from the group and it wasn't until Mer saw the string of a bikini top around her neck that she realized it was a woman. The hair on both sides of her head had been shorn, and geometric patterns shaved into it. She'd fashioned the remaining hair into a samurai-worthy topknot. The effect added fierce inches to her tiny frame.

Mer stepped forward and held out her hand. "Welcome to the Aquarius Dive Shop. I'm Mer."

"Pleasure." She pumped Mer's hand. "I'm Phoenix."

A male student dropped his bag on the dock and called, "Hey, Professor. Do you want me to go check us in?"

"Thanks, I got it," Phoenix answered, and then turned back to Mer. "There's always one bucking for brownie points." She let out a bark of a laugh that sounded remarkably like a seal.

"Come on up. I'll get you squared away while your students stow their gear on the boat." Mer pointed to Taylor on the deck of the thirty-foot Island Hopper. "We're on the *Dock Holiday*."

"Ha!" Another seal bark. "Round 'em up!"

Fifteen minutes later, they cast off.

Taylor captained the boat and Tom served as deckhand, leaving Mer with nothing to do but nervously scan the horizon for pirates as the small vessel bumped along the waves to the dive site.

The students huddled around their professor as she spoke over the engine noise. They all held onto rails but Phoenix. She stood in the center of the deck, her legs absorbing the motion of the boat.

A wave of nostalgia crashed over Mer. Perhaps she'd been too hasty in her decision to take a hiatus from academic life. She missed the sense of accomplishment that accompanied a discovery, missed her undergrad days, when every class afforded an opportunity to appease her curiosity. She edged closer.

"The *HMS Winchester* was nine hundred and forty-four tons of British man of war built in 1693," Phoenix said. "Her keel was an impressive one hundred twenty-one feet, and she had a thirty-eight foot beam." She chopped her hands through the air as if outlining the dimensions of a box. "Most importantly for us, she had an armament of sixty cannons."

A brunette with a long braid scrunched her face. "What's the big deal about cannons?"

Phoenix tossed the question to the group. "Anyone?"

A sunburned blonde fluttered her hand, but the young man from the dock answered first. "They don't deteriorate."

A suck-up *and* a know-it-all.

"Actually, they do," Phoenix said. "Just at a much slower rate than the wood that made up this particular ship."

The students wore varying levels of interest on their faces, but Phoenix's enthusiasm remained strong and her hands flew in time to her words. "The *Winchester's* cannon was the clue to the ship's identity."

"How did a cannon help identify it?" This time a heavyset young man posed the question.

"Cannons were the bling of the high seas. By the end of the sixteenth century, bronze edged out iron. It was expensive, but a far superior material for ordnance. Cannons were embellished and engraved. Occasionally, the guns even had nicknames. Put that all together and cannons are a nautical archeologist's dream."

Phoenix lectured several minutes more as the boat traveled north across gin-clear water. A low profile speedboat rushed toward them, its hull slapping the water. Mer dashed to the port rail. It wasn't until the speedboat steered a wide berth around them that she relaxed.

They were nearly at the dive site when Mer's curiosity got the better of her. The students had underwater slates, tape measuring reels, and rulers. One student prepped a camera. But what they didn't have were specimen containers, lift bags, or the means to retrieve or protect any artifacts. "Not collecting anything today?" Mer asked Phoenix.

"There's not much left. Some cannonballs, a few pins, a pile of ballast stones, but they're hard to find unless you know what you're looking for. A lot of coral can grow in a couple of centuries. But that's the point of this lesson."

"What is?" Mer asked.

Phoenix grinned. "Learning to recognize what nature wants to hide. Besides, collecting in the Keys requires permits. Getting them can be a nightmare."

"Even for academics?"

"Oh, it can be done, but you've got overlapping jurisdictions here. There are sixty-three thousand plus acres of protected water in John Pennekamp Coral Reef State Park. Then there's the Key Largo Coral Reef National Marine Sanctuary—not to be confused with Pennekamp, which is actually inside the federal boundaries. All in all, you've got approximately twenty-nine hundred square nautical miles owned by the government."

Mer whistled.

Tom glared at her and hollered, "Hasn't Leroy schooled you about whistling?"

"I'm a work in progress."

Phoenix laughed and jerked her thumb at the deckhand. "Let me guess. He probably has a problem with women on board, too."

"Surprisingly not. He just puts on a good show. You ever had Cuban coffee?"

"I live in Miami."

"Then you know the type. Strong. A tad bitter. Best enjoyed in small doses."

"Ha! Anyway, the Division of Historical Resources grants archaeological research permits. Mostly to museums and universities. They're a lot easier to get than exploration and recovery permits. In theory, those go to any Schmoe who can convince the state they deserve one, but in reality, it takes a well-funded salvage company to comply with the regulations these days. Either way, the state oversees the whole production. Helps to preserve the archaeological integrity of the site, but frankly, I think they just want a piece of the action."

"Action?"

Phoenix raised an eyebrow. "Academics recover artifacts, looters bring up treasure."

"What happens if you find something but you don't have a permit?"

"Unless you want a Class Three Felony on your record, you can look but don't touch. Wrecks located in state waters belong to the state—which pissed off a whole cadre of salvors who'd operated under the Finders Keepers doctrine since man started plying the seas."

"From an archeological standpoint, it sounds like good legislation."

"Personally? I love it." Phoenix swept her arm around the horizon. "But the ocean's a big place. Hard to patrol. Tomb raiding occurs underwater, too."

Tom held up both hands and flashed his fingers. "Ten minute warning!"

The boat exploded into a hub of activity. Students pulled on wetsuits, rifled through gear bags, and double-checked their equipment.

Phoenix peeled off her T-shirt, exposing a breathtaking tattoo of a bird surrounded by flames that covered her back.

"Which came first, the tattoo or the name?" Mer asked.

"Ha!" she barked. "You'd be surprised how many people don't make the connection. The fire came first. Which is why I spend so much time in the water. You splashing with us?"

Mer pulled her wetsuit up over her shoulder. "I'm going in. Maybe take some photos."

Phoenix looked up from her gauges. "Alone?"

It was a good question. Recreational diving was done in buddy teams—two or more divers who stayed close enough together to assist each other in the event of an emergency. Charter boats insisted on it, unless divers could prove they'd had additional training and carried redundant gear in the event of equipment failure. "I'm certified self-reliant," Mer answered.

Tom leaned his head between the two women. "Dr. Cavallo is a marine scientist, too."

Phoenix waited for clarification.

Mer rolled her tank valve open and checked her air pressure. "I'm a teuthologist. Earned my doctorate at UCSB, did most of my research in the Arctic, studying the biogeography of Arctic cephalopods."

"You tracked octopuses. Nice." Phoenix resumed her gear check. "Sure you don't want to help ride roughshod over a group of baby scientists?" She chucked her chin at Mer's pony bottle. "It's a lot easier than schlepping an extra air tank on a reef dive."

Why not? Plus, she liked Phoenix. It was nice to hang out with another academic. Especially one who knew the plural of octopus was octopuses, not octopi. "I can circle the herd. Make sure none wander off."

"Thanks. Once they start their site diagrams, their focus on each other goes out the window."

Taylor motored to the GPS coordinates of the *HMS Winchester*. Unlike the reefs at Molasses and French, there were no mooring balls on the Elbow to mark this particular site. She found a nearby sandy area and came to a dead stop while Tom lowered the anchor over the side. The boat settled into the current and floated over the top of the reef.

Mer stood at the edge of the swim platform, slipped on her fins, and lowered her mask onto her face.

Taylor cut the engines and gave her the thumbs up. "Pool's open!"

Mer entered the water with a giant stride and scattered a school of blue tangs. They quickly regrouped and sheltered in the shallow reef.

She loved this moment, when everything around her surged with life. In truth, it made her feel insignificant. One small creature in a vast ocean. It put her troubles in perspective and made them seem manageable. Almost.

Dry air hissed through the regulator and filled her lungs as she descended the anchor line to the sand. Bubbles tickled past her ears when she exhaled. At the bottom, she checked the set of the anchor and waited for the professor and her students.

Cold water trickled down the neck of her wetsuit and she shivered. In the Keys, the changing of the seasons was marked by the thickness of one's wetsuit. She wore a three-millimeter, but it was almost time to break out the five and retire the thinner one until spring.

The divers rallied at the anchor. Phoenix shot a compass heading and set off.

Mer lingered, enjoying the solitude underwater. The barrier reef that protected the Florida Keys was the Nation's only coral reef. It sheltered twenty-five percent of all known marine animals and they all appeared to be out to welcome the divers. Mer's gaze swept the area, searching for signs of an octopus.

Phoenix took the group on a tour of the reef. Mer skimmed the seafloor, peeking into the nooks and crannies as she followed the students. A school of grunts congregated under a ledge, moving forward and back with the surge.

The students had their work cut out for them. The elkhorn and stony corals reached nearly to the surface in places, the product of over three hundred years of growth. Given the choice between looking for iron pins on a reef and a needle in a haystack, Mer figured the odds probably favored those covered in straw.

When they returned to the starting point, Phoenix released the students in buddy teams. They parted ways, their heads down as they searched the crags for clues of the wreck.

Mer slowly kicked and glided over the reef. Bright sunshine sliced through the water, casting lacy shadows through the purple sea fans. A cluster of painted tunicates with their ethereal chrysanthemum petals formed underwater bouquets that rivaled any flower found topside. And yet they were invertebrates, not flowers.

She froze. Oscar had plucked flowers for her from behind a church. Bijoux had mentioned the Catholic Church's food bank. Oscar wore a crucifix—and St. Justin's might provide more than a meal to a man in need.

It was a long shot, but suddenly she couldn't wait for the dives to end. She might be able to talk to Oscar after all.

Phoenix swam over to Mer. She pointed two fingers at her eyes and then directed Mer's attention to a crevice between two overhangs. At first glance, it looked the same as the rest of the area. She ignored the tiny wrasses that played hide-and-seek among the fauna and scrutinized the lumpy structure of the reef and its contours. The uniformity was the clue. Nature didn't build uniform reefs.

She smiled as she finned over a mound of coral-encrusted coconut-sized cannon balls.

Phoenix raised her finger vertically in front of her regulator, swearing Mer to secrecy, and swam to another section of the reef.

Mer remained a moment longer. She had to appreciate the irony. Her entire life had recently exploded, and now, she'd found peace with three hundred-year-old cannon balls.

The ocean was a fascinating combination of history and life, revelations and secrets, danger and comfort. And sometimes, one experienced them all in the same day.

Mer's hair was still wet when she entered the gym a few minutes before six. She'd driven by the church, but the lot was empty. No Oscar, no cars, no one. Even the food pantry was closed.

She took a sip from her water bottle and walked through the cardio and weight rooms to an area in the back of the building. The Keys had more jails than gyms, which considering her recent burglary, suggested there really was trouble in paradise.

Several women and a couple of men were stretching. Mats lined the floor and mirrors covered the walls. Stations with heavy bags, speed bags, and a giant tire dotted the perimeter. A sparring ring dominated the rear corner. She was willing to bet her paycheck that the Marquis de Sade had nothing on this place. It was perfect.

A lithe teenager breezed in and threw her bag against the wall just as the instructor roared his first command. She looked familiar. It took two burpees before Mer placed her. Gabriella, Detective Talbot's daughter.

Another four burpees and she no longer cared. As it turned out, learning to kickbox started with a lot of the four-part modified push-ups, followed by too many squats, and an unending circuit of sit-ups. Sweat trickled down the side of her face. Halfway through the warm-up she wondered if anyone in the room knew how to operate the defibrillator. By the time the instructor transitioned to punches, Mer had mentally drafted her will.

"Your stance is all wrong. Look at the instructor. Bend your knees." The freckle-faced Gabby ran circles around her. Literally.

Mer stepped out her legs, bent her knees, and envisioned decking the fresh-faced teenager. It carried her through the simple punches.

Then came the combinations. Two punches punctuated by hooks, uppercuts, kicks.

"Seriously?" Gabby torqued into her uppercut. "Haven't you ever thrown a punch before?"

Talking wasted air, but she managed a hoarse response. "Never had to."

Gabriella rolled her eyes so dramatically she should have won an award. "Your thumb goes outside your fingers. Throw a punch like that and you'll break your thumb."

Mer rearranged her fist and threw two more shadow punches.

"Stop. Just stop. Are you right handed?"

Mer nodded.

"Put your left foot slightly in front of your right. Stay on your toes." She demonstrated, and her auburn ponytail bounced. "Now, you want to have a straight punch. The first two knuckles should hit first. Don't lead with your pinkie."

"Why not?"

That earned Mer a jaw drop. "It'll collapse your punch and you'll end up with a boxer's fracture."

"Ladies!" the instructor yelled. "Socialize on your own time."

Gabriella grabbed Mer's arm. "Come here." She led Mer away from the people dipping and punching in perfect precision and stopped in front of a heavy bag. She sized it up. "This one will do."

The bags all looked alike to Mer. "How do you know all this?"

"My dad's a cop." Gabby pulled a pair of fingerless gloves from her duffle, and then hit the bag with a series of jabs, crosses and hooks.

"Your turn." Gabby tossed Mer her sweaty gloves, crossed her arms, and stood back.

Knocking the snot out of a heavy bag was a lot harder than it looked and her first hits were awkward. Tentative.

"Try this." Gabby demonstrated in slow motion without hitting the bag. At least she didn't quote Shakespeare like her father.

Mer tried again. This time the punch landed on the bag with a satisfying thud.

"Just like that, but harder," Gabby ordered. "That's it. Keep going."

Mer fell into a rhythm. Each hit reverberated through her body. Primal.

The gym receded. Gabby disappeared. Mer torqued her hips,

punched through the bag, and imagined landing blows on the assholes who had ransacked her home. The swinging bag knocked her off balance. She returned with a growl and slammed her fist into the bag in a quick double punch.

A tap on her shoulder startled her. She spun, acutely aware of her surroundings again.

"Remind me not to spar with you. By the way, I'm Gabby."

Mer gulped air like a beached fish. "I know. We've met."

Tiny lines formed on the young woman's forehead. "We have?"

Mer peeled off the gloves. "Well, maybe not technically. I'm Mer Cavallo. You were in my house on Thanksgiving." Still no recognition. "The burglary?" she prompted.

"Oh, wow. That was you? Sorry I didn't recognize you." Gabby took the outstretched gloves and jammed them into her gym bag. "Dad said you were a doctor."

That surprised her. Not that he'd said she was a doctor, but that he'd mentioned her at all. "A teuthologist."

"You specialize in teeth?" She pulled a towel from the bag.

Mer's mouth twitched. "Octopuses. I'm a marine scientist."

"That's cool. I've been diving since I was ten. Dad taught me."

"Your father is an instructor?" Although considering his position on the sheriff's dive team, she shouldn't have been surprised.

"Long time ago."

Factoring in the girl's appearance, a "long time ago" looked to be about six or seven years. Mer grabbed her own towel and tried not to wince. "I work at the Aquarius Dive Shop. You'll have to come out with us someday."

"Sure." She slung her bag over her shoulder. "I'll say hi to my dad for you."

Mer was still trying to figure out how to respond when Gabby left.

14

Mer woke up the next morning tired, sore, and hungry—a grumpy trifecta that could only be remedied by an all-you-can-eat buffet, a deep-tissue massage by a woman named Helga, and going back to bed—none of which figured into her plans for the day. She settled for buying a cup of coffee and a donut from the gas station. Four unladylike bites and a sip later, her body and mind were back in sync.

Time to find Oscar. She licked her fingers and turned north.

Few things in Key Largo soared higher than the Saint Justin Martyr Catholic Church bell tower. The cross at its pinnacle rose above the treetops and served as a landmark from the highway. Mer puttered through the parking lot searching for Oscar's car and had almost completed her loop around the church complex when she spied his white Corolla tucked into the corner by the butterfly garden.

She tapped her knuckles against the passenger window, but there was no movement inside. Cupping her hands around her face, she peered through the window tint.

No Oscar. Nothing to suggest he was living in his car, either.

She straightened and glanced around her. Mer's relationship

with the Church was complicated—ironic, considering the collar her brother Franky wore. It had been the topic of more than one of their conversations. Entering the inner sanctum rarely made her to-do list. Plus, she wasn't really dressed for the occasion, although if there was a God, He probably wasn't all that hung up on fashion.

Pocketing her keys, she tromped toward the entrance to the church and paused at the statue of Christ that towered over the immersion pool. Unlike its twin located in fifteen feet of water in Pennekamp Coral Reef State Park, this one wasn't covered in fire coral.

Mer entered the vestibule, a corporeal purgatory one had to pass through to achieve the nave. So far, so good. The handle felt warm under her hand. She hoped it wasn't the precursor to lightning.

Inside, she sucked in her breath. It was as if somehow the colors and beauty of the Keys had been captured and set free under the raftered roof. Ocean blues, calming sands, stained glass that sparkled with the vibrancy of reef fish cavorting in the shallows. The room radiated comfort.

No wonder Oscar had sought its shelter.

He sat in the corner, hunched over the pew in front of him, his face hidden. A rosary dangled from between his clasped hands, moving in time to his Hail Marys.

For the first time, doubt crept into Mer's mind. Maybe she should wait outside. It seemed rude to interrupt someone at prayer. But there was something about his posture that stopped her. The slumped shoulders, the bowed head. It was more than an attitude of worship. He appeared defeated. Unmoored.

She knew that feeling. As much as she wished otherwise, the coin could wait. Oscar needed a friend.

Mer sat at the end of his pew. He wore the same rumpled clothes he'd worn the day she met him on the dock.

As if feeling her scrutiny, he glanced up, his eyes big behind his clunky glasses.

"Hey," Mer said softly.

He immediately straightened and slicked back his hair. "Meredith. What are you— I did not know you were Catholic."

Best not go down that road. "I came here to find you."

His brows drew together. "Me?"

"Bijoux told me there was a problem with your paperwork."

He drew his hands into his lap. "The problem is I do not have any."

"That seems a gross oversight for an archivist."

He blinked several times. "Yes."

What was wrong with her? Even when her intentions were good, she managed to say the wrong thing. She tried again. "How can I help?"

He exhaled and his whole body deflated. "There is nothing anyone can do."

"Of course there is. We're two smart people. I bet we can figure out something."

He continued to thumb the beads, although his lips had stilled.

"Why are you here?" Mer asked.

He held up his rosary. "I find comfort in the Church."

It sounded like an honest admission, so why did she think he was stalling? "I meant in the States."

"Ah." He shifted on the pew. "Why does anyone leave home?"

She pointed to the massive stained glass window to their left, depicting Jesus walking on water. "Some leave to spread the gospel. I left because of my research."

"I once told you it was for the adventure."

Something in his voice was off. "You did." She gambled. "But it's probably a sin to lie in church."

"It is a sin to lie no matter the place." A faint smile touched his lips and then faded. "But adventure would not be a lie."

"Nor, I suspect, the whole truth," she pressed.

"No." He removed his glasses and slowly cleaned the lenses with his shirt. "All my life, I have wanted my father to be proud of me."

"You're a scholar. Of course he's proud."

He replaced his glasses. "My father is a man of the military. Not books. My first remembering of him is when he shoots his gun into the air to celebrate the *Triunfo de la Revolución*— our independence day." He lifted his gaze to the life-sized crucifix suspended over the altar. "My brother was his favorite. He would have followed my father."

"Why didn't he?"

"He is dead." Oscar tilted his head, but his eyes remained on the cross. "That leaves me. Coming to America. There is hope here."

The quiet of the nave pressed around them.

"Many Cubans, they dream of a life in America," he said. "It is not easy for Cubans to fly to America, but they can fly to Ecuador. Many walk the thousands of miles through Mexico to cross the border with other Mexicans." He glanced at Mer. "Like the journey of your coin." He resumed his study of the cross. "But there are many dangers in such a long journey and it is hard for the old. Hard for the very young. It takes money. Many cross into America with little. Coming to America, it cost me everything."

Mer clasped her hands. His was a story shared by thousands.

He sighed. "There is a legend in my country. The Legend of the Thirteenth Galleon. I mentioned it on the boat." His thumb absently stroked a bead. "Not many know of it."

He hesitated so long that Mer wondered if he meant to continue to keep it a secret. "You said it was cursed."

"Cursed. Yes." He picked up the rosary again. "The story begins in the fifteenth century, and tells of an ancient ship that sailed from my country."

Three hundred years before King Philip minted his coin.

"She was a beautiful ship, made all of gold, with silk sails that looked like clouds. Heavy with gold and gems, she was a gift to God —a request for redemption—but then came a great storm and she sank." A profound sadness settled in the lines of his face. "I would need to find that ship to make my father proud." He blinked as if waking from a dream. Disoriented. "I am sorry. What about you? Why are you in the Keys?"

"What makes you think the Keys aren't home?"

"It is my educated guess." Levity returned to his face. "I have seen where you live."

Indeed he had. At its worst. The devastation haunted her, but Oscar waited for an answer. Several reasons came to mind, but they all seemed too personal to share. "I wanted to be warm." A safe reason that had the added benefit of being true. "I spent two years in the Arctic on a research project, but then funding ran out. I've always wanted to dive in the Keys." She shrugged. "Here I am."

"Warm."

Morning sunshine flooded through the window and splashed bright colors on the marble altar. A year ago, she lived in the Arctic. There, everything appeared in sharp relief. No ambiguity. Here, life was saturated. She didn't know what to wring away in order to absorb more.

"Will you stay in the Keys?" she asked.

He cocked his head as he considered the question. "Yes. For the near time." He rubbed his hand over his heart. "Someday, maybe I can go home."

That word again. Home. Oscar had left his, and dreamt of going back. Hers had been destroyed—all because of a coin. A coin she still knew little about. But that was about to change.

"Oscar."

He bowed his head over his rosary. "I am tired. Please. I ask you to leave me to the peace of this place."

"But—"

"All I possess is my pride. I do not wish to also lose it."

She stood. Uncertain. "Do you have somewhere to sleep?"

His fingers tightened around the beads. "I am staying with Bart Kingston."

She didn't know the name, but at least he had a place to stay other than his car. It erased some of her worry. "Will you contact me if you need anything?"

His eyes filled with tears. "You are a kind woman, Meredith Cavallo. I hope I do not have that need."

15

The conversation with Oscar left her pensive. Despite everything that had recently happened, she still had a roof over her head, still had the means to feed and clothe herself. Still had a job. Oscar had his pride, and that had turned into an obstacle for those who wanted to help him.

A loud growl from her stomach prompted Mer to pull into the gas station for another donut, then just as quickly she changed her mind. It wasn't hunger she needed to satisfy.

Her thoughts returned to the coin. Maybe she needed to broaden her search, put it in context to its world. After all, if Oscar wouldn't talk to her, perhaps King Philip would.

At ten o'clock, Rosa unlocked the library door and held it open for Mer. "Hey there. You're back. More coins to research?"

"Switching it up. King Philip the Fifth of Spain."

"Well, aren't you the edgy one today." She followed Mer to the reference desk and tucked around the counter. "Let me see what we have."

Rosa dug a pencil from the mass of dark hair piled on top of her head and scribbled numbers on a scrap of paper. "Do you need me to show you where it is?"

Mer took the proffered paper. "I can find it. Thanks."

The section on Spanish colonial history consisted of precisely three books. Two more than she expected to find in a small municipal library in the Keys. She gathered them all and found a table by the window.

Years of research had taught her to scan vast amounts of information. Headings, bullets, first and last paragraphs. That's where to hunt for the treasure buried in a document.

As she read, a story of empire building unfolded, but it was the trade routes that caused her to read the passage again.

Mexico.

Oscar had mentioned something about the coin traveling across land like Cubans trying to immigrate. Did he mean a trade route? In the eighteenth century, the Spanish mined precious metals from the Mexican interior and packed them to Veracruz where they were loaded onto ships for transport back to Spain.

And Mexico City had a mint.

She disappeared into the stacks, found the coin catalogue from the day before, and returned to her desk.

Excitement surged through her. She had assumed the M on the coin represented the mint in Madrid. What if it really meant Mexico City? She flipped through the countries and stopped at Mexico.

Her eyes scanned the page and fell upon the four *escudos* coin first. Identical design but smaller in size.

Then she found the eight *escudos* "portrait dollar."

Using the eraser end of her pencil, she traced the three entries. Two from 1732 and one from 1733. All were annotated as rare, and no numbers indicated mintages. A note followed the three dates. She read it and dropped her pencil.

"Holy shit."

A woman at the next table shushed her, but Mer ignored her.

She closed the catalog and proceeded to do the one thing that librarians around the world hated: she re-shelved the book. Additional coin catalogs lined the same shelf. Some covered different eras, some specific countries. One specifically detailed gold coins. She pulled that from the shelf and a thin pamphlet fell to the floor.

Coins of the Spanish Treasure Fleets. Underneath the title in smaller letters it read 1715 and 1733.

Mer sucked in a quick breath.

Treasure fleets.

She crossed her legs and sat in the aisle.

It wasn't Oscar's legendary Thirteenth Galleon, but it was every bit as exciting.

The pamphlet rendered the coins in line drawings. The next section described denominations and her interest piqued but quickly cooled when it described equivalencies. Did it really matter that eight *reales* made up one *escudo*?

The next paragraph answered her question. An *escudo* was sometimes referred to as a doubloon. Pieces of eight.

It all clicked. Colonial. A time when pirates roamed the seas, especially along the Atlantic Coast and in the Caribbean. The portrait dollar was a milled coin, while the others weren't, but they were all in circulation at the same time.

"Yo ho, yo ho."

Mer practically levitated to the reference desk. "New topic, Rosa. Do you have any information on nautical archeology?"

"Nautical archeology or treasure hunting?"

"Both, I guess," Mer said. "Local to Florida if there is anything."

"If there's anything?" Rosa laughed. "You're not from around here, are you?"

The observation stung.

"People have always hunted treasure in the Keys." Rosa set down the book she was sorting and disappeared into the stacks. "We have a couple of books on the various fleets that beached along the Keys and further up the coast. You know that's why the Jupiter area is called Florida's Treasure Coast? Right?"

"I didn't." On impulse she asked, "Have you ever heard of the Legend of the Thirteenth Galleon?"

The librarian didn't even break stride. "I'm not familiar with that one. Maybe it sank in the Carolinas. There are a bunch of wrecks up there, too." She studied the numbers on the bottom of the spines. "Okay, you start here." She dragged her finger over two spines. "And end here. We had more, but every time we get a new title, someone adds it to their personal collection."

The two books sagged against each other.

"You can find more books at the History of Diving Museum in Islamorada. But if you really want to know about treasure hunting, you should talk to Skipper Biggs. He's worked the coast here for years."

"Where can I find him?"

"He owns the Bilge. Just don't go there by yourself."

The Bilge. Wonderful. Still, she had been there once before and had lived to tell the tale.

Mer called Detective Talbot on her way to the Bilge and was surprised to connect with the man rather than his voicemail on a Saturday morning.

"You're never going to believe this," she said.

"Try me."

"The coin I gave you? It's worth fifty-four thousand dollars."

Talbot whistled.

She could barely contain her excitement. "There are fewer than a dozen known to exist. It needs to be in a museum, not an evidence locker."

"Need I remind you that it's evidence?"

"Of what? Seems to me it's found property. That makes it mine, right? I mean if no one claims it. And frankly, I can't imagine too many people wanting to explain to the police how their rare coin ended up in a bundle of drugs. I'll waive my right to it. Give it to a museum."

"You draweth out the thread of your verbosity finer than the staple of your argument."

"Quote Shakespeare all you want, Detective. There's nothing wrong with my argument."

"Except that the coin is still evidence."

She rolled her eyes, but was unwilling to admit defeat. "What do you know about Philip the Fifth?"

"Based on the coin, I'm pretty confident he was King of Spain in 1733."

"Nothing gets by you, does it?"

"I'm a detective."

Mer pulled into the gravel lot of the Bilge and parked next to a paddle shop, facing the bay. "Philip had a difficult time of it when he took over the Spanish throne. For one, he was French."

"I can see how that would be problematic."

"Hence the War of Spanish Succession which pitted just about all of Europe against France, Spain and a handful of German States."

"How do you know all this?"

She wanted to believe his voice was tinged with admiration, but suspected it skewed more toward skepticism. "Library."

"Is this what you do for fun?"

Two boats were already tied up to the small wooden dock behind the bar, their owners relaxed on the patio, drinking. She wondered if they'd mind if she joined them.

"I think we can agree that wars are expensive," Mer said.

"If they're anything like divorces. Yes."

"Imagine losing whole countries in the property settlement." She drew a big breath. "Well, to augment the royal coffers, Spain had set itself up in the New World. They controlled most of South America, Cuba, significant ports in the Caribbean, parts of Florida."

"Is this where you get to the treasure fleets?"

She sputtered to a stop. "You know about them?"

"I've been diving off the coast of Florida my whole life. Of course I know about them."

All her enthusiasm ebbed. "Oh."

"But you encapsulated two hundred years of Spanish Colonialism brilliantly," he added as consolation.

So she had that going for her. "Is this like a square grouper—everyone knows about them but me?"

"Kind of."

Mer leaned her head against the steering wheel. "Was there any part of this you didn't know?"

"That I had a fifty-four thousand dollar coin in evidence."

Mer cut the engine and the air conditioning stopped. A young couple carried kayaks to the small launch at the water's edge.

"I suppose you know about the Legend of the Thirteenth Galleon, too."

"Nope, that's a new one. What about it?"

"Never mind, not important." She slammed the door a little too hard when she got out. "Well, this conversation didn't really unfold as I thought it would, but what do you think?"

"About what?"

The man was impossible.

"You have a very valuable Spanish Colonial coin in your possession that dates from the same year that a fleet of Spanish galleons wrecked along the Florida Keys." She leaned against the side of the Subaru. "A *treasure* fleet. Doesn't that spark your curiosity?"

"What sparks my immediate interest is the Florida—Florida State game that starts in an hour."

"What about all the other coins?"

"Last I knew we just had one."

"Exactly. Where are all the other coins from that year?"

"I'll keep an eye out. If any of them show up on the field, I'll let you know."

Growing up with two older brothers, she'd learned at a young age not to get between a man and his football. She might be able to talk reason to him after the game, but now? Not a chance.

"Go 'Noles," she said.

Hopefully Skipper Biggs wasn't a football fan.

16

The Bilge occupied waterfront property, but no one would ever mistake it for a romantic rendezvous. No one ever went there for food, either. They didn't serve any.

Mer stood at the threshold until her eyes adjusted to the murk. It looked every bit as dank as the first time she'd visited. The gloom reminded her of the surging darkness of a deep wreck. Benign if a diver took all the appropriate safety precautions, dangerous to the uninitiated.

The room appeared empty, although she couldn't be sure with all the shadowed nooks and crannies. She headed toward the bar. A dull brass rail girded the dark wood. As she neared, a cragged man of indeterminate age blustered through the door of what appeared to be a small office to the right of the wall of bottles.

"What can I get you?" His voice had a bit of a rasp, like an engine in need of attention.

"I'm looking for Skipper Biggs."

"I meant, what are you drinking?"

"Oh, a water, please."

"With what?"

"Excuse me?"

"Bourbon, whiskey, what?"

"Ice would be great."

His perpetual squint narrowed further. "You on the job?"

"Which job?"

"Don't play funny with me, girlie. You a cop? FWC?"

It took a moment for her mind to translate the acronym. Florida Fish and Wildlife Conservation Commission, which was technically the FFWCC, but the bartender didn't look as if he'd appreciate the distinction. "No. Just here on my own."

"Cost ya a shot a question."

"You're kidding me."

"Take it or not. Makes no never mind to me."

"That's absurd."

He shrugged and turned away.

"Wait."

In all her thirty-three years, Mer had never been drunk, although her brothers gave it a good run on her twenty-first birthday. Two and a half margaritas and a fit of giggles later, they'd relented. But Skipper Biggs was neither a cop nor a priest and at the moment, he wore an expression that clearly conveyed she could take his offer or leave it. She glanced at her watch. Not quite noon. Great.

"Could I have a chardonnay instead?"

"Don't got it."

"Pinot Noir?"

"Ain't that kind of joint."

"What do you have?"

He slammed down a bottle of Jack Daniels.

Great. Best be precise. She pulled on the barstool. It was bolted to the ground. Probably to keep it from being used as a weapon to bludgeon the surly guy behind the bar.

"Are you Skipper Biggs?"

He poured a shot of Jack and slid it in front of her. "Yup."

"I want to ask you about portrait dollars."

"That ain't a question."

This was harder than she expected. "What do you know about 1733 Spanish portrait dollars?"

His eyes cut between her and the shot glass and back again. She brought it to her nose and the fumes cleared her sinuses.

"Best shoot it. I ain't got time for a sipper." The gold earring in his left ear glinted in the light that sputtered from a neon beer sign behind him.

Mer shot the Kentucky bourbon and the bite brought tears to her eyes. "Could I have a Coke, please?"

A glass of questionable cleanliness materialized on the bar. "I'll give you that question on the house." He squirted a dark liquid from a hose into the tall glass and filled the shot glass a second time. "You're a shot behind." He waited for her to tip it back and said, "They're rare."

She was hoping for something she didn't already know. "You ever find any?"

Bourbon splashed into the glass. "Only in books."

The door opened and a slice of light slashed the gloom. A beefy guy with no neck, trailing an odor that didn't originate from a cologne bottle, slid onto the stool next to Mer.

Skipper leaned forward. "Can't you see that stool's taken?"

The man backed off to the other end of the bar. "Sorry, Skip, didn't know she was special."

A warm glow tingled from her toes and took up residency in her lips. She was special.

Skipper pulled a beer from the cooler and in a practiced move, removed the cap and sent it end-over-end into the trash. He placed the bottle in front of the other patron. When he returned, Mer held out her empty glass.

"So where's the rest of them?" She shot the bourbon before he even answered. "Every year, Philip minted thousands of coins. Where are they?"

"Girlie, if I knew the answer to that we wouldn't be having this little set-to."

She beckoned him close and whispered, "I found one."

Skipper set the bottle of Jack behind the bar. "Located the Thirteenth Galleon, did ya?"

Her foot slipped off the foot rail. "You've heard of the Thirteenth Galleon?"

He plunged a glass into soapy water and turned it upside down on a bar rag. "I heard 'bout it. Sure. Heard about El Dorado, Atlantis, and Big Foot, too."

"Tell me about it."

"That ain't a question and it's too early for bedtime stories."

"You think it's true?" Whatever *it* was.

He leaned against the back counter and crossed his arms, not bothering to refill her glass. "Girlie, some say there's four to five thousand shipwrecks sittin' in Florida waters. Pirate ships, merchants, galleons, transports, and slavers. All just waitin' to be found. Suppose one of them could be the galleon."

"Can you teach me how to find a treasure ship?"

He dragged the bottle out again. "Teaching's easy. Finding's harder."

"You ever find any?"

This time he tipped the bottle. "Treasure paid for the Bilge."

"How?" She shot the glass. "How do you find a ship?" Her words were starting to run into each other.

"You gotta listen. To fishermen. To locals. To those silly-ass tourists combing the beach. You wait for storms to do the heavy lifting for you by stirring things up, throwing it on the shore." He snorted. "What you don't do is listen to some fool blabbering on about a treasure ship. People who really think they're on to something? They keep their pie-holes shut."

The empty glass sat on the bar in front of her in a little puddle. She'd lost count of the number of times he'd filled it, but her lips were numb.

"Will you help me? I drank all your silly shots."

He squinted at her. "If there was a thirteenth ship full of treasure, there'd be records of it in the archives of Seville. Just like all the other ships in the fleet. There ain't. Pretty sure you can figure out my answer from that."

Skipper's answer stoked her curiosity. But he was all wrong about the thirteenth galleon. A fifteenth century legendary ship wouldn't sail with an eighteenth century fleet. Would it? Her brain felt fuzzy. Maybe she could track down Oscar again. Bet he wouldn't even make her drink. She tried to focus. Who had he said he was staying with? Someone smart. No, not smart. "Bart! Do you know where to find Bart Kingston?" she blurted.

Skipper pushed away from counter. "We're done here."

"But I've got more questions."

He leaned into her face. "I ain't got more time."

His breath held the scent of toothpaste. Mint. Which didn't really complement Kentucky bourbon. They stared at each other and Mer started giggling.

"What's so funny?"

"That'll cost you a shot." She tried to wink, but ended up closing both eyes, which just made her giggle harder.

He didn't appreciate her joke. Or maybe he just ignored it. "You got a cellphone?"

"Yup." She dug in her wallet and pulled out several bills that landed in a crumpled heap. She sorted through the pile, but the numbers didn't add up in her head. "Will this cover it?"

Skipper plucked a few bills from the pile and pushed the remainder back. "You're drunk. Call someone."

"I'm not drunk." She slid off the barstool and had to hold onto the brass railing until her feet pointed the right direction. "Thank you, for your time." She hiccupped, and then smiled. "You really weren't all that helpful. You act all crusty—which can't be good for business—"

"Hold your beans, girlie."

"But you have a very nice voice," she said, vaguely aware of the interruption.

He wagged his finger in her face. She tried not to laugh, but he looked so serious.

"That mouth of yours is gonna get you in trouble, you don't keep it good 'n tight. Best you forget anything you learnt about that legend. Now git."

17

The sun blinded her as she crossed the parking lot to her car. The effects of the alcohol chased her through the dusty lot and ran circles around her, making her dizzy. Calling someone seemed like a great idea. She was still thirsty. The day was young and she felt fantastic.

A vision of Selkie danced in front of her. Lean, long, hard. Her pulse picked up. That's what this party needed. A Selkie.

Even with his number on speed dial, it took several tries before she succeeded in placing the call.

"Hey there," he answered.

"You're so sexy."

He laughed. "There's a conversation starter. Where are you?"

"Anywhere you'd like me to be." She toyed with her hair. "Feel free to use your imagination."

"Mer, are you okay?"

"Fabulous." She sang the word. "I think you should take me to bed." So much for filters.

"Are you drunk?"

"Would you take advantage of me if I said yes?"

The line buzzed with what sounded like a sigh. "I can't take advantage of you if I don't know where you are."

She giggled. "Good point. I'm at the Bilge." The line went silent and she held it out in front of her face to hear it better. The seconds ticked on the call, so she put it back to her ear. "Hello?"

"What in the world are you doing there? No, not important. Is Skipper there?"

"Of course he is. Did you know he owns the place?"

"Good. Stay with him, he'll protect you until I get there."

"I don't need protecting. I'm in my car. Waiting. For you. You. *You*."

"Get out of the car. You're risking a DUI. Walk back to the bar while we talk."

"Which do you want me to do first? Get out of the car or walk in the bar? Hey that reminds me of a joke. A goldfish, a stingray, and a shark walk into a bar..."

"Get out of the car."

A burp built up in her throat and she covered her mouth. "I love it when you get all forceful."

"I'm not being forceful."

"You're so cute. No. You're too tough to be cute. You're gorgeous. But you already know that, right?"

"Are you out of the car yet?"

"Y-e-s..." She fumbled for the door handle and pulled herself off the seat. The horizon jumped, making her body feel like a ship in a storm. She took a heading on the door and launched herself. "If you hurry, I'll make it worth your while."

She tripped on the threshold, but righted herself.

"Are you inside?"

"Yup, Mr. Bossy-pants. Which for the record, I'd like to get into."

"Let me talk to Skipper."

"I already talked to him. He's not all that helpful."

"Just hand him your phone. Please?"

The floor rolled as she bumped toward Skipper. "Since you said 'Please.'"

She leaned one elbow on the bar and her body sagged next to it. "Hey Barkeep. Selkie wants to talk to you."

Skipper gave her a sideways squint, but took the phone. "Yeah." He held the phone to his ear for another thirty seconds, or maybe a couple of minutes. Mer lost count, but he eventually gave her back her cellphone. She set it on the bar. He slid it closer to her. "Put it in your pocket."

"When did everyone become so bossy?"

A stray beam of light squeezed through a dirty window and hit a bottle of vodka. Mer traced the refracted stripes on the bar and tried to recall the order of colors in a rainbow. The next thing she knew, Selkie stood at her side.

"Hey, I know you." Her words slurred. "When'd you get here?"

She rotated her wrist, but couldn't read the watch. Too much effort. She rested her head on the smooth wood and inhaled beer fumes from a generation of spills. She closed her eyes and kept one foot on the floor, hoping it would stop the spinning.

Skipper's gruff voice said, "She came in asking questions."

"You offer her the going rate?"

"Yup."

"Looks like she asked a lot of questions."

Selkie sounded amused, which didn't make any sense. She'd asked very serious questions.

Skipper again. "If I'd know'd she was yours, I would've cut her off about a fifth ago."

"Thanks for looking after her until I got here," Selkie said.

"Girlie needs a shorter leash."

Selkie laughed, deep and sexy. "That'd take more than the two of us."

"Not at the moment."

A hand grabbed her wrist and the next thing she knew her body was doubled over Selkie's shoulder and her face was bouncing against his back. "Nice view." She giggled.

Skipper's gruff voice followed them through the bar. "Careful now she don't puke. Least not in here."

Selkie drew the curtain with a flourish and sunshine poured into his bedroom.

Mer squinted, but too much light seeped under her lids and attacked her brain. "Is that necessary?"

"Probably not, but after babysitting you all night and rebuffing your amorous invitations, I have to admit, it's kind of satisfying."

Struggling to a seated position, she noticed her clothes weren't on her body the way she'd left them. "And my clothes just happened to come off?"

"No, that was during your striptease." A dreamy expression settled on his face. "I didn't stop that."

Mer flushed to the roots of her hair, which at the moment, hurt. "This is not the way to convince me to move in."

He sobered. "Skipper told me you were asking after Bart Kingston. He's bad news, Mer."

"Who?" The whole memory of the Bilge replayed out of focus.

"Never mind, we can talk about it later." He handed her a frothy drink that smelled like old socks. "Here, drink this."

"What is it?"

"Better you don't know."

The pulse in her temple struggled to break free of her skin. "Smells like revenge."

"I promise you'll feel better."

She brought it to her nose and her stomach lurched. "I'd rather wallow in my misery."

"Suit yourself." He opened another curtain.

She cringed. "I don't think I like you right now." Gripping the glass with trembling hands, she drank the potion in a series of gulps, afraid if she stopped, she'd never have the courage to take another swallow. It slid down her throat like mucus.

Selkie crossed the room, opened the bathroom door, turned on the light, and then stepped aside. He studied his watch.

Mer's stomach rumbled. "You poisoned me."

He continued to study his watch. "Nope. You did that to yourself."

Another ominous growl rose up from her belly. Her eyes widened. She threw back the sheets and sprinted a jagged path to the bathroom, slamming the door behind her. She barely made the toilet before she retched.

"Seventeen seconds. That may be a new record," he spoke through the door.

"Go away."

"I promised you'd feel better. There's a pitcher of coconut water on the counter. When you're finished doing—" He waited while she heaved again. "What you're doing. Drink that."

"My days of listening to you are over."

"I recommend drinking all of it," he said. "You're dehydrated. It'll help replenish your electrolytes."

"I need to borrow your gun."

"Trust me. The worst is over."

"Not for you, it isn't," she promised.

"Take your time. When you're ready. I'll have eggs for you. You need the amino acids."

"When did you become a doctor?"

He laughed. "I just have more experience with this than you do."

Mer swiped her hair off her face and twisted it into a loose knot at the base of her neck. The least he could have done after provoking this bit of porcelain worship was hold her hair.

The tile floor cooled her skin. She eyed the pitcher on the counter above her, not sure of her ability to reach it without triggering another round of veneration. Still, the throbbing in her temple had subsided some, and the light no longer seemed to stab into her brain like an urchin spine.

She grabbed the vanity and pulled herself upright. The earth continued on its axis with no discernible deviation. A crystal tumbler sat by the pitcher. He probably should have put out a plastic one. She poured a glass.

Light shone through the crystal and illuminated the pulp in the coconut water. The thought of drinking another Selkie concoction left her somewhat less than enthusiastic. She sniffed the brim and waited for a stomach lurch that never came. Tentatively, she sipped the water, then refilled the glass, and drank that, too.

The heft of the tumbler felt heavier than the delicately etched glass should, and she was surprised her earlier tremors had disappeared. She still wasn't inclined to give Selkie props, but she did feel a bit better.

Better enough to figure out why the mere mention of Bart Kingston set everyone on edge.

18

The shower did wonders for her disposition. Brushing her teeth elevated her status to almost human. Her clothes still smelled of the Bilge, so she swiped one of Selkie's button-down shirts from the closet. Blue. Bijoux would be proud.

She wandered into the kitchen. Selkie had changed into cargo pants and a T-shirt. A black duffle sat by the door.

"I got a page while you were showering," he said. "I don't know how long I'll be gone. There's a key on the table. Stay as long as you want."

The sick feeling came back. She knew very few details of Selkie's job beyond that he was an instructor at the Naval Air Station in Key West. Those duty days were planned in advance. It was the random times his pager went off that worried her. Sometimes he left for days at a time. He always returned tired and quiet from those trips. Other times, he was gone for a matter of hours. He tended to come back from those trips amped, as if too much activity had been crammed into too little time, and the adrenaline hadn't had a chance to dissipate.

She pushed the key in a small circle on the table. "Why won't you tell me what agency you work for?"

"I work for the Navy."

"Yes, but what do you *do* for them?"

"Things I can't talk about." He hefted the duffle and the items inside shifted with a metallic clank. "You know that."

She looked him in the eyes. "You probably shouldn't have taken up with an inquisitive woman, then."

"Probably not, but I'm really glad I did."

She placed her hand over his heart. "Be careful."

"Always." He leaned over to kiss her. "You should wear blue more often. That shirt never looked so good on me."

"Hurry back," she said.

He dropped his hand to the doorknob. "Before you even know I'm gone."

Which was a lie. She knew he was gone the moment the door clicked shut. The house echoed with emptiness. Or maybe that was just her heart.

She ate her eggs outside and was amazed to realize she was hungry. She cleaned her plate and contemplated her day. She could go back to bed, but, if you counted passing out, she'd already slept over fourteen hours. Oscar might be at St. Justin's but on a Sunday morning, so would a thousand other congregants. Best wait until tomorrow for that. The library was closed. Besides, she'd already scanned every book on Colonial history, treasure hunting, and coin collecting it had. That left the History of Diving Museum. The librarian had mentioned it had a book collection.

She opened the Internet browser on her phone. The museum opened at ten o'clock.

The first thing that came into view was the massive dive helmet on the History of Diving Museum sign. The second was the sprawling underwater seascapes that covered the building with manatees, manta rays, and whale sharks.

Inside, the lobby served double-duty as the gift shop and

smelled faintly musty, a holdover of things recovered from wet environments.

An older couple waited at the register. The museum docent took their cash and turned all the bills until they faced the same direction before filing them into the drawer. When it was her turn, Mer paid her admission and then located the book display.

The shelves held a variety of books: personal essays, biographies, sea creatures, reef biodiversity, and equipment. On the bottom shelf, she found books on the Spanish treasure fleets. Mer pulled one from the shelf and flipped through the pages.

"If you're interested in treasure, you should try lifting the silver bar we have inside," the docent said as she hovered behind Mer.

"You have a display on this?"

"Oh, yes. Art McKee and his crew worked the coast down here." She plucked a paperback from the display and moved it over two books. "He's considered the granddaddy of all Florida salvage divers." She held out her hand. "I'll hold that book for you if you like. I highly recommend going through the displays first. If nothing else, you don't have to carry anything while you're looking." She curled her fingers several times until Mer handed over the title.

A second employee came out of the back carrying a carton. "Hey Dr. Mer." Gabriella Talbot set the box on the counter. "Sore?"

Sometimes Mer forgot how small Key Largo really was. Tourists overwhelmed the roads and created crowds, but a mere ten thousand or so people called the island home. And outside of the resorts, it wasn't unusual to run into familiar faces. "A little."

"I figured. Well, welcome to the museum. First time?"

"Actually, yes."

"You'll love it." Gabby opened the flaps. More books.

The docent slid the box away from Gabby. "Why don't you show your friend around the exhibit?"

"Sure."

Gabby held open the hatch-shaped door and they plunged into a hallway dedicated to the earliest accounts of diving. At any other time, Aristotle's description of a diving bell would send Mer into geek nirvana. Today? Not so much. She was on a mission to find clues. Gabby, on the other hand, wanted to point out every information placard.

"You don't have to babysit me," Mer said.

"No worries. This way I won't have to listen to her tell me how I stocked the books wrong." Her hair brushed her shoulders. "I come back here all the time."

"She mentioned a treasure room?"

"Just beyond the South Florida displays. Go ahead. I'll catch up."

That was all Mer needed to hear.

Mer loved museums. Like Gabby, she tried to absorb every snippet of information the curators deemed worthy of knowing. She promised herself she'd return when she could study the exhibits, but at the moment, her pace rivaled a baitfish evading a barracuda.

She practically skidded into the display. The area wasn't much larger than a living room, but the walls were lined with display cases bursting with artifacts. A magnetometer hung from the ceiling over a blue banner exalting *Treasure!* The far wall had a life-size diorama of a diving-helmet-clad salvor wielding a metal detector over a pile of ballast stones.

A video about the Spanish fleets played on a loop in the corner. She held the old-fashioned telephone receiver against her ear and caught the video mid-narration. She listened through the end and it automatically restarted.

A lot of the information she already knew. Twice a year, Spanish fleets had left their homeland laden with European goods and set sail for the New World. There, they offloaded the European goods and picked up New World goods to take back. Preyed upon by other nations and pirates, Spain developed a convoy system, consisting of armed escorts for the merchant ships.

The narrator explained that the fleets split in the Caribbean. Some ships headed to Cartagena and Portobelo, while the others sailed for Veracruz. When they had exchanged their cargos, the ships rallied in Havana and embarked on the return trip together, under guard.

Havana.

In 1733, the Spanish fleet had embarked on their voyage home from the Cuban port on Friday, July thirteenth.

From Havana.

Where Oscar worked in the archives.

Skipper had said there wasn't any record of a thirteenth galleon in the Spanish archives. A tingle shot through her body and raised the hair on her forearms. What if the records were someplace else?

Someplace like Havana.

Mer gathered all the books they had on the treasure fleet and carried them to the register.

Could there really be a link between the coin she'd found and the Thirteenth Galleon? The discrepancy in time bothered her. Oscar had said the legend began in the fifteenth century, and the coin hadn't been minted until 1733.

Unless Oscar had lied.

The clerk tucked a flier into the bag and it jutted out the top. "It's late notice, but considering your purchase, you may be interested." She lifted the bag and handed it to Mer. "The International Society of Maritime Archeology is holding its annual fundraiser. Winslet Chase is speaking."

"The event's tonight," Gabby added.

"Who's Winslet Chase?" Mer asked.

The clerk's eyes turned dreamy. "He's a modern day treasure hunter—and really good looking. Also the foremost authority on everything you just bought."

Mer glanced at the flier. "A thousand dollars a ticket?"

"It doesn't matter," Gabby said removing the flier. "I called for one of the museum patrons yesterday. They're sold out."

"At a thousand dollars a pop?" Mer paid just over a grand for her apartment and that covered a whole month. "Who has that kind of money to spend on a dinner?"

"It *is* black tie," Gabby said, as if that justified the expense. "Do you own a gown?"

"No."

"Then it doesn't really matter what it costs, does it?"

The girl's logic was unassailable.

"Besides, like I told you, it's sold out. Too bad, though," Gabby continued. "The keynote sounds interesting. The lore of treasure hunting."

Mer still couldn't get beyond the price tag for the event. "Treasure hunting has always been alluring," she said absently.

"Not lure," Gabby said. "L-o-r-e," she spelled out the letters.

"Let me see that." Mer snatched the flier from the teen's hands.

The Lore of Treasure Hunting and How It Informs Nautical Archaeology. The headline framed a photograph of a handsome man in profile with wind-tousled hair, his eyes searching an endless stretch of ocean.

"No way," Mer whispered.

"Told you it sounded interesting."

Mer barely heard her. "I need to get in."

19

Bijoux opened the door to her home, but before she could speak, Mer blurted, "I need a dress."

Her boss opened the door wider. "From what I've seen of your wardrobe, you could use several."

"This one has to be nice enough to make the door guy overlook the fact that I forgot my invitation."

"Forgot?" Bijoux fluttered her hands and the jade bracelets on her wrist clacked. "Never mind. I suspect I do not want to know."

"Probably not." Mer walked into the living room. Most everything had vintage appeal; plush pillows, lush fabrics, and the occasional contemporary piece brought it all together with an inviting warmth that reminded Mer of Bijoux herself.

Bijoux pursed her lips and studied Mer as if she were a side of beef. "I need more information. Cocktail? Business casual? Red carpet? Cannes?"

"The Annual Gala for the International Society of Maritime Archeology."

"Your wetsuit won't suffice?"

"Last year's event was in Paris. At a little place called the Ritz."

"No neoprene then." Bijoux's finger tapped faster. "Where are they planning on holding it this year?"

"The Florida Keys Art Museum."

"That is not the Ritz."

"The guest list includes three Academy Award winners, two current senators, one former president, and Don Shula."

The tapping stopped. "Who?"

"Former Miami Dolphins coach."

"Ah. Local flavor."

"No, that is provided by Chef Hervé of Maison du Soleil," Mer said.

"No expense spared. When is this soirée?"

Mer dropped her chin. "Funny thing, that."

A long sigh escaped Bijoux's lips. "So...it is tonight?"

Raising her eyes again, Mer grabbed Bijoux's hands. "I really need your help. I can't do something like this on my own."

"Why do you want to go?"

"The speaker is Winslet Chase."

"The treasure hunter?"

Mer nodded. "Rumor has it, he's located a wreck that would make every other treasure hunter's find look like couch change."

"Why is everyone so obsessed with treasure?" Bijoux waved her arms. "Never mind. What time is this event?"

"Two hours."

"Evidently, Madame Scientist now believes in miracles."

"It isn't a miracle when you call in the best."

"That." Bijoux poked a painted fingernail in Mer's face. "That is how you are going to get past the doorman without an invitation. Remember how to do that." She dropped her hand. "Now, wait here."

A moment later, Bijoux returned holding a sapphire blue dress suspended from a padded silk hanger. "It is essentially strapless, so your shoulders shouldn't be a problem."

"What's wrong with my shoulders?"

"Nothing. Most models don't have as much upper body strength as you do."

"I lift tanks."

"Yes. And models lift jewelry." She slid the dress from the hanger. It rippled like the Atlantic on a calm day, catching the light, reflecting the clouds.

Mer caught her breath. "It's beautiful."

"Try it on."

The front of the dress appeared self-explanatory. Whaling constructed a rigid bodice, but the low back didn't appear to have much of anything except a single horizontal strap that seemed too thin to hold everything together. "I don't know how."

Bijoux opened a narrow zipper that Mer hadn't seen.

She read the name on the label and gasped again. "I can't wear this. Even I know that name."

"Of course you can," Bijoux said.

"If something were to happen to this dress, I couldn't afford to fix it."

"It was a gift from the designer."

"You know—"

"Yes. Are you going to try on the dress, or just wear the shorts you've got on?" She turned her back to Mer to give her a modicum of privacy.

Tiny crystals covered the fabric. Clutching it to her chest for just a moment, Mer reveled in the princess feel of the gown. She smoothed it over the couch, and then kicked off her shoes and shucked off her clothes. The heavy fabric slid down her body, the silk lining cool against her skin. She pulled the little zipper, but couldn't get a grip without the front of the bodice falling forward. The straps hung limp. Mer was completely flummoxed. "I need your help."

Bijoux faced Mer again. "The hair will be next. One thing at a time."

Holding the bodice up with one hand, Mer patted her unruly waves. "What's wrong with my hair?"

Bijoux levered the zipper and the fabric snugged around Mer's hips, leaving the rest of her back bare. "You cannot wear a dress like this with hair like that." She stepped in front of Mer and took the straps. "Pretend these are armholes and slide your arms through."

Mer did as she was told. Bijoux connected the concealed clasp and adjusted the straps so they lay flush across her shoulder blades.

"Now. Let me see."

Fabric pooled at Mer's feet. The bodice swept low across her chest and a rectangular cutout revealed more of her cleavage than most bikinis.

"Perfect," Bijoux said.

"Dragging three inches of material is hardly perfect."

Bijoux extracted a pair of strappy sandals from a felt bag.

"Oh no." Mer backed away from the horror in Bijoux's hand. "I trip in sneakers. There is no way I could pull that off."

"There's no time to hem the dress. This is your only alternative."

"I'll kill myself in those."

"You Americans. Always so dramatic. They are just shoes."

"They're stilettos. Last time I checked those were considered dangerous weapons."

"Wear these and the doorman won't even notice you don't have an invitation. They are Christian Louboutins. Commonly known as leave-ons."

"Why is that?"

"Because you can take off everything else." Bijoux thrust the shoes into Mer's hands. "Put them on."

Very gently, Mer settled onto the couch and bent over to buckle the tiny strap around her right ankle. The sandal molded to her foot and her calf muscle popped. "My feet hurt already."

"You must stand before you can claim that. Besides, a little sacrifice will remind you of your goal."

"My goal is to speak to Winslet Chase. See if he's heard of the Legend of the Thirteenth Galleon."

"And you must wear the shoes to do that."

"These shoes scare me."

Bijoux clucked her tongue. "Says the woman who dives with sharks. For fun. Now we must tend to those toenails."

The woman at the door had an air of affluence more cloying than her perfume. Any last vestiges of hope that Mer's borrowed leave-ons would get her across the threshold withered.

One couple stood in line ahead of her. The man's burgundy cummerbund matched his wife's gown. She'd slung a fur stole nonchalantly across her shoulders—a completely unnecessary accessory given the evening heat. Thank goodness Mer's own gown was strapless. She could already feel beads of sweat rising. But that was nothing compared to the discomfort radiating from the borrowed red-soled shoes of Satan. Bijoux had told her most women would kill to own a pair. Mer was ready to kill anyone who delayed her from taking the damn things off.

And that job belonged to the four-foot-ten-inch kewpie doll guarding the door.

The line behind Mer stretched back to the limos. Everyone held heavy cream parchment invitations. Everyone except Mer.

The couple ahead of her moved inside and a wash of blessed air conditioning breezed across Mer's shoulders.

Ms. Kewpie smiled at Mer from a face that looked as if all the wrinkles had been ironed out of it. "Welcome to the International Society of Maritime Archeology fête." Her accent was Bostonian, and Mer wondered briefly if she had come over on the Mayflower.

"Good evening."

"May I see your invitation, please?"

The dreaded question. The one Mer had spent two hours trying to figure out a plausible way to dodge. "I'm sorry, I left it in my limousine." Which was probably the first time her eight-year-old Subaru had ever been thought of in those terms. She'd parked it in the back lot with the service trucks, drawing a look or two from the tuxedoed waitstaff. The walk to the front in heels had nearly crippled her.

"Oh, that is a shame. Let me check our guest list." She consulted an iPad. "Your name?"

The woman held the tablet at eye-level, which gave Mer an unimpeded view of a blurry screen. No help there. For a split second she considered dropping one of the Robber Baron names, but no self-respecting Vanderbilt, Carnegie, or Rockefeller would toddle like a newborn on four-inch heels. "Meredith Cavallo."

"Cavallo. Cavallo. Ca-vall. O. I'm sorry, could it be under another name? Your business, perhaps?"

"No. Dr. Mer Cavallo. Please check again."

"I am sorry, Dr. Cavallo. Perhaps your chauffeur could bring the invitation to the door? I'm sure we can resolve this as soon as I see the invitation."

A shadow passed behind the tiny woman and Mer craned her neck to look in the face of a very serious, very large, very intimidating doorman. Put a Super Bowl ring on his finger and he could have been one of Shula's defensive linemen.

"Nice shoes," he said.

Mer smiled. He did not.

"Thank you, I'll just walk back and get it myself," she said.

Ms. Kewpie didn't respond, but instead turned and held out her hand to accept the next guests' invitation. "Welcome, Mister and Missus Morgan. Enjoy the festivities."

Maybe she should have dropped an industrialist's name after all. It worked for the Morgans.

Mer clutched the railing as she descended the stairs and stepped onto the gravel path. Great for flip-flops, not so wonderful for heels. But every place in the Keys had gravel pathways. Dig an inch below the topsoil and the whole archipelago was one big chunk of oolitic limestone, which a mere hundred-and-fifty-thousand years before had been a living coral reef. Give or take a millennium.

Her heel turned slightly and her ankle absorbed the shock. "Wear the shoes, Bijoux said. You'll be fine, she promised. Right."

The Subaru came into view and she extracted her keys from the tiny silver clutch Bijoux had insisted she carry. A curl escaped Mer's simple chignon, and she blew it out of her eyes. How on earth did she think she'd bluff her way into an A-list event? A doctorate didn't count for anything when the yardstick measured wealth.

One of the catering guys leaned against the back wall of the building and took a deep drag on his cigarette while he watched Mer's painfully slow progress across the treacherous terrain.

He emptied his lungs of smoke in a long exhale. "The entrance is around the corner."

"I lost my invitation. They won't let me in."

"And you all dressed up with no place to go."

"I'm just a walking cliché." And not a very good one at that.

The caterer ground the ash of his cigarette off against the wall. "Nice shoes, by the way."

"Be happy you're not wearing them," she said. "You guys need help?"

"How about I just let you in?"

Mer's heel dragged across a small root and she threw her arms wide to catch herself. "You'd do that for me?"

"Hate to see someone as beautiful as you, stranded on the outside looking in."

Her conscience jabbed her. "You should know I never really had an invitation."

"Makes it all the more fun, now don't it?" He winked and Mer noticed he wore eyeliner. Maybe a touch of rouge.

"I won't get you in trouble?"

"My break's about over." He dropped the cigarette stub into the breast pocket of his chef coat. "You want in or not?"

A smile unfurled across her face. "Yes, please."

He held the break room door for her. "Good luck."

She smoothed the curl back into place. "How do I look?"

"Like you belong. Now go before I change my mind."

"Thank you." She stepped onto the linoleum of the break-room floor and her foot slid across the slick surface.

The caterer caught her by the elbow and steadied her. "Honey, you're going to have to own this if you don't want to find yourself right back out the front door. Look, I perform in one of the burlesques in Key West, and if I can pull off being a woman, so can you. Now straighten up. Get your balance and for the love of Cher, smile."

20

The museum exhibit hall sparkled with jewels, with crystal, with thousands of white lights winking like stars high above the heads of the hundreds glammed up for the festivities. A string quartet played discreetly in the corner, providing music for the couples twirling on the dance floor. Stoic waiters passed among the guests with trays of canapés and flutes of champagne.

Mer entered the exhibit room as if she owned the place—shoulders back, chin up, and smile firmly in place. She accepted a crystal flute from a passing server and her hips fell into a natural sway. Nothing could stand in her way.

Except the exceptionally large lineman working security.

"Good evening, again, Doctor," he said.

"Good evening." She tried to peer past him, as if to get someone else's attention, but even with five-feet-nine-inches of natural height and four inches of heels, she still saw only the fabric of his substantial suit jacket. "Excuse me, I see my friend."

"I still need your invitation."

"She's with me." Detective Talbot stepped from behind the security guard.

The man's whole demeanor changed. "Of course, sir." He left in the direction of the door.

Mer watched the exchange. Or rather she gaped at Detective Josh Talbot. She'd seen him in slacks and dress shirt, and run into him when he'd worn shorts, but nothing prepared her for the figure he cut in a tuxedo. Elegant. Poised. Confident. No doubt about it. The man rocked a suit.

"Dr. Cavallo, you look radiant." He took her free hand and steered her toward a corner away from the crowd.

He stood close enough that she could see the flecks of mystery in his hazel eyes, their lightness so striking against his darker skin. Sea grass, she decided. All the colors of sea grass resided in those mesmerizing eyes.

"I seem to have rendered you speechless," he said.

"I could say the same about you. I mean, handsome. You look handsome." She mentally slapped her forehead.

He swept his arm to encompass the exhibit room. "All the world's a stage, and all the men and women merely players." A mischievous spark lit his words. "And what part are you playing tonight? I didn't notice your name on the guest list—I would have remembered that. So, are you someone's plus one?" He arched an eyebrow. "No, I think not, or I wouldn't have found you engaged in a conversation with a member of the security team. That leaves party crasher."

Mer studied her toes. Bijoux had painted the nails a deep crimson. Each time she caught sight of one of the violently colored piggies, she thought she was bleeding. A distinct possibility, considering the shoes.

"Why are you here?" he prodded.

Stalling, she sipped her champagne. The alcohol soured in her stomach, an unwelcome reminder of her recent visit to the Bilge. She decided to come clean. "I think I might have discovered what's so important about that coin, why someone would destroy my place to recover it. I thought if I cornered Winslet Chase, I could make him answer some questions."

Talbot tilted his head back and laughed. "Make him? Unless you overpower him with your beauty, I don't think you'll be able to make him do anything."

The laugh pricked her pride. "A compliment and an insult both delivered in the same sentence. I see you haven't lost your charm, Detective."

He sobered immediately. "This isn't a game."

"And yet ever since I pulled a smuggled coin out of the sea, I seem to be the pawn in a game of chess with rules that everybody understands except me."

"Crooks don't follow the rules."

"Who do you think broke into my house?"

He hesitated. "With no forensic evidence, we may never know."

"But..."

"But..." he drew out the word. "I'm not a huge fan of coincidence and on the heels of finding a gold coin stashed with drugs, I'm fairly certain the incidents are connected."

"So, I'm in the crosshairs of a smuggler."

"Which is why you need to let us do our job."

Her cheeks burned. "Whoever did this is a thug. How smart can he be?"

"Don't confuse smart with cunning. They are two entirely different traits. One is a level of intelligence. The other is the ability to read human nature and twists things to one's advantage. You are smart. You are not cunning. You don't have that mean streak."

"I don't know how to take that."

"It's a beautiful night." He took the glass from her hand and set it down on a cloth-covered high table. "May I have this dance?" He held his hand out, palm up. "I'll do my best not to step on your toes."

"Literally or metaphorically?"

"I'll leave that to you to decide."

"Unless they're playing the Hokey Pokey, I don't think you want me out there."

"Would you rather I arrest you for trespassing?"

She placed her hand in his. "What delightful incentive you offer, Detective. Isn't that called bribery?"

"Bribery works the other way. This is coercion. An almost certain abuse of my power as an officer of the law."

He led her to the dance floor. The music changed. Slower. Languid. He placed his right hand in the small of her naked back and held out his other hand in invitation. "Relax. This is a waltz, not a cha-cha."

A waltz, she told herself. Nothing more. She rested her free hand on his shoulder, and the sparkling clutch dangled from her wrist.

"Ready?" he asked.

"As if I had a choice."

"That's the spirit!" He swept her onto the dance floor. Pressure from his hand directed her body and she found herself in step with his movements. The tempo cued her speed.

"Can you even arrest me when you aren't on duty?"

"What makes you think I'm not working?"

"I hardly imagine the county pays its detectives to waltz."

He pulled her closer and his thighs touched hers. "Maybe I'm undercover. What better way to blend in?"

She tried to ignore the contact. "So you're using me."

"Seems to me you should be thanking me. I'm fairly confident my officer was going to escort you to the door."

Touché. *Dammit.* They one-two-three-stepped around the dance floor. "Why'd he listen to you?" She said above the strains of the music.

He shook his head as if coming out of a daze. "You lost me."

"Guido. The officer. He couldn't leave us fast enough."

Confident, controlled, elegant Detective Talbot returned. "Because I wrote the operational plan for this shindig. And I outrank him."

"Oh."

"But if it makes you feel better, I could have arrested you even if I weren't on duty." The lines around his eyes deepened as he smiled. "One of the perks of the job."

The music quickened to an ankle-twisting tempo and Detective Talbot swung her to the edge of the dance floor. "Dare I ask?"

Mer peered past his shoulder. "I don't think Guido's going to let you."

The large deputy strode toward them like a linebacker in search of a quarterback. "We've got a problem."

Talbot released Mer's hand. "Don't go anywhere."

She donned her best Little Bo Peep expression. "And miss all the fun?"

The detective squinted an unspoken warning, and then excused himself.

As soon as his back was turned, Mer scanned the crowd, but she didn't recognize a single person. Certainly not Winslet Chase.

She hobbled her way through the throng and entered the *Lignum Vitae* room. It had been filled with historical art depicting the horror of the two hurricanes that had devastated the Spanish fleets. Curious, she wandered through the gallery room. The most recent painting had been added to the collection last year to commemorate the three-hundredth anniversary of the 1715 hurricane. Others dated back to the eighteenth century.

One painting in particular stood out. Painted a mere four years after the event, the artist had captured the angry skies and lashing winds that tormented a galleon. Massive waves buffeted a second ship rendered in ghostly outline in the background. Historians attributed the painting to Berdugo, which might mean something to an art historian, but meant nothing to her. She was more interested in the identities of the two ships: *El Infante* and the *San José*. She was even more interested in finding the elusive Mr. Chase—and he wasn't here.

She crossed under a large arch and entered another gallery, this one designated for the silent auction. Tables laden with *objets d'art* lined one wall, while easels supporting Wyland and Guy Harvey paintings lined the opposite one. She absently perused the displays, paying more attention to the changing sea of faces that swirled around her than the high-priced pieces. Near the end of the row, a bronze mermaid captured her attention and she paused. Hair floated in a delicate mass around the mermaid's naked torso, her hand raised in greeting. *No.* The melancholy expression suggested a moment of farewell. Regret. It was compelling, and Mer wished she had the disposable income to purchase it. She brushed her hand along the base of the statue. Unlike the other auction figurines, this one lacked a bid sheet.

"Art should create a yearning, no?" The words came from a man in a wheelchair behind her. A tribal tattoo emerged from his sun-streaked hairline on the left side of his face, then disappeared under the collar of his impeccably tailored tuxedo. He studied her over the rim of his snifter. Sipped his drink. Smiled.

In a room full of exquisite items, he was possibly the most breathtaking of them all.

"It is the same with a beautiful woman." His wheelchair inched forward and he rested his foot against her calf.

She half-stepped to the side.

"Art must make your heart race, consume your thoughts, until all you can think about is how you are going to possess it," he finished smoothly.

Ew. She wished he hadn't spoken. "Isn't it enough to admire it?"

He laughed. "How parochial you are."

Mer had been called many things in her life, but parochial wasn't one of them. His assessment left her piqued. "Let me guess. You must be the artist."

"No." He held out his glove-clad hand. "I'm Winslet Chase."

Mer gulped. The thumbnail promotional photo she'd seen that depicted him on the bow of a boat had failed to prepare her for meeting the treasure hunter in person. She shook his hand. "I'm sorry I didn't recognize you."

"It's the chair."

"Excuse me?"

"People expect explorers to be taller," he said. "With fewer wheels."

"Water's buoyancy is more forgiving than earth's gravity."

"Exactly. Too many people allow their perceptions to limit their abilities."

Perhaps she had misjudged him. "I'm looking forward to your presentation this evening. I wonder if I might ask you a couple of questions?"

"Of course."

"Your success rate for locating shipwrecks is phenomenal. What do you do differently?"

"Romantics search for Atlantis. I hunt ships that have documented provenance. A historical record of their existence. I know they actually exist before I start looking for them."

"Interesting stance, considering your keynote."

"Not if you know where to look. Shipwrecks are found above ground. Then it is merely a matter of retrieving them."

She relaxed and an ironic smile twisted her lips. "Simple."

"Simple, yet rarely easy," he agreed. "It is a pleasure to meet you, Dr. Cavallo. You are as charming as I was led to believe."

Mer's scalp prickled. "You seem to have me at a disadvantage."

"I was told you'd be here tonight. I said that's impossible. Your name was not on the list. But my friend was adamant." He swept his upturned palm in a dramatic arc in front of him. "And here you are."

His scrutiny unnerved her. "Who told you I'd be attending?"

The lights flickered and conversations in the room hushed. From the doorway, a waiter announced that dinner would be served in the Seminole banquet room in ten minutes. Chatter resumed and the crowd surged around Mer and Winslet as couples headed for the dining room. A blink later and the gallery had emptied except for a few lingering art aficionados.

"Shall we?" he asked Mer. "I'd be delighted if you'd dine with me."

"I believe you were going to tell me who said I'd be present tonight."

He sighed. "Suffice it to say we have a mutual acquaintance, Dr. Cavallo." He brushed an imaginary piece of lint off his lapel. "And apparently, a mutual interest."

"I don't think we do."

His gaze hardened. "Don't play coy, Meredith. It's beneath you."

"This conversation is over."

He blocked her path with his chair. "It's over when I say it is."

Her legs trembled under the heavy dress. Wheelchair or not, the man frightened her. Unless she ripped off her stilettos, she wasn't capable of outrunning him—and even then her damaged feet might not be up for the challenge. She scanned the room, hoping to see Talbot. Hell, she'd settle for Guido. Neither deputy was among the stragglers drifting off toward the dining room.

"How much truth do you ascribe to the Legend of the Thirteenth Galleon?" he asked.

She swallowed a gasp. Her goal for the evening had been to meet and speak with Winslet Chase. Ask him that very question. In her mind, it had been a very different encounter. "How—?"

"Do you think the legend is grounded in truth?" he pressed.

He obviously thought she knew more about the legend than she did. No sense dispelling the illusion. "By definition, legends are unauthenticated. Otherwise they'd be history."

"That's a dodge."

"What do you care?" Heat pulsed through her body, but she preferred that to the cold fear it replaced. "Legends don't interest you, remember?"

"What if I told you that there's proof of its existence in this very museum?"

"I'd say if that were true, the ship would have been found a long time ago."

"And I would have agreed with you, if it weren't for the recent discovery of the ship's manifest. I believe that particular treasure is residing in an evidence locker in the Monroe County Sheriff's Office."

The room tilted. Mer put her hand on the table to steady herself. "You can't possibly suggest that someone stuffed the long-lost manifest of a legendary treasure ship into a bale of drugs and tossed it into the sea?" But she knew that was exactly what happened. The brittle paper. The multiple Dons. They weren't names. They were Spanish titles.

"Who am I to say?" he answered.

She narrowed her eyes at him. "What's your role in all this?"

"I'm a treasure hunter. The obvious answer is I seek treasure."

"Indulge me. What am I missing?"

"The ocean is a dangerous place, Dr. Cavallo. But you know that."

"Are you threatening me?"

"Don't be ridiculous. I would never do something so cavalier. We're just getting to know each other. I wouldn't expect you to enter into a business relationship with someone whom you know nothing about."

"I'm a scientist and I teach scuba. I don't need a business partner for either endeavor."

"Piffle. What you want doesn't really enter into the equation." He placed his empty glass next to the mermaid statue. "She reminds me of you. That wistful look, wanting something beyond her reach." He grasped the hand rims of his wheelchair. "Now if you'll excuse me, I believe there is a white-wine-poached lionfish waiting for me in the dining room. Are you sure you won't join me?"

"Positive."

He smiled and it dazzled with danger. "I said I'd share something about myself. I'm the kind of person who doesn't let obstacles prevent me from getting what I want." He wheeled several feet, before he spun. "Oh, dear. I almost forgot. Some chap named Oscar accosted me in the parking lot. He asked me to tell you that he needed to talk to you. He'll be waiting by your car."

21

Mer limped toward the museum entrance. Most of the gala attendees were dining in the banquet hall. In another forty-five minutes, Winslet Chase would address the audience.

The kewpie doll gatekeeper had abandoned her post and a female deputy manned the front door. It had been such an ordeal to get in, Mer was hesitant to step out. Did A-list soirees require a hand stamp for reentry? She had no experience to draw on.

But Oscar waited and damn if she didn't have a slew of questions to ask him.

The deputy smiled as Mer approached. "Leaving us so soon?"

Mer shook her head. "I'm finding the company a bit stuffy. Just popping out for a breath of fresh air."

"It's a beautiful evening," the deputy said, diplomatically. She held the door for Mer. "Be careful."

Music followed Mer into the night. The warm ocean breeze wrapped around her bare shoulders. Tiki torches illuminated the pathway but did nothing to obscure the star-filled sky. Paradise.

She lifted the hem of her dress so it didn't drag across the gravel as she picked her way around the museum to where she'd abandoned her car. Each step tortured her already pained feet.

How long had Oscar been waiting, and how did he know she'd be inside? She slowed. Bijoux was the sole person who knew Mer's whereabouts. Had she told Oscar? But who had told Winslet Chase? He said he'd been "accosted." That certainly didn't give the impression he knew Oscar. She considered the possibilities. Talbot hadn't known she'd be there until he had saved her from being unceremoniously ejected. Selkie had been activated for duty earlier that morning and didn't know of her plans.

So how had Winslet Chase known she'd be at the gala?

A dark shape leaned against her car. A man, clutching his ribs and taking short, shallow breaths.

"Oscar." Gathering her dress in both hands, she hurried to his side. "You're hurt."

Pain darkened his brown eyes. "I'm sorry, Meredith."

"Sorry?" She fumbled with her purse. Grabbed her cellphone. "You need medics."

Oscar put a mangled hand over hers and stopped her from dialing. "No. You must not. Please. Listen."

"You need—"

Oscar yanked the phone from her grasp and slid it across the roof of the Subaru. "He will kill me." He collapsed against the car again and cradled his broken hand. "And you, as well."

A chill that had nothing to do with the breeze trickled down her spine. She dared not breathe. Didn't move or blink. But her mind whirled. She tried to slow it down, to make sense of the chaos. Without moving her head, she swept her eyes across the landscape, tried to locate the threat that darkness and night noise hid.

She lowered her voice. "Can you walk? We need to get inside."

"We cannot. He watches."

"Who does? I don't understand."

Oscar winced. "Bart." He half-turned and lifted his chin toward the hardwood hammock that lined the edge of the property. A figure emerged from the shadows. His arm hung by his side, but he held something that glinted in the moonlight.

"He has a gun," Oscar said. "You must listen to me."

Mer grabbed his arm. "No, you listen to me. There are deputies inside. Undercover officers. All we have to do is get to the other side of the car. Yell. They'll come running."

"The music. They will not hear us."

She opened her purse and rummaged for her car key. "We've got to get out of here!"

"Stop!" He crumpled to the ground, dragging her with him.

Both driver-side tires had been slashed. She kicked away from him, her heels skidding across the gravel.

He held up his good hand, as if trying to calm a spooked animal. "They will not hurt you if you do as I say. The coin." His voice sounded dull. Defeated. "You must get it."

It didn't make sense. "The coin?"

"They think it is the key to the Thirteenth Galleon."

She rolled onto her knees and heard the dress tear. "Why do they think that?"

"I told them so. To protect you."

She forced herself to remain still while every instinct screamed at her to get as far away as possible. Common sense told her she'd get three feet and either trip or get shot. Could she trust Oscar? He'd just dragged her to the ground—but he was trying to help her. Or so he said. Mer stared up at the stars. Oscar was not the gentle academic she had imagined. "Oscar. What the hell is the Thirteenth Galleon?"

"A bribe. To King Philip. Sent by a group of churchmen to convince him to—" he struggled to find the right word. "Change for the better the Alhambra Decree. But that is not important. The ship! It is real."

Real. Nothing about this evening felt real—except the fear roiling in her gut.

"In the archives. I found an old ship record book." His words gathered speed. "It is buried with papers of no consequence. The binding, it is old. Cracked. Under the leather, hidden, are three things—a note, a list of names, and a coin. The galleon is real."

"If the coin isn't the key, what is?"

"You."

She gasped. "Me? *You* found it!"

"I found proof of the Thirteenth Galleon, but you, you have the clue."

"I don't have anything."

A sharp whistle sliced through the music.

Oscar whispered. "There is no more time. Please." Tears filled his eyes. "You must find it."

She leaned against the side of the car. "I don't know how to find a sunken ship."

"You know someone who does."

Winslet Chase. Her new business partner. The thought filled her with more fear than Bart in the bushes.

Oscar reached for the window jamb and struggled to stand. "This is my fault," he said. "I am very sorry I brought this trouble to you. Look for the clue. You will see it when you return. Now, you must walk me back."

She almost laughed, but her mouth was too dry. "Back to Bart Kingston? Not a chance in hell."

"Do what he says. He will not hurt you."

"Right. Because a smuggler always keeps his word."

"He will not hurt the key." He offered Mer his hand.

She refused. "But he may want to keep it."

Two more short whistles rent the night.

Oscar grabbed her by the arm and roughly pulled her upright. "We must hurry. The patrol will return in two minutes."

"I'm not going anywhere." She wrenched free of his grip. "Not with you. Not to Bart."

His whole body trembled. "Please forgive me."

Cold metal pressed into her naked side.

"You must walk with me," he said.

Tears formed but she blinked them away before they could spill. "Who are you?"

"I am who I said." He prodded her toward the darkness. "I am Oscar Vigil. I am an archivist. Now, you must trust me."

Fight or flight. The gun in her side took away the choice. Her heart raced. With any luck, she'd pass out before she got to the mangrove. Then what would they do?

A ghost materialized from the shadows. Thin. Wiry. Wearing a ball cap. She'd seen this guy before. But where? Her heel scraped against a sprinkler head and she stutter-stepped forward. Close enough to recognize the Met's logo on the cap. The guy from the grocery store.

"*You're* Bart Kingston?"

"Safety tip. You shouldn't keep your wallet in an outside pocket."

"How do you know...?" Dots connected in her head. She whirled on Oscar. "You've been in this since the beginning."

Rage clouded her judgment. She widened her stance and cocked her arm.

Bart laughed. "Don't be too hard on him. He didn't have much choice."

Oscar lowered his hands. The pipe he'd held against her side dropped to the ground with a dull thud. He closed his eyes and waited for the blow.

No gun. The implication registered before her mind even processed the sight. Bart. The threat was Bart.

She twisted, throwing all her weight into the punch. Bart's nose crunched under her fist.

Then all the stars in the sky rained down behind her eyes in a burst of pain.

Mer struggled to her hands and knees. Swayed. Spit grass from her mouth, unsure how it got there.

"Stupid woman." Bart rubbed his knuckles against the thigh of his jeans. He towered over her and drew his leg back.

Oscar grabbed his arm. "No. The patrol. There is no time."

Bart backhanded Oscar with the butt of the gun and sent him reeling against a coco-plum tree. "Don't touch me again."

He leveled the gun at Mer. "Get the coin." His foot shot out.

The blow drove the breath from her body. She clutched her belly and retched.

"Get the coin, or your friend's a dead man."

22

M er held an icepack against her right eye as she sat on the bumper of the ambulance. Red and blue light danced against the museum walls and made the crystals of her dress shimmer purple. She shut her good eye. "I need a ride home."

"I still think you should go to the hospital. Let them check you out," Talbot said.

It had been nearly two hours since the attack. Two fun-filled hours recounting the betrayal of a friend, the attack of a madman, and what? A business proposition to go into treasure hunting?

She lifted the icepack off her swollen eye. "Are we through?"

He sighed. "Give me a minute. I'll drive you home." He hailed the female detective. "Get with the curator. I'm going to need the surveillance video."

Guido lumbered over to the ambulance. "The K-9 tracked Kingston and Vigil to the road. Found some overlapping tire tracks. CSI's snapping photos, but no way to tell if they're the right ones."

"Bart Kingston drives a black Ford pickup truck," Mer said. The memory of headlights drilling into her mirror from the Thanksgiving pursuit filled her mind. "Lifted."

Guido flipped through his notebook. "That jives with motor vehicle records. Patrol's *en route* to the address on file. It's in Marathon."

Talbot nodded. "Good."

"Oscar was in an old Corolla. White. Pretty beat up," Mer said.

Talbot addressed Guido. "Wasn't there a Corolla stolen in Stock Island about a week ago? Maybe we'll get lucky with a plate."

"On it." The deputy retreated.

"What about Winslet Chase?" Mer asked.

Talbot answered, "He's being interviewed now."

"He's in this up to his neck." Fatigue overwhelmed her. "There's no way Oscar would approach him." Unless they were all in this together.

Deputy Cole materialized from the shadows, and before she could stop herself, she spat out, "What's he doing here?"

Talbot glanced up. "He's been here all evening. Part of the perimeter team."

Cole walked over to Talbot. "I finished interviewing Chase. He said some guy approached him in the parking lot and asked him to pass a message to this one," he said, pointing at Mer. "Chase thought he was a gardener or something and didn't think anything more of it until he was speaking to the Doc here and realized she was the one the guy was talking about."

"Where's Chase now?" Talbot asked.

"Probably on his way home. He gave a description of the guy, but didn't know anything else. I let him go."

"Of course you did." Mer rolled her good eye and her swollen one valiantly tried to follow. "Did it occur to you to ask him about the Thirteenth Galleon?"

Cole turned his back on her and continued to talk to Talbot. "Chase said he was bidding on silent auction items when Dr. Cavallo came up to him. Started hitting on him."

"Bullshit," Mer said. "He approached me."

Cole ignored her outburst. "He wasn't interested, but she

wouldn't take no for an answer. That's when he remembered the gardener, made the connection, and sent her outside."

Mer spoke over Cole's shoulder to Talbot. "I'll wait for you over there." She gathered Bijoux's shoes in her hand and walked barefoot across the grass and waited at the edge of the parking lot. The last thing she wanted to do was listen to Deputy Cole and Detective Talbot discuss her fictional flirting.

Her thoughts ran to Oscar. At the church he had looked bewildered. Lost. She stitched together his words, trying to weave them into a semblance of truth. America was the land of opportunity, of adventure. It would take finding the Thirteenth Galleon to redeem himself in his father's eyes. At the time, she thought it was hyperbole, but Oscar's only reason for being in the Keys was to find the galleon. After realizing the coin was gone, his sole purpose in asking Bijoux for a job was to get close to the woman who had found the bale. Her.

She'd been so grateful when Oscar returned her wallet, not realizing that he'd been in league with Bart Kingston to steal it in the first place. When Bart had discovered the coin wasn't inside, they must have quickly devised a Plan B—and Mer had voluntarily told Oscar where she lived. Invited him to dinner. He knew she was working the sunrise charter. Hell, she did everything but help the two of them ransack her apartment.

The icepack's chill had leached into her skin and settled in her heart. Oscar had betrayed her. It was stupid, but she'd trusted him. He was an academic—and in her world, that meant something. He'd capitalized on her idiocy, and his actions tonight had drawn her further into danger.

The crunch of gravel announced Talbot's arrival in his dark colored Impala. Mer opened the door, but he dashed to her side and helped her into the passenger seat. She leaned her head against the window, reveling in the coolness.

The car dipped as he took his seat. "Are you certain I can't take you to the hospital. What if you have a cracked rib? A concussion?"

"Nothing the doctors can do about either one." And she didn't want to think about what a hospital bill would cost. The repair bill for a torn and grass-stained designer dress was worrisome enough.

He placed the car in gear and eased down the museum driveway.

Twenty-odd miles and she'd be home. Twenty miles to screw up her courage and tell him what she'd held back earlier. What she hadn't wanted to disclose in front of other people. But she had to tell him. A life was at stake. Maybe even her own.

Mer broke the silence. "There's more." She studied her reflection in the passenger window. The woman who stared back was nearly unrecognizable. She had a choice. Continue hurtling herself headfirst in a game where there were no rules, or trust Talbot and come clean with what she'd learned tonight.

"More what?" He turned north on Overseas Highway.

"More than what I told the other deputy earlier." She held the tattered edge of her dress together and wished she could gather her frayed thoughts as easily. "I need the coin back."

He laughed. "And you expect me to hand it over to you just because you asked for it?"

"No." Her fingers brushed the hollow of her throat before she remembered she wasn't wearing her seahorse pendant. "I hope you'll hand it over to save a life. Bart told me to get him the coin."

"And if you didn't?"

"He'd kill Oscar."

Talbot straightened. "Did he tell you how to contact him when you got it?"

Mer shook her head and then realized he couldn't see her in the dark interior. "No. Maybe he doesn't really expect me to be able to get it."

"Yes, he does."

"I think we can both agree that my covert infiltration skills need work. Even Bart should realize that breaking into the sheriff's evidence locker is beyond my ability."

"It's not in the locker."

"The safe, vault, whatever you put it. That's not the point."

"It is the point," Talbot said. "The coin in the property room is fake."

"Why would there be a fake coin in a bundle of drugs?"

"Oh, I suspect that coin was real enough."

"I'm confused." Fatigue robbed her of her ability to follow the conversation. "Are you saying that the coin I gave you wasn't the coin Cole booked into evidence?"

"That's the million dollar question."

"You can't be serious." She shifted in the seat, ignoring the pain the movement provoked in her side. "Isn't there a system or procedures or something? How could this happen?"

"Cole said he booked the gold coin. The property tech confirmed that he received a gold coin. After you informed me of the value, I arranged to have an expert evaluate it. He laughed when he saw it, said he could go into any souvenir shop in the Keys that sold pirate toys and buy the same doubloon."

"It wasn't a doubloon. I gave you a gold, 1733, eight *escudos*, milled portrait dollar."

"And I gave the coin you handed me to Deputy Cole."

"So Cole switched it?"

"He swears he booked the coin I gave him."

"Which means he thinks I gave you a fake."

"Bingo."

"But you know I didn't." Her voice climbed with outrage.

"I believe you didn't, but I never examined the coin before I gave it to him."

"So you have doubts." A heavy feeling pressed against her chest. She'd thought they had moved beyond that. It made telling him the rest more complicated.

"What I know is that the coin in evidence is fake. Either Cole booked a phony coin or someone gained access to the evidence locker and swapped it out. So the real question is did Cole know the coin he booked was fake? He says no."

"Why would I give him a fake coin? The coin was lost. I didn't have to admit I'd found it again."

"Plausible deniability."

She blew the stray curl off her face. "Now you sound like Cole."

"It's his theory. On the surface, it appears that you turned in the coin. In reality, you're a whole lot richer and your business partners are none the wiser."

Business partners. The phrase echoed in her head in Winslet Chase's voice. "If that's the case, how does Bart know the coin was swapped?"

"Good question."

"Here's an even better one. Where's the real coin?"

"Tonight's antics indicate that Bart thinks you have it," Talbot said. "Or at the very least you know how to get it."

Her mind circled back to another question. "Who is Bart Kingston?"

"A mid-level smuggler. His mother lives in Marathon, though I doubt he's stupid enough to be there when the deputies arrive."

A hollow feeling started in her stomach. "What kind of smuggler?"

"He's not discriminating. Anything that will turn a profit. Drugs, people, you name it."

The hollow feeling spread and threatened to swallow her. "Mid-level?"

"Smuggling is a hierarchy," Talbot said. "Bart's in the middle and that makes him more dangerous. He has to keep those below him in line and impress the higher-ups."

"He's got a plan to impress the boss, all right," she said. "He's bucking to deliver the treasure of the Thirteenth Galleon."

"You missed the keynote, but according to Winslet Chase, there's no such thing."

Her doubt vanished. "There is, and I have the proof."

23

"I have a theory. Actually, it's more of a hypothesis," Mer said.

The Overseas Highway forked in Tavernier and a wall of densely woven foliage rose up on either side of the road as they continued to drive toward Mer's home.

"I'm not a scientist," Talbot replied. "How about we stick to the standard English definition?"

She fiddled with the heel of one of the shoes in her lap. "This could take a while, and you'll probably want to take notes."

"We're a bit overdressed for Denny's," he said. "Although, they serve breakfast twenty-four seven."

The thought of food turned her stomach. "If you don't mind, I'd rather talk at my place."

"At least give me a tidbit to tide me over."

"What I'm about to do may break the law, and I'm debating whether or not to tell you."

"Wow." He rubbed the back of his neck. "You know I have to act upon what you tell me."

"Hence my reluctance."

The car hit a bump in the road. Pain stabbed her side and she drew a sharp breath between her teeth.

He slowed. "Sorry."

"For what? You didn't hit me."

His knuckles tightened around the steering wheel. "About that. What the hell were you thinking? Punching a guy packing a gun. He could have killed you."

The outburst surprised her. "There wasn't a whole lot of thinking going on."

"That's painfully obvious. One kickboxing class doesn't make you Wonder Woman." He glanced at her, but the interior of the car was dark and she couldn't read his expression. "Gabby told me she'd run into you at the gym," he added.

"So I gather." The last thing she needed was a lecture. Suddenly, the thought of sharing the same space with a person who doubted her integrity was too much. She needed distance from Talbot. From thoughts of the coin. From everything about this messed up night.

The Overseas Highway had few traffic lights, but the one that controlled the intersection at Atlantic Boulevard flashed yellow and then red, despite the absence of cross traffic. Talbot stopped at the crosswalk and Mer pushed her shoulder against the door and practically fell from the car before she could maneuver her sore feet under her.

"Thanks for the ride." She slammed the door, the movement spurring a new round of pain. She'd contemplate the childishness of her behavior later— when she could see out of both eyes, draw a deep breath, and walk without a Quasimodo shuffle.

Mer ignored the red light and hobbled across the intersection. Talbot activated his emergency lights and followed her, matching her tortured pace.

He rolled down the window. "Get in the car."

Every muscle in her body ached, both from squaring off on a punching bag and being used as one. Nothing sounded better than climbing back into the car and letting him drive her the last mile to her home. "Go away, Detective."

"I can arrest you for jaywalking."

Mer kept walking. "Don't forget perjury, obstructing an

investigation, and misappropriation of found property. Cole will be thrilled."

"You have to be under oath to perjure yourself."

She stopped so he could appreciate the full effect of her glare.

"I don't have time for this." He raised his voice to be heard above the engine. "Please just get in the car. Look, I'm sorry."

The stilettos bumped her thigh as they dangled from her hand. "For what?"

He goosed the accelerator and angled the car across the sidewalk, stopping within inches of her and blocking her path. "The remark about kickboxing. That was out of line and I'm sorry. I'm off my game. I got a call earlier. Cops busted up a party. My...Gabby was arrested." He pinched the bridge of his nose as if he had a headache. "'Tis a happy thing to be the father unto many sons."

Mer wasn't ready to make nice. "Maybe so, Shakespeare, but you've got a daughter." She leaned through the open window. "Apparently one you can't control."

He grabbed the steering wheel with both hands and stared straight ahead.

Her head throbbed with shame and she ran her hand over her swollen eye. "That was uncalled for. I'm sorry. She's not my daughter."

He wore the expression of a child who had lost his dog and his world had ground to a wretched end. "She's not mine, either."

Surely he didn't mean his words literally? But the rigid set of his shoulders convinced her he had. What little energy Mer's body held in reserve fled, taking all of her anger with it.

The door handle weighed a ton. She opened the door and sank into the passenger seat. In the dark, she laid her hand on his forearm.

He shook off her touch and jammed the car into drive. They rode the rest of the way in silence.

The detective's Impala bounced across the driveway gutter.

"Sorry." Talbot veered to the left side of the dual driveway and parked.

It was the first word he'd spoken since the bombshell about his daughter.

"Lots of sorries tonight," Mer said. "I'm sorry, too."

He ran his hand over his shorn hair. His loosened bow tie and rumpled tux erased years from his appearance, and he looked like a morning-after prom date. At least that's how she imagined a prom date would look after spending a night on the beach, waiting for the sun to rise. She hadn't gone to her prom, so it was supposition.

He cracked open his door, but didn't get out. "I should explain."

"It's none of my business."

"She's my daughter." He drew a breath. "I'm just not her father."

A handful of inches separated them, yet he seemed to be a world away.

"I don't understand," she said softly.

"It was my senior year. Gabby's mom and I, we were a fling. Nothing serious, you know? And then..."

"It got serious."

"She was pregnant. I wanted to do the right thing. Bought a ring." He glanced at Mer. "Hasty marriage seldom proveth well. So I guess it's a good thing she refused."

He worried his bowtie and it came off in his hand. He folded the material into a neat square.

"When Gabriella was born, everything changed. She was my daughter." A ghost of a smile warmed his face and then faded. "The first time I held her I fell in love."

"She's a wonderful young woman. You've done well."

"Gabby's a terror on the soccer field." Pride entered his voice. "She's going to Nationals this year with her school." He crumpled the cloth in his hand. "Did you know that hospitals put those plastic identification bracelets on babies, too? They do," he answered for her. "Name, birthday, blood type. Turns out Gabby has type A blood. Funny, since her mom and I are both O positive."

Mer grasped the implication immediately. Two parents with type O blood could only have a child with the same blood type. Anything else was a genetic impossibility.

He shook out the material and started to refold it. "I decided then it didn't matter. My dad...well, let's just say I didn't want to be like him." He laughed, but it held no mirth. "Tonight Gabby got picked up at a party. Not the end of the world. She wasn't hurt and the deputy notified me right away. But it's kind of hard to pick up your kid when you're on a special detail, so I called her mother." He paused as if trying to pick the right words. "She went *off*. Blamed me for not intervening. Asked me what kind of dad I was. I snapped. And for the first time in fifteen years, I flung it in her face."

"Does Gabriella know?" Mer whispered.

"God, I hope not." He kicked the door open the rest of the way. "You see, Dr. Cavallo, I do trust you." For a moment it looked as if he wanted to say more. "Let me make sure you get inside okay."

Ever the gentleman. Even in distress. "This isn't a date," she said gently.

Some of the tension left his shoulders. "I can assure you, if this were a date, you would have had a better time tonight."

"You set the bar pretty low."

He managed a tired smile. "Let's get you inside." He came around to her side of the car and offered her his hand. "For the record, I don't think you swapped the coin."

She placed her hand in his and allowed him to draw her upward. "Thank you. That means more to me than you know."

Together they hobbled toward the door. Mer unfastened the jeweled clasp on the evening purse. At least something had remained unscathed. Her key hid under the wadded piece of paper Oscar had left tucked into the driver's window of her Subaru. "Do you need to take care of things at home? Because I have a story to share with you, if you have the time." She gripped the key.

"Emotions are too high tonight. Gabby's safe. That's all that matters."

The porch light next door clicked on and Selkie rounded the corner. "Mer?"

Her mood lightened. She hadn't expected to see him tonight, especially when his car wasn't in the driveway. He must have parked in the garage.

In a flash, he was at her side. And just as quickly, he processed her disheveled appearance, swollen face, and torn dress. Without a word, he turned to Talbot. His eyes glanced at the detective's open collar but settled on his hand at Mer's elbow.

"Am I interrupting?" his voice held a frostiness foreign to the Keys.

"Not at all," Talbot said. "I was just seeing Dr. Cavallo home from the gala."

"A gala doesn't explain her injuries."

She stood between the men and glared at Selkie. "I'm fine. Thanks for asking."

Selkie spoke around her. "I assume there was security. Who was the incompetent running the operation?" he demanded.

"Me," Talbot replied. "May I?" He took the key from Mer's hand and opened the door.

"Congratulations. A stellar job."

Talbot faced Selkie. The absolute stillness in his stance belied the tension that fairly crackled between the two men.

It was the final straw. Oscar kidnapped. A black eye, hurt ribs. Two slashed tires. One dress worth more than her college education, torn. And now she had Talbot and Selkie acting like tomcats scrapping over a piece of fish.

"Enough!"

Both men looked at her.

"I'm going to change clothes. Then I'm going to sit in the backyard and talk about treasure. If you don't want to be there, fine. If you do, try not to kill each other before I come outside."

She shuffled into her apartment and slammed the door.

Men.

She unfolded the paper from her purse and reread the copy of the manifest she'd transcribed the night before Thanksgiving. The name was there.

Berdugo. Mateo Eques de Soto y Berdugo.

When she reemerged, she wore sweats and a T-shirt and carried a half-full bottle of wine, two salvaged coffee mugs, and a water bottle for herself. The Adirondack chairs had been pulled into a circle.

Mer handed the wine bottle and mugs to Selkie. He poured a mug and then offered the bottle to the detective.

Talbot waved it away. "I'm still on duty." He locked eyes with Mer in warning as he took out his cellphone and selected a recorder app.

Settling into her chair, she drew a deep breath and winced. "I don't have proof for everything, but I've been piecing together this puzzle and I think it started in Cuba. With Oscar." Her hands trembled as she raised the water bottle and took a small sip while she gathered her thoughts. "He told me tonight that he had found proof to support that another ship had joined the 1733 fleet that left Havana and wrecked along the Florida Keys. A ship that local legend called the Thirteenth Galleon."

"Chase said it didn't exist," Talbot said.

Selkie glared at Talbot. "Don't interrupt."

She'd be grateful for Selkie's support if she didn't suspect his comment was more a dig at the detective than a show of support for her. "Oscar worked in a government archive. He said he'd found the coin, the manifest, and a note hidden in the binding of an old ship log. I never saw the note, but Oscar believes it points to the true clue."

"The coin?" Selkie asked.

Mer dug into her sweats pocket, and then unfolded a piece of paper. "The manifest." She looked at Talbot. "After Bart and Oscar fled, I went back to my car. This piece of paper was shoved into the window of my driver's door. It's the list that was stolen off my desk. But I'm getting ahead of myself."

The sloping Adirondack offered no respite for her aching ribs, but she was too tired to get out of the chair. "Oscar said he'd come to the Keys by boat. I think that boat belonged to Bart Kingston and that somehow Bart got hold of the coin and the manifest."

"And the note?"

"I have no idea how the note fits in—or if it still exists." Mer tilted her head back. The moon outlined a sky full of clouds. "There was a squall the night before Leroy and I pulled the drugs out of the water. They lost the bale and that's when Bart's scheme began to unravel."

"Wouldn't it be Oscar's scheme?" Talbot asked.

"I don't think so. Maybe originally, but Bart is definitely calling the shots now."

"And you know this how?"

"Oscar had been badly beaten." Images of his mangled hand and the sound of the gun striking his head sent a chill down her spine. "But he was too scared to try to escape. He told me they—whoever they are—believe the coin is the key. But that was false information that he'd fed them to throw them off the trail. He said that I was the key—"

Selkie slammed down his cup. "You?"

"Not me *per se*, but because I had the actual clue. The manifest. Which Oscar stole from my home, but never shared with Bart. The real manifest was almost completely destroyed. But if they thought it had any value, they would have gotten it at the same time they stole the real coin."

"I'm confused," Selkie said.

"The coin in evidence was replaced by a fake one—I'm investigating how that happened," Talbot clarified.

"But Mer's a suspect."

Talbot shrugged. "It was found property to begin with. It really doesn't matter what she turned in. The importance is how it relates to the bigger story." He shot out of his chair and started pacing in a small circle. "But I'm missing something."

"Other than a coin?" Selkie asked.

"We keep saying they—Bart and his compadres. Up until tonight,

I thought he was a suspect in somehow stealing the coin. But if he thinks Mer stole it—"

She held up her finger. "For the record—"

Talbot waved away the rest. "That means he had nothing to do with the switch."

"Which means there's someone else involved," she said.

Selkie broke in. "Someone with their own endgame."

"After tonight, I'd add Winslet Chase to the list," Mer said. "He asked me about the Thirteenth Galleon, so I find it completely disingenuous that he told a crowd of people it didn't exist."

"How would he switch the coin?" Talbot asked.

Good question. "Cole?" It came out as a whisper. She didn't like the man, but accusing a police officer of illegal conduct didn't sit well. The media made it sound as if they were all corrupt, but she knew better. Her brother and Talbot proved it.

"God, I hope not."

"But it's a possibility," she added.

The detective looked miserable. "I can't rule it out."

"Oscar had the manifest. Could he have palmed the coin, too?" Selkie asked.

"I turned in the coin after the burglary," Mer said. "No. I think Oscar is being coerced to help, and he's trying to foil them. Bart stole my wallet at the grocery store. And it was Bart and Oscar who burglarized my home. Oscar found the page of names I'd transcribed from the manifest photo, and he tucked it away before Bart noticed."

An uncomfortable thought occurred to her and she shifted in the chair. She'd accomplished what she'd set out to do. She'd discovered who burglarized her home. She knew the reason behind it and the value of the coin. Yet she also knew there was more to learn. And the remaining secret loomed larger than her little world. If Oscar was right, it involved the Church, a king, and a treasure.

If she weren't in so much pain, she'd acknowledge that solving the mystery sounded intriguing. "There's one more thing. I may have figured out the clue Oscar hinted at."

Talbot stopped pacing and Selkie leaned forward. "Why do you say that?"

Knowing the link and understanding the clue were two very different things, but there had to be a connection. It was too coincidental. The canvas had been painted a mere four years after the hurricane.

"There's a painting in the museum by an artist named Berdugo. I'm pretty sure he's on the manifest."

24

Rain sluiced off the balcony that sheltered her patio and hammered the Adirondack chairs they'd sat in last night. She'd slept in fits. Every time Mer moved, something hurt, so she tried to lie still. And while her limbs obeyed, her mind refused to quiet. It raced through possibilities, spun arguments, and jumped to conclusions—a triathlon of shoddy reasoning.

Over the past few days, she'd unearthed a trove of information that left her far better informed about the importance of the coin and manifest, but no better equipped to extradite herself from their continued intrigue.

By ten a.m., and after hours spent squinting at information on her phone, she'd learned one thing: coffee made from brown-colored crystals sucked.

Mer closed the browser, dragged a comb through her unruly curls, and grabbed her keys. She cursed. A critical component of her plan to get good coffee was still in Islamorada with two slashed tires and decorated with evidence tape. A glance at her phone confirmed that Talbot hadn't called to release it yet.

Her to-do list kept growing: save Oscar, foil Bart Kingston, avoid Winslet Chase, solve the riddle of Berdugo, find the Thirteenth

Galleon, rebuild her home, retrieve her car, buy new tires, and get a decent cup of coffee. She rubbed the back of her sore neck. Her ability to accomplish anything on the list hinged on coffee.

Desperate times called for desperate measures. She swapped her flip-flops for running shoes, although in her current condition, the closest she'd come to a run would be an aggressive shuffle. Even factoring in a margin of error, she calculated the mile walk to the gas station would take about three days.

She opened the door and came face to face with Bijoux's raised fist. Both women took a startled step backward.

Bijoux recovered first. "I heard." Her hand dropped to her side and her eyes filled with concern. "Should you be up?"

"I need coffee."

"Why do you not brew your own?"

"I don't have a coffee grinder, coffeemaker, or coffee."

"That does complicate things." Bijoux brushed the hair back from the side of Mer's face. "When I suggested you add color to your life, I meant with your clothes."

Lifting her shirt, Mer revealed the purple and blue contusion on her side. "Wait a few days and I'll be experimenting with yellows."

"*Mon dieu.*" Bijoux's lips pressed into a frown. "Whoever did this is a coward."

Mer invited her boss inside. "Your dress..." Draped across the foot of her bed, the designer gown gleamed in the morning light like a bruise. She'd assessed the damage earlier. It wasn't as horrible as she'd supposed last night—the tears were all along seams—but of everything she'd borrowed from Bijoux, she wished she'd damaged the damn shoes. "The strap and hem are ripped. The side is torn. There are grass stains everywhere."

Bijoux waved her hand dismissively over the gown. "It is only a dress."

"I'm so sorry. I'll pay for the repairs."

"Don't be absurd. I'll send it back to Jean-Paul with a note." She faced Mer. "I came by to make certain you are truly all right. See how much time you will need before you should come back to work."

"I'm ready."

"If that was meant as a joke, it isn't funny. Based on your appearance, it will be some time before you will lift tanks."

"But—"

"The weekend is done. It's a slow time of year. Based on the current reservations, the *Dock Holiday* will run two mornings and one afternoon trip this week. We won't need the *LunaSea* until Saturday. And Kyle is delighted to help in the store."

Mer narrowed her eyes at Bijoux and the other woman burst out laughing. "Perhaps delighted is too strong a word."

"Perhaps. Can I buy you a cup of coffee?" Mer asked.

Bijoux wrinkled her nose. "Not if it is from that dreadful gas station."

"You're driving. My car is still in Islamorada."

"Perfect. We'll go to Café Moka, and then you can make arrangements for your car."

"Can I run something by you?" Mer asked.

"Of course," Bijoux answered.

Light poured into the cafe through French doors. The espresso machine hissed while they waited for their drinks.

Mer started to slump against the counter, but the pain from her ribs brought her upright. "Oscar mentioned that the Legend of the Thirteenth Galleon arose after a group of churchmen raised a bribe for King Philip to change the Alhambra Decree."

"Oscar." Bijoux's bracelets clacked with her agitation. "I would not have thought him capable of such treachery."

"I've given Oscar's participation in this a lot of thought. I'm convinced he's trying to protect me."

"He needs to try harder."

"You didn't see him last night. He was scared. And yet he still found the courage to try to intercede when Bart threatened me. Think about it. Oscar grew up in a country where people could disappear in the dark of night. Then he hooks up with Bart Kingston —a man who can definitely make people disappear. Oscar wouldn't stand a chance against such a thug."

"You are letting him off too easy."

"He's going to die, if I don't help."

The barista slid their cups to them with a smile and turned back to the machine.

Bijoux made no move toward her coffee. "What is this decree?"

"The expulsion order that King Ferdinand and Queen Isabella signed during the Spanish Inquisition." Mer collected her latte and scone. "It commanded all Jews to abandon the kingdom of Spain— or face death."

"I can see why churchmen would want to change that."

"Except it was the Church that was pushing for the decree, so why would they try to invalidate it?"

Bijoux picked up her cup. "Perhaps there was a faction that allied with the Jews."

"Here's where it gets interesting. Oscar said the legend started in the fifteenth century."

Bijoux paused at the creamer table and pulled two napkins from the dispenser. "What year was the edict?"

"Ferdinand and Isabella signed it in 1492." Mer nibbled the edge of her orange-cranberry scone.

"The ship sunk over two hundred years later. How could that be connected?"

"I don't know," Mer admitted.

"What about the manifest? Were any of the passengers Catholic?"

"Probably. Europe was overwhelmingly Catholic at the time."

"Your argument needs more substance."

The loud espresso machine delayed her answer, but Bijoux was right.

"I need more coffee for that."

Bijoux held open the door. "You need sleep, not coffee."

The flat tires imparted a forlorn tilt to her Subaru. Fingerprint powder smudged her driver window and a dark smear of blood streaked her door where Oscar had jammed the folded manifest.

"Do you want me to wait until the tow truck driver arrives?" Bijoux asked.

"No. The dispatcher said it'd be an hour. That will give me time to go into the museum and study the painting again. You're more than welcome to join me."

"Watch you stare at a painting? Fortunately, I have other errands that require my attention."

Mer hugged Bijoux. "Thank you."

"Get some sleep. I'll check on you tomorrow."

"You don't need to do that."

"No. I do not." She wagged a finger in Mer's face and her bracelets kept time. "Sleep."

She nodded.

Satisfied, Bijoux drove off and Mer trudged to the entrance of the museum. Unlike last night's debacle, today all she had to do to enter was buy a ticket. The lady at the register even smiled at her—although she may have been trying to mask her horror at the bruise that covered half of Mer's face.

She shuffled her way to the *Lignum Vitae* Hall. When she got there, a velvet rope blocked the entrance and employees were breaking down the exhibit.

Mer hailed a curator.

"The exhibit is on temporary loan to Winslet Chase," the man stated officiously.

"The whole thing?" Wow. Winslet had some pull. Unfortunately, he also had the Berdugo. She had to think fast. "A charming man." The words practically choked her. "I met him last night at the gala."

At the mention of the A-list fete, the curator's demeanor immediately changed. "A riveting keynote."

She tucked a curl behind her ear, exposing the bruise. "I'm afraid I missed it. You see, I was the woman assaulted on your museum grounds. A most unfortunate event, wouldn't you agree?"

Some of the starch left his spine.

Channeling her inner Bijoux, she stood as straight as she could, which due to her ribs, was considerably less than vertical. "When I spoke with my counsel this morning, I assured her that the museum shouldn't be held accountable." Referring to Bijoux as counsel may have been a bit misleading, but her boss *had* dispensed advice, just not on accountability. "Of course, I was devastated to miss the two things I had most wanted to see last night. The Berdugo painting," she pointed to the empty space on the wall, "and Winslet's presentation."

"It's—" He cleared his throat. "It's your lucky day. We recorded his entire speech."

"After all that occurred last night, it would make me very happy to receive a copy of it."

"Of course, Miss...?"

She held out her hand and hoped the curator wouldn't shake it too vigorously. "Doctor." Gatecrashers usually didn't command the same level of respect as legitimate A-listers, and with any luck, he'd be satisfied with a title. "You must have documentation on the painting in your inventory. I'd like a copy of that too, please."

"I'm sorry, that's priv—"

"I'm certain that sharing a photograph won't break any rules. After all, it's merely a depiction of what you displayed." She'd picked up a southern accent to go with her smile. Why, she hadn't a clue. Maybe she really had suffered head trauma.

"It will take just a few minutes to copy the presentation onto a disc. Unless you require a different format?"

She no longer had a laptop, but she didn't want to quibble. "No, thank you. That would be wonderful." He'd taken two steps before she stopped him. "I almost forgot. Do you have the artist's bio?"

"Actually, there isn't one. The only thing we know about him is his surname."

Selkie was grilling dinner in his backyard when Mer rounded the corner of his house. "I found the link!"

He flipped the single piece of chicken and doused it with a bit of his beer. "You need to let law enforcement handle this."

"Aren't you even a little curious?" She came up behind him and wrapped her arms around his middle.

"No." He sidestepped out of her grasp.

She tried again. "I watched the lecture. The one Winslet Chase gave."

"How did you—? Never mind. I don't want to know."

She hadn't eaten since her scone and latte that morning and the smell of grilled chicken made her mouth water. "He talked about the legend."

"I don't want to hear this, Mer."

She continued undeterred. "There's really not much to tell. Of all the legends, he kind of paid the Thirteenth Galleon short shrift. Stingy considering how much he wanted to talk about it with me. Which in light of everything that's happened, suggests he doesn't want anyone else poking around the legend."

"Sounds like good advice. You should take it."

"But what he did mention—"

"Doesn't interest me."

"I think the clue is in the painting."

"I don't care, Mer."

"Why not?" She took a step back. "When you know this means so much to me?"

He turned back to the grill. "You're a smart woman. It shouldn't be that difficult to figure out."

"You have a master's degree in communication." She tried to keep the hurt from her voice. "Humor me."

"I don't want to talk about it." He twisted the knob in the wrong direction and the flame jumped before he extinguished it.

She stared at his back. "All right." But it wasn't. "Do you want me to come back later?"

"I've got plans. The pub's holding a gala."

The barb found its mark. "Why are you being so pissy? Is this about last night?"

He took the chicken from the grill and dropped it on his plate. "Let Josh do his job, Mer."

"You didn't think that was such a good idea last night."

He banged shut the lid. "You make me crazy. I leave for fourteen hours and when I come home I find the woman I love dressed to the nines, with another man, and she's hurt. You didn't even try to call me."

"Is this about me, or that you weren't there to keep me safe?"

He held up his plate. "My dinner's getting cold."

Dismissed. Her mouth opened and shut like a fish out of water, but no sound came out. She started to tell him what he could do with his *dismissal*, but stopped. What was the point? She smoothed her T-shirt and said coldly, "Sorry to have bothered you."

The slap of her flip-flops marked her retreat.

His words followed her. "You looked beautiful."

She tensed. "What?"

"Last night. Even after all you'd been through. You still looked beautiful."

Something inside her snapped. "No." For a moment, that was the only word she could muster. And then the moment passed. "You don't get to banish me with one breath and compliment me with another. I did nothing wrong last night. And I refuse to apologize." She stepped closer then stopped. "I don't have all the answers. Hell, I don't even know all the rules, but this isn't working. Not for me. Not anymore."

"I shouldn't have said that."

"I'm not sure exactly what part of the conversation you're referring to, but it doesn't really matter. You did say it."

The tongs clacked as he squeezed them shut and carefully balanced them on the grill shelf. "Where does that leave us?"

"You're a smart man." She threw his earlier words back at him. "It shouldn't be that difficult to figure out."

25

The Bilge opened at eleven, and Mer was outside the door the next morning when the key turned at 10:58.

Skipper squinted at her. "Looks like someone opened a can of whoop-ass and your face got in the way."

She pushed past him. "Bart Kingston."

He rammed a wedge under the door to hold it open. The slant of the sun accentuated the crags of Skipper's face and glinted off the hoop that cupped his left ear. "Told you, he's bad news." He grabbed the leg of an upside-down chair, pulled it off a high top table, and set it on the floor.

"No. Actually you didn't." She dropped her backpack onto the floor and curled her fingers around the leg of another chair. "You didn't tell me about the Thirteenth Galleon, either." She flipped over the chair. The weight of the wood pulled her injured muscles and the chair landed heavily on the concrete floor.

"I'll thank you not to break my furniture."

"Winslet Chase—"

"Ain't no better than Bart Kingston," he finished for her.

"He seems to think I'd be a good business partner. Trouble is, I don't much care for him. In fact, I dislike him so much that you look good by comparison. Which is why I'm here."

"You're barking up the wrong tree, girlie. I ain't looking for a business partner. And if you got any sense, you'll stay away from Chase."

"What do you know about Winslet Chase?"

"You opening a tab?"

"Not a chance in hell."

A faint smile played at the edges of his lips. "Yeah, well, I'll give you this on the house. Used to work with the bastard. A wreck up Jupiter way." He righted another chair. "He's smart. Good with the investors."

Winslet Chase and Skipper Biggs? That couldn't have lasted long. At least not without injury. Two type-A personalities had to butt heads.

"So what was the problem?"

His mouth twisted as if he'd swallowed rancid milk. "The man's a liar and a thief."

He grabbed another chair, but Mer held onto one of the other legs. "You're a treasure hunter."

"Used to be."

"Once a pirate, always, no?"

He yanked the seat from her grasp. "This your brand of charm?"

"There's a painting in the Florida Keys Art Museum. The *Lignum Vitae* Hall to be precise."

He cleared another table. "I reckon there's several."

Mer gathered her backpack and claimed a barstool. "This one depicts *El Infante*, the moment she bilges on the reef during the hurricane." She rummaged in the bag. "In the background, there's another galleon battling the storm. Historians labeled it the *San José*, because the *San José* sank closest to *El Infante*."

"So?" He flipped the last of the chairs and retreated behind the bar.

"You know your ships. You tell me."

She slapped the photocopy of the Berdugo painting onto the bar.

"Don't need a painting to tell me what's wrong with that. The *San José's* a Spanish merchant ship. A *nao*, not a galleon."

A thrill ran through Mer. "Exactly."

"That's it? That's your evidence of the Thirteenth Galleon?"

"When the weather cleared," Mer said. "*Capitana* was stuck on another reef nearby. She's a galleon. Historians gave the artist a pass. Simple mistake. Artistic license. Whatever."

Skipper dropped bins of sliced lemons and limes into a compartmentalized container. "You got 'bout thirty seconds before I throw you out." He yanked a plastic jar of maraschino cherries from the bar fridge.

"I've never been in a hurricane, but I've been in a tropical storm. Visibility sucks. And that was on land. Throw in some waves? There'd be no way the artist could have seen the *Capitana*. She was too far away. So what galleon is in the painting?" She leaned against the bar. "Last week, I pulled a square grouper out of the ocean. Inside, I found a portrait dollar. The only wreck those coins have ever been recovered from was the *San José*. But this wasn't one of them."

He put down the spoon that he was using to dig for cherries. "Alright, girlie. I'll bite. Where'd it come from?"

"The *Archivo Nacional de Cuba* in Havana. That's why no one has ever found record of the galleon in the Spanish archives. The records were buried in Cuba."

He narrowed his eyes. "How you know all this?"

"Our buddy Bart Kingston smuggled the archivist into the Keys." She paused, confident she had his attention. "Know what else was with the coin?"

"I'm riveted."

"A manifest for a galleon. One that wasn't in the official list of ships, because no one was supposed to know it existed. The artist was on that ship. He was leaving a clue to where she went down."

"So what's the clue?"

"I don't know. I thought you might be able to tell me."

Skipper laughed—a joyous, little-kid laugh that sounded out of place in the Bilge. He grabbed a cocktail napkin and wiped his eyes. "Time's up."

Mer squared her shoulders, ignoring the dart of pain. "No."

He crumpled the napkin. "Ain't your choice."

"Selkie vouched for you. Leroy said you're honorable. I don't see it, personally, but I trust them. I need your assistance to find this ship."

"Don't believe everything you hear." He tossed the napkin in the trash.

"I have to find it."

"Girlie, you don't know the first thing 'bout salvage."

"I know enough to go to an expert."

He leaned against his old-fashioned cash register and folded his arms. "Don't you think if a galleon went down off the Keys it would have been found—like all the others have?"

"No one was looking for it. You said it yourself. There are thousands of wrecks off the coast."

"The 1733 fleet hit the reefs. Shallow enough that the Spanish salvaged their ships right after they sank."

"If that were true, there would be more than five known portrait dollars." She let the words sink in. "There aren't."

She could tell that made an impression on him.

"You telling me it sank in deep water?"

"That would explain why it wasn't salvaged immediately by the Spaniards."

"You got a boat?"

Selkie's thirty-six-foot Dorado, the *Devil's Advocate,* would be perfect. Wide swim platform, galley, sleeping berths. If only... "No."

"Huh. You think about the number of divers you'll need? Deck space? Fuel costs?"

Mer attempted to speak, but he cut her off.

"Let's talk outfitting a boat. Gotta have an air compressor, metal detectors, a magnetometer, passive sonar, coolers, buoy markers, anchors—you'll need three of them babies."

Her heart sank. "Three?"

"How else you gonna stabilize the boat once you turn on the blowers?"

"Blowers?"

"Mailboxes." He set his elbow on the Berdugo photo and leaned into Mer's space. "The things that look like shiny PVC elbows you mount on the stern to swing over the props." He clucked at her confusion. "Acts like a giant leaf blower to clear off the silt and sandy overburden that's hiding what you're trying to find."

Mer mouthed an "Oh," but no sound came out.

"You just expect to dive an area with a bucket and find what you're looking for?"

Add a bucket, and yes, that was a fairly decent summation of her plan.

He straightened and grabbed a bar rag. "State ain't gonna be too keen on you poking around in their sanctuary, either."

Finally, something she could refute. "I'm just looking. I don't plan to keep any of it."

"You say that now, but treasure is trouble. Not the finding of it. What it does to the soul. Turns honest men to cheating. It don't matter on who—his wife, his partners, investors, himself. It's an ugly business. Gold changes people. Just ask Winslet Chase."

"I'm not doing this for the treasure."

"Whatcha doing it for then?"

"To save a man's life. Reclaim my own."

"That won't pay a crew. Anyone worth their salt's gonna need something that pays the bills."

She felt as if she was drowning. "What's your price?"

"Girlie, I ain't for sale."

Everyone had a price. Not everyone wanted money. Maybe Skipper's price was hidden in his earlier warning.

"If we don't find it, Winslet Chase will."

26

Mer wiped her hands along the sides of her capris. This was no different from any other presentation. She knew her talking points. She'd double-checked her facts in the hours since her visit with Skipper. Learned a few new things.

Outside, the sun retreated. She switched on the light. Soon the Aquarius training room would be filled with people. *Friends.* But they'd have questions. Hard questions.

She'd taken more care with her appearance than usual, wearing white capris and a black-and-white silk tank—the one her mother had chosen for Mer to wear under a business suit when defending her dissertation. Today, she'd even tamed her hair, and it fell in soft curls around her shoulders.

Maybe she should have prepared a PowerPoint presentation.

Leroy entered first.

"Well, don't you look prettier than a pat of butter meltin' on a short stack." The straw in the corner of his mouth waggled as he spoke. "Other than the bruise, that is."

Her hand automatically touched her face. "Bijoux's always after me to add color to my life."

"I'd wager she meant something else," he said.

"Probably." The red had deepened into mottled blues and purples that no amount of powder would hide. She'd tried. "Thanks for coming."

"Wouldn't miss it." He made an elaborate show of looking around the room. "I was promised pizza."

Mer stood with her back to the whiteboard and inhaled deeply. "Sadly, you were misinformed."

"Ah, well. Already here, might as well take a load off." He pulled out a chair and sat.

Detective Talbot walked in next. He wore tan shorts and a dive T-shirt.

"Casual Tuesday?" Mer asked.

"My schedule was adjusted because of the gala."

"I didn't mean to interfere with your day off."

He stood in front of a poster of a sandy beach in Bonaire and struck a pose with his hands on his hips. "Justice never sleeps."

Bijoux stood in the doorway. "But the last I knew, detectives did."

"True. But I'm hungry, and a little birdie told me there'd be food."

"According to the boss, that's bad info," Leroy said.

Talbot found a chair in the back of the room. "'Tis an ill cook that cannot lick her own fingers."

Leroy crossed his arms, but there was mirth behind his beard. "Now that you mention it, I don't remember much finger licking on Thanksgiving."

Mer glared at Leroy, but addressed Talbot. "You know you can leave Shakespeare at home when you go out."

"Quoting Florida statutes isn't nearly as interesting." He slid the chair the remainder of the way across the carpet. "Doesn't impress women nearly as much, either."

Bijoux asked Mer. "Are you expecting anyone else? If not, I'll lock up."

Seven minutes past the hour. "I don't think they're going to show."

Over the course of the last several days, she'd lived with changing information, new hypotheses, and downright speculation. She'd sorted through the data and organized it into a possible timeline, simplified the mass of possibilities. She'd tried to find blind spots, and correct errors. Now—

"You'll never plow the field by turning it over in your mind."

Ha. Leave it to Leroy.

She capped and uncapped the dry-erase marker. "This is a tale that starts in 1492," Mer said.

"Excellent," Talbot said. "I'll understand the vernacular."

Mer ignored him. "The night of the gala, Oscar said a group of churchmen bribed King Philip to modify the fifteenth century Alhambra Decree that expelled Jews from Spain."

"It was still in effect two centuries later?" Talbot asked.

Mer nodded. "Fast forward to the 1730s and a painting by an artist named Berdugo. Originally, my research didn't generate any hits on the man's full name, but the surname belongs to a long line of Sephardic Jews—many of whom went on to become illustrious rabbis during their lives."

"They're the churchmen?" Leroy asked.

Mer nodded. "After being forced from their homeland, some of the clan went to Morocco and others relocated in Mexico and became merchants. But most trade routes lead to Europe."

"A problematic issue if you are not allowed into Spain," Bijoux noted.

"Precisely. The Berdugos didn't want to change the decree. They wanted to rescind it. And by the eighteenth century, they had the one thing the current King of Spain needed. Cash."

Mer drew an outline of the Florida Keys and placed an island in the lower right of the whiteboard. "Not to scale."

"Obviously," Bijoux agreed.

"Although the exact amount isn't recorded, they amassed a treasure large enough to persuade King Philip to rescind the prohibition against Jews returning to Spain. All they had to do was get the money to him."

She drew an X on the upper portion of the island. "That's where

Cuba comes in—Havana, to be exact. Every year, a fleet of ships traveled to Spain from the New World. Pirates targeted solitary ships, so the Berdugo clan threw in their lot with the 1733 fleet."

"Not a good summer for sailing," Leroy said.

"No, it wasn't. The fleet was caught in a hurricane almost immediately. One ship remained afloat, and a few more were refloated after repairs. Most of the ships ran aground on the reefs dotting the Keys."

"Their locations are all well-documented," Talbot said.

Someone knocked on the door and Bijoux excused herself.

"If this galleon was part of the fleet, why hasn't it been discovered?" Leroy asked.

"No one was looking for it," Mer said. "Since it wasn't salvaged contemporaneously, the ship probably went down in deeper water."

"Evidence?" Talbot asked.

"Very little. And unconventional."

Talbot rocked until the back of his chair touched the wall. "How unconventional?"

"Well, it's legendary." Mer bolstered her courage with a deep breath. "But here's the thing. There are suddenly a whole lot of people looking for this galleon. Oscar. Bart Kingston. Winslet Chase."

"Who said in public that the Thirteenth Galleon was hogwash," Talbot reminded her.

"True, but that very same night he tried to convince me to partner with him. That got me thinking. Many legends are grounded in truth. A secret galleon filled with gold morphs into a golden ship with clouds for sails. But there's more." Mer circled the X on the board. "Let's start with Oscar, an archivist from Havana who found a very rare coin, a manifest of names, and a note. The coin speaks to the treasure, the manifest confirms the ship, and I have no idea what the note—"

Bijoux ushered Skipper into the room.

"Guess it's a good thing I showed up, then. Eh, girlie?"

Relief coursed through her. "As long as you didn't bring alcohol."

Skipper sat. "Ain't here to socialize."

"Then I'll cut to the chase." Mer returned to the front of the room. For all his gruffness, the success of her plan hinged on Skipper's participation. "The Thirteenth Galleon is real and I'm going to find it."

Talbot leaned forward. "Just for the sake of argument, let's suppose this ship really does exist."

"It does," Skipper interrupted. "Chase contacted me about a week ago. Claimed new evidence had been found. Wanted me to help him find it."

Mer could hardly breathe. "What kind of evidence?"

"Supposedly some super-secret squirrel message from a spy on one of the other ships." He dug a note from his pocket. "I quote, 'The seas rose, night fell. Our brother now guards Neptune's gifts. All lost, but hope.' Knowing Chase, there's more, but that was the bait he dangled."

"If Chase knows about the note." She tapped her pen against her palm. "There's a good chance he knows about the Berdugo."

"Not necessarily," Bijoux said. "He claimed the entire exhibit. That hardly seems to suggest he knew of a single painting's significance."

"Because he doesn't have the manifest," Talbot said.

"Because Oscar risked his life to steer them in the wrong direction," Mer corrected. She paced in front of the whiteboard. Finally, she uncapped the pen and wrote several names on the board. "Oscar found proof of the ship. But to actually find the wreck, he had to get to the States."

"Enter a smuggler." She drew a line between Oscar and Bart. "Bart transported a Cuban archivist to the Keys and somewhere along the line, he figured out that Oscar had a coin—and had clues to find more. But locating treasure is hard work. All Bart really had to do was sell the information to someone who *could* find it."

"Winslet Chase." Talbot approached the board and grabbed another pen from the tray. "But Bart couldn't produce the goods. The bale fell into the ocean—maybe during the transfer from a mother ship, maybe it just bounced out in the storm—doesn't matter. What matters is everyone thinks Mer is the go-to gal to find this wreck."

Skipper crossed his arms. "So what's the plan?"

"Simple," Mer said. "Find it."

Leroy stroked his beard. "Seems a bit lacking in detail."

Mer retrieved the photo of the Berdugo painting from her backpack and Talbot held it up while she taped the paper to the white board. Something about the painting bothered her. "Skipper, you said the seas rose as night fell, right?"

"The seas rose, night fell. No 'as.' Least that's how Chase told me."

"Something got lost in translation." She tapped the pen against the board, leaving a trail of small dots. She paused mid-tap and grinned. She wrote NIGHT in big letters along the crooked coast she'd drawn of Key Largo. "It's not night." She added a K. "Chase said *knight*. This explains why I couldn't find any record of Mateo Eques de Soto y Berdugo. He's not the artist. He's the knight—Eques in Latin. He was on the treasure galleon, but it sank and presumably took him with it." She shuddered. "He couldn't have painted the ships."

Talbot leaned against the front of one of the tables. "Then who did?"

Mer practically danced with excitement. "I bet if we examine the manifest of the El Infante, you'll find another Berdugo. Heck, there was probably a Berdugo on every ship. They weren't spies. They were insurance."

Someone else knocked on the door and Bijoux excused herself again.

Mer kept talking. "If something happened to the treasure, chances were at least one of them would know the details. And figure out a way to retrieve it later."

Phoenix swept into the room like a gale, her topknot slightly askew. "Sorry I'm late. Your message came in while I was underwater. And traffic on the stretch sucked." She dropped her bag, took a seat, and kicked up her feet onto the table.

"Everyone," Mer said. "This is Phoenix. She's an underwater archeologist and professor at the University of Miami."

Skipper pushed himself up. "Girlie, before you go off half-cocked, a word?"

Bijoux stepped in. "I'll complete the introductions."

As soon as the two were out of the classroom, Skipper spun on her. "You can't include her."

"I already have," Mer replied.

"Then you're gonna be shut down before you even start." He leaned into her space. "Where's your buddy Oscar gonna find himself then? Huh?"

"What are you talking about?"

"She's an archeologist."

"And a professor," Mer said. "What's the problem?"

"For starters, what you're planning to do is south of what the state considers legal. You got an exploration permit?"

"No."

"State ain't gonna give you one either. Leases for the waters 'round the Keys have been divvied out for years. Poking around a Marine Sanctuary? That's governed by federal statutes. You think some professor's gonna risk her position 'cause you've got a treasure itch you gotta scratch?"

"Why did you come today?" Mer asked.

"I don't mind getting a little dirty if the cause is good. Not everyone has my sensibilities."

"You know there's a cop in there, right?"

"Jesus, Mary, and Joseph! Why don't you buy yourself a pair of handcuffs and save everyone the trouble?" He stomped back into the training room.

Mer lingered in the shop. Skipper was right. She had no right to drag her friends and colleagues into something that endangered their livelihoods or safety.

The people in the classroom looked at her expectantly as she walked in. She still had the dry-erase pen in her hand and she placed it on the tray.

"I don't have an exploration permit." She cleared her throat and spoke louder. "I'm going to search for a treasure galleon that most people think doesn't exist. I'm not searching for the gold, but to save a man's life. Maybe get my own life back." She pulled out a chair and collapsed in it. "I have no right to ask any of you for help. My intentions are good, but..." She looked at Skipper. "Not everyone has my sensibilities."

No one moved.

"That's it? I drove all this way for a speech?" Phoenix craned to look at the other people in the room. "I mean it was a nice speech and all, but I'm pretty sure I can make up my own mind about whether to participate. So if you don't mind, get on with it."

"I'm serious. There could be significant consequences," Mer said.

"Amateurs." Phoenix pulled her feet off the table and strode from the room.

How long would it be before the others followed?

"She'll be back," Bijoux said and dipped her head toward the professor's bag. "She only took her phone."

"We all have our reasons for being here, Dr. Cavallo. I want to catch a crook," Talbot said. "There may be a way we can combine forces. A way that keeps everything aboveboard."

"We're dealing with smugglers, burglars and kidnappers." Her voice lowered. "They shot at us. I can't ask you guys to face that."

Leroy snorted. "You're as tough as a one-eared alley cat, but you aren't going to be able to do this on your own." He dug out his phone and dialed. After a short pause he growled, "I'd like to order some pizzas."

The room erupted in chatter as everyone suggested toppings. Mer took it all in. She was the little fish in a big ocean of amazing people. This was her school.

She retrieved her wallet and slapped her credit card on the table. Leroy waved his hand over the card as if he could generate enough wind to push it away. Mer set her jaw and slid the plastic closer.

He scowled, but read off her number into the phone. "Don't

forget the anchovies." He gave the dive shop's address and hung up. "Now." He handed Mer her credit card. "You were saying?"

From the first day she'd met Leroy, he'd taken her under his wing. He could be blunt and crotchety, but she never once doubted his integrity. Her throat felt tight. "Right." She leaned over, picked up the pen, and refocused. "I'm under surveillance. Bart knew when I was grocery shopping and on the boat. Winston knew I'd be at the gala. What we need is a decoy."

"Two boats, two crews," Talbot said. "One that's really searching. The other one floating on top of a false site."

"At this point, how do we know which is which?" Bijoux asked.

"The answer is in the painting." Mer unrolled a nautical chart across the front table and pinned it open with her wallet and a reef-fish identification book. "The *El Infante* is in the foreground of the painting, already bilged on the reef. Historically, we know that occurred here." Mer pointed to spot on the chart marking Little Conch reef. "She lies in fifteen, sixteen feet of water. Seaward, the reef drops fairly quickly—within a half nautical mile or so, you're in a hundred feet of water." She went back to the painting. "The ship off the *El Infante's* starboard side is the Thirteenth Galleon."

"Loaded with treasure, she'd sit pretty low," Skipper said. He squinted at the painting. "She's built like a galleon I salvaged in the Marquesas. Drew eighteen feet. Even if the waves ranged twelve to fifteen feet, that means there's a whole lot of reef this one could've kissed."

"She had to have sunk in deeper water," Mer said. "Otherwise, there would have been survivors, and salvage efforts."

Skipper sidled between two tables to get to the front of the room and stopped when his nose was about a foot from the photo of the painting. "She's already going down."

Leroy joined him at the whiteboard. "Well, if that don't beat a hog flying."

The chart forgotten, they all clustered around the Berdugo.

Bijoux tapped her manicured finger against her lips. "Wouldn't that mean the galleon sank in shallow water after all?"

"Ever been in a car wreck?" Skipper asked.

Talbot elaborated. "The involved vehicles end up in all kinds of positions, depending on the angle of the strike, the velocity of travel, and things like friction."

"We know where the *El Infante* ended up—" Leroy started.

Mer finished the thought. "The painting shows their relationship."

Skipper continued to study the painting. "That's more information than I've had for some of the other wrecks I've found."

"Ha!" Phoenix barked from the doorway. "You guys figure out where we're looking yet? Because I just made it legal."

27

The room smelled of pepperoni, grease, and excitement. Mer and Talbot pushed two tables together and Leroy set down a stack of three pizza boxes. Bijoux laid out plates and napkins, while Phoenix distributed water bottles. Everyone talked at once.

"Two Mers?" Leroy said. "I have a hard enough time dealing with one."

Talbot opened the closest box. "That's going to be the hardest part of the operation. I can find a deputy who looks like Mer, but capturing her personality..."

Mer slid a piece of pepperoni pizza onto her plate. "I was so close to liking you."

"Such an injury would vex a saint."

"Worry not. The feeling's passed."

"We said it earlier. Two boats, two crews." Talbot chose a slice of Canadian bacon and pineapple. "People see what they expect to see. If we have Mer's lookalike get on a salvage boat and head out to a site, to all outward appearances, Mer is on a treasure hunt."

"I understand the decoy part, but the logistics are fuzzy." Mer sprinkled a liberal dose of red pepper flakes onto her slice. "I'm under surveillance. They'll know when I arrive at the dock. We have to assume they're watching. If we send the decoy on the salvage boat, what boat am I getting on and how do we look for the galleon?"

Phoenix held up her hand and gulped down a bite. "I can't speak to the decoy action, but if it helps, we can use any boat to conduct a search. All we need to do is drag a magnetometer behind it. No sense burning fuel in a larger boat when a smaller one will work for this phase."

"So," Bijoux said. "The *Dock Holiday* would work?"

Phoenix nodded. "Absolutely. I'll just be collecting data. We can stow some dive gear in case we finish the survey early, but until we find a promising site, we don't need salvage equipment. Quite frankly, since we're just trying to locate and not recover, there's really no need to have a salvage boat at all."

"Except to make it look good," Talbot said.

Leroy removed the straw from his mouth and tucked it into his shirt pocket. "You ever seen Skipper's boat?"

"What's the matter with my boat?" Skipper demanded, squinting at Leroy.

"Let's just say she looks better from a distance." Leroy scooped two pieces of pizza out of the box, covered them with a layer of anchovies, and folded them together. He took a big bite and stared back.

The silence stretched and Mer feared the operation was going to be scrapped before it began.

"Aye," Skipper finally said. "She's not much of a looker, but she's mine."

Talbot wiped his hands on a napkin and tapped a note in his phone. "Skipper, you in? Can we use your boat as the decoy?"

"I'm still here, ain't I?"

That was half the equation. Mer considered the options. Few people holidayed in the Keys during the first week of December. By mid-month, the roads would become congested—and when schools closed for winter break, a crush of tourists from snowy climes would descend on the islands, eager to shed their layers and wear shorts.

There really wasn't a better time. She'd have to dip into her savings, but this was her operation. She should shoulder the expense. "Bijoux, can I charter the *Dock Holiday* for the next couple of days?"

"No."

Mer felt as if she'd been kicked in the gut. Did Bijoux not think she was up to it? "I can't afford the *LunaSea*."

Bijoux unscrewed the cap of her water bottle. "The *Dock Holiday* isn't scheduled until Sunday. As long as I don't get a charter request, she's yours to use."

The enormity of the offer humbled Mer. "I'll reimburse you for the fuel."

"You will not," Bijoux said then patted Mer's forearm. "We don't often have the opportunity to be a part of history. I would like to contribute."

History. This was more than saving Oscar. Finding the Thirteenth Galleon would add a page to the history books. The thought sent a shiver through Mer. "Thank you."

"We have the boats." Talbot looked around the room. "Do we have the crews?"

"I've been in this since the start, hate to miss the ending," Leroy said.

Talbot nodded and shifted his hawk gaze to Skipper.

"You don't think you'd get my boat and not me, do you?"

"Not a chance," Talbot said.

Phoenix scrunched her forehead. "Not to be a naysayer..."

"Then hold your beans," Skipper said.

The professor ignored him. "Pulling a magnetometer is no easy task."

"I can vouch for Leroy's skill," Mer said.

"It's not his driving skill I'm worried about." She lifted the container of anchovies to her nose and sniffed. "Seriously. You eat that?"

Leroy rescued them from her grasp, fished out one of the tiny fillets, and dropped it into his mouth.

"Anyway," Phoenix continued. "Conducting a survey is precision work. The equipment needs to maintain a steady depth over changing terrain, all without getting caught up on the reef. Captain, you ever pull one of these before?"

Leroy swallowed. "Can't say as I have."

"Skipper?"

"What kind of question is that? Course I did."

"So here's the issue." Phoenix wiped the grease from her mouth. "If the salvage boat is the decoy, we need Skipper on the other boat."

"That's not part of the deal," Skipper said.

"Can't we train Leroy?" Talbot asked.

"It's not a matter of training. It's a function of time. I can have a grad student cover some of my classes, but not many. If we're going to do this, we need to get good data on the first pass."

"Is it realistic to think we can find something that's been hidden for centuries the first time out?" Mer asked.

"Ha! Not even remotely," Phoenix answered. Then she grinned. "Sure would be nice, though."

"If things work out as I hope," Talbot said, "it won't be necessary. With any luck the decoy will draw Bart and company out of hiding."

The scope of the operation kept expanding. "Which means you'll have other deputies with you, right?" Mer asked. When Talbot nodded, she continued, "So including you, that's what? Three deputies by the time you get a decoy for me? Will you be able to make that fly?"

"I can try. But even if I convince the brass, it won't be an open-ended operation. I'll have a week. Tops."

A week. Mer had never tried to locate a shipwreck before, but she had tried to find octopuses. Even knowing how to interpret the clues to their whereabouts, the creatures didn't always want to be found—and they were real. Swathed in legend, the Thirteenth Galleon was still a hypothetical.

"I'm a bit confused," Mer admitted.

"The first step in recovery is to admit it," Leroy teased.

Mer knocked aside an anchovy and stole a piece of pepperoni from the slice in front of the captain. "The question remains. How can I be on two boats at once? They know when I'm on the dock. They'll certainly know when I leave it."

"We can do the switch at sea," Talbot said.

Bijoux cocked her head. "If they are monitoring Mer that closely, would they not see the exchange?"

"Not if the boat doesn't stop."

"Doesn't stop," Mer repeated.

Talbot cleared his throat. "What if we send Skipper out to the reef on the *Dock Holiday* early. We put the decoy deputy on the salvage boat but hide her in the V-berth until it's time for the switch. Meanwhile, Mer shows up on dock, does her morning routine, gets on the salvage boat, and Leroy takes it out. Everything looks normal. But then he swings by the reef, drops Mer close to the boat, and keeps going. Mer swims underwater to the other boat, climbs aboard, *et voilà*. Mer is now on two boats at the same time."

Leroy leaned forward. "In full scuba gear? No way in God's green earth I'm dropping anyone off a moving boat. Too dangerous."

Scenarios zinged through Mer's mind. Most didn't end well. "What if you cut the engines? Act as if you're taking a wave head-on. Can you cut it back hard enough to throw it in neutral, while I step off? Then kick it back into gear."

"You ever jump off a moving boat?" Leroy asked.

"No."

"Even if I can cut it back, you're going to slap the water. Hard enough to rip your mask off and tear the regulator out of your mouth. Smack the back of your head with the tank."

"Maybe you should discuss this with Selkie," Bijoux said. "I imagine he has experience with this type of operation."

Selkie. Yes, he probably did have this type of specialized training. But damned if she was going to ask him for advice.

"I'll do it," Mer said.

"Has your cheese slid off your cracker?" Leroy asked.

She considered his words. "Maybe. But there's way too much at stake to worry about a bit of a hard landing."

"Seems to me you've had enough injuries lately, you shouldn't be aiming to collect any more."

A pained expression flashed across Detective Talbot's face. "There's an element of risk for everyone here. I'm not going to minimize it, and frankly, I'm not sure my sheriff's going to sign off on this. But the bad guys will be after us, not you. Any of you can bow out at any time. No questions asked."

"I'm in," Mer said firmly.

Leroy pushed his plate away and leaned back in his chair, his arms crossed. "Well, then I guess I'm in, too. Someone has to make sure the propellers don't chop you into chum."

Mer decided against a third piece of pizza.

"I was never out," Phoenix said. "How dangerous is it to gather data?"

Skipper squinted. "You and me are going to be on the same boat."

"Ha! Bring it."

Mer's brow knit with a new concern. "How do I get back to the salvage boat at the end of the day?"

"You don't," Talbot explained. "You'll be coming in on the charter boat. Dress in something flamboyant. When you get to the dock, come upstairs. You and the deputy will exchange clothes and poof! Mer's back on the dock."

"Why can't she do that in the morning?" Leroy asked.

"If Mer's going to be made, it'll be on the dock." Talbot wadded up his napkin. "I might be able to get a lookalike, but there's a good chance she's not going to know how to handle lines. It'd be easy to train binoculars on a person from across the canal. Harder at sea—at least without giving away your position. If we have any chance for this to succeed, they have to believe Mer is on the salvage boat. That said, I'll leave the choice to her."

"One problem," Mer said.

"What's that?" the detective asked.

"I don't have anything flamboyant."

Bijoux smiled. "I do."

28

Talbot was waiting for Mer inside the Aquarius Dive Shop when she reported to work two days later.

"You sure about this?" he asked.

It had taken him a full day to get clearance, and she wasn't about to back out now. "Absolutely."

He handed her a cup of coffee. "Better drink quick then."

The white paper cup leached warmth and she peeled back the plastic lid. "Smells wonderful, thanks."

"Deputy Mercurio's already on Skipper's boat." He'd swapped his normal detective garb for shorts and deck shoes. "She'll stay in the V-berth until you're ready. She's a little shorter than you but she has frizzy hair. It'd be pretty hard to distinguish you from each other in a lineup."

Her hand patted the mass tumbling from the ponytail port of her ball cap. "The Arctic didn't have nearly as much humidity."

"Bijoux gave Mercurio some crew gear. You'll be wearing the same T-shirt, same ball cap. We got her a pair of Oakleys."

"Kind of hard to conceal a bulletproof vest under a bikini." Mer grinned.

"Which is why she won't be taking off her T-shirt."

Mer swallowed her coffee in a scalding gulp. She'd meant it as a joke, but his expression clearly conveyed he took this very, very seriously.

"What worries me is the exchange."

The exchange. His term for when she suited up in scuba gear and jumped off a moving boat. To be honest, the prospect excited her. Not that she was in a hurry to tell her mom about it. "Piece of cake."

"Well then, the plot is laid." He gave her arm a reassuring squeeze.

"You can tell me to mind my own business, but how's Gabby? Is she okay?"

He seemed surprised at the question. "She's good. It's all good." But his voice lacked conviction. He opened his mouth as if to speak, but then sighed. "She's grounded, so I'm currently Public Enemy Number One."

"Well, of course you are. Wasn't it Shakespeare who said, 'Parenting oft sucketh?'"

"Sounds like him." His smile revealed his chipped incisor. "See you tonight."

"Aren't you going, too?"

"I'll be on the department's patrol boat."

"Oh." She'd thought he'd be on the *Dock Holiday*. With her.

"Don't worry. The bad guys will be after us, not you."

A refreshing change of pace. She toasted him with her coffee cup and left.

Downstairs she took a moment and drank her coffee. All things considered, the plan had merit; a bit unconventional, but solid. Thanks to Phoenix and her network, they all wouldn't end up in Admiralty Court for poaching someone else's lease. All the subterfuge would end. The cops would rescue Oscar and arrest the appropriate criminals. Her life would return to normal.

No, not normal. That would require Selkie.

She dropped her empty cup into the trash bucket and collected her scuba gear bag and a tank from the equipment room. The weight pulled on her sore muscles, and she struggled to remain upright while she carried the gear to the dock.

Bijoux owned a long stretch of dockage along the canal with plenty of space to accommodate the two charter boats. Adding Skipper's thirty-six foot salvage boat, the *Finders Keepers*, made for tight quarters, especially with the boat's dual twenty-four-inch aluminum blowers and dive platform. But the *Dock Holiday* had left about an hour ago to moor on Grecian Rocks.

Mer paused by the salvage boat. Leroy jumped down from the flybridge and took her gear from her. "I tell you, if dumb were dirt, you'd be about an acre."

"You'd do the exact same thing—and you know it."

"Doesn't mean I want to watch you do it. How are you planning to jump off a moving boat if you can't even tote your own gear?"

The straw in his mouth spun so fast she expected it to knock her hat askew.

"I was carrying my gear just fine until you grabbed it. Besides, getting off won't be the tough part." She sat on the gunnel, swung her legs over, and stood. "Wow. Not a lot of room to move around."

Two large gear tables took up the center of the deck, and a bench near the port stern had spaces for five scuba tanks. Most salvage divers worked off a surface-supplied air source, and a hookah dive system was mounted on the starboard side, complete with hose reels and regulators. A large bucket in each corner held an anchor line. Steel cables stretched from each of the two blowers to a winch mounted between the main and upper decks. Two plastic tubs made it appear that the boat was ready to accept any artifacts that Mer—or in this case, the deputy—brought up from the depths.

"Gotta make it look good," Leroy said. "Now go meet yourself."

Mer crossed the deck and entered the cabin.

A woman wearing clothes that matched her own stood in the galley pouring a cup of tea from a thermos.

"Hey there. You must be Dr. Cavallo. Captain Penninichols said I'd recognize you by your shiner." She twisted the container's lid closed and held out her hand. "I'm Deputy Mercurio. Call me Gina. Better yet, call me Mer."

Mer shook the deputy's hand while gaping at the bruise on the woman's face. "Please tell me that's makeup."

"Smudged mascara, blue eye shadow, and a hint of lipstick." She laughed. "Tea? I've got enough for two."

"No thanks, your partner brought me coffee."

Gina's brows rose slightly before she adopted a more neutral expression. "I'm sorry I can't help you out with the boat prep, but when the time comes, I'll help you into your gear so you're not twisting those ribs more than you have to."

"Thanks, I appreciate that. Actually, I appreciate it all." She wanted to say more, to acknowledge that this woman was placing herself in harm's way for someone she didn't know. But Mer didn't know how to put it into words.

"No trouble at all. It's not often I get paid to spend time on the ocean."

"Being bait," Mer reminded her.

"Quit your worrying. We've got this." She steered Mer toward the cabin door. "Go be seen on deck."

"I'll be back when we're underway."

Gina retrieved her tea. "I'll be here."

Outside the cabin, the morning sun bounced off the canal. Mer lowered her sunglasses over her eyes. The boat had two control stations, and Leroy was at the helm on the main deck.

"Not too late to rethink this," he said.

"And do what? Wait for Bart Kingston to come find me again? Go into business with Winslet Chase? I don't think so."

He squinted at Mer. She stared back. Finally, he settled his straw in the corner of his mouth. "Well then, let's see what this tug can do."

She managed the lines, Leroy managed the engine, and together they managed to get *Finders Keepers* off the dock. Mer stood next to him while they traveled the canal. He radioed to make certain their way was clear as they approached the dogleg at Crash Corner, and then continued through the turn. From there it was a straight shot out of Port Largo into the Atlantic Ocean.

"Think they'll take the bait?" Leroy's voice startled her.

"Hope so." Mer scanned the area. They had to be there, somewhere. Watching. "Until now, they've known everywhere I've been. I'm worried they'll know the northern site is bogus."

"If they knew where to find the galleon, they wouldn't need you now, would they?"

She bit her lip. "Winslet Chase is a smart man."

"Guess we better act like we know what we're doing then." He dropped his hand on the dual controls as he neared the end of the canal. "Skipper's already on site. We'll head out and then bear north. I'll take you as close to the dive site as I can. When you're ready, I'll power down, but we'll still be moving. Soon as you splash, I'll be on the move again."

"I'll be fine."

"Then it's time you got ready." He increased speed. "I set up the decoy gear while you gals were gabbing. Gina has yours all set up in the cabin. You got time for a safety check. Remember you need to be over-weight so you'll go in negatively buoyant."

It was going to happen. Suddenly her stomach churned as if she'd swallowed an entire school of grunts and they were doing their best to swim out of her belly.

"You can scrap this any time before you splash, but if you're going to do this..." Leroy said. "Well, best get going."

A head bob was all she could manage. She took her empty gear bag and entered the cabin. Gina held Mer's mask and a bottle of defog. Her assembled gear was propped by the couch.

"Showtime!" The deputy set the items in the galley sink. "Let's get you ready."

Mer sat on the cabin couch and slid her feet into her wetsuit and drew it up to her waist. Thrusting her arms into the sleeves, she shrugged it up over her shoulders. "Zip me?"

Gina grabbed the lanyard and pulled.

The restricting neoprene made breathing difficult and Mer

practiced a few deep breaths while Gina lifted Mer's gear onto the couch.

Mer turned the air on, checked her gauges and confirmed the weight. She flayed the buoyancy compensator vest open and sat on the couch. Gina guided her arms through the BC and helped cinch it up so Mer didn't have to twist.

"I defogged your mask and here are your fins," Gina said. "The gunnels are fairly high. If you can, stay low. I'm going to move up to the bow and prance around a bit. Hopefully, anyone watching will be tracking me. The quicker you can do this, the better."

"Got it." Mer said.

Gina handed Mer her mask. "Captain, how we doing?" she shouted.

"Two-minute warning."

"Anyone on the horizon?"

"Just the *Dock Holiday*."

"Alrighty." Gina did a last minute examination of Mer's equipment. "I'm leaving. Count to ten and go. You'll be great."

And she was gone.

Mer counted the beats. Ten interminable seconds that she ticked off with her dive watch. She settled her mask over her face and wiggled her jaw to make sure she could equalize her ears on the way down. Satisfied, she opened the cabin door. The *Dock Holiday* floated off starboard and she shot an estimated bearing to the other boat.

Leroy throttled back and gave her a nod.

Mer walked across the deck, slipped on her fins, and strode off the platform into the endless blue of the Atlantic.

29

T he water greeted Mer with a slap that reverberated all the way into her fillings and flooded her mask. Maybe she *should* have asked Selkie for advice.

With the extra weight she wore, she sank quickly. The drone of *Finders Keeper's* engines cut through the water. Even though she knew the boat was traveling away from her, her brain couldn't decipher the direction of the sound.

First things first. Mer feathered air into her vest to slow her descent. Now, safely away from the slicing propellers, she needed to stabilize her buoyancy and start her swim. She tilted her head back and cleared her mask. The snorkel was gone. In hindsight, she should have removed it. Lesson learned.

Leveling her compass, she focused on the dial, adjusted her position, and kicked. No red and white dive flag flew over her position to warn people of her underwater presence. She needed to keep deep enough to avoid any incoming boat traffic until she arrived at the *Dock Holiday*.

Powerful kicks propelled her across the sand and over an eel garden. Hundreds of small pencil-thin brown eels poked their heads out of their burrows and swayed in the surge. They reminded her of prairie dogs. Her shadow swept over them, and they disappeared in a blink.

Grecian Rocks, a half-mile long spur and grove reef, loomed in front of her. A shallow reef, it earned its name because at certain tides, the coral jutted above the water and was often mistaken for rocks.

She found the encrusted cannon embedded in the reef. It served as her landmark and placed her about seventy-five feet south of where she wanted to be.

Too early for other dive charters, the waters held only the noises of the reef—clicks, crunches, and the surf crashing against the shallowest corals. Confident she was safe from boat traffic, she surfaced. The *Dock Holiday* bobbed on the nearest mooring. Phoenix stood on the deck wearing shorts and a bikini top. As soon as she sighted Mer, Phoenix swung her arm in an arc and tapped the top of her head with her fist. Mer returned the signal indicating she was fine, and then ducked under water to avoid the surface chop while she swam the rest of the way to the boat.

At the swim platform, she handed her fins to Phoenix.

"You want to shuck your tank in the water?" the archeologist asked. "I can haul it up. Save you some wear and tear on your body."

"I just hit the water from a moving boat. I can climb the ladder."

"Ha! I suppose you can."

Mer pulled herself up the aluminum ladder. Water shed from her gear as she paused at the top. Skipper stood at the helm watching *Finders Keepers* shrink in the distance.

"It's a sad day when a captain watches his boat disappear without him." He narrowed his eyes. "You better be right about this, girlie."

No pressure.

Phoenix walked Mer to the bench and guided her tank into the holder. "Good thing you're here. Another ten minutes and we'd have killed each other."

Skipper tossed a handful of sunflower seeds into his mouth. "What'd you call 'em? Philosophical differences?"

"Surprised you remembered that, being multi-syllabic words and all," Phoenix shot back.

"Only takes half the syllables to say you're wrong."

Mer swiveled her head between the two of them and briefly wondered who'd win if they came to blows. Hopefully, she'd never find out. Mer eased out of her gear and gingerly tugged the wetsuit to her waist. The sun was still low on the horizon and stingy with warmth.

"Your dry bag is on the dashboard," Phoenix said.

"Thanks." Mer stowed her fins under the bench and clipped her mask to the wet BC, tucking her gauges out of the way in case the tank shifted. She pulled on a T-shirt, but left her wetsuit at half-mast. "So, what's next?"

"Ain't going nowhere if one of you don't unhook us," Skipper barked.

This was going to be a long day.

Mer released the mooring line and Skipper set course for the *El Infante*.

He spit shells into a cup. A stray hull stuck to his front tooth. "Time to mow the lawn."

Off the reef, he opened up the engines and the boat bumped across the swells at a brisk pace.

Mer shouted over the combined noise of wind, engines and thumping hull. "Mow the lawn?"

"Girlie, you're gonna have to learn the lingo if you go salvaging with me."

Phoenix interjected, "We're not salvaging anything. We're here to discover and preserve."

"Your fancy museums would be empty, weren't for us."

"There's more to a site than treasure. How do things relate to each other? Who did they belong to? Salvors don't give a fig about historical significance. If it's not shiny, who cares? Treasure hunters are nothing but glorified grave robbers."

"Don't see how writing a university paper on it makes it any less grave robbing."

Phoenix squared off on Skipper, as fired up as the bird tattooed on her back.

Mer interrupted. "I'm not going to learn the lingo if no one tells me what it means."

Skipper glanced over his shoulder at her. "Mowing the lawn—"

"Geez, at least give her context." Phoenix pointed at a torpedo-shaped device tucked under the port bench, "That is a cesium-vapor marine magnetometer, otherwise known as a fish. When it passes over ferrous material, it detects the change in the earth's magnetic field. This one belongs to the university and costs more than the GDP of some third-world countries."

"Don't know what was wrong with mine," Skipper said.

"Other than it being on another boat?" Phoenix swung her backpack off the dashboard and pulled out a laptop. "Once we get inside our search area, we'll lower the fish into the water and tow it behind the boat. Give or take, each row will be a mile long. Then we'll jog over about seventy-five feet and take another pass. We keep doing that until we've surveyed the whole area."

Simple and repetitive. "Mowing the lawn," Mer said.

"Bingo. Provided you have a captain who knows what he's doing, the data you collect is amazingly accurate. The trick is keeping the magnetometer about ten feet above the seabed."

"You think it's as easy as following lines on a screen, you're welcome to try your hand at it," Skipper groused.

Phoenix leaned closer to Mer and lowered her voice. "I can already tell just from watching him that he knows his stuff. No sense giving him a false sense of importance though."

"How does the fish log the hits?" Mer asked.

"Downloaded direct to this computer. It's pretty zoomy." She slapped the cover of her laptop. "Each magnetometer reading is stamped with time and position info. We're looking for a sine-wave spike, followed by a dip, and then it should even out at baseline again."

"Sounds fairly straightforward."

Phoenix propped her sunglasses on her head. "Only because

computer software translates the majority of the data. Fortunately, we're searching a relatively shallow area. Provided we don't get hung up on reefs, we can still pull ten or so knots. When we're through mowing, we'll dive the hits, poke around a bit. Maybe get lucky."

Mer didn't believe in luck. Hope without hard work rarely led to success. She believed in the scientific method—but to date, her methodology for finding a legendary ship left a lot to be desired. She didn't have enough facts to employ deductive reasoning as a method of elimination. Instead, she found herself in the wild-ass guess territory of the scientific community: abductive reasoning.

If there were a ship, then its *likeliest* location would be within these parameters. Sure, the hypothesis was still based on the best information available, but when the evidence was drawn from a legend, a painting, a mystery, and an egomaniac in a wheelchair parsing out a cryptic message, how accurate could the hypothesis really be?

They didn't need luck. They needed a miracle.

30

They'd been mowing the lawn for hours and the sun had passed its zenith. Until they had coordinates to dive, Mer could do nothing but stay out of the way and try to avoid getting sunburned.

At first, she watched Skipper. The first two times she'd interacted with him, he'd been behind a bar—a man of indeterminate age whose expression suggested that he'd just as soon kick a patron out of the bar as serve her.

A different man stood at the helm. He didn't wear sunglasses and his squint deepened the lines radiating from the corner of his eyes. While he wasn't exactly smiling, the stubborn line of his mouth had relaxed. Wrap a bandana around his head, give him a flintlock or saber, and with his wide-set stance and gold hoop earring, he could be a pirate.

Phoenix's earlier words reminded Mer that the task at hand was not an easy one. Skipper maintained course, monitored his depth, adjusted his speed, and kept the magnetometer in position over a constantly changing seafloor.

He turned for another pass, the fish swinging wide before settling behind them.

"A photo'd last longer." He shoved another handful of sunflower seeds into his mouth.

Mer blushed. "How long have you been a captain?"

"How old are you?" he asked.

"Thirty-three."

"Add a couple years to that."

"Navy?"

"'Til I got kicked out."

Phoenix sat sideways on the bench opposite the helm, her back to the bulkhead. She cradled her computer on her lap and held a deli sandwich in her hand. "Let me guess. Following the rules turned out to be a tad difficult?"

"Suppose you could call it that. They found out I joined at sixteen."

"I might come around to liking you yet," Phoenix said. She bit off a mouthful that would make a thirteen-year-old boy proud.

"And to think I managed all these years without your approval."

Phoenix returned to her computer, occasionally letting loose a bark when the magnetometer registered a particularly strong hit.

Mer grabbed another of the sandwiches from the cooler and extended it to Skipper. He shook his head so she unwrapped it for herself. The ocean air always made her hungry and things that tasted mediocre on land often tasted far better at sea.

"Hey Skipper." Phoenix crumpled the paper sandwich wrapper into a ball and handed it off to Mer to throw in the trash bucket. "Run one more pass, would you?"

"That'll take us over the *El Infante*."

"I know. I want a comparison reading."

Skipper swung the *Dock Holiday* and paralleled the shore for one final pass.

At the end of the mile, Phoenix stood and wedged the computer on the left side of the dashboard. "That's a wrap." She twined her fingers behind her back and straightened her arms into a stretch. "Time to reel in our fish."

Skipper placed the props in neutral. Mer managed the cable and when it neared, Phoenix hauled the magnetometer into the boat.

"I can do a quick analysis," Phoenix said. "Identify a site to dive before we head in. But I'll have a much better idea of what's going on out here after I run the data tonight." She pointed at the half sandwich Mer was about to put back in the cooler. "You going to eat that?"

"All yours."

"Thanks." The professor studied the computer screen while she chewed. "I think we should start here." Phoenix tapped the screen. Taking another bite, she spoke around the turkey. "I'll print maps for us to use tomorrow, but this hit is practically right underneath us." She shared the coordinates with Skipper.

"Tell me what to do." Mer had explored plenty of shipwrecks in her life, most of which were steel-hulled and clearly identifiable as ships. By comparison, the dive on the *Winchester*, when she'd first met Phoenix, illustrated how efficient time was at ravaging wooden vessels, chewing away at the timbers until only pins, ballast, and inorganic artifacts remained to tell the tale of shipboard life. Still, her body hummed with excitement. After all the imagining, the hoping, the planning...they might actually find the wreck.

Phoenix polished off the remainder of the sandwich and wiped her hands against her shorts. "Hold that thought." She disappeared into the V-berth and returned holding two handheld metal detectors. "Ever use one of these before?" She passed one of the detectors to Mer.

It had a long handle with an arm brace at one end and an angled flat disk at the other that resembled a miniature steering wheel. A small yellow waterproof control box attached to the middle. "My dad combed the beach after storms when I was a kid. I played with his metal detector once or twice," Mer said.

"Same idea except these work underwater. Wave it back and forth over the sand, under ledges. It'll squeal if it detects anything we need to take a closer look at." She indicated the controls. "On, off. The needle gauge will help you pinpoint your target. Pretty simple.

Best thing about this particular beaut is it ignores minerals." She handed Mer a pair of headphones that looked no different than those used above ground. "Self explanatory, I hope."

Skipper called over his shoulder. "We're here."

In short order, they anchored, hoisted their dive flag, and the two women geared up.

"Expanding circle, grid, jackstay?" Mer named off the common patterns. "How do you want to search?"

Phoenix shouted over her shoulder, "Hey Skipper, how close are we to the coordinates?"

"Any closer and you'd be the coordinates."

Phoenix leaned over the side. "Visibility's good. How about we use the anchor line as ground zero. You go north, I'll go south and we'll do independent U-search patterns. Meet back at the center each turn. That way we won't be knocking into each other. Find something interesting, bang your tank."

"Sounds good."

Mer entered first. The water washed the warmth of the day off her body. She surfaced to the side of the platform and treaded water until Phoenix entered, then Skipper handed them the detectors and headphones.

Mer looked at Phoenix. "Ready?"

The woman nodded. In unison, they dumped the air from their BCs and descended to the bottom.

⋯⋯⋯⋯⋯⋯⋯

Mer and Phoenix regrouped at the anchor. They clapped on their headphones, switched on their metal detectors, and swam in opposite directions. They'd agreed on a fifty-kick cycle before turning a quarter turn east, finning a body length and returning. If all worked out, they'd come face to face again, and then repeat the process until Phoenix called it quits. Then they'd return to the anchor line and complete the same search pattern westward.

Mer snugged the brace against her forearm as she swept the metal detector in gentle arcs in front of her. She floated about a foot off the bottom, but the metal detector skimmed the sand. Silt billowed in little puffs around the disk, leaving particles suspended in the water column.

The headphones muffled the already muted sounds around her. Despite feeling the press of water against her body, the lack of sound somehow distanced her from the experience. The rhythmic back and forth of the metal detector coupled with counting her fin kicks lulled her into a near meditative state.

She approached the end of her first length and stared off into the distance. Somewhere out there was a shipwreck. If not the Thirteenth Galleon, then another ship. Another story.

On a day like today, it was hard to imagine the ocean as anything other than a gentle cradle, as soothing as a lullaby. But ships rarely bilged against the reef on calm days. They might languish in the doldrums, but they didn't tear the bottom of their ship apart and sink.

No, that required storm-whipped waves and wind that shredded sails and snapped masts. Currents that pushed ships into the shallows, grinding them against razor-edged corals, and then dragged them back to sea.

She turned a quarter turn, and swam a body length, and turned again.

Warning signs usually preceded storms. Wispy mare's tails high in the sky. A freshening wind. Confused seas. More than once, she'd seen Leroy peer into the unknown and chomp his straw. "Smell that? There's foul weather brewing."

Captains of the 1733 shipwrecks had surely read the signs, too. They'd known before they embarked that hurricane season was upon them. They had felt the freshening wind. But Philip needed his gold. And so they'd sailed.

A ping startled her and her breath caught. She swept the detector over the same spot, zeroing in on the target. The tone steadied. Could this be it? She held the detector off to the side and fanned her hand above the spot, swishing the loose sand away. An eternity passed before the water cleared.

Nothing.

She cleared away more sand and swung the detector back over the shallow indentation. The needle jumped in time to the tone.

This *could* be it. Her pulse beat in her ears, trapped under the headphones. For the first time it seemed real. She was a treasure hunter. Up until now, the search had all been academic. But this...in a moment, she could be staring at a piece of history. Holding a coin. Or a nail. Or perhaps a golden chain a passenger had fashioned to avoid paying taxes on his wealth.

She pressed her eyes closed. They had to recover a coin. A 1733 portrait dollar minted in Mexico City, to be precise. Anything else could be from the debris trail of the *El Infante*.

And she wanted to be the one to find it.

Even underwater, her face warmed. But it was true. She wanted to be the one who found irrefutable evidence of the galleon. Not to claim a portion of the loot, or even to save Oscar. She wanted to find the Thirteenth Galleon to prove she was right.

She put aside the detector and redoubled her efforts to clear the sand. At last she uncovered a jut of metal. Her hopes dissipated with the silt. A grid. Too uniform to be historical. She yanked the corner and pulled free a broken lobster pot.

Served her right. The ocean held generations of lost and cast-off items. She was far more likely to recover trash than a single coin. Plus, it shouldn't matter who found the galleon, her hypothesis would still be validated.

It shouldn't matter, but it did.

Picking up the metal detector, she snugged it against her forearm again. Bubbles vented past her face and raced upward, expanding as they neared the surface before they finally burst.

She had work to do.

Phoenix had already started down another row by the time Mer arrived at the end of her own. She jogged over. They weren't pulling magnetometers, but they were still mowing the lawn.

By the end of the dive, Mer had recovered two more lobster traps, one reel, a broken dive knife, several cans, a lawn chair frame, and a cellphone, but nothing to suggest that a treasure galleon had sunk in the area nearly three hundred years prior.

They ascended together, stopping at fifteen feet for a safety stop to allow their bodies to shake off some of the nitrogen they had absorbed during the dive.

Buoyancy was a skill that new divers struggled with, and they constantly filled and emptied their BCs with air. Experienced divers rarely touched their inflator hose and could alter their position in the water through breath control.

Mer rolled onto her back and removed the regulator from her mouth. The outline of the boat above them barely blurred. Puffing out her cheeks, she released an explosive *puh*. The bubble ring formed a pewter crown that shimmered until it disappeared in the brightness of the sun slanting through the water.

She righted herself and checked the remaining time on her dive computer. Phoenix hovered, her legs crossed like a genie in her bottle. The final seconds counted down and Mer signaled for Phoenix to go up first. When she was safely on board, Mer swam to the ladder, took off her fins, and climbed into the boat for the second time that day.

"Guess what I found?" Phoenix said as soon as Mer stripped off her mask.

"A coin?" She couldn't keep the excitement from her voice. Not being the first to find a portrait dollar didn't sting as much as she thought it would.

"Ha! I would have banged on my tank for that, and we'd still be down there." Phoenix looped the bungee cord over the tank valve. "Musket ball."

Mer secured her own gear. "Significance?"

Skipper spit a sunflower hull into his cup. "We're practically on top of the *El Infante*. A musket ball don't mean a thing when you have a debris trail half a mile long."

"Are we going back down?" Mer asked.

"Not unless you want your alter-ego to spend the night on Skipper's boat." Phoenix toweled her hair. "They can't come in until we do."

She glanced at her watch, although the slant of the sun on the horizon told her everything she needed to know. This late in the year, the sun set about 5:30.

There'd be no more dives today.

31

Mer smoothed her hand across the front of her dress. Sheer and billowy, it looked more like a negligee than a bathing suit cover-up. Bijoux must have loved picking it out. She piled her hair on top of her head, smashed a broad-brimmed hat over the mass, and swapped out her Oakleys for a pair of oversized glamour sunglasses. Lastly, she slid her feet into a pair of espadrilles.

She felt ridiculous.

Phoenix entered the V-berth and whistled. "No one's going to mistake you for a professor." She handed Mer a large straw tote. "I'll take your backpack. Don't want to spoil your new look."

"For the record, I don't like my new look."

"You'd turn a lot of heads in South Beach."

Mer thinned her lips. "That changes absolutely nothing."

Skipper stuck his head into the V-berth. "I didn't sign up for no night shift."

"Guess that's my cue." Mer shoved her crew gear into the tote and passed Phoenix the backpack. "Just leave it upstairs, I'll collect it when I get to be me again."

"Channel your inner Kardashian, you'll be fine."

Mer slung the tote over her shoulder. "What's a kardashian?"

"Seriously? Never mind. Catch you tomorrow."

Mer adjusted her glasses and headed for the shop. The wedged espadrilles were better than stillettos, but she still held the handrail on the stairs for balance.

Inside, a Christmas tree covered in dried sea stars and sand dollars crowded the door. The tinny tones of a steel band hammering out a version of "Jingle Bells" followed her as she walked toward the dive classroom.

Detective Talbot stood in the front of the room, leaning casually against the lectern and speaking with Deputy Mercurio, who sat on the front table, her legs swinging. His eyes widened as Mer walked into the classroom, and he quickly diverted his attention to the report he held in his hand.

Mer shut the door with her foot and ripped off her hat. "Did it work? Did they take the bait?"

"Never saw a soul," Gina answered. She still wore the Aquarius dive shirt, although she'd taken off her ball cap.

Mer tossed the straw tote onto the closest table and it landed with a muted thud. "That's disappointing." Mer folded the oversized sunglasses. "For all we know, they could have followed us."

Talbot and Gina exchanged glances, but Talbot spoke, "Did you see anyone today?"

Mer kicked off the espadrilles. "We were trolling a pretty popular area. A couple of fishing charters, a pleasure craft or two. No one that seemed to pay us any undue attention."

"Good," Talbot said.

The air conditioning in the shop cut through the sheer fabric of the cover-up. Mer pulled her T-shirt and shorts out of the tote and placed them on the table. "Same plan for tomorrow?"

Gina picked up her hat and inspected the brim. "How'd the scuba entry go?"

Mer stepped into her shorts and fastened them under the cover-up. "Well, it wasn't a total yard sale." She drew the fabric over her head. "But I lost my snorkel and there's a distinct possibility I knocked a filling loose."

"Holy crap!" Gina jumped off the table.

Mer spun around, clutching the cover-up to her chest. "What?"

Both Talbot and Gina stared at the bruise on Mer's side.

She dropped her arm to block their view of the yellow-tinged purples, feeling naked despite the bikini top. "It looks worse than it feels."

Gina slapped Talbot in the chest. "You knew it was this bad?"

Talbot cleared his throat. "Dr. Cavallo is quite capable of determining what she wants, or is willing to do."

Mer willed her heart rate to return to normal. "Thank you." She shoved her arms into her T-shirt and drew it over her head. "But no one's answered my question. What's tomorrow's game plan?"

Talbot rolled up the report he held in his hand. "You'll be doing the same thing."

"That makes it sound as if someone else won't be," she said.

Gina grabbed the cover-up. "You ever think of becoming a cop?"

Mer shook her head. "I don't like getting shot at."

"We try to avoid it, too." She grinned at Mer and said to Talbot, "Turn around."

He did and Gina stripped to her one-piece bathing suit and donned the cover-up. She slid her ballistic vest into the tote sideways and covered it with a towel.

"Okay." The deputy twisted her hair into a high ponytail and tucked it under the broad brimmed hat. She glanced at her watch. "Better get going."

Mer handed her the sunglasses and sandals. "See you tomorrow?"

"I'll be there." Gina slipped her feet into the wedged shoes, put on the glasses, and left.

Jimmy Buffet took over from the steel band and sang about cheeseburgers in paradise. Mer's stomach growled.

"Hungry?" Talbot asked.

"A somewhat regular occurrence, I'm afraid." She claimed the spot on the table that Gina had vacated and sat cross-legged with her back against the wall.

"Category Three serves a mean burger." He paused. "We can debrief over dinner."

A burger sounded great and it'd be good to accomplish two tasks at once—but duty called. "I'm still on the clock. Now that I'm Mer again, I've only got a few minutes before I need to help put the boats to bed."

"Right, of course." He unrolled the report. "I can't share a lot, but I thought you needed to know. Cole's disappeared."

She straightened into alertness. "Deputy Cole?"

"I'll know more after tomorrow. He put in for emergency leave—his mother's health."

She relaxed. That wasn't nefarious, that was a man responding to the realities and responsibilities of life. "I hope it's not serious."

"She's dead."

"That's horrible. Dead?"

"As a doornail."

The detective's delivery was without inflection, and despite her dislike of Deputy Cole, Talbot's flippancy struck her as grossly improper. "You're being quite cavalier."

"His mother passed away four years ago, so I'm a bit suspicious about the emergency aspect."

"Oh." She slumped against the wall. "There's more, isn't there?"

"Yes." He rerolled the report and sat on the table next to her. "Because of the coin, I did a bit of digging."

Mer's hunger disappeared.

"Cole's parents divorced when he was thirteen," he said. "A month later, his mother remarried. Had another child two months after that."

The math raised more than eyebrows.

Talbot continued, "Cole has a half-brother."

She knew by the expression on his face that she wasn't going to like the answer, but she asked anyway. "What was his mother's name?" she whispered.

"Agnes Chase."

She made the connection immediately.

"Winslet's mother."

The familial relationship of Deputy Cole and Winslet Chase gnawed at Mer as she helped wash down the boats for the night. The implications of the bond followed her home. They perched on her shoulder as she grilled a cheese sandwich and drank a glass of milk.

And they woke her up at one o'clock in the morning.

Who knew what information had passed between the two men and how long they'd been communicating. From the moment she and Leroy had pulled the smuggled bale onto the *LunaSea*, Cole had known the status of the coin—when it was believed lost, when she'd recovered it.

No wonder he'd been uncooperative when her home was burglarized. He'd probably stood watch while Bart and Oscar ransacked the place. Talbot's unexpected arrival could have been problematic for him. Accusing her of being a drug dealer was a nice touch.

Cole had also been on perimeter patrol the night of the gala, the same night Oscar and Bart conveniently escaped detection. And Deputy Cole "just happened" to interview Winslet and then let him go.

The scariest prospect of the men's relationship was what it meant to the treasure operation. Could Cole have read all the police reports that Talbot had filed? She suspected so. Which meant the operation was compromised.

The thought drove her from bed. She pulled on a lightweight hoodie and shorts and wandered outside. Out of habit, she glanced over at Selkie's house. Her anger had dulled into something else. Something she'd spent the last two days trying to define. Something she didn't want to think about. Not now.

The grass was damp under her bare feet and for the first time this season, the temperature was predicted to drop into the sixties. UGGs weather for the natives. But she had to admit, wearing shorts in December did not suck.

Two days shy of full, the gibbous moon would set soon, but the fading reflection lit the underside of gathering clouds.

The grass gave way to sand and Mer perched on one of the boulders that lined the water's edge and stared out to sea.

The Thirteenth Galleon hid somewhere in those depths. Cole, Bart, Oscar, and Winston hid somewhere else. She was the sole person exposed in this dangerous game of hide-and-seek.

And it made her feel oddly alive.

Maybe Selkie was right. Scars were battle badges. Proof of resilience and perseverance. She traced her fingers along the puckered skin on her thigh. She was a survivor.

It didn't lessen her fear. Frankly, she didn't want it to. Selkie was right about another thing. Fear kept her safe. When her gut clenched and the hair on the back of her neck stood up, higher reasoning just got in the way. Fear was primal. And it was her friend.

Tomorrow, she would resume the search for the Thirteenth Galleon. She would do what she could to mitigate the risks, but she would not back down.

She had to find a coin and replace the one stolen from evidence. Turn it over and save Oscar.

A large wave crashed against the rocks and misted her face with salt.

The whereabouts of the stolen coin remained a mystery. Cole's disappearance certainly didn't bolster his assertion of innocence. The coin's value made it an attractive target, but selling the portrait dollar would be risky. The evidence custodian had access, too—but unlike Cole, that employee hadn't fled on a fabricated pretense. Nor, presumably, did that person have connections to a well-known treasure hunter.

The clues snapped into place. It was so obvious.

She slid from the rock and retraced her steps to her apartment. At her touch, the home screen on her telephone glowed and she disconnected it from the charging cord. A twinge of guilt made her hesitate, but she pushed it aside and dialed Talbot's number.

His sleepy voice answered after the first ring.

"They aren't in cahoots," she said without preamble.

"Dr. Cavallo?" He cleared his throat.

"Yes."

She heard rustling through the phone as if he was struggling to sit up in bed. "Are you okay?"

"Of course I am."

"Okay, because normally when I get a call in the middle of the night, someone is either headed to the hospital or the morgue."

"Cole and Winslet Chase. They're not colluding. They're in opposition."

"You know it's one-thirty in the morning, right?"

"Winslet thinks I have the coin—or at the very least that I can recover it."

"And that you'll be seeing Deputy Mercurio in what, six hours?"

Her frustration mounted. "Do you want to hear this or not?"

He yawned loudly. "By all means. Please. Convince me that Chase and Cole aren't in..."

"Cahoots," Mer finished for him.

"Technical term?"

She pushed open the sliding door and stood framed in the doorway. "It's a perfectly serviceable word, and quite frankly, given your profession, I'm surprised you're not more familiar—"

"I'm quite aware of its definition."

"Then, why on earth—"

"I'm hanging up now."

"Winslet Chase doesn't know where the coin is. He thinks I can get it." The words poured out in a rush that she hoped would forestall him from disconnecting. She continued to speak into the ensuing silence. "Since Cole stole the coin, that means not all the information is being shared between the brothers."

"You're assuming Cole stole the coin."

At least he was still listening. "Well, of course he did."

"And you know this how?"

"Abductive reasoning," she said.

"I'm sure I'm going to regret this, but what?"

"Occam's Razor." She pulled the door closed behind her. "When dealing with multiple hypothesis, go with the explanation with the fewest assumptions."

"Kiss."

That wasn't a word she expected to hear from Detective Talbot. "Excuse me?"

"The kiss principle. Keep it simple, stupid—K-I-S-S."

"I'll stick to calling it abductive reasoning."

"I suspected as much. Now, please, for the love of Shakespeare, get to the point."

"I didn't steal the coin. That's a fact. It's also a fact that both the evidence custodian and Cole had means and opportunity to take the coin. I'll even grant you that they both could have been driven to steal it for financial gain."

"But?" he prompted.

"Cole has a much better motive. Revenge."

Talbot shifted and the rustle of bed sheets was unexpectedly intimate.

"That presupposes he was wronged," Talbot pointed out.

"Imagine being a teenager and discovering that your mother doesn't love your father any longer. Then to make matters worse, you find out that she's already replaced him with another man."

"Thy father slew my father, therefore, die?"

"She's pregnant by one man and still married to another, so metaphorically-speaking, yes. Now imagine how you'd feel when your new and unwanted sibling arrives and monopolizes your mother's attention. I'm thinking that could create a great deal of animosity and jealousy. To make matters worse, baby brother grows up, becomes a successful treasure hunter, an international sensation, while you—"

"Join an honorable and noble profession and become a superhero in a green uniform."

"You're a superhero. He's a jackass."

"You're letting your personal feelings influence your argument."

She crossed the patio, stood in the center of the lawn, and curled her toes into the damp grass. "I'll admit, I don't harbor any warm fuzzies for the man, but it makes sense. I think Cole is working both sides."

"If he's double-crossing his brother, what's his endgame?"

"Foiling his brother? Finding the treasure? Avenging his father for his mother's duplicity?"

"That's a lot of possibilities."

She tilted her head back and stared at the stars, freshly emerged in the wake of the setting moon.

"It's his time to shine."

32

"Treasure hunting sucks," Mer said. "It's not at all like the movies."

"Be glad." Phoenix dug a stack of Oreos from the bag and extended it to her. "Indiana Jones got mixed up in a lot of shit. Although Lara Croft found Daniel Craig. That wouldn't suck."

They sat side-by-side wrapped in towels, with their backs against the gunnel, and their faces angled to the sky, trying to capture the sun when it broke through the lowering clouds. The *Dock Holiday* rocked above their next dive spot.

"For the record, this is why I didn't pursue archeology," Mer said. "Time is very skilled at hiding things. The ocean is even better. Between the two, they've crushed my innate sense of optimism."

"That's because you haven't found anything yet." The package rustled as Phoenix grabbed another handful of cookies. "Find a piece of history. You'll be hooked."

They had already splashed three times, and their surface interval required another forty minutes to pass before they could go back in for a final dive.

"You know Skipper's never going to forgive us if we find something and he's at the other site."

"He wanted to be on his own boat." Phoenix stuffed another cookie in her mouth. "*Finders Keepers*. What kind of a name is that?"

"Truth in advertising," Mer said.

"Treasure hunters don't care a fig about history."

Leroy carried over a length of line and sat on the opposite bench. "It's been my experience that salvors know more about history than most professors."

"But they don't *care* about it," Phoenix said. "They learn just enough to figure out where something's located. It's the gold they want. The glory. Not the knowledge."

"You can't lump all treasure hunters together." Without looking, he twisted the line's ends into a carrick bend. "There's a big difference between Skipper Biggs and Winslet Chase."

Mentioning the two men's name in one breath reminded Mer. "Did you know they once worked together?"

Leroy shook out the line. "Winslet made quite a reputation for himself in those days."

"Another crook," Phoenix said. "Just in a prettier package."

"What happened?" Mer asked.

"Short story is Skipper saved his life."

"And the long one?" she pressed.

"Back in the day before the State tightened up regulations, Skipper held the lease to a Civil War-era wreck down Marathon way." He double looped the line and swung it absently against his calf. "Winslet was just starting out. Skipper took him under his wing, became partners."

"They ever find the wreck?"

Leroy threw the line to Mer and it landed in her lap like a coiled snake.

"They did. That's when the trouble started."

She shook out the supple braided-cotton line. Great for practicing knot tying. Not at all like the scratchy polypropylene attached to their floats and tag lines. "What happened?"

"You remember how to tie a trucker's hitch?"

Mer secured one end of the line around the leg of the dry table and pulled it taut. "Keep talking."

"Skipper wanted to do things by the book," Leroy said. "He ran a tight ship. Chase, not so much."

Mer formed a loop in the middle of the line and twisted it behind, around and back through the loop. "A characteristic he hasn't outgrown." She pulled the knot tight.

"They'd already collected some artifacts—"

"You mean stole," Phoenix said.

"That's not Skipper's style. He had his permits." Leroy's straw spun a couple of rotations before he continued. "He wanted to do things systematically, but it was late. They knocked off for the day. Next morning, his boat was gone."

Mer loosened the line. "Let me guess..."

"Skipper borrowed a friend's boat and set out. Sure enough, he found his boat anchored over the top of the wreck. The mailboxes were in the water and Chase had already blown the site clean."

Phoenix snorted. "So much for systematic." She wadded up the empty cookie package.

"No one was on deck. After a while, Skipper decided to strap on a tank and check things out for himself. That's when he found Chase. Pinned."

"Pinned?" Phoenix's hand hovered over the trashcan.

"Fool had blown so much away from the wreck that he uncovered some of the ironclad structure. While he was exploring it, the surge shifted. It collapsed. Caught Chase like a rat in a trap."

Mer shuddered. "Good thing Skipper came along when he did." Drowning was something she wouldn't wish on anyone. Not even Winslet Chase.

Leroy's typically merry face darkened. "You'd think that would earn him some gratitude. Chase was a breath away from empty. Skipper gave him his tank. Made a thirty-foot free ascent."

"Right on," Phoenix said.

"Grabbed another tank, came back down with a crow bar. Managed to unpin Chase. He was bleeding pretty badly. Caught the interest of a bull shark. Skipper made a choice and blew through his safety stop."

Recreational diving always suggested a safety stop, but a diver could spend a lot of time at thirty feet before nitrogen built up in his body to the point of detriment. But add in a free ascent, exertion, and stress, and sometimes bad things happened. "He got bent."

"Yeah. He took a hit. More important, he got Chase to the surface and onto the boat. Saved his life."

"But?"

"Chase saw dollar signs. Sued. It was Skipper's boat."

"That Chase stole!" Phoenix said, indignant.

"Courts didn't see it that way. They were partners. Unsafe business practices and other nonsense. Chase lost the use of his legs. Skipper lost everything. His house, the boat." Leroy spit over the side. "The insurance settlement set Chase up pretty good, though."

"What about the Bilge?" Mer coiled the line and wrapped it with a couple of turns.

"That came later. Skipper's a stubborn one. Rebuilt everything. Even bought his boat back."

"The *Finders Keepers*?" Phoenix asked. "I wouldn't have thought he'd want it after all that."

Mer thought back to Skipper's grim expression in the Bilge when they spoke about his ex-business partner. "It was more than the boat," she said. Reaching into the coil, she selected a loop from the running end and pulled it up and over the mass. Cinched it tight. Finished, it resembled a noose. "Skipper didn't want Winslet Chase to have *his* boat."

The wind freshened. Mer tasted the metallic heaviness of impending rain.

Leroy eyed the horizon. "It'll be close."

The increased wind shortened the period between swells and the seas seemed confused, attacking the small boat from all sides.

One more dive.

Truth was, she was ready to go home. Instead of finding the Thirteenth Galleon, the whole day had been dedicated to determining where it was not. Statistically speaking, their next dive had little hope for a more exciting outcome.

"It's going to be rough by the time you come up," Leroy said. "Sure you ladies want to do another dive?"

"Doesn't matter to me," Phoenix answered.

The repetitive diving had taken a toll on Mer. Her side hurt. The thought of heading in, getting warm, and calling it a day held enormous appeal. But with the deteriorating weather, their prospects for diving tomorrow dwindled—along with her ability to help Oscar.

"We're going to get wet either way." Mer threw the line back to Leroy. "Let's finish what we started."

Time was running out.

The next morning, Mer stood in her living room with the broom cocked over her shoulder like a baseball bat. Her senses strained. She'd thought she'd seen something—and it moved. She edged closer to the kitchen and forced herself to breathe.

Rain slid off the carport and pounded the driveway. It had fallen nonstop since yesterday evening. The noise filled her apartment with discord.

Every impulse was to run. Create distance. But then what? Call Selkie? No. She wasn't a damsel waiting to be rescued. She could do this.

A rap on the door startled a squeak from her. She backed to the door, never taking her eyes off the intruder.

"Who is it?" she called.

Bijoux's voice carried through the door. "I come bearing gifts."

Mer balanced the broom against her shoulder and unlocked the deadbolt.

Bijoux entered, but stopped when she saw Mer. "You know they work better when the bristles are pointed down."

"Not for this job."

Florida was home to an abundance of insects. Mer understood the role they played in a healthy ecosystem, but she didn't particularly enjoy sharing her living space with them. Especially ones that had four times as many legs as she did. The glossy black spider in the upper corner of her kitchen peered down at her like an eight-legged overlord. She didn't want to squish it, but one of them had to go.

"Did you know you have a package by your door?" Bijoux said.

Mer sidled closer to the spider. "I'm not expecting anything."

"That does not negate the fact that you have a package by your door." Bijoux held a brightly wrapped and slightly soggy gift, and she set it on the table.

Mer swept the broom across the ceiling. The spider dropped onto the counter and Mer jumped backward.

"Impressive. I did not know you could fly," Bijoux said.

The spider scurried behind a wooden pepper mill and disappeared under a copy of the local Free Press. Mer swore under her breath. "Shouldn't you be at work?"

"It is a stormy Saturday. No one is at work." Bijoux said. "I'll get your other package. You appear otherwise engaged."

Steeling herself for a vicious counter-attack, Mer lifted the edge of the paper.

Bijoux returned and hefted a large rain-splattered box onto the kitchen counter. It landed with a thud. "They both have eight legs. How can a woman who studies octopuses be so afraid of spiders?"

"You can contemplate the irony later."

"Would you like some help?"

More than life itself. "I've got it." Mer gingerly dragged the paper away from the wall.

Bijoux snorted and bumped Mer out of the way, and then picked up the paper. A full-page advertisement for Keys News covered the back cover and the spider clung to Wendy Wheeler's face like a freakish mole. "Sink or outside?"

"Outside." Goosebumps pebbled Mer's arms and she rubbed them away.

"You probably shouldn't visit Haiti," Bijoux called over her shoulder as she opened the door. The tumult of rain filled the apartment, and she flicked the newspaper to rid it of the stowaway. "You would not like the tarantulas. Or the banana spiders." She came back inside. "I suspect you would not enjoy the centipedes, either."

The goosebumps returned.

Bijoux tossed the paper onto the table. "Since I already know what I got you, you should open your mystery box first."

The carton was large enough to hold half her belongings. "That's odd," Mer said. "There's no shipping label."

"Has your landlord returned from London?"

"No."

"Maybe you should call the handsome detective."

They stared at the box.

"It's not ticking." Mer grabbed a paring knife and sliced the tape. The flaps popped open, exposing a sea of packing peanuts. Mer reached in.

Bijoux stopped her. "Let me. You shouldn't be lifting heavy objects." She removed a bubble-wrapped figurine. Styrofoam peanuts clung to the plastic and fell to the floor.

Mer slid the box aside, and picked at the packing tape with the paring knife.

"It is not surgery, Madame Scientist."

Mer worked a corner free and pulled. The plastic fell away in sheets until only a soft flannel drawstring bag remained around the item. Mer released the tension and the bag dropped, pooling around the base of the mermaid from the silent auction.

Bijoux sucked in her breath. "She is exquisite."

Mer tore her attention from the statue and rifled through the peanuts, searching for a note. Nothing.

"Who is your admirer?" Bijoux asked.

Mer answered without hesitation, "Winslet Chase." The statue was taller than Mer remembered. Gracefully balanced. Bijoux was right. The artistry was exquisite. She pushed the bronze away from her as if it were the man himself and it bonked against the cabinet. "He told me the mermaid reminded him of me."

Bijoux tapped her chin with a manicured nail. "Not so much physically." She waved her hand in the air as if to spin her thoughts into words. "More of a posture, an attitude. She is beautiful."

"I don't see the resemblance," Mer said flatly. But she did. Not anatomically—for one thing, Mer had legs—rather it was the yearning captured in the mermaid's outstretched arm. So many things beyond reach. "I need coffee."

Bijoux spun and retrieved the damp, gaily wrapped package she had brought with her and extended it to Mer. "Merry Christmas."

"You're two and a half weeks early."

"Happy Hanukkah."

"Closer, but still two weeks away," Mer pointed out.

Undeterred, Bijoux tried again. "Housewarming."

Mer contemplated that option, but shook her head. "I've been here too long."

"Consider it an *après*-burglary, last-chance-before-I-take-it-back, gift."

"Ooh." Mer accepted the gift. "I've never received an *après*-burglary gift." She held it next to her ear and gave it a shake. "I wonder what it could be."

"Fair warning. I used plenty of tape, so if you are your usual meticulous self, I'm going to make myself comfortable."

An explosion of damp red and green curls cascaded down the sides of the package and hid massive amounts of cellophane tape.

"You did that on purpose," Mer said.

"Of course. You are lucky. I considered duct tape. Merry Christmas."

Mer set the gift down and threw her arms around her friend. Bijoux's tight spirals of shoulder-length hair smelled of coconut and something musky. Exotic. "Thank you."

"It is not so beautiful as your statue."

Mer broke free. "Perhaps not, but you are." She bent over the package to hide the flush that rose to her face. Sliding her fingernail into the fold, she picked at the tape. Bijoux sighed, but Mer ignored her. At last, she had a small pile of shredded tape. She peeled away the heavy paper and revealed a French press.

"I took the liberty of opening it and placing a bag of ground organic Haitian blue coffee inside." Bijoux picked up the discarded ribbon and ran a curl through her fingers. "For the future, you will need to get a grinder. Life is too short for poor coffee."

A coffee pot. The thoughtfulness made Mer smile. She filled the kettle and set it on the stove, then washed the press. "May I interest you in a cup?"

"What a silly question. Why do you think I gave you Haitian coffee?"

The coffee bag crinkled as she opened it. Mer held it to her nose and inhaled deeply. Rich and earthy. The kettle bubbled and hissed and finally whistled. She poured the water over the grounds and the scent filled her small apartment.

Mer pulled two chipped ceramic cups from the cupboard. One had the eagle and anchor of the U.S. Navy on it and her heart clenched. "Unfortunately, I don't have any cream. Or sugar."

"Up until a moment ago, you didn't have coffee or the means to make it either."

"Life is looking up." Mer pressed the coffee and poured, then handed Bijoux her Gryffindor mug. Selkie's mug warmed her hand, but failed to chase the cold feeling from her gut. "Why would Winslet Chase give me the mermaid statue?"

"He's trying to intimidate you in a way that would sound ridiculous if you complained." Bijoux dropped her voice to mimic a man's, but only succeeded in adding a sultry note to her silky voice. "All I did was give her a gift. Since when did that become illegal?"

"Maybe I'm going about this all wrong and I *should* become his business partner. Convince him he doesn't need Oscar."

"Do you honestly think that would work?"

"No." Mer stared into her coffee. "But what if we don't find the galleon? What if they decide keeping Oscar alive is riskier than killing him?"

"You are not responsible for the decisions made by others."

The rain continued unabated. Mer caught herself drumming her fingers against the mug and she set it down. She needed to get back in the water. *Do* something.

"Oscar believes I'm smart enough to unravel this legend. What if I'm not?" Before Bijoux could answer, Mer drew the bag around the mermaid and pulled the drawstrings tight. "I'll contact the museum and have them return the statue."

"You will not." Bijoux loosened the bag again. "For one thing, you don't know for certain who gave it to you. Perhaps it is from Selkie."

The thought saddened her. No. It wasn't from Selkie. They had avoided each other since their blowout. It was as if neither of them knew how to bridge the chasm. The one that spanned twelve years, new love, and old hurts.

"Then she's going outside." Mer lifted the statue. It weighed less than a dive tank, but still pulled on her muscles. She went through the sliding door by her bed to avoid walking in the rain and placed the mermaid on the teak patio table. Stepping back, she regarded the placement, and then turned the statue so she faced the ocean. Wistful. Perhaps they were kindred spirits.

The Keys valued their natives. Mer's grandparents weren't Florida Crackers. Her parents didn't help build the Flagler railroad. Hell, she hadn't even known what a square grouper was until she'd pulled one onto the boat. And look what came of that.

Mer returned to the kitchen and retrieved her coffee. Despite knowing the reefs better than most locals, she was a mainlander. An outsider.

Like Bijoux.

She squinted at her friend, searching for clues to her success.

"What?" Bijoux asked.

Scuba instructors were a dime a dozen in the Keys and even though Bijoux paid better than the other shops, Mer made barely enough to cover expenses. She'd never own a home here. The insurance alone would bankrupt her.

"I am not sure I like that look on your face," Bijoux continued. "It usually means trouble for someone. And as we are alone, well, you can understand my concern."

"How long have you been in the U.S.?"

"On and off, about ten years."

"Do you go home frequently?"

"Just once, when my mother died. Soon after I arrived in New York." Her eyes took on a faraway look. "I had not yet earned enough money to bring her to the States. Then, it was too late."

"I'm sorry." A pang made Mer realize how much she missed her own family.

"You would have liked my mother. She was fierce. Haiti can be a difficult place for one who is not."

"From Haiti to New York. That must have been shocking."

"Not as shocking as my new life. New York was my base. I traveled. Mostly Paris. Milan, London. Six months in Tokyo. My booker got me into some of the big shows during Fashion Week." The corners of her mouth lifted. "Even you would recognize some of their names."

Mer tilted her head. It made sense now. The posture and the poise. The dress.

"Modeling is a difficult life. I was lucky. I chose to leave. Not all are given that dignity."

She'd known Bijoux since she started working for the dive shop, but in those months, Mer had come to appreciate her sharp intellect and generous heart—all wrapped up in bright sarongs, headscarves and a regal bearing that made heads turn. Bijoux spoke flawless French, Haitian Creole, English, and probably more Japanese than she let on. But Mer knew little about her friend's life. It was a subject Bijoux rarely broached.

"What else don't I know about you?" Mer joked.

"I've been homeless."

Mer's cup clacked against the counter. "I'm sorry."

Bijoux sipped her coffee leisurely. "For what?"

"I didn't mean..." She didn't know what she meant and the confusion unsettled her. "I've always had a roof over my head. I've been hungry, but I've never known hunger." She topped off Bijoux's cup and then her own. "I've seen homelessness, but it's never touched me."

"Ah, but it has," Bijoux said. "You just never felt it."

"When did you come here?" Mer asked.

"I bought the shop two years ago. The transition from New York City to the Keys." Bijoux burst into laughter. "Now *that* was shocking."

"You've made it home."

"Home is not a place, Madame Scientist."

The last of Mer's savings was earmarked for a ticket to visit her parents at Christmas. But even California didn't feel like home anymore. The gin-clear water of the Keys did. Not the island, but the blue water surrounding it.

That's where she belonged. That's where she felt at home.

"I need a boat," she blurted the thought out loud.

"A boat," Bijoux repeated. "The *LunaSea* and *Dock Holiday* are not enough for you?"

"To live on." Mer tasted the truth in her words and found she liked it. "I need a boat. Here in the Keys. Among friends and fishes."

"A boat."

"I don't want to pay rent all my life. I've lived on boats before. I don't own much." She walked around her apartment, assessing. She paused next to the massive walnut desk. "This won't fit. But think about it. I'm a scientist. There's a research center in our backyard. So is the National Oceanic and Atmospheric Administration. Mote Marine Lab has field stations in the Keys. REEF has offices just down the road. I could do it, Bijoux. I could make a life here."

"You already have."

Mer pressed her lips together. "No, I've been marking time. I was only supposed to be here until my next big opportunity whisked me back into academia. Then I was going to leave."

"What is that saying about best-laid plans? I seem to recall you turned down a research position."

Excitement tingled through Mer's veins. She dumped the dregs of the coffee beans out into the trash, grabbed a sponge and washed the coffee beaker vigorously. "Exactly. I turned down the offer." She stopped mid-swipe and turned off the water. "Why did I do that?"

"Are you asking me or are you thinking aloud?"

She abandoned the coffee press in the sink and dried her hands on her shorts. "I wanted to explore another side of my life. I wanted a community, a family. I wanted to see if things would work out with Selkie."

"He cares for you very much."

"He does." For a moment Mer wished she didn't care. "But I never forgave him for how things ended."

"It is not so long ago that it can't be addressed."

Tears threatened. "This is for an offense that took place years ago."

Bijoux answered slowly. "That is a long time to harbor ill feelings."

"I didn't realize..." Mer picked up the sponge again and lowered it into the coffee pot. Bubbles formed along the water's edge and leisurely burst one by one. "Selkie is an honorable man—overprotective, but driven by good intentions. He apologized. I accepted." She poured the soapy water over the plunger. Coffee grounds peppered the bottom of the sink. "I accepted, but I didn't really forgive. I certainly didn't forget. I just knew he'd run away again. From me."

"He does not strike me as the type of man to run away from anything."

"Not anymore." She splashed water to wash the remaining grounds down the garbage disposal, and her voice dropped to a whisper. "And he can't run away from me...not if I run away first."

"Sometimes we forgive people so we, ourselves, can move forward."

"Sometimes," Mer mused aloud, "forgiveness requires taking a step back."

34

S unday dawned gray but dry, and everyone assembled for another day of hide-and-seek with the treasure galleon. By the fourth dive of the day, Mer was ready to concede that the galleon was winning. Not that she wanted to give up the hunt, but it seemed fair to acknowledge that a three-hundred-year head start certainly lent an advantage.

As a researcher, she'd spent a considerable amount of time searching—for answers, for specimens, for funding. Even in her field of study, octopuses were notoriously difficult to find. Yet nothing prepared her for the mind-numbing task of searching for buried treasure and swinging a metal detector back and forth.

She adjusted her grip and finned to a new spot around the edges of the reef. Back and forth. Her arm ached with the repetitiveness of it.

Mer had been four years old when she first saw the ocean. She'd stood at the water's edge and giggled as the surf rolled over her toes. She'd tagged along behind her brothers as they explored the tide pools. Everything moved. Crabs skittered. Soft anemones closed around her finger when she poked them.

The water had pushed a shell toward her. When she picked it up, a tiny octopus squirmed across her hand. Fascinated, she held still, watching it bunch and pull its way across her skin. She dipped her hand back into the water and the sea creature swished its legs together and jetted into a crevice.

From that moment, she'd been hooked.

Even today, being in the ocean humbled her. Underwater, she had to acknowledge her deficiencies. She couldn't see without a mask, couldn't smell. Touch was experienced at a distance, through gloves, or wrinkled fingertips, if at all. The sea tasted of salt and grit. Water muffled sound, hid its origination.

The metal detector squealed. Mer jerked to attention and spied a little garbage heap of shells beside a small crevice in the coral. A midden. Few creatures in the ocean tidied up after themselves as octopuses did, and often the first clue to their whereabouts was the stack of empty shells and crab carapaces piled neatly outside their dens.

She set down the metal detector. After nothing but recovering trash, she needed an octopus to brighten her day. Hovering over the reef, she peered into the crevice. A single eye stared back at her, its horizontal pupil looking like a dash painted across a white marble.

Mer smiled so widely that water crept into her mask.

The octopus' gill slit fluttered as it drew water in and out to breathe. Its color remained neutral, a sure sign she hadn't startled it.

She removed her glove and placed her naked finger at the edge of the den. Two of its arms uncoiled and settled on her skin, the suckers tasting her. Curious.

Octopuses had personalities. Some were shy and retiring, others bold and inquisitive. Gently, she drew her hand back, hoping to coax it out of its den.

It released its hold.

Mer placed her hand a bit further from the den and waited. This time the arms that reached out did their best to pull her in, twining around her wrist, touching the neoprene of her wetsuit, but returning to her naked skin.

Finally, it emerged, flowing like a waterfall over the coral. *Octopus vulgaris*. One of the few octopuses that ventured out onto the reef during the day. Mer automatically checked its third right arm for a *ligula*, but the suckers went all the way to the tip. A female, then.

The octopus settled next to the metal detector, as if reminding Mer of her current job.

Fine. She picked up the detector and swung it over the section of reef that held the den. It alerted again, the noise harsh in her ears.

The sound must have bled beyond her headphones. The octopus flashed red and jetted a short distance away before spreading her mantle and mimicking the colors of the corals. Mer set aside the detector, not wanting to distress her new friend, but not knowing what to do next.

Most likely, the detector had alerted on yet another piece of trash, either drawn into the den by the octopus, or something that had spent so much time in the ocean that coral had encased it.

A third possibility occurred to her. She ascended a few feet to be able to study the crest of the reef. Crevices slashed the top. Small items could fall through the reef, and remain protected from discovery and the rigors of surge.

She bit her mouthpiece, swam back to the sand, and pushed the disk of the detector under the ledge. She listened to the alert as she waved the device back and forth. Each direction rewarded her with a tone.

Digging her flashlight out of her pocket, she shined the beam under the ledge and pressed her cheek as close to the sand as her equipment allowed.

Nothing.

Not that she'd expected to discover a chest overflowing with gold and jewels, but it would have been nice.

Still, something had triggered the detector.

She peered into the darkness again, her gaze following the glow of her light. No morays. Normally passive creatures, an eel protecting its territory could take off a finger, and she'd grown rather attached to hers. She drew her glove back on and worked her arm into the crevice.

Her hand dug into the sand and sifted the grains through her fingers. The soft particles covered a hard stratum that resisted any attempts to explore further.

Her computer beeped, reminding her that in a few minutes, she'd have to rally at the line with Phoenix and they'd head up. Call it another day. Check off another site on the map.

Several feet away, the octopus watched her.

Mer floated back up to the level of the cephalopod's den. Octopuses tended to relocate every couple of days. The hunting must be good here, at least in terms of crabs.

The scientist in her couldn't resist and she wiggled her hand into the lair and patted around. Loose shells shifted under her fingertips. The octopus moved closer and flashed red with excitement.

She stilled, barely breathing.

Octopuses piled their leftover shells outside their den.

Carefully, she scooped up the objects and slowly withdrew her hand.

For a moment, she stared at her closed fist, afraid to open it. Afraid to confirm that she'd found a slovenly octopus that had forgotten to take out the trash. Until she opened her hand, she could be holding anything—the underwater equivalent of Schrödinger's cat—she held both treasure and trash. Slowly, she unfurled her fingers and almost inhaled her regulator.

Three gold coins sparkled as brightly as the day they were minted.

In Mexico.

In 1733.

35

Phoenix was right. Finding treasure was far more enjoyable than searching for it.

Mer stared at the coins for over a minute, marveling at the pronounced milling along their edges and the detail of the portrait. Finally, she set the portrait dollars on the reef and with shaking hands she unhooked her surface marker buoy from her vest. It took three tries before she managed to clip the line from her reel to the bright orange tube. She released a small blast of air from her alternate regulator into the bottom of the inflatable buoy and set it free. The reel unspooled and the buoy gathered speed as it neared the surface.

Suspended in the water column, Mer turned onto her back and let the surge rock her. The surface gleamed sixty feet above her, a shimmer of blue and gray with stray sunbeams piercing the water in angles. She was the only person in the world who knew beyond doubt that the Thirteenth Galleon had metamorphosed from legend into history. The three portrait dollars confirmed it. And for just a moment, she wanted to hold the stunning knowledge close.

The ramifications of the find would fall to someone else. She had a coin, and that meant Oscar would be safe. Her part would soon be over. Archeologists and historians would be busy for years and Phoenix would be in at the ground floor.

The dive computer alerted again. Time to go up. Phoenix would already be at the line or perhaps on her safety stop.

Still, she hesitated. Plenty of air remained in her tank and this was a moment to treasure.

Finally, she flipped over and wound the reel around a rock, careful not to damage any coral. They had the GPS coordinates for the site, but this reef wasn't familiar. The buoy was as close to marking an X on a treasure map as she could do.

Edging closer to her den, the octopus reclaimed one of the shiny portrait dollars. The suckers passed the coin toward her mantle as if it were on a conveyor belt. Gathering the remaining two gold disks, Mer tucked them into the pocket of her vest.

The octopus dropped her coin—no longer interested in an item that wasn't edible—and jetted away, disappearing into another crevice. Mer turned the coin over in her palm. Perhaps she should leave it as tribute. Compensation. A gift for another diver to discover, so someone else could experience the level of elation that goes with plucking gold from a sea of blue. Phoenix would call her crazy for leaving such a valuable artifact behind, now that she had already disturbed it.

She returned the coin to the den. It wasn't the first time someone had considered her crazy, and probably not the last.

Now it was time to share the news.

The anchor line rose out of the sand as Mer drew near. Phoenix hovered halfway between Mer and the boat, already on her safety stop. Mer ascended slowly, her bubbles outpacing her. At fifteen feet, her computer automatically started to tick away the seconds.

Phoenix glanced at her own gauges and signaled to Mer that she was heading up.

The desire to share the news almost prompted Mer to delay her, but the very real possibility of removing the coins from her pocket and having them slip through her fingers convinced her otherwise.

Two and a half minutes more and she could share the news on deck with Leroy, too.

The growl of a boat engine made Mer look up in surprise. The *Dock Holiday* rocked on the surface and Phoenix's silhouette disappeared as she pulled herself onto the boat.

The noise increased. Even underwater, Mer could tell that the boat was traveling fast.

Idiots.

Dive graphics on the *Dock Holiday* clearly identified their vessel as a scuba charter and Leroy always flew a dive flag when he had divers in the water. Other boats were supposed to give them a wide berth—or at the very least, greatly reduce their speed. The approaching boat was doing neither.

Mer glanced at her computer as the final seconds of her safety stop elapsed. The roar of the engines surrounded her. When she looked up, the hull of a long narrow boat came into view. Three engines churned the water behind it as it swung a wide circle around the *Dock Holiday*. The wake buffeted the smaller charter boat from all sides, and the swim ladder stabbed into the water.

Her stomach roiled. She'd seen a boat like this before. The day she and Leroy had found the square grouper.

The buoy. She closed her eyes inside the mask and groaned through her regulator. Surface marker buoys served two purposes: to broadcast a diver's position or mark an area. If Bart learned she'd found the treasure, everything would change, and he'd have no reason to fulfill his end of the bargain regarding Oscar. Worse, he'd eliminate witnesses. And two of her friends were already in the line of fire, topside.

Mer descended and retraced her path to the reel. Fear quickened her breaths and she tried to calm herself to conserve air. The deeper she swam, the sooner she would run out of air—but she didn't want to get anywhere near the slicing props, nor did she want anyone on the boat to see her. They had probably already noticed the marker, so her only hope was that they were too busy circling the *Dock Holiday* to record the GPS coordinates.

She unsheathed her dive knife. Holding the titanium blade gave her a modicum of comfort. The yellow reel stood out in marked contrast to the sand-colored rocks that pinned it to the ocean floor. Mer sliced through the string attached to the buoy and the surface marker floated from the site.

The reel presented another problem. If she left it in place, and the boater above had marked the spot, it would act as a neon sign with a "Look Here" message. If she took it with her, the severed string might raise questions she'd rather not answer.

More than three thousand patch reefs dotted the waters surrounding the Keys. Mer did her best to sear the details of this one into her brain. She used a barrel sponge, brain coral, and the octopus den to triangulate the location. That would have to do.

The octopus was nowhere to be found. She grabbed the two coins from her pocket and stuffed them into the recesses of the den to join the third. She didn't know what she'd face when she surfaced, but being caught with two gold portrait dollars would ruin any chance of plausible deniability.

Doubts crept into her mind and kept her on the reef. Nothing but her own paranoia suggested that Bart was at the helm of the circling boat. No one beyond a select few knew the *Finders Keepers* was a decoy, and most of those people were either on the boat or diving with Mer.

But her gut argued otherwise. Sure, where there was water one could always find careless boaters, but this was a crappy day in December on a no-name reef. And what about Deputy Cole?

She retrieved one of the coins and slipped it into her neoprene bootie, flexing and arching her foot until she felt the smooth metal slide toward the toe. It might come in handy as leverage.

Collecting the reel, she set out once again for the boat. The anchor jumped at the end of its line and she was glad the reef was far enough away to escape damage. She dropped the reel in the sand. Divers lost equipment all the time. At least this way, if someone found it, the reel's location wouldn't give away any more information.

The cigarette boat still circled the *Dock Holiday*, but it was moving slower now. The engines gave a low rumble like thunder on the horizon—a warning of storms to come.

Dread added a metallic taste to the air she sucked from her tank. She'd done all she could to keep the Thirteenth Galleon's secrets. She had to go up.

Or drown.

The rocking boat meant Mer's timing had to be perfect. Grab the ladder without a proper foothold and six feet of aluminum railing would slam into her already injured ribs. Miss the ladder altogether and she risked having it come crashing down on her with all the weight of the *Dock Holiday* behind it. Usually, the time between swells could be predicted, but the wake from the circling boat destroyed that.

Waiting until the cigarette boat crossed in front of the *Dock Holiday's* bow, she thrust the metal detector toward the surface. Through the water, she saw Phoenix lean over and felt the tug as the archaeologist grabbed it. Mer released the device and immediately pulled her fins off. She looped them over her wrist and held her position until the stern drove the ladder deep into the water. Darting forward, she grabbed the ladder with both hands and planted her feet on the bottom rung. The *Dock Holiday* bucked and reversed course. Her biceps strained as the water dragged at her and tried to pull her back.

The boat stabilized for a moment, and she shimmied up two rungs and held on for another ride.

Leroy rushed to her aid. "Wait for my count." He looked beyond her to the waves.

She clung to the ladder. Her breaths squealed through the regulator, but she didn't dare remove it in case she lost her grip and fell backward.

"Here comes a break," Leroy said. "Three. Two. Now!"

He grabbed her under the arm and helped haul her onto the dive platform. Another swell hit the boat. Leroy pulled her into a bear hug and braced himself against the railing for balance.

Mer glanced over the captain's shoulder at the other boat. A Picuda.

The man at the helm powered down the engines.

Phoenix swiped the bench clean and motioned to Mer. "He's stopping!"

The speedboat bobbed about twenty yards behind the dive boat.

Mer stumbled to the bench and fell onto it, dropping her fins on the deck. She spit out her regulator and ripped off her mask.

Phoenix drew the bungee cord over the top of her tank. "You okay?"

Mer snapped a quick nod. Within seconds, she released her buckles and stood. "It's Bart, isn't it?"

"Up 'til now, he hadn't been close enough to tell," Leroy said.

The *Dock Holiday* dragged anchor at the mercy of the swells. Mer shadowed her eyes with her hand and squinted at the speedboat. The blue hull barely distinguished itself from the sky above and the water below. Inside the open cockpit, the captain stood and faced them.

Bart Kingston.

Mer's pulse jumped. The last time she'd encountered the smuggler, he'd shot at her. Instinctively she ducked, and dragged Phoenix with her.

"What do they want?" Phoenix whispered.

Mer peeked around the transom in time to see Bart raise his arm. "We're about to find out."

36

They were dead in the water.

Mer pushed Phoenix under the bench. The hull might not stop a bullet, but at least Bart wouldn't know where to shoot.

Leroy hunkered under the bench on the other side of the boat.

The swells calmed, no longer frothed by the speedboat, and the anchor bit into the seafloor again. But from their hiding places, none of them could reach the radio. There was no way to outrun Bart and no way to call for help.

"Hey Doc. Show yourself," the smuggler shouted.

Leroy vehemently shook his head.

"Come out, come out wherever you are," Bart sang.

"Don't even think it, Cavallo," Leroy said.

The non-skid deck dug into her palms and she wondered if her legs would hold her upright if she stood.

Bart slapped something against the boat. The sound rang out like a shot. "You're pissing me off." His voice held more menace. "You don't want that."

No. She didn't.

"What are you doing?" Phoenix stage-whispered. "Don't—"

Mer blocked out Phoenix's voice and Leroy's worried face, and stood.

Bart held a black object in his right hand, partially concealed behind the gunnel. He raised it to eye-level. She clutched the rail for support.

Binoculars.

Her legs nearly buckled with relief even as she felt the crawl of his gaze settle on her. He had to see her fear. Know he was the cause. Revel in it. She stood straighter and jutted out her chin. *Fuck that.*

After an eternity, he lowered the binoculars.

The Picuda's motors roared to life and the boat idled closer.

Her knuckles whitened around the rail. She refused to hide. Let him come. Let him try something.

Ten yards from the stern, he gunned the speedboat into a sharp turn. Mer ducked, but the rooster tail of seawater crashed over the stern of the *Dock Holiday* and drove her to the deck.

Soaked, Phoenix scrambled to her side. Her fingers dug into Mer's biceps. "What the hell just happened?"

Mer sat back as the Picuda receded. The howl of its engines faded on the wind. "They know where I'm not. They know about the ruse."

Leroy hauled himself upright. Salt water dripped from his beard. "I'm beginning to believe you really are bad luck on a boat."

The adrenaline dump left her shaking. "For the record, I'm blaming Phoenix. I wasn't on the boat when this all started."

"No, but he waited for you." Phoenix sat on the deck with her back against the bench. "Pretty sure that means I'm in the clear." She laughed, but it lacked her usual exuberance.

"Did you radio anyone before I came up from the dive?" Mer asked.

"More concerned about getting you out of the drink." Leroy offered Mer his hand and helped her stand.

Her legs wobbled. "How'd he know we were here?"

"He's a pirate. Who knows what kind of intel he has." Leroy

pressed the water from his beard and walked to the helm. "At least we didn't have anything worth plundering. When I saw your—"

"We should pull anchor." Mer locked eyes with Leroy and gave the slightest shake of her head. The gold coin scorched her sole and she had an unfathomable desire to keep its existence secret.

Leroy narrowed his eyes, but remained quiet.

Phoenix yanked off her booties with shaky hands and drained the water from each one. "For once I'm glad we got skunked."

The surface marker buoy had disappeared from the horizon. Without tension, it had probably keeled over and was awash on the current. But Leroy had seen it. He'd been on the boat. She didn't know why, but she hoped Phoenix had been too busy stowing her gear to notice the marker.

Mer addressed Leroy, "Ready to weigh anchor? We're sitting ducks if he decides to return."

"Waiting on you."

And it wasn't for the anchor.

———

The engine noise rose to a high pitch as Leroy pushed the dive boat to her limits. Mer stood at the bow and braced herself against the rails. Seawater dripped from her hair, off her nose. Her legs absorbed the pitch and yaw of the bucking deck as the boat fought through the swells.

The bow offered no protection. She should be under cover. Thinking. Trying to make sense of her conflicted thoughts. But the spray stinging her face and the ache in her legs reminded her she was alive.

She liked that.

Each time she moved her foot, the coin pressed into her skin. Skipper's words haunted her. Treasure was trouble. Not the finding of it, but what it did to the soul. Well, she had found it, and no one but she knew it. Yet somehow, in a vast ocean, Bart had come upon their location.

Phoenix sat on the main deck, silent. Her topknot had come down and wrapped in a towel, she looked as innocent as a small child. But what did Mer really know of the woman? Only that she worked as a university professor, which meant she was overworked and underpaid. Would the archeologist help exploit a site for profit if it meant going against everything she professed to care about? Mer had been hoodwinked by one academic lately. Reading people was not her strong point. Maybe Winslet Chase had made Phoenix an offer she couldn't refuse.

Because one thing was certain: Bart Kingston knew their location.

The sun started its descent and the sky was a soup mix of clouds. As they approached the dock, she was no closer to understanding her reluctance to share the coin with Phoenix.

Talbot came down the stairs as Leroy swung the *Dock Holiday* around and squeezed the small charter boat between the other two vessels.

The detective handed her the bowline. "You're soaked."

"Good thing I'm wearing my wetsuit." She wrapped the line around the cleat and moved aft.

Talbot followed her and passed the spring line under the rail. Mer pulled the boat snug against the dock. "Is Gina upstairs?"

"She's waiting to exchange clothes."

"You can tell her not to bother. We had a bit of a run-in with Bart on the high seas." She read the alarm in his face. "Everyone's fine."

The concern morphed into annoyance. "Why am I just hearing about this now? You had a radio."

"Long story. Let me finish here and I'll meet you upstairs and tell you the whole sordid tale."

He didn't move. She thought she heard a sigh, but it was lost under the creak of the boat against the dock bumpers.

"You sure you're doing okay?" The concern was back, softening his hazel eyes.

Mer bled the air from her regulator. "I think I'm starting to get used to the adrenaline."

"That's not a good thing."

Phoenix stuffed her towel into her dry bag and tossed it onto the dock next to Talbot. "Do you need me for anything? I just want to go home."

Talbot pulled out his phone and punched up a recorder app. "Sounds like I need to get a statement from you before you go."

Phoenix leaned over the side and spoke into his phone. "Some guy in a big-ass boat showed up. Lapped us 'til we were dizzy. Left." She disappeared into the V-berth and reemerged carrying her gear. "Anything else?"

Talbot glanced at Mer for validation.

"Other than the fact he's wanted, I don't think Bart committed any new crimes today." Mer loosened the tank strap and lifted her BC off the tank. "Well, other than ignoring the dive flag."

The detective moved forward to help Phoenix from the boat. "Let me get your phone number. Can I call you tonight if I need to follow up on anything?"

"Sure." She recited the numbers, but ignored his outstretched hand. "I'm begging off the dive tomorrow. I have a lecture in the morning."

"No worries. I'm shutting down the operation," Talbot said.

"Best news I've heard all day. I'll catch up with you guys later." Phoenix scooped up her other bag and tromped off toward the parking lot.

The tide placed the boat level with the dock. Mer stepped off the stern, dumped her gear into the rinse bins on the dock, and returned to the boat to collect her tanks.

Talbot moved to help her. "Forsooth—"

"If you quote Shakespeare right now, I may resort to violence."

"I'm still recording."

"It'll take more than a phone to save you."

"Duly noted." He stashed the phone in his shorts pocket.

Leroy did a quick check around the helm, and then joined them on the dock. "I must say, I've had fun before, and today wasn't it."

"I think we can all agree on that," Mer said. She pulled her two tanks from their holders. The movement didn't hurt nearly as much, and she realized it had been a week since the gala. Seven days since meeting Winslet Chase, since being duped by Oscar, since Bart Kingston had punched and kicked her black and blue.

What a difference a week made. Last Sunday she'd been scared. Now she was pissed.

Leroy took the tanks from her. "Never seen you wear your wetsuit this long. Your toes are going to be nothing more than shriveled up prunes."

She shut the hatch on the V-berth and locked it. "I imagine they will be." Mer dragged her backpack off the dashboard and slung it over her shoulder.

"Makes a person wonder why you're still wearing it."

She swept her hand in an after-you gesture and followed the captain off the boat. "Far be it for me to leave a question unanswered."

Talbot crossed his arms and leaned against the dock piling, right under the sign warning divers to watch their step. "What are you two trying not to say in front of me?"

Water splashed over Talbot's deck shoes as she dragged her equipment from the rinse bin. "Let me stow my gear in the equipment room, and I'll meet you in the classroom. I have some news to share."

The first thing Mer noticed when she entered the classroom was the outline of the ballistic vest under Deputy Gina Mercurio's Aquarius crew shirt. It reminded her of the stakes.

Gina gave her the once over. "Nice wetsuit."

Leroy sat against the wall. "Are you going to tell me why you sent up your surface marker? Thought something had gone wrong. Then Phoenix popped up and said you were on your safety stop."

Talbot had dragged a chair around to the front of the room and sat with his elbows on the table and his hands cupping his face, as if he had a headache.

She suspected she was about to make it worse. "Is Skipper still around?"

"I cut him loose already," Gina said. "Do I need to call him back?"

"That's okay. Bijoux?"

"I'm here." Her boss swept into the room. "Why are you still wearing your wetsuit?"

"Yes, Cavallo," Leroy asked with feigned innocence. "Why is that?"

Mer bent over and unzipped her right bootie. "I can't take off my wetsuit without first taking off my booties."

"You dodging the question, or is this going to be another one of your long-winded explanations?" Leroy asked.

She reached her hand into the toe, careful not to spill the trapped water. "I didn't want to take off my booties."

Leroy tipped his chair against the wall. "Wake me when you get to the good part."

The coin felt heavier than a modern coin. Heavy with history. It saddened her that Phoenix wasn't here to share the moment, but that was partly Mer's own doing. "I found this today on the reef." She handed the coin to Leroy.

The sound of chair legs hitting the floor ricocheted around the silent room. Then everyone in the room started talking at once.

"Is it?"

"Well, I'll..."

"A portrait dollar?"

"*Mon dieu.*"

Everyone but Mer huddled around Leroy. Their voices rose as they passed the coin between them. Marveling at the same things she had underwater. They were all a part of the history now.

"You were marking the spot." The usually nonplussed captain looked slightly dazed.

"I was. That was the plan, anyway. Until Bart arrived."

"How did you know it was him?"

"I didn't. At least not definitively. But I saw the length of the hull. The three motors. It seemed too much of a coincidence for it to be anyone else. But how did they know where we were?" She repeated the question she'd asked on the boat.

"Wait a minute," Gina interrupted. "You had a run-in with Kingston?"

"He circled the boat until I came up from my dive, then he idled off our stern." She removed the second bootie, hopping on one leg to keep her balance. "Called me by name. He had binoculars. The logical conclusion suggests he was verifying my presence on the *Dock Holiday*. Which meant he knew I wasn't on the *Finders Keepers*."

"Son of a bitch," Gina whispered, then cleared her throat. "This changes everything."

"It can't," Mer said.

"That's not your call, Dr. Cavallo." Talbot typed notes into his phone. "We deployed the patrol boat to watch the *Finders Keepers*. All along, we figured that would be the boat they'd make a move on. We don't have the manpower to watch both boats."

"You don't have to. You're forgetting—I found a coin. Actually, three of them."

"Three?" Leroy slid the coin across the table and it stopped in front of Mer.

"I contemplated leaving them all behind, but we needed one." She held up the coin. "This is how we're going to get Oscar back."

"You're not going to get anyone back," the detective said. "We've been compromised. It's too dangerous."

Mer set the coin down. "How *did* we get compromised?"

"Even a blind squirrel finds an acorn now and again." Leroy interjected.

Mer shook her head. "I have a hard time believing they just happened upon us, especially when we went to all the trouble to make it look as if we were miles to the north."

"You're suggesting someone tipped them off," Gina said.

Mer thought of Cole, Phoenix, and Skipper. "We can't discount the possibility."

"All along, they've been one step ahead of us," Talbot said. "It's as if they knew what we were doing, and where we were, as soon as we began."

The answer slapped her with its obviousness. "They're using GPS trackers." It all fit. "They used one in the bale, the boats, my car." She smacked her fist against her thigh. "How did we miss that?"

"You didn't." Talbot pushed back his chair and stood. "I did. From now on, this is a law enforcement-only operation."

"You planning to swear me in?" Mer asked.

"The plan was meant to keep you out of harm's way, not put you in the middle of it."

They couldn't scrap the plan. Not now. Not when they were so close to saving Oscar. "Do you want to take my statement now, or tomorrow night?" She tried to sound casual, but the challenge in her voice was unmistakable.

Talbot's hand lingered on the back of his chair. "Why would I talk to you tomorrow night?"

Mer stepped into his personal space. "Because by that time I will have spoken to Winslet Chase, met with Bart Kingston, and rescued Oscar Vigil."

"Oh, boy." Leroy tipped his chair against the wall again. "I swear. We need a popcorn machine in this shop." He turned to Bijoux. "I'll even pitch in."

"The state allows me to take people into protective custody if I deem them a danger to themselves," Talbot warned.

She didn't flinch. "At the beginning of this operation you said it was up to me to determine what I was capable of."

"That was before you turned into an addle-pated lack-wit."

"I'll match my wits against yours whenever you're ready, Detective."

Talbot reached into his back waistband and dangled a pair of handcuffs in front of Mer's face.

Mer inched closer, her pruned toes nearly touching his deck shoes. "Double dog dare you."

"With pleasure."

Bijoux and Gina sprang into action at the same time. Gina slid between the two while Bijoux grabbed Mer by the shoulders and dragged her backward.

"You're shaking," Bijoux said, her voice silky with reason. "Your wetsuit is frozen. Why don't you go change? Get dry."

"Regain some of the wit you apparently lack," Leroy added.

Gina whispered something to Talbot. He flushed, but his posture visibly relaxed.

The damp neoprene sapped the warmth from Mer's body and stole her energy. She didn't want to fight. She just wanted this all to end. They were so close. She had to convince them it would work.

"All I have to do is call Winslet and tell him I've found the galleon. I've got proof. The coin."

Gina appeared poised to intercede again. "How's that going to save Oscar?"

"Bart said he'd kill Oscar if I didn't give him the coin. Problem is, he's never told us how to contact him. But if he and Winslet are in cahoots like we think they are, calling one is as good as calling the other."

"What makes you think they'll let you go?" Gina asked.

"No one wants *me*. They want the galleon," Mer said. "Plus, I'm hoping you guys are going to swoop in and arrest them."

"How?" It was the first word Talbot had spoken since threatening to handcuff her.

"Don't you have some electronic thingy you can use to find out if there's a tracker on the boats?"

"We prefer to call it a thingamajig."

She didn't know if he was coming around to her way of thinking or just being sarcastic. "Can you check the boats before we go out tomorrow? Confirm that they tracked us?"

"You're not going out tomorrow."

"You can't stop me from diving," Mer said. "So let's table that issue."

Talbot implored Bijoux. "You control the boats."

"Yes, Detective, but I do not control Meredith. She works for a dive shop. That means at some point she will again be on the reef. Would it not be better if she were under your supervision when that inevitability occurred?"

Mer could tell Bijoux's words made more of an impact on the detective than her own. "I can help you end this."

"Once more unto the breach?" Talbot asked. "No. The potential price is too high."

Mer picked up the portrait dollar. "Not if we do it right."

"You must have one doozy of a plan," Leroy said. "I'd kind of like to hear it."

The captain gave her the opening she needed. "We can assume

they've been tracking the boats for at least two days. One to follow the *Finders Keepers* and another to realize the *Dock Holiday* was mapping an area and we were diving the hits. We use that to our advantage."

"How?" Talbot repeated.

"They don't know we've found the coin yet. We act as if we're diving a new site in the morning—just like every other morning we've been out. Then we pick a spot—you pick a spot—that gives you the tactical advantage and we park the *Finders Keepers* over it."

"It's the ocean," Gina said. "There isn't much tactical advantage anywhere."

"There is." Talbot darted out of the room and returned a moment later carrying a chart. "If we choose a site here for the salvage boat." He tapped the map and then swept his finger over to a new location. "We can use the backside of Tavernier Key to stage the patrol boat. At the first sight of Bart or Winslet, you sound the alarm and we'll be there in a flash."

Mer drew her brows together. "That's a fair distance from where we've been dragging the magnetometer."

"It's there or nowhere," Talbot said. "If you stay in the area you've been working, it will lengthen the response time. I won't have it."

Gina studied the map over Talbot's shoulder. "It'd be safer to snatch them on land," she said. "Easier to contain them. More backup's available."

"We've been turning over rocks. He's not in the Keys." Talbot scrubbed his face. "For all we know, he's commuting from the Bahamas. The Picuda is designed for quick crossings."

"What about Winslet Chase?" Leroy asked. "He's got a high profile. He ought to be easy enough to roll up."

"Chase hasn't gotten his hands dirty enough yet. He's offered Dr. Cavallo a job and delivered a message. It isn't even enough for a warrant."

"You know he's up to his eyeballs in this," Mer said.

"Knowing it and proving it are two different things. Judges are sticklers for something called probable cause."

"Then this is your best bet." The wetsuit and the audacity of the plan chilled her and she started to shiver. "We're beyond the need for subterfuge. So let's give them what they expect. We're hunting treasure. Drop the mailboxes. Make it look as if we've blown the site. What do we have to lose? They know where we mapped. It wouldn't take more than a few days to reconstruct the work we've done and find the galleon themselves."

"Then why wouldn't they get rid of Oscar and just wait us out?"

"Because I'm going to warn Winslet that if he goes off-script, I've made arrangements to announce the GPS coordinates of the legendary Thirteenth Galleon to the world. He wants the glory too much to let that happen." She willed Talbot to understand. "You know they're monitoring the marine radio. Let's invite them to the party. Tell them if they don't deliver Oscar, posthaste, we're going to blab the news."

"Posthaste?" Leroy eyed Talbot. "I'd say you're rubbing off on her."

The screen of Talbot's phone lit up with a text. He glanced down. "I've got to go brief the brass. No promises, but either way I'll come back and see if I can locate tracker signals on the boats."

"What about my car?"

"I can swing by the house and check later." He looked more tired than he had an hour ago. She seemed to have that effect on people. It wasn't one of her better traits. "You might as well drive it home. It would seem odd if you suddenly changed behavior. But consider staying with your neighbor."

They both knew which neighbor he meant.

He left and the energy in the room fizzled. Holiday music dripped from the speakers.

"What now?" Mer finally asked.

Gina collected her bag. "Change out of your wetsuit. Go home. Celebrate finding the galleon."

Leroy stood and intentionally bumped her on his way to the door. "And try to make it through the night without stirring up a hornet's nest."

"We both know the improbability of that," Bijoux said. She rolled up the chart and rapped Mer on the shoulder with it. "But I would be grateful if you at least tried."

Mer delayed Gina while Leroy and Bijoux left the room. "What about the coin? Shouldn't you book it for the night into evidence for safekeeping or something?"

"Nope." Gina dug through the bag for her keys. "Not evidence of a crime. It's your problem."

"Oh." Mer fidgeted with the cuff of her wetsuit.

"Something else bothering you?" the deputy asked.

Mer wrapped her arms around herself. "I just wanted to apologize."

"For what?"

"I put you in an awkward position earlier. Detective Talbot and I...I mean... We don't always play well together." She sighed. "I swear that man brings out the worst in me."

Gina failed to hide a smile. "No worries."

They walked toward the door.

"I'm curious. What did you say to him to calm him down?" Mer rubbed her arms in an attempt to bring some feeling back into them. "I might need to use it someday."

Gina stood in the threshold of the shop and the door chime kept cycling until she stepped back. "I told him if he wanted you in handcuffs so bad, he should at least have the courtesy to buy you dinner first." She stepped through the door before Mer could sputter a response and called over her shoulder, "See you tomorrow."

Mer retraced her steps until she shadowed Bijoux's office door. "I don't understand men."

"If it makes you feel better, Madame Scientist, we are enigmas to them as well."

"No. Not really." She held up the coin. "Can we lock this in the safe, tonight?"

"Of course." Bijoux placed her pen down on a stack of paperwork. "Would you like to spend the night at my house?"

Mer contemplated the offer. "Thanks, but I'm going to pass. I need to take care of some things tonight." Selkie topped the list.

Her boss leaned back in her chair. "Be honest with him."

Mer started to utter a denial, but changed her mind. "I intend to."

Bijoux spun her chair and opened the cabinet door behind her, revealing the office safe. She spun the tumblers. "You seem certain your plan will work tomorrow."

"I *hope* my plan will work." Mer handed the coin to her friend.

"So do I. Now go home." Bijoux placed the coin in the safe and tumbled the lock.

"You coming?"

"Not yet. I have my own things to take care of."

"Don't stay too long," Mer said.

Downstairs in the equipment room, she peeled off her wetsuit and for the first time in hours, drew on dry clothes. She'd kill for a hot bath. Maybe later. After all was said and done.

She hung her gear, grabbed her backpack and locked the door behind her.

Night noise followed her as she walked to her car. Music from the pub at the end of the canal drifted over the water. Behind the wheel, she pulled her phone from her backpack and held it for several minutes before screwing up the courage to text Selkie.

He answered almost immediately. "I'll be waiting."

Unto the breach, indeed.

38

M er picked up champagne on her way home. She'd made history and she was thirsty. It made showing up on Selkie's doorstep less awkward. Plus it was a safe bet that he had champagne flutes.

She paused in front of his massive door with her knuckles at the ready, and then lowered her hand. This was silly. She was only here to talk. To apologize and set some ground rules. With any luck, they could get back to normal—only better.

Condensation beaded on the champagne bottle—a common occurrence in the Keys, even when winter humidity was at its lowest. She readjusted her grip and realized she was stalling. Mer straightened and drew a deep breath. No one was forcing him to meet her. That meant something—unless he was just humoring her. She took a step back and dragged her fingers through the seawater tangles in her hair. Maybe she should have cleaned up first so she looked more presentable.

Finally she raised her free hand and knocked.

"I'm out here."

The champagne bottle nearly slipped from her grasp.

"I didn't mean to startle you." He leaned against the corner of the house, half hidden by the shadows on the wraparound deck.

"I'm a bit jumpy lately." She hoped he hadn't seen her indecision at the door, but he didn't miss much. Before he could misconstrue her actions, she blurted, "I wanted to say I'm sorry."

She wanted to say a lot more, but best to start out small.

He emerged from the shadows. "With champagne?"

"I also wanted to share some news with you."

"Must be good news if it warrants bubbly."

"I found the galleon." Awe tinged her voice. She still had difficulty believing it. "The Thirteenth Galleon. It's real."

"Congratulations!" He wrapped her in a bear hug and lifted her feet off the ground, then lowered her almost immediately. "Shit. I'm sorry. Did I hurt your ribs?"

"I'm good." The length of her body still pressed against his and she breathed in the comfort of his scent. She'd missed him. "Celebrate with me?"

His hand sought hers. "Come on back, tell me all about it."

Her trepidation fled. It was going to be all right. "I found it because of an octopus."

"Why am I not surprised?"

She followed him onto the rear deck, rearranged the throw pillows, and sank into one of the teak patio chairs. "I recovered three portrait dollars. They had fallen through the reef. If it hadn't been for the octopus, I'd never have figured out they were *in* the reef."

"I'm happy for you, Mer." He took the bottle and tilted it to read the label. "Shall I?"

She shook her head. "I'll do it."

He laughed. "Wow. This is a day of firsts."

His words stung. For a reason she didn't want to ponder, it became imperative that she open the bottle herself. "I'm quite capable."

Selkie held it up and to the side, like a child keeping a toy from his younger sister. "It's not a big deal. I know it scares you."

"Lots of things scare me." She held out her hand. "Give me the bottle."

"All yours."

It was a hollow victory. She'd never actually opened a bottle of champagne before. Probably for the same reason she hated opening a sealed tube of pre-made biscuits or her irrational dislike of Jack-in-the-boxes. Anticipating explosions set her teeth on edge.

The bottle felt heavy. Dangerous somehow. She pulled off the foil. "Did you know that it's the industry standard that the wire cage is twisted six times?"

He reclined on the chaise and folded his hands behind his head. "You don't say."

Mer untwisted the wire securing the cork. "Not five, not seven—"

"I get it. Six."

She slid the cage off and clamped her fingers down on the cork.

"I'd be glad to help you with that," Selkie said.

She sucked in a breath and pushed harder on the cork.

"Uh, the objective is to get the cork *out* of the bottle."

"Every year scores of people go to the hospital because of champagne cork accidents. Mostly on New Year's Eve."

"Give it here." He grabbed the bottle.

For a moment they played tug-of-war. What was she doing? This was supposed to be a celebration, not a war of wills.

"Fine." She released the bottle. "You do it."

"So which is worse? Popping the bottle or asking for help?"

"I like to be self-sufficient."

"So asking for help."

Two seconds. *Two seconds* and already she regretted backing down. "I just wanted to celebrate."

"That doesn't require another person. What do you really want to say, Mer?"

The breeze played in the palms and carried on it the scent of night blooming jasmine.

"I *want* to say I love you."

The intensity of his scrutiny unnerved her.

"But?" he prompted.

She owed him the truth. "I'm not sure I should say it to you."

His gaze cut away as if he no longer appreciated her candor. "Huh." He tilted the bottle. "I would have chosen a weightier red for this conversation."

"Look at me." She put her hand against his chest. His heart pulsed beneath her hand and she marveled at the evenness of it, while the erratically beating heart in her own chest ached. "Please."

He shook off her hand.

"You scare me," she admitted.

Hurt flickered across his face. "What?"

"Because of what happened the first time we fell in love."

"You can't let that go, can you?" He dropped the cage back over the top of the champagne bottle and twisted the wire. Once. Twice. "Six times, right?"

"Up until recently, I thought I had forgiven you. But I hadn't. I was a kid when we fell in love. When you left, I buried myself in my studies. But I never licked my wounds. I ignored them. Then they healed over and I didn't think of you again."

He winced. "I'm sorry."

"But all that's changed. I've been thinking about you—about us —a lot lately," she said. "Did you know there are five parts to an apology?"

A rueful smile softened the angles of his face. "Is this like the six twists of the champagne cage?"

The tension eased fractionally, but enough for her to poke fun at herself. "I quantify things. It's what I do." Her hand worried the seahorse pendant at the base of her throat. "You should also know I'm not trying to hide anything. I'm here because I think this is important."

"I know that, Mer."

"An apology is first and foremost an expression of regret."

"I said I was sorry."

"For many people, that's as far as it goes. But they never actually accept responsibility. They deflect it. Or worse, they ignore it," she said.

"I've already said it was all my fault."

"Stop." He wasn't going to make this easy. She didn't want him to. "Let me finish. Please."

The breeze toyed with the foil wrapper and he caught it before it dropped off the table. "Sorry." But he said it as just a word, with no meaning behind it.

"A true apology is complicated," Mer said. "Some people will say they're sorry when they're not. They just want the conflict to go away. But an apology has to be genuine. It has to make things better."

"You can't make restitution for hurt feelings," he said.

"The last step is to ask for forgiveness."

"I've done that. I've done all of that."

"You've done most of it. But *I* haven't." She curled her legs beneath her. There was more. Drawing a breath, she dove in. "Selkie, when you came back into my life, I wasn't confident enough to be honest with you about how badly I'd been hurt before and I'm sorry. It was wrong for me not to express my concerns and fears." Her words were stilted, but she had to get the feelings out. She had to make him understand.

He moved toward her and she held up her hand. "I'll try not to do the same thing in the future, but quite frankly, I don't have the skills to do this cold turkey, and I know I'll backslide. Confrontation is difficult for me. At some point, I'll probably screw up again—but I'll do my best not to." She drew a big breath and blew it out. "Will you please forgive me?"

"No."

Her throat constricted and she unfolded her legs. Even though she'd prepared herself for this reaction, it still hurt. "I understand." There was no reason to continue with the rest.

"I don't think you do," he said. He scratched the stubble on his jaw. "This has been a difficult week. Without you."

"It's been hard on me, too." She missed sharing the events of their days. Missed hearing him hum while he shaved. Missed the way he brushed his fingers over her forearm right before he reached for her hand.

"You were the one who asked for it," he reminded her.

"Is that enough reason not to forgive me?"

"It's been my lot in life to fall in love with strong, independent women." He stared beyond her, lost in the darkness. "It's easier to pretend I can't forgive you than it is to acknowledge that I can't protect you."

She tucked her hands under her arms. "That's about the dumbest thing I've ever heard."

"I've dedicated my life to protecting all I hold dear. My family, my country, and my men. You. I've failed at every turn."

"How can you say that?"

"No one aces SEAL training. But I did well enough to get noticed. My sister had dubbed me Selkie when we were kids. The whole Irish thing. But that, combined with my new job made me think the whole thing was ordained." He laughed mirthlessly. "Hubris."

"You can't protect everyone."

"The summer we first met, I was broken. My body. My confidence." His fingers brushed her scar. "I know what you're going through."

She held her breath, not wanting to say the wrong thing. The helicopter crash had affected him—she'd known that—but not how much. He still talked about it with such pain.

"What you don't know is that I lost two men on that mission. I had to prove to the Navy that I was worth keeping. But I had to convince myself first. Your brother talked about you all the time. I felt like I knew you before he'd even introduced us. But I wasn't prepared for you. Turns out you're capable of scaring people, too. Or at least me."

She bit back the obvious question. It no longer matter why he had left her, then.

"My bones mended. I healed. The Navy sent me to school. I've spent a career trying to make up for letting them down. Letting my men down. Their families."

"Did you pull the trigger on either man?"

He reared back. "What? No!"

"No." She sought his hand. "Then you're blaming yourself for something you didn't do."

"That's the point. I didn't protect them." He cupped her face in his hand and tucked a wild curl behind her ear. "That brings us to you."

"You've never failed me." But even as she said it, she knew it wasn't true.

"Did you know that Josh taught me how to scuba dive?"

The abrupt change in the conversation yanked her back to the summer they'd fallen in love. They'd spoken of diving together. He was already certified. She wasn't. "That means you've known Detective Talbot longer than you've known me."

"He was working on a dive boat in Key West. A snot-nosed twenty-one-year-old, barely old enough to drink. I was twenty-three and an Annapolis grad. Cocky as all hell and about to enter SEAL training. I figured knowing how to dive before they threw me in the water would be a good thing. Josh and I hit it off right away."

"Why are you telling me this?"

"He's a good man." Selkie smiled. It nearly reached his eyes. "The champagne's getting warm. Let me grab some glasses." He disappeared into the house.

Last night's moon was full. Tonight its tarnished glow waned, but the illumination threw her world into stark perspective.

By the time he returned, she'd opened the bottle. She felt a sad elation. Being alone was better than being with the wrong person, but it still meant being alone.

He stared at the cork and then lifted it and tenderly folded it into her hand.

She started to cry.

"I love you, Meredith Elena Cavallo."

She cried harder. She'd never meant to cause him more pain. They'd both suffered enough. "I'm so sorry."

"There should be four other parts, you know." He squeezed her hand briefly, and let go.

Her chin trembled. "I know."

"Promise me you'll be careful."

She could only nod.

39

Mer woke an hour before her alarm. Her first look in the mirror nearly sent her back to bed, and no amount of cold water remedied her puffy face, red eyes, or wild hair. Instead she called her mother.

Her parents wouldn't be home from their two-week cruise until tonight, and the call went straight to voicemail. It didn't matter. Mer wanted to hear her mother's voice.

The beep caught her off-guard. She sputtered a message and closed with, "Love you both. Give Pops a hug. Talk to you soon. I'm going for a run." Which was a phrase she'd never uttered in her life.

A run.

Once the initial shock wore off, it didn't seem like such a horrible idea—a painful one but not horrible. Running had health benefits. It couldn't possibly make her look any worse, and she already felt crappy. Perfect.

She dug her shoes out of the back of the closet.

The streetlights glowed, but Key Largo still slept. She took a few tentative steps, her footfalls overly loud in the quiet. No lightning sparked from the sky to smite her, so she quickened her pace. It didn't take long before each breath sounded like a consumptive chest rattle.

A Chihuahua barked at her from behind the wrought-iron gate of a multi-million dollar home. On the left side of the street, boats lined the canal, parallel parked along the dock allotted to every property. She eyed each boat she passed, wondering how it would be to live on it. Most offered accommodations larger than her apartment and cost in the high six figures—about four figures out of her price range.

She huffed to the end of the road and punched the security code onto the pad. The ornate wrought iron gate opened and she set off again before fully regaining her breath.

Ocean Cay had never struck her as a long street, but it seemed an eternity before she saw the passing cars that marked the Overseas Highway. She cut south through a hotel lot and jogged past a row of wooden kiosks used by dive, fishing, and tour companies. She descended the stairs to the narrow canal dock.

A crimp in her side slowed her pace as she drew abreast the *African Queen*. Its new life as a tour boat for movie buffs made it one of Key Largo's biggest attractions.

Another few hundred yards and she'd be at the dive shop—sweaty, nearly two hours early, and unprepared to face the day. Not that she'd planned on staying. She was only halfway through her run.

Her lips twitched. She was actually running.

A fish jumped in the canal, startling her out of her reverie, and she stutter-stepped into a puddle.

Maybe running was a bit of an overstatement. Really, it was more of a fast shuffle. Still, breaking into a sweat counted for something and she hadn't thought of Selkie in at least fifteen minutes.

The dock connected restaurants, tiki bars, and hotels along the water. She zigzagged around a small boat launch and onto the dock owned by Bijoux. At the picnic tables, she stopped and leaned over, her hands on her knees. Tears and sweat dripped onto her legs. When had she started crying again?

"I didn't know you were a runner."

Talbot's voice came from the top of the stairs. Mer wiped her eyes before straightening.

He cleared the last three steps with one stride. "Are you okay?"

A squadron of pelicans skimmed the water of the canal in a silent V formation.

She tried to smile. "I'm just overjoyed someone called me a runner."

"Is this about today?" he asked. "You don't have to do this."

She leaned against the wooden table and stretched her calves. "I thought we already had this conversation. Not contemplating going without me, are you?"

He sat on the bench. "That crossed my mind, but no. It all hinges on you."

"Then why are you here so early?"

"You were right. There's a tracker on each boat. I wanted to make sure no one tampered with anything before we went out today."

"You've been here all night?" she asked, but his wrinkled clothes confirmed her suspicion.

"Too much at stake. We've only got one shot."

"With luck, that's all we'll need."

"Doubting your plan, Dr. Cavallo?"

"Scientists always build in a margin for error, but it won't be necessary this time."

"Thou art wedded to calamity."

"Not today." Her legs were starting to cramp, and the lightening sky reminded her she had to run home and get cleaned up before reporting for work. She pushed away from the table.

"I stowed a satellite phone in the V-berth," Talbot said. "That way if we need to, we can talk without being overheard." Talbot stood. "Promise me you'll be careful today."

His request reminded her of last night's conversation with Selkie. She knew it was time to leave before she began crying again. "Nothing but."

She sprinted until she knew she was out of sight and then

slowed. She had to push Selkie out of her mind. He wasn't going to be of help today, and other people were putting themselves at risk. She owed it to them to be focused.

By the time she'd arrived home, showered, and driven back to the shop, it had turned into a Chamber of Commerce morning. Picture perfect. Her mother would say it was a good omen. Mer took it as a proof the Keys had beautiful weather.

Bijoux retrieved the coin from the safe and handed it to Mer. "Are you sure you want to take this out on the ocean?"

"No. But on the off chance I have to produce it, I want to be prepared."

"If all goes as planned, you won't have to." Bijoux hugged her. "*Bonne chance.*"

Mer closed her hand around the coin and went downstairs.

Talbot wasn't on the dock and Leroy had his head buried in the engine compartment of the *Finders Keepers*.

Mer addressed the captain's backside. "Today's the day."

Leroy capped the oil container and wiped his hands on a rag. "You got your mind made up, I see."

"We're almost done." The thought thrilled her.

Leroy's cellphone rang, but he ignored it. "Seems to me, you've done your share."

"All the more reason to see it through."

His straw bounced accusingly. "I swear, if I threw you in the ocean, you'd float upcurrent just to spite me."

Mer managed a smile. "Not on purpose."

A rust-bucket of a Buick careened into the parking lot. A second later, Skipper Biggs bore down on the two of them. "What's this I hear about contacting Winslet Chase?"

"How did you learn about that?" Mer asked.

Skipper dismissed her and looked to Leroy for an answer.

"That's the plan," Leroy said.

"It's the only way I know of to show him this." Mer's hand disappeared into her pocket and came out holding the portrait dollar.

Skipper worked his mouth as if he were shifting dentures. "Is that what I think it is?"

"Cost you a shot to find out," Mer said, even as she handed him the coin.

Skipper stared at the portrait dollar in the middle of his palm. "I'll be damned."

"Don't suppose there's ever been much doubt about that," Leroy said.

"Where'd ya find it?"

"Last spot we were at yesterday." She drew Skipper aside and briefed him about yesterday's events. "And so, yes, I'm going to have a little chat with Winslet."

"I see. And you figured you'd set up the *Finders Keepers* to make it all look good."

"We don't want them to be suspicious. If it looks as if we just found the wreck, it ought to be enough to lure him in."

"Oh, he'll take the bait, all right," Skipper said. "The man can't resist making the most of someone else's work."

"As soon as we see them on the horizon, we'll alert the Sheriff's Office. They'll be staged a minute away."

"Chase isn't going to come alone."

"That's the sheriff's problem."

"And whose problem do you think it'll be before they get there?"

"Leroy's and mine."

"Well now, that's your first mistake."

"Excuse me?"

"It's my boat."

A tickle of foreboding made Mer anticipate his next words.

"And your plan ain't worth beans if you ain't got my boat." Skipper crossed his arms. "And you ain't got my boat 'less I'm the captain."

"But—" Mer began.

"Choice is yours."

Mer and Leroy exchanged looks and then Leroy handed Skipper the rag. "Guess I'll mate."

"Do you even know how?" Mer asked.

"I'll watch while you demonstrate."

Bijoux hurried toward the trio. "Leroy, I need to speak with you. It's about your wife."

He paled. "Is Maggie okay?"

Bijoux glanced at the others.

"We're all friends here," Leroy said.

"A dispatcher from the Sheriff's Office tried your cell. Maggie was in an automobile collision and they're transporting her to the emergency room. He said a deputy will meet you there." Bijoux barely paused for a breath. "Do you want me to drive?"

"No." He shook his head as if dazed. "Did they say anything else?"

Concern softened Bijoux's voice. "She's a strong woman. Go."

He gave a curt nod. "Mer, walk with me."

Without waiting, he headed toward the parking lot.

Mer fell in step beside him. "I'm sorry, Leroy. I hope she's okay."

They were almost to the truck before he spoke. "You best watch yourself, today. I'm not going to be out there with you."

"No, but Skipper will be."

He dug in his pocket for the truck keys. "He's got more sense than he lets on. If he tells you to do something, don't think twice. Today isn't a day for scholars. It's for scrappers."

She gave him a quick hug. "That's for Maggie."

40

C onch Wall, Conch Reef and Little Conch Reef offered divers three very different dive sites, despite the similarity of their names and their proximity. Experienced divers chose the northernmost site, where Conch Wall's vertical reef met the sand at ninety feet. In the middle, Conch Reef allowed divers to explore Gorgonians and barrel sponges, and it was the closest most people ever came to the restricted area around the Aquarius Reef Lab. The southernmost site, Little Conch Reef, sheltered the remains of *El Infante* and was shallow enough to snorkel.

Skipper motored northwest of Conch Reef and threw an anchor in fifteen feet of water. The site had the advantage of being close enough to where they had been searching to forestall suspicion, while being far enough from the *Thirteenth Galleon* to protect the discovery.

"Don't see why you need to splash," Skipper said.

Mer yanked the zipper of her wetsuit closed. "They seem to know our very thoughts. I don't want to do anything to deviate from the other days."

"Without the professor, seems to me we already have."

"All the more reason to make the rest of this look normal." She ignored Skipper's surface-supplied rigs in favor of her own equipment and donned her gear. "I hate leaving you alone, though."

"No need to worry about me. I ain't the one with a coin in my boot."

No. That dubious distinction belonged to her. And the coin would remain there until she saw Oscar. She indicated the metal detector on the deck. "Maybe I'll find us something else."

"Girlie, if you find more treasure, I just might propose."

"Considering the magnitude of the question, it will cost you more than a shot."

He tore the top off a fresh package of sunflower seeds. "Marriages always do."

The *Finders Keepers* had a narrow swim step and an open-rung swim ladder off the stern, but most of the real estate was occupied by two industrial-sized blowers, which unmistakably identified the vessel as a salvage boat.

Mer sat on the transom and swung her legs around until she was facing the ocean. Without Phoenix, she would dive alone. She lowered her mask, tested her regulator, and made a giant stride into the ocean.

Skipper handed her the metal detector. "Happy hunting, Missus Biggs."

Clapping the headphones around her ears, she descended.

No eels. No stingrays. Nothing broke the monotony of the sand. She halfheartedly swung the metal detector, but not even trash registered on the console. The current had picked up and in the shallow water, the surge pushed and pulled at her body. She sculled her fins slightly to stay in place.

The concept of time had always fascinated Mer. Like a state of matter, it could act as solid, liquid, or gas. Time was as fluid as the ocean, fleeting in moments of joy, tedious when burdened by anticipation—and at the moment downright inert.

She checked her gauges for the third time. Twenty minutes. Not nearly long enough to qualify as a typical dive. She started to hum ninety-nine bottles of beer on the wall. At fifty-two, she quit and ascended.

"Shaving it a bit close, ain't ya?" Skipper took the metal detector from her outstretched arm.

"It felt like forever." She hooked her fins over her wrist. Unlike the *LunaSea*, this ladder had a central support and rungs that extended from both sides. Theoretically, one could climb it wearing fins, but she preferred the stability of foot-to-rung contact.

Within minutes, they were underway. Skipper took a northwestern heading to navigate closer to Tavernier Key where Talbot and the patrol boat were staged. Although outside of the area where they'd dragged the magnetometer, it was as far from the key as Talbot would authorize. She hoped the location didn't tip off Bart and Winslet Chase.

The game plan for the second site included a dive, some excitement on deck, and then dropping the blowers into the water. There was no reason to activate them. Even if they were working a legitimate salvage site, the blowers would be overkill in fifteen feet of water. The elbow-shaped pipes were designed to direct the prop wash of the twin engines onto the site and blow it clean. This shallow, it would be like using a sledgehammer when a feather duster would do the trick.

Skipper anchored the boat and Mer entered the water. She couldn't stop thinking about how this afternoon could play out. As long as they released Oscar, she would be satisfied. He'd gotten her into this whole mess, but he was as much a pawn as she was. No, her wrath was directed at Bart Kingston and Winslet Chase. They were the puppeteers in this drama. She still didn't know how large a role Deputy Cole played, but it didn't matter. He'd fled. He was the Monroe County Sheriff's problem now.

Phoenix remained an enigma. She had a legitimate excuse for not being on the boat today, but after yesterday's confrontation, was it feigned? Of course, most normal people wouldn't want to return to an endeavor that forced them to interact with armed smugglers. But frankly, Phoenix wasn't normal—and Mer desperately wanted to believe the professor had a lecture to present.

Doubt plagued her the rest of the dive. Even the sudden appearance of a rare Kemp Ridley sea turtle failed to lighten her mood.

Finally, enough time had elapsed for Mer to surface and she clambered aboard. Out of habit, she checked her air pressure. Because the first dive had been short and shallow, she hadn't breathed enough of her supply to warrant changing the tank. Even after the second dive, she still had nearly a third of her pressure left. Mer looped a bungee cord around the yoke of the tank to secure it to the makeshift tank rack, and peeled the wetsuit down to her waist. She'd break down her equipment on the way home, once this fiasco was finished.

"Ready?" Mer hoisted the bow anchor and the *Finders Keepers* bounced in the current.

"Yup. The blowers are going to need three anchors to make it look good."

"Tell me what to do," Mer said.

"Normally, we'd drop a buoy over the site as a marker, but it doesn't really matter where we end up."

"Could have told me this before I hoisted the bow anchor."

"You got a lot to learn, girlie. That one's set last." He squinted against the horizon. "Go ahead and drop the port anchor."

Mer lowered it into the water.

"We're going to pay out about a hundred and fifty feet of line. I got the line marked in fifty-foot increments. Let me know when it hits."

Mer called out the markers. "Done."

"Drop the starboard anchor. Same drill." He turned the boat toward port and goosed the engines. "Then move on up to the bow. When I tell you, pay out the bow anchor."

She positioned herself and waited for his command.

"Now," he shouted.

She dropped the third anchor.

He shut down the engines, and in the silence Mer heard waves slap against the hull.

"Grab port, I'll man starboard," Skipper said. "Now it's just a matter of taking in the lines 'til we're set good and steady."

When they finished, the three anchors formed an upside down T, with two angled off the stern and one in front of the bow.

"Now for the mailboxes. I'll winch them down. You'll need to lock 'em in place with cotter pins so they don't bounce."

"Okay." She studied the blowers as they lowered. "I give up. Where do the pins go?"

"Underwater. Put on your mask. You'll see the hole."

Great. She worked her arms through the wet neoprene, found her mask and jumped in. Without weight, the wetsuit increased her buoyancy and she flailed to stay under. She jammed the pin into the latch for the port blower. After a quick breath, she repeated the process on the starboard one.

"Anything else while I'm down here?"

"Not until we pack things up for the night."

The time had come. Mer climbed back on board and picked up the radio mic. She didn't know the name of Bart's boat. Winslet Chase might not even be monitoring the channel.

"No use getting all worked up," Skipper said. "Either they're out there or they're not."

She depressed the microphone talk button, waited a second, and spoke slowly, "*Finders Keepers, Finders Keepers, Finders Keepers,* calling *Picuda Bart, Picuda Bart, Picuda Bart.* Over."

The radio crackled with static, but no response. Two minutes later, she repeated the transmission. And then again after two more minutes. Nothing.

Disappointment soured her stomach. "Now what?"

"Wait fifteen minutes, try again."

The satellite phone Talbot had given them rang. Mer answered.

"We heard you loud and clear," Talbot said.

"No offense, but it wasn't you I was trying to reach."

"Bet you'll be plenty glad to see us when Picuda Bart shows up. Nice call sign, by the way."

"If I annoy him enough, he's bound to respond."

"I always do," Talbot said with a laugh. "We'll be monitoring, but if they show up unannounced, get us on the phone."

That possibility hadn't occurred to her. Bart had the data from the GPS tracker. He could be on his way this very moment.

"Dr. Cavallo?"

"I'm sorry, what?" Mer ran her fingers through her hair.

"No heroics. If any boat gets close, call us. They might be in something other than the Picuda."

"I'm just bait. This is your bailiwick. I just wish they'd show up so you can finish this."

Skipper threw his cup of sunflower shells into the trashcan and stood. He peered intently at the horizon.

Mer moved next to him, the phone still against her ear. "Hold on a second." She lowered the phone. "What do you see?"

Skipper raised his arm and pointed. "Girlie, best be careful what you wish for."

It took several seconds before the hull of the speedboat distinguished itself from the horizon.

Mer tightened her grip on the phone. "They're coming."

"Be there in a flash."

Talbot's voice was reassuring, but there was no doubt; the race was on, and the Picuda had a head start.

The racing boat drew closer, its engines screaming with speed. Three men crowded the cockpit. Two looked like modern-day bandits, wearing sunglasses and neck gaiters pulled up to mask their faces. Even so, she recognized Bart. He still wore his faded Mets cap. The captain sat at the helm. Winslet Chase? The fabric around his face hid any hint of a tribal tattoo. The third man was Oscar.

Mer tore her gaze away from the men to glance toward Tavernier Key. Talbot's boat was just a speck.

The Picuda won by a mile. The captain throttled back and waved. "Ahoy! A merry life and a short one," he shouted the pirate greeting. "I come bearing gifts."

Arrogant with an edge of menace. It had to be Chase.

Bart hauled Oscar to his feet. His hands were bound behind his back.

"This can't be good," Skipper muttered.

Bart forced Oscar to sit on the gunnel.

Mer sucked in a breath. "They wouldn't—"

Before she could complete the thought, Bart shoved the bound man. With no way to check his momentum, Oscar slammed into the ocean and disappeared under the surface.

"Bastard." Mer grabbed her fins and mask.

"Wait." Skipper seized her by the biceps. "They don't want him, but they may want you. Those engines hit you, only the sharks are gonna be happy."

Mer yanked free of Skipper's grasp. "He's going to drown."

Oscar surfaced. He tilted his head backward. Sputtered for air. His body bobbed to the uneven tempo of his wild kicking.

The captain craned in his seat and watched Oscar thrash. He raised his head toward the crew on the salvage boat. Even from behind dark glasses, Mer felt his piercing stare. "I'm here to collect my treasure."

He idled the Picuda closer to the *Finders Keepers*, narrowly missing Oscar.

Bart tossed a line at Skipper. "Permission to board," he said sarcastically.

Skipper made no effort to catch it. "And if I refuse?"

The captain, his face still covered, remained seated. He casually leveled a gun at Skipper's chest. "We're coming anyway."

The waves from the boat swamped Oscar and he started to choke. His head barely remained above water.

"The deal was the coin for Oscar." Mer removed the coin from her bootie, held it up, and then placed it on the workstation table. "I'm going to get him before he drowns."

Cautiously she moved toward her gear. If Oscar went under, she'd need the tank for the search. She shrugged into her BC and settled it onto her back. Her hands shook as she donned her equipment. She missed the buckle and cursed silently. When it clicked, she tightened the straps.

Skipper cut his eyes toward Mer, giving her time to sit on the transom before he reeled in the line. The Picuda bumped against the *Finders Keepers* as she entered the ocean.

She surfaced and oriented on Oscar. Fifty feet of choppy water separated them.

Out of the corner of her eye, she saw Bart jump from the Picuda to the deck of the salvage boat.

The patrol boat was coming, but Oscar needed her now. She closed the distance, but not soon enough. His head slipped underwater.

"No!" Mer dumped the air from her BC and descended.

The Picuda's engines churned the shallow water into a murky soup that cut visibility to nearly nothing but he must be close. She had to find him.

Oscar materialized in front of her like a mountain rising from the fog. His eyes were closed and his kicks feeble. She came up behind him, snugged her arm under his, and fought for the surface.

Their heads broke the water and Oscar choked a breath, gasping for air.

Mer removed her regulator. "I've got you. You're safe, now."

He continued to cough and retch.

"Trust me, Oscar." She cradled his head against her chest. "I'm right behind you. Listen to my voice. Everything will be all right."

His body relaxed.

Kicking backward toward the boat, she continued to talk to him. She tried to shield his face from splashes so he wouldn't panic again. "We're almost there. As soon as we're at the boat, I'm going to cut apart your wrists, okay? I'll need you to hold as still as you can."

He nodded.

She glanced over her shoulder. Bart was on the deck, toe-to-toe with Skipper.

Mer kicked the final few feet to the platform. The transom blocked her view of the men. She put Oscar's feet on the bottom rung of the ladder and unsheathed her dive knife. "Remember, keep still." She pinned his body against the ladder to stabilize him and then slid the knife between his wrists. A quick upward thrust cut the plastic tie.

Mer helped him up the ladder and then hoisted herself onto the swim platform.

He'd gotten onto his hands and knees, but couldn't manage more.

"Take a deep breath. You're okay now." She said the words aloud, hoping to convince them both.

"This is one coin," Bart shouted at Skipper. "Where are the rest?"

"Stay down," she told Oscar, and then peeked over the transom.

Bart raised his fist and Skipper dropped into a fighting stance. The captain of the Picuda trained his gun on Skipper.

Mer jumped up. "Skipper doesn't know. I'm the one who found them."

Oscar struggled to his feet next to her.

The patrol boat bore down on their port side.

Bart heard it, too. He spun and then snapped back and decked Skipper. "It's a setup!" He turned to Mer and pulled a knife from his waistband. "You bitch!" He jumped toward her.

Oscar pushed Mer, placing himself between her and Bart. She stumbled sideways. Clawed for balance.

Heard a gunshot.

Fell.

And the ocean swallowed her whole.

41

H er mask flooded from the force of the impact and the regulator dangled behind her as she sank. The retort of a second shot echoed through the water. She flinched and fought the urge to surface.

Air.

Leaning to the right, she brushed her hand against her thigh and then swept her arm in a wide arc. The hose settled into the crook of her elbow and she shoved the regulator into her mouth, purged the water from it, and drew a big breath.

The engines of the Picuda roared to life, stirring up the ocean. Blinded, she readjusted the mask, then tilted her head back and exhaled through her nose to displace the water. The *Finders Keepers* floated above her. She was under the swim platform. Safe from the three massive outboard engine props that minced the water.

With any luck, the patrol boat—

The water around her exploded. The fury ripped the regulator from her mouth and stole her mask. The shriek of the *Finders Keepers* engines filled her head. Crowded out reason.

Sand and debris pelted her. The prop wash pinned her to the seafloor. Held her captive.

The blowers.

She didn't dare open her eyes. Relentlessly, water and sand pounded against her. The pressure knocked the air from her lungs. Like an underwater hurricane, she was trapped in a maelstrom.

Mer plunged her hands into the sand. Her shoulders bunched and she drew herself forward, muscles straining. She needed air. Her diaphragm pulsed. She knew it was a matter of seconds before instinct overpowered logic and she inhaled water.

She anchored herself with one hand and swept her other hand behind her. No regulator. Nothing. Mer forced her hand upward. She fought against the pressure until she felt the yoke of her tank. Grabbed the low-pressure hose and drew it through her fingers until she found the regulator. Shoved it in her mouth. And then she bit down—hard—so not to lose it again.

Her fingers hit the purge valve. Blasted the water from her mouthpiece.

She drew a breath.

Then another.

The mouthpiece fluttered against her lips from the constant energy that swirled around her.

She clawed her way forward, inch by inch. Breath after breath. Deep and rapid.

Without a mask, she couldn't read her gauges, but she knew she'd sucked the tank nearly dry.

Which meant she had to surface.

And face the man who had just tried to kill her.

The water roiled. Before she could surface, she had to free herself from the crush of the blowers. She kept her eyes closed to protect them from the whirling debris. Her progress was slow, but at last the pressure abated.

The cacophony created by the blowers prevented her from discerning other noise—which meant she could be swimming directly into the whirling props of the Picuda or even the patrol boat. Ideally, she wanted to surface under the bow of the salvage boat, tucked in close so that nobody topside would see her. Then she could figure out what the hell had just happened and what fresh dangers awaited her.

There had been two gunshots. Bart had a knife. Even now Skipper and Oscar could be injured. She needed to get back on the boat.

Drawing a breath got harder. She had one, maybe two, breaths left in the tank. She risked opening her eyes to orient herself. Floating particulates and her unbound hair obscured everything but the fact that there was nothing above her. She had no idea how far she was from the boat. Or how long she'd be exposed before she could hide.

The blowers finally stopped. The quiet disoriented her even more than the noise.

She sucked in one last breath.

Out of options, she kicked toward the light.

Mer surfaced on the port side of the *Finders Keepers,* about ten feet from the hull. She drew a breath and submerged again, swimming the short distance underwater. Her hand brushed the hull and she stayed as close to the boat as she could without clanking any of her gear against it. Slowly, she raised her head out of the water.

The wind had increased and the boat bounced in the chop. She kept one hand against the hull, afraid to push too far away from the boat. She strained to listen. Her heart pounded against her ribs with such force she was certain it would give away her hiding spot.

Still touching the hull, she edged up to the bow.

Until she knew who had control of the boat, she didn't want to announce herself. The only thing she had going for her was an element of surprise. And that wouldn't buy her much. She took stock. Her dive knife had survived the storm and was still attached by its sheath to her BC. Other than the fish identification slate she had in her pocket, that was it. She'd lost her mask, snorkel, and surface marker buoy.

A shadow fell on the water. Fingers wrapped around the bow railing above her.

Her heart leaped into her throat.

At last a voice broke through her fear. Female, but unintelligible.

Silently, Mer shimmied around the bow to the starboard side. The Picuda was gone. In its place was the patrol boat.

Another voice, male this time. "Girlie's tough. She'll be up."

Skipper's voice had never sounded so good.

"I'm here!"

Detective Talbot leaned over the railing. "Thank God. Are you okay?"

"I think so." She'd been too busy to check for injuries.

"Told you," Skipper said.

The patrol boat blocked her way and she retraced her path around the *Finders Keepers* until she arrived at the stern. Talbot stood on the swim platform. Even though he was in shorts, it was the first time she'd seen him in a uniform. He reached over to help her to the ladder. Concern creased his face. "No bullshit now. You're sure you're not injured?"

She handed him her fins and pulled herself up the final step. "I'm fine."

Bart sat with his hands cuffed behind his back and his legs straight out in front of him. Buckets and equipment had been knocked over, and the deck looked as if they'd landed a thrashing sailfish. Gina knelt next to a motionless man.

"Oscar." The word escaped Mer's mouth as a moan.

She sat on the transom and swung her legs around, unbuckling her BC as she went. Shrugging the vest off one shoulder, she swung the tank to the side and dropped it on the deck. She fell to her knees next to the unconscious man.

His T-shirt had been cut away, but blood stained the white cloth. Gina pressed a bandage against his upper chest just below the shoulder joint. An oxygen mask covered his face, but his breath barely fogged the inside, and underneath it his skin was ashen.

"How bad?" she croaked.

Gina avoided her eyes. "Gunshot wound. No exit wound. Gloves are in there." The deputy chucked her chin toward the open first-aid kit. "I need you to watch him for a minute. Okay?"

Mer nodded. "Whatever you need." The latex gloves tugged at her wet skin. She rolled her hand onto the bandage as Gina rolled her hand off. Mer had seen her fair share of trauma—living on a research vessel, everything short of surgery was taken care of on board. But gunshot wounds were given short shrift in training. Call for help, stop the bleeding, and treat for shock. In that order.

"We need to get him to a hospital," Mer said.

Gina stood. "Helicopter's *en route*." She turned toward Talbot. "Let's get Kingston onto the other boat before the bird gets here."

Mer leaned over and grabbed another bandage and applied it on top of the saturated one under her hand. At least it wasn't a sucking chest wound, but it still precluded raising his legs to treat for shock. She drew the first aid-kit closer and rifled through the contents. Her hand settled on a space blanket and she tore the package open with her teeth.

Talbot dragged Bart to his feet. "Don't do anything stupid. That man dies and you're on the hook for murder."

Bart stepped onto the gunnel of the salvage boat. "I didn't shoot him."

Talbot handed Bart off to Gina, who latched onto his arm and drew him into the patrol boat. "Might as well have," she snapped.

Mer attended Oscar. Her gloved hands shook as she laid two fingers against his neck and felt for his pulse.

Skipper shuttled back and forth between the deck and V-berth, stowing fenders, lines—anything that could become a projectile—and lashing everything else in place.

"It's going to feel like a hurricane when the helicopter comes in." He collected the first-aid kit, and drew the space blanket off Oscar. "Don't need anything fouling their engines." He stowed everything in the V-berth and secured the hatch.

The rhythmic thump of helicopter blades made Mer search the sky. *There.*

The pilot hailed Talbot on the radio to coordinate the approach.

The detective hung up the mic. "It's about to get really loud." Talbot drew Skipper aside. "Gina's not a captain."

"Looks like you better get on your own boat then, leave me to mine."

"The Stokes litter—"

"Boy, I got this." Skipper unwound one of the two lines tethering the boats together and held on until Talbot unlashed the other and jumped into the patrol boat.

The helicopter approached from the stern and angled to give the pilot the best view of the deck. The rotor wash whipped Mer's hair and she threw herself prostrate across Oscar's body to protect him. The noise and swirl of energy felt like being trapped under the blowers all over again.

The pilot backed off a bit and then hovered about fifteen feet over the water. A crewman wearing a helmet, harness, and flotation device jumped from the copter into the water and swam to the boat. Aboard, he approached Mer.

"Gunshot wound, shallow respiration, thready pulse," she shouted.

He asked a few more questions and signaled the crew chief. The helicopter altered its position, hovered over their port side, and lowered a sled-like object identical to the rescue litter they'd used on the research vessel.

The medic leaned close to her ear and yelled. "They're going to dip the Stokes litter and then touch it to the side of the boat. Do *not* touch the litter before it's grounded, or we'll be taking two people to the hospital. Understood?"

She nodded.

"Okay. I'm going to leave you for just a moment."

The litter bumped against the hull. The medic reached over and guided it onto the deck and disconnected it from the hoist hook.

"Captain!" the medic shouted. "I need your help."

Skipper stepped forward.

"We'll treat him in the air, but I need your help getting him secured on the litter."

He positioned the Stokes litter next to Oscar then motioned for Mer. "The Cap'n and I will lift him. I need you to push the litter so the backboard is underneath him." He positioned himself at Oscar's head and directed Skipper to the feet. Together, they lifted the injured man far enough for Mer to maneuver the Stokes litter into position. The medic secured several straps across Oscar's body, and signaled the crew.

A moment later the litter was hooked. The winch took up the slack and the medic guided it off the deck. The litter spun like a leaf dangling from a web until it disappeared into the dark maw of the bay door. Once they had Oscar safely aboard, the line dropped again to pick up the crewman.

The helicopter began moving before the medic was completely inside. He scrambled in, the bay door closed, and the timbre of the rotors changed as the helicopter gained speed. Mer's ears rang with the *whomp whomp whomp* as the copter disappeared into the sun.

"They're going to want us to follow them in." Skipper glanced over his shoulder at the patrol boat. "I'm guessing they'll need statements, and some fool will want to take a look at the boat. Even though their evidence just got blown halfway to the Bahamas."

"I suppose they will." For the first time, she noticed his swollen cheek. "Are you okay?"

He simply grunted.

She peeled off her bloody latex gloves and stared at the horizon, trying to regroup. The patrol boat bobbed in the chop. Talbot had his man. Oscar was no longer in the clutches of smugglers. Yet this wasn't how it was supposed to play out.

She closed her eyes, but instead of darkness she saw Oscar's pale face. This whole fiasco had started and ended with a single coin and a man's quest to make his father proud.

But she'd undertaken her own quest. She'd sought to identify the person who had destroyed her home, and along with it, her chance to create a normal life.

Or so she'd told herself. What she'd really wanted was to identify someone to *blame* for her failure to make a home in Key Largo.

And that honor belonged to her.

42

It was after seven o'clock when Mer arrived home, barely able to breathe through the tightness of her chest. Night noise chattered around her, but it only served to make her feel more alone.

Oscar had protected Mer from Bart's knife, only to be shot by Chase.

Ironically, if it hadn't been for Bart turning on the blowers, the patrol boat would have roared right past the *Finders Keepers* and chased the Picuda, but Talbot had spotted the frothing water and knew something was wrong. Confronted by two deputies with guns, Bart had surrendered.

Once they'd returned to shore, Gina had taken Mer's statement and insisted medics check her for injuries. Meanwhile, Talbot had transported Bart to the Sheriff's Office to be interviewed and booked. The crime scene investigator had taken several hours to process the boat. By the time Skipper and Mer returned to the dock, the shop had closed, but Bijoux remained to greet them. She'd wanted to know the details of the day.

The Picuda had vanished. Winslet Chase was in the wind.

The light outside Mer's door had burned out, casting the area in shadows. A palm frond scratched across the driveway and jangled her already frayed nerves. Key in hand, she approached the door. The handle and deadbolt still glimmered with newness.

A small box wrapped with an ornate metallic bow leaned against the threshold.

A whimper rose to her lips and quickly morphed into a growl. She spun around, trying to pierce the silvered moonscape and ferret out an enemy that came and went as silently as smoke.

She raced to the end of the driveway. Puddles of light from the street lamps illuminated an empty road. On the other side, the boats in the canal creaked and strained against their lines. Water slapped hulls. Nothing out of the ordinary.

Except the package at her door.

Winslet Chase.

She stepped behind her car and studied the box. Unlike the carton the statue had arrived in, this was small: about eight inches long, five inches wide, and two inches thick. The container didn't appear to have any embellishments other than the bow, a wide silver ribbon that shimmered like broken glass in the moon shadows. She should call Talbot. So said her rational mind. But it was her limbic brain in control at the moment. And it was pissed.

She marched to the door and kicked the package aside. It slid onto its back with a slap.

And then it began to ring.

The phone rang thirteen times, before Mer's pulse settled into a rhythm that wasn't life threatening—a definite improvement over explosive, but her heart still beat at twice its normal rate.

She stared at the package. The contents seemed self-evident. The ringtone had been programmed to mimic an old-fashioned ringer, the kind her folks used to have hanging on the kitchen wall.

Winslet Chase wanted to talk.

Well, she wasn't ready yet.

The phone fell silent.

Rational thought returned in snippets, but the idea pushing all others aside was the need to notify Detective Talbot. With a sigh, she grabbed her own phone from her backpack and dialed his number. The call went to voicemail. She tried Deputy Mercurio. Same thing. Not surprising—today's events must have required a fair amount of paperwork. She tapped the phone against her chin and then dialed the non-emergency line of the Sheriff's Office.

The dispatcher answered in a rush, confirmed Mer didn't have an emergency, and put her on hold. A Caribbean steel band rendition of "Let it Snow" played in her ear.

Finally the dispatcher returned. "What can I do for you?"

"I'm trying to get in touch with Detective Talbot."

"Let me transfer you to his voicemail."

"No, wait," Mer said. "I've already left him a message. I need to file a report."

"What's the problem?"

"Someone left a strange package on my doorstep."

"Did you recently order anything?" She sounded harried.

"No."

"Are there any markings on it? Shipping labels?"

"No markings. Just a bow."

"A bow. You mean, like a gift?"

"Exactly," Mer said.

"You want to have a deputy to respond because you got a gift?"

Put like that Mer could understand the dispatcher's skepticism.

"I've had a spate of trouble lately." Which was an understatement, but she desperately wanted to avoid recounting the entire affair to the dispatcher. "Look. Detective Talbot knows all about it. He wanted me to report anything unusual."

That seemed to get through to the woman. "We've got a major incident unfolding. It might be several hours before a deputy can respond."

"Fine." Mer gave her the address and hung up.

Now what? Sleep was definitely out of the question. There was no way she'd be able to relax, knowing the box was outside her front door. She glanced up at Selkie's. Dark. Not that asking him for help was an option anymore.

That left opening the damn box.

She rummaged through the back of the Subaru for her first-aid kit. For the second time that day, she donned surgical gloves.

The reason eluded her, but she didn't want to take the package inside her home. Instead, she pushed aside the medical kit and a blanket to create space in the hatchback. Carefully, she set the package inside the car. It hardly weighed anything. The dim interior light danced on the ribbon as she slid it off the box.

She paused. Talbot would probably give her holy hell tomorrow. But her curiosity won out. He'd get over it.

Or not.

Without the ribbon, nothing remained to secure the box. All she had to do was lift the lid. Her hands hovered over the edges. Small as it was, all manner of unsavory items could be inside with the phone.

Schrödinger's cat.

She shook her head. There was no cat—dead or alive. There never was. It was only a thought experiment to explain quantum superposition. This was a box. Containing a phone.

Steeling herself, she lifted the lid.

A phone.

It seemed anticlimactic. After all, she'd heard it ring.

Nestled in a swath of fabric, the small flip phone reminded her of a model she used to own. This one was dark gray and had a message screen. The screen blinked.

She had a text message.

43

The message icon pulsed bright red. Mer stared at it.

Finally, she opened the phone. The text originated from a blocked telephone number and consisted of a short message and a string of numbers.

Call me, Winslet.

It wasn't as catchy as "Call me Ishmael," but then again, Winslet didn't require two hundred thousand words to get his point across—he wasn't through with her.

She stared at the numbers as if they held the key to his whereabouts. The 305 area code serviced an area that stretched from Key West to Miami. Considering he'd left the damn thing on her doorstep, there was a good chance he was within those boundaries as well. But why call from a blocked number when he gave her his number in the text?

Nothing ventured, nothing gained. She dialed the number. Almost immediately, she regretted it and hung up, but not before the line rang once. Talbot would have a conniption. It was bad enough she'd opened the box; placing the call would probably push him over the edge.

Still.... Today hadn't played out as she'd planned. Oscar had been shot. Skipper punched. This was an opportunity for Mer to finish things without jeopardizing anyone else.

One problem. She was vastly outgunned.

No doubt about it, she should have left the box unopened. Her Pandora-level curiosity had served her well in science, but this wasn't an experiment. Mer collected the ribbon, cardboard, and phone. She carried them into the house and locked the door behind her.

It was too late for coffee, so she set down the phone and filled the kettle for tea. She needed sleep, but she was too amped up and at some point a deputy would arrive. Maybe the chamomile would soothe her frazzled nerves.

She dropped into a wicker chair and waited for the water to boil. To the casual observer, her home showed no signs of being violated. But the gouged desk, the torn curtain, and the bent hinge on the cabinet door—the scars were there, if one looked closely.

The kettle whistled and she startled, catching herself rubbing her thigh.

Enough of the maudlin thoughts. Returning to the kitchen, she dropped the last tea sachet into her Gryffindor mug. The boiling water hissed out of the spout and splattered as she poured. Inhaling the tea's delicate scent, she waited for it to work its magic and override the crush of emotions.

Of course, it might help if she actually believed in magic before she tried to summon it.

The wind strengthened and even inside, she heard it tear through the palms.

Air currents in Key Largo were a far different phenomenon than the wind she'd grown up with in Santa Barbara. There, the Santa Anas blew for days through the canyons in maniacal gusts of heat that made everything brittle and dry—chaparral, skin, and nerves, alike. The Santa Anas howled with heat, inflaming passions until they combusted. Here, the wind felt heavy, saturated with warmth. It knocked into things with a physical force, battering houses, whipping palms, filling sails, and raising waves.

Despite its destructive power, Mer had an affinity for wind. She admired its power and enjoyed when it tugged on her hair. The wind buoyed her spirits aloft, even as it reminded her of her marvelous insignificance.

She removed the tea bag. The first sip burned her mouth. The gift phone rang again and she jerked so violently, she splashed hot tea on her hand. Should she answer it and play by his rules, or annoy him by ignoring the call?

She opted for the latter. Her mother would call her petty. She preferred to consider it a dignified silence. Plus, there was a good chance that if the deputy didn't get there soon, she'd cave in and call, just to appease her curiosity.

To distract herself, she opened the browser on her own phone and searched for the local news channel. The dispatcher had mentioned a major incident. Maybe that would give her an idea if she should wait for the deputy or go to bed.

A red "Breaking News" banner scrolled across the top of the Keys News website. Mer clicked the video link and turned up the volume. Wendy Wheeler. Great.

"The Monroe County Sheriff's Office tactical team have surrounded the home of famed treasure hunter Winslet Chase after a boat involved in an at-sea shooting was discovered docked at his northern Key Largo property."

Thank goodness Mer had put down the tea.

She backed the video up and started it again. The wind whipped Wendy's perfect bob into a not-so-perfect snarl, and she had to hold her notepad up to protect the microphone.

"Law enforcement has the area cordoned off, but we're here in a neighbor's backyard to bring you exclusive footage of the standoff that began early this evening." The camera panned away from Wendy and focused on the Picuda in the canal behind the sprawling home. Off screen, she continued speaking. "If you're just tuning in with us, we're on the scene of a SWAT standoff with famed treasure hunter Winslet Chase. Few official details regarding the incident are known at this time. We spoke via telephone to a member of the Sheriff's Office who declined to give his name because he's not authorized to speak on behalf of the department. Unofficially, the deputy said Winslet Chase is wanted in connection with the shooting of a rival treasure hunter in the marine sanctuary. No word on that man's condition."

Contradictory emotions flooded her body—anger over the senseless shooting of Oscar and triumph that Winslet had nowhere to run and would soon be in custody.

The camera cut back to Wendy. She snapped the microphone to her mouth. "Lots of unanswered questions remain. Has Winslet the treasure hunter turned rogue pirate? Will he parlay with negotiators, strike his colors, or abandon ship to salvage his reputation? Check back for updates on the continuing saga. Live from Key Largo, I'm Wendy Wheeler, the key to Keys News."

Vintage Wendy. She could have her own drinking game: a shot for every silly question asked.

Annoyance morphed into relief. His house was surrounded. It would be hard—perhaps impossible—for him to escape. Winslet would get tired or come to his senses. Even now, he was probably arranging for some high-priced attorney. One thing was certain. She wouldn't be talking to a deputy about the gift on her doorstep anytime soon.

She picked up the flip phone. Her rational self knew calling Winslet didn't rank as one of her brighter ideas. She set the phone back down and spun it in small circles on the table while she watched the news footage again. Were Talbot and Gina there? It was too dark to tell. She hoped they weren't in the line of fire.

She spun the phone again. She had a direct line to Winslet Chase. He'd had a reason for giving her the phone. Maybe he'd listen to her. The phone wobbled to a standstill. Before she could stop herself, she flipped open the phone and dialed the number.

The phone rang, but no one answered. Apparently, the SWAT team had his undivided attention.

She finished her tea and rinsed the mug, and then dialed the number again. Still no answer. She turned off the light and headed toward the bathroom to get ready for bed.

A gust of wind rattled her bedroom slider, followed by a crash of wood on the concrete patio. She peeked around the curtain. The mermaid statue still gazed wistfully toward the ocean, but one of the patio chairs had blown over and its cushion was bumping its way across the yard, making a break for the ocean.

Mer unlocked the slider door and wind howled through the crack. She slid it open and a sharp gust of wind ripped through the curtains and rifled the papers on her desk. She stepped outside and closed the door behind her.

Clouds skittered across the waning moon and dappled the lawn in ever-changing shadows. The cushion blew into the darkness toward the kayak launch. Mer darted across the lawn, the grass chilly under her bare feet.

Moonlight broke through the clouds and Mer stopped. Stared.

The pillow rested against the hull of a beached kayak.

She had a visitor.

44

Mer took an involuntary step backward and retreated into the shadow of the tall hedge. Everything looked sharper. The wind toyed with a sea-grape leaf, tossing the broad oval end-over-end across the lawn in a slow-motion dance. But Mer's mind moved at lightning speed.

The kayak was empty. No paddle. No life jacket. But its presence meant someone had been in her yard recently. They could be watching her at this very moment. About forty feet of no-man's land yawned between her and the sliding door—a door obscured by shadows.

She could creep along the hedge, but the prowler might have slipped into her home while she was outside. She shivered. Had the wind really knocked over the patio chair?

Selkie's home remained dark, and getting to it would require cutting across a moonlit swath of lawn, and then running up the fence line to the driveway. But then what? Her cellphone was on her nightstand.

The hedge at her back was an impenetrable barrier of woven foliage that hid a cinder block wall. No escape there. She eyed the ocean. The seabed was a combination of coconut-sized rocks, depressions, and sea grass. No problem to kayak over it—provided one had a paddle—but not deep enough to swim in. It would be hell to walk across without breaking an ankle or falling.

Her best bet would be to shimmy along the shadows as far as she could, and then make a break for the driveway. Run to a neighbor's house to call the police.

She slid one foot forward and inched her way toward the house.

The beam of a flashlight bobbed along her driveway, coming from the street. She sucked in her breath and pressed herself against the hedge.

Three knocks, rapid and authoritative.

She didn't dare move. The wind filled the ensuing silence.

Another three knocks. "Monroe County Sheriff's Office," a male voice said loudly.

Relief made her legs weak. "I'm back here!"

One of the branches caught in her hair. She yanked it free and stepped into the moonlight, walking toward the driveway. The deputy came around to the patio and trained his flashlight beam on her face. She raised her hand. "Do you mind? I can't see."

"Sorry." His footsteps neared, but he didn't lower the flashlight.

The voice sounded familiar. He snapped his chewing gum.

The gum. Oh, no, no, *no!* She spun. Deputy Cole grabbed her in a wristlock and drove her face down into the ground. The flashlight landed on the grass beside them. His leather belt creaked as he moved. She twisted. The handle of his gun glinted above the holster.

"Good to see you again, Doc." He jammed his knee into the small of her back and knelt, his boot close to her face. "Quit resisting. You're under arrest."

She spit grass out of her mouth. "Bullshit." She tried to buck him off, but he cranked on her wrist until she thought it would break.

"I figured you'd be too smart to fall for that." He increased the weight on her back until she could barely breathe. "Dumb enough to believe a deputy would be knocking at your door, though."

He must not know she'd called 9-1-1. She had to stall. *No.* She had to get away.

"Think about your career," Mer said. "You don't want to do this."

"Wrong again." He snapped his gum. "If you're as smart as Talbot says, you'll tell me where the treasure is."

"There is no treasure."

He applied more pressure to the twist lock. "Next time you lie, I'm going to break your wrist."

"I gave it to Bart."

"You gave him a single coin. Where's the rest of it?"

One piece of the puzzle clicked into place. "That was you sitting at the helm of the boat." Not Winslet. *Cole* was the one who'd shot Oscar. "But the boat...the police have Winslet's place surrounded."

"Who better to take the blame? It was easy enough to leave the boat there. Kayak over here. And when they search his place, what do you suppose the deputies will find?"

"The coin you stole from the evidence locker."

"A gold star for the doctor." His weight shifted. He opened something on his belt and metal clinked. "I know the coin you gave Bart isn't the same one I had. That means you found more. I'm only going to ask nicely one time. Where did you find the treasure?"

Dread pulsed through her body. She had one chance. She had to make it count.

Overriding every rational impulse, she let the tension drain from her limbs, making it appear that she'd surrendered. "Don't hurt me. I'll tell you what you want to know."

"Maybe Talbot was right about you after all."

His grip on her wrist loosened ever so slightly. It would have to be enough. Using the ground as leverage, she tensed every muscle in her body into an explosive twisting buck. The force knocked Cole off balance. His hand landed inches from her face. Wrenching free of his weight, she rolled onto her back and drew both legs toward her chest and kicked. With all the fear-infused power she could muster, she drove her feet into his side, and sent him sprawling. She crab-walked backward and then sprang to her feet and sprinted toward the house.

With a snarl, Cole barreled into her from behind. The full force of his weight slammed her into the ground and her head barely missed the edge of the concrete patio. Pain erupted in her knee. She kept fighting.

He yanked her left arm away from her body and slapped a handcuff against her wrist bone and ratcheted it closed. Mer sobbed and drew her other arm under her chest.

He punched her in the ribs. "Stop fighting. You're under arrest."

Headlights raked across the driveway. A car door opened. "What the hell? Let go of her!" Selkie commanded.

"He's got a gun!" she screamed. "Get down!"

Selkie charged toward them, his body a clear target silhouetted against the headlights.

Cole released her arm. He shifted and the gun slid out of his holster with a whisper that roared louder than the wind.

Mer twisted. Desperate, she windmilled her arm toward the deputy. The empty handcuff bashed into his cheek.

Cole raised the gun and fired. The muzzle blast burned against the night sky. The retort nearly deafened her.

Selkie stutter-stepped, but kept coming. He drove his shoulder into the deputy and knocked him away from Mer.

Both men regained their balance. Selkie lunged forward, and they merged into a tangle of limbs fighting for control of the gun.

Mer grabbed Cole's shoulder. He snapped his elbow back, striking her in the face. Blinded by tears, she stumbled backward and crashed into the teak table.

A second gunshot severed the night.

She watched in horror as Selkie crumpled to his knees. Cole raised the gun and pointed it at Selkie's head. Instinctively, she grabbed the mermaid statue and swung it like a bat. It connected against Cole's skull with a sickening thud. He fell to the ground, senseless.

Mer dropped the statue and pried the gun from of the deputy's hand. Selkie had collapsed, his eyes closed. His car headlights spotlighted the pulse in his throat. It was beating impossibly fast.

She lifted his T-shirt and stifled a gasp. A gaping wound tore through his side.

"Can you hear me?" She pulled off her own shirt and wadded it against the wound. He didn't move. "I have to call for help. I'll be right back." His stillness and silence frightened her more than the fight had.

Her legs felt disconnected from her body as she stumbled into the house. The buttons of her phone blurred and it took four tries to enter the emergency number. The call connected, but the dispatcher's voice had an underwater quality to it.

Mer returned to Selkie within moments. He hadn't moved. Her knees buckled and Mer collapsed next to him. His pulse had grown faint. She couldn't see his chest move. A weight crushed her heart. "Hurry," she whispered, willing the ambulance to arrive.

Mer tried to staunch the bleeding with pressure. "Don't you dare die on me. You hear me? We've got unfinished business, you and I." Tears dripped off her chin.

Wind swirled Mer's hair. The headlights burned behind her and her shadow crawled toward the ocean as if trying to escape into the restless water.

"I love you," she said. But he couldn't hear her.

45

Mer sat in the empty waiting room, in a chair pulled beneath the window, with an icepack on her knee. She hadn't bothered to turn on the light. Too many thoughts crowded her mind, all of them screaming for attention.

"You know you should get your leg looked at." Detective Talbot stood silhouetted in the doorway. He still wore the uniform shorts and polo shirt he'd worn on the boat. Fatigue weathered his face.

"Not until he's out of surgery." She drew her good leg up to her chest. Her other knee didn't bend. "Not until I know he's going to be okay."

"It could be hours."

"It doesn't matter if it's days," she snapped, and then drew a deep breath. "I'm sorry. I..." She rubbed her hand over her face, wishing it were a cloth that would wipe the slate clean. "Did you have more questions?"

He shook his head. "I didn't want you to wait alone." He pointed to another chair. "May I?"

He waited until she nodded, and then dragged the dilapidated chair to the window. His gun belt scraped the armrest as he sat.

They both stared at the window. The darkness outside reflected the light that seeped in from the hallway behind them and transformed the pane into a mirror. Concern etched Talbot's face.

Mer looked away. "How's Leroy's wife?"

"She's fine," Talbot said. "It was a bogus call to get Leroy out of the way."

"Smart," she said. "And Oscar?"

"He came through the surgery just fine."

They descended into silence again. Someone was watching television and the sitcom's laugh track bled through the wall.

"How did you get to the house so fast?" Mer finally asked.

"Bart."

She picked at the grass stain on her shorts. "I don't understand."

"Bart wasn't much for talking. But Gina came in during the interview. A tip had come through Crime Stoppers about the Picuda."

"Cole reported it to throw everyone off his trail."

"We didn't know it was a diversion then. Anyway, I used the information against Bart. Told him it was just a matter of time before we had Chase in custody. Then we'd get the real story and any chance he had to cut a deal would disappear."

"That worked?"

"Bart turned green. I thought it was because he figured Chase was going to rat him out. Wrong. He realized Cole had set up Chase, and Bart didn't want to be next. After that, I couldn't shut him up."

"So all along, it was the two of them?"

"I can't go into the details, but yes. Cole turned a blind eye to Bart's activities in exchange for a kickback."

"A symbiotic relationship," she said. "One is an apex predator, while the other feeds off the scraps, but both benefit from the interaction."

"Sounds accurate."

She readjusted the icepack. "But that still doesn't explain how you beat the medics there."

"I was *en route* before you called dispatch." His police radio crackled with a transmission. He paused to listen and then continued. "At the end of the interview, Bart revealed Cole's intentions to murder you. I called. You didn't answer."

"You thought the worst."

"I feared the worst, but I should have known better," he said. "Cole seriously underestimated you."

The thud of the statue hitting his skull shivered up her arms, the memory as sickening as when it had actually happened. "He's dead, isn't he?" But she knew the answer.

"Yes."

She locked eyes with him in the window's reflection. "Please let me see Selkie before you arrest me."

The air conditioner clicked on for another cycle and a muted phone rang at the nurses' station. Finally, he cleared his throat. "I'm not here to arrest you, Mer."

It was the first time he'd called her by name.

"There are a lot of moving parts to this investigation, and it's going to take some time to wrap up, but no. Cole was a dangerous man who was going to kill you. You're not the bad guy here."

Relief stripped her of her ability to speak for a moment, but then she noticed his stricken face. "I'm sorry. This must be hard for you. You worked with him."

"He betrayed a lot of people who trusted him." His jaw hardened. "No one hates a dirty cop more than the cops who wear the same badge."

"Cole pointed the gun at..." Mer said. "He was going to kill..." The image of the gun at Selkie's head overwhelmed her. Tears ran unchecked down her cheeks. "Selkie saved my life."

"You repaid the favor."

She ached. "I never got to tell him I love him."

"He knows."

"How can you say that?"

Talbot broke eye contact. "Because I told him." He cleared his throat. "You're shivering. I'll go get us some coffee." Without waiting for her response, he rose and headed for the door.

"Josh?" She whispered.

He stopped in the threshold.

"Thank you," she said.

46

Mer stuck a pencil down the air splint on her leg in a futile search for the itch that was robbing her of her last vestiges of sanity. After everything else that had happened over the last several weeks, going crazy just seemed like the cherry on a demented multi-tiered cake. Or was that icing? She repositioned the pencil and rammed it down for another try. *Non-itch splint, my ass.*

Limping, she'd dragged the Adirondack chair into the shade of the palm. It was an uncharacteristically cool day. Selkie would be wearing his Annapolis sweatshirt. Navy was playing in the Armed Forces Bowl. Of course, blazing heat wouldn't prevent him from showing support for his alma mater.

The game started in a few hours. Until then, Selkie had said he needed to catch up on some business.

Which left her staring at the Atlantic.

Their relationship had entered a new stage. Time would tell what that meant, exactly. In the short term, he would try to protect her, as he was wont to do, and she would remind him she was self-sufficient, as she was wont. Meanwhile their guardian angels would get together and drink.

A large wave hit the boulders and spray shot into the air. Somewhere in that vast ocean the Thirteenth Galleon lay hidden.

The sea had reclaimed her treasure. At least for now. Both known coins had been recovered. One from Bart and the other from Winslet Chase. Phoenix had told Mer that the State had revoked the exploration permit for Conch Reef in order to evaluate the galleon's cultural and archeological significance. She'd used air quotes around the reason. In theory, Mer had a stake in the coins she'd found. But Mer agreed with Oscar. They needed to be in a museum. For now, the Monroe County Sheriff's Office was again the portrait dollars' custodian.

The Cuban government had already petitioned to have the original coin returned—along with their disgraced archivist. Oscar hadn't yet learned whether the current immigration laws would allow him to remain in the States, nor the legal repercussions of his actions. Regardless, he was still recuperating in Miami, and in no condition to travel.

She'd never forget the yearning she'd seen on his face the day they'd spoken at the church. All he'd wanted to do was make his father proud. Instead, he'd jeopardized his ability to ever return home.

A car door slammed. The slap of flip-flops grew louder, and then ceased. Someone knocked on her door. "Mer?"

She recognized Bijoux's voice and relaxed. "Back here."

Bijoux rounded the corner wearing a rainbow-hued caftan, an armful of bangles, and oven mitts. She carried a casserole dish. "I figured you were home. I brought over some of my famous *poulet creole*. It's a Haitian stewed-chicken dish. I put the Scotch bonnet on the side for you sensitive types."

"I don't think I've ever been accused of being sensitive."

"A Scotch bonnet pepper is hotter than a habanero."

"Who knew I was so delicate?"

Bijoux smiled. "May I put it there?" She used her foot to point toward the outdoor dining table.

The table looked empty without the mermaid statue. For the unforeseeable future, the Sheriff's Office considered it evidence.

"Sure." Mer pulled herself out of the sloping deck chair. "I'll get plates."

"Sit. I'll get them."

Before Mer could argue, her friend disappeared around the corner.

The scent of the dish flavored the air, at once sweet and spicy. Her mouth began to water.

When Bijoux returned, she held a box overflowing with decorative paper plates, cups, and napkins. Leroy and his wife, Maggie, dogged her heels. Each of them bore pie totes.

Maggie bustled forward and claimed a portion of the table. "I hope you like cherry. But if not, I've baked a Key lime, too. Oh, and of course, pumpkin. Two actually."

Gabby flounced into the backyard and dropped an aluminum foil-covered dish on the table. She threw her arms around Mer in an enthusiastic hug that nearly knocked Mer off her good foot. "Hey, Dr. Badass."

Gabby's father followed at a more sedate pace.

Mer looked from one face to another. "Would somebody please tell me what's going on?"

Josh Talbot raised a wine-carrier containing six bottles. "Isn't it obvious?" He set them down and then looked toward her neighbor's house. "Selkie upstairs? I should check the score."

"The game hasn't started yet," she shouted to his retreating back. But then the sound of even more cars in the driveway distracted her.

"Hey, Seahorse. Look who I ran into at the airport."

Her brother's voice made it into the yard before he did.

"Franky!" Mer hobbled forward and then froze. "Mom? Pops? What—" Tears filled her eyes and she couldn't finish before she found herself enveloped in the arms of her family.

"We were in the neighborhood," her father said. "Thought we'd drop by for dinner."

Mer felt dizzy as if she'd somehow found herself back at the Bilge and had two shots warming her belly. "How did you—?"

"I made your favorite," her mother said.

The aroma of caramelized honey took Mer back to family holidays. "When did you have time to make candied yams?" She squinted at her mother. "How long have you been here?"

"Honey," her mother lovingly smoothed an errant curl out of Mer's face. "We just got here."

"We got into town, though, late last night," her father added and winked. He put a breadbasket on the crowded table.

Her mom turned to her dad. "Dean, honey, do you mind going back to the car? I left the cranberries and the relish plate in the backseat."

Bijoux arranged the plates, utensils, and napkins to one side, creating a buffet. Dishes crowded the edge of the table, leaving room in the center. "Your mother told me all kinds of stories about you while we cooked this morning."

"Oh, really?" Mer raised her eyebrows at her mother.

"One of the perks of motherhood, sweetheart." She patted her daughter's arm, not the least bit contrite.

"This has to be the place. I can hear them all the way from the street!" Phoenix entered the yard wearing a Santa hat and holding the hand of a pudgy brunette with a dazzling smile. "Hey everyone, this is my wife, Amanda."

Amanda raised her hand shyly.

Phoenix handed Mer a small gift. "I promise it's not a phone. Ha! Skipper here yet?"

"Not yet." She shook her head. "Wait, who else is supposed to be here?"

Bijoux swept by on her way to the kitchen. "He'll be here in about a half hour. His relief bartender called in sick."

Gabby tapped a playlist on her phone and propped it on the windowsill. The patio pulsed with activity and the holiday music blended with laughter and chatter as her friends and family introduced themselves to each other.

Franky scrutinized the feast. "Looks like we're missing something." He tapped his index finger against his chin. "Something big."

"A turkey, perhaps?" Selkie said. He leaned on a cane as he slowly walked down the driveway. Talbot followed, carrying a roasting pan so big it made his biceps pop.

"The bird needs to rest about ten more minutes," Selkie added. "Trust me when I say you don't want me to make the gravy."

"That's my cue." Mer's mother disappeared into the kitchen behind Talbot.

Franky bumped his shoulder against Mer's. "Surprised?"

"Surprised?" She narrowed her eyes. "How long have you been planning this?"

Her brother shrugged. He pulled his cellphone from his shorts pocket.

"Aren't you supposed to wear your habit everywhere?" Mer asked.

Franky selected a number and dialed. "Nuns wear habits. Priests wear cassocks. Or jeans. Hey, we're here. Hold on." He handed the phone to Mer.

Dazed, she held it to her ear. "Hello?"

"What's up, Doc?"

Mer smiled despite her other brother's hokey greeting. "Hey, Vito."

"Sorry I'm not there for the shindig. I'm working a pretty big investigation at the moment. I could use your help if you want to come back to California, though. Help me crack the case."

Mer perused her backyard. It overflowed with happy people. Her people.

Loved ones, all of them.

She reached for Selkie's hand. "No, thanks. I think I'll stick it out here."

ACKNOWLEDGMENTS

I discovered something about myself while writing *Beached*: I enjoyed blurring the lines between fact and fiction.

For the curious, here are some facts:

King Philip V's ill-fated Spanish treasure fleet left Havana on Friday, July 13, 1733, and within days was overtaken by a hurricane. The shipwrecks dot the Atlantic edge of the Florida Keys and their locations are historically well documented.

Likewise, the Alhambra Decree of 1492 is an actual expulsion order that commanded Jews to either convert to Catholicism or leave Spain.

The 8 *escudos* gold "portrait dollar" is an extremely rare coin—so rare it made me wonder where the rest of the cache was and how I could go about finding it.

Here's where the facts get murky:

Sources say in 1492 Rabbi Don Isaac Abravanel offered King Ferdinand II and Queen Isabella I a bribe to rescind the expulsion order. This offer was supposedly overheard by the Spanish Inquisitor-General who burst in on the meeting and accused the monarchs of selling their souls for a few pieces of silver. The comparison to Judas Iscariot so shamed the monarchs, they nixed the deal.

And so began the *What-if* game. What if I added three hundred years, chose a new monarch, and mixed in a pinch of colonialism? A bit of fine-tuning and the Legend of the Thirteenth Galleon coalesced.

Now that I had a legend, I needed help making it a reality.

Commercial salvage rights in Florida waters are strictly regulated and new permits are exceedingly rare. I'm indebted to Tommy Vawter, the Director of Operations at TreasureWorks, for graciously identifying the major lease holders and explaining how the process works. Lest anyone think I wasn't paying attention, please note I took considerable liberties to make Mer's operation legal.

Thank you to J.T. Coyne, CAPTAIN, USN (Ret), for sharing his insight on helicopter rescues and the dangers such operations entail.

The value of a person willing to brainstorm, proofread, dispense advice, lend support, or simply share a glass of wine should never be underestimated. A toast to Autumn Blum, Dr. Deidre Chang, Lisa and Gerry Carroll, Lynn Prince, Norma Hansen, and a couple of folks who were too shy to be named. You all rock.

A continued debt of gratitude is owed to my agent, Helen Breitwieser of Cornerstone Literary. Her encouragement and guidance has set me on a new and exciting path.

My deepest appreciation to Mandy Mikulencak, for her unwavering support, critical feedback, wicked grammar skills, and good humor. No one could ask for a better critique partner or friend.

I may work in isolation, but I am never alone. I am blessed to have an amazing family that stretches from California to Colorado. My husband, David, may be the last person on this list, but he's the first person in my heart. Thank you. For everything.

I hope you enjoyed *Beached*. There is no greater honor for a writer than to have readers who come back for more. If you liked *Beached*, please share the news with others. A review is a powerful way to show your support and I would be truly grateful.

ABOUT THE AUTHOR

A retired police captain and FBI National Academy graduate, Micki Browning writes the Mer Cavallo Mysteries set in the Florida Keys. Her debut mystery, *Adrift,* was nominated for an Agatha award for Best First Novel and has won both the Daphne and Royal Palm Literary awards. She also writes short stories and non-fiction. Her work has appeared in dive magazines, anthologies, mystery magazines and textbooks. She lives in Florida with her partner in crime and a vast array of scuba equipment she uses for "research."

To learn more about Micki, visit her website—and while you're there, join her newsletter for the most up-to-date info about events, new releases, and behind-the-scenes-peeks!
www.MickiBrowning.com

facebook.com/MickiBrowningAuthor

twitter.com/MickiBrowning

goodreads.com/Micki_Browning

bookbub.com/authors/micki-browning

ALSO BY MICKI BROWNING

Adrift ~ The first Mer Cavallo Mystery

Short Stories:

"String Theory" *Mystery Weekly Magazine*

"Sleighed" *Mystery Weekly Magazine*

"Thicker than Water" Busted! Arresting Tales from the Beat

"F is for Fruitcake" Happy Homicides 6: Cookin' Up Crime